Dedicated to John, my husband,
For having faith in me.

Hatred stirs up strife,
but love covers all offences – Proverbs 10, xiii

# Chapter One

Lily Thorpe stood looking over the Mersey, a stiff breeze blowing her dark curls about her face. Her dreamy gaze took in the fussy little tugs ushering out a towering white liner past the line of the docks, which provided most Liverpudlians in some way or other with their livelihood, and out to the open sea. Not so long ago a German airship had flown over the river; some would rather it had stayed away, looking on it with suspicion, but she could understand the Germans wanting to see one of England's greatest ports, only second in size to London. There wasn't anything Lily liked more than to come down to the Pierhead where there was always something to see. Even if the ships had not crowded the river, the ceaseless movement of the water had an hypnotic quality that drew her.

Lily was suddenly conscious of the rising wind as oily waves slapped against the wooden landing stage. She took her eyes from the river and looked for her sister and brother. May was not far away. Lily seized her hand and shouted to Ronnie: 'Come away from the edge! Here's the ferry coming in.'

Her younger brother ducked beneath the thick metal chains which were supposed to keep the adventurous out and sauntered towards her. He was thin-faced, brown-haired and wiry, but small for his eleven years. 'Jimmy Gallagher learnt to swim by being thrown in at the deep end,' he informed her.

'Well, don't you be trying it here,' said Lily grimly. 'You'll freeze to death in five minutes.' She grasped the collar of his jacket and held him firmly.

The three of them watched as ropes, thick as a man's arm, were thrown from the ferry to a couple of men on the landing stage.

'Why do we have to watch?' cried May, who was fairer than her brother and a year younger but who often had more to say for herself. 'I'm cold!' She huddled into the well-worn red coat, which her other sister, Daisy, had cut down for her, and stamped her feet.

'Sea air's good for you and it'll blow the cobwebs away,' said Lily, squeezing her hand. 'Besides it's educational watching the ships coming and going. Think of all the cargoes that are unloaded . . . tobacco, grain for feed and the breweries, timber, sunflower oil for cattle cake . . .'

'And think of the places!' Ronnie's voice was rapt. 'Don't you wish when a hooter blows we could be on one of them ships crossing the bar and heading for the open sea?'

'I want to go home,' moaned May. 'You can keep your ships.'

'You're an unnatural Liverpudlian!' teased Lily, but she turned her back on the river and looked up at the clock on the Liver Building. It really was time to go. 'I used to yearn like crazy to travel when I was young,' she mused.

'Don't you now?' asked her brother.

'Chance would be a fine thing!' She smiled wryly, considering how her mother dying after May's birth had stopped her dreams.

They puffed their way up the open gangway to avoid the crowds from the ferry, who in the main were heading for the covered passengerway. The tide was in and below them the water with its distinctive smell of salt, oil and mud surged in the gap between the landing stage and the wall of the Pierhead. Faraway places with strange-sounding names, calling, calling, she thought.

'I'd like to see the animals,' said Ronnie. 'Tigers and elephants!' He made a trumpeting noise.

Lily shushed him because as they reached the top of the gangway she was aware someone was speaking. The voice was strong, powerful, and spoke the King's English with a distinct colonial accent. He was obviously new among the Bible thumpers who did their best some Sundays to convert those using the ferries or simply taking a stroll. She paused. He had attracted quite a crowd. She edged her way nearer to the front, dragging May with her while Ronnie followed more slowly. She was surprised to see he was dressed in some kind of habit, and stopped, prepared to listen to what he had to say.

'We're not staying, are we?' said May loudly. 'I want me tea and I'm tired!'

The preacher's head turned in her direction and Lily saw he was about thirtyish, with weatherbeaten skin and a mop of wavy bleached fair hair with a funny little tuft that stuck up from his crown. 'Man – and girl – shall not live by bread alone but by every word of God,' he paraphrased. 'Jesus said, come on to me all that are heavy laden and I will refresh you.'

'I wouldn't mind some bread right now, wack!' yelled someone in the crowd. 'How about one of those miracles like what Jesus was supposed to have done?'

The corners of the preacher's mouth lifted. 'Do you just happen to have five loaves and two fishes, brother?'

Lily smiled. 'You could see if the Isle of Man boat's in? Perhaps you could do something with a kipper?'

There was a ripple of laughter.

He looked at her and the expression in his eyes was amused. 'A challenge!' he shouted.

But before he could say more an elderly woman said, 'Oh leave him alone! He's got a lovely voice and I like listening to it. Yer a load of heathens, the lots of yous. A trip to church'd do yer all good, only it would probably collapse with the shock.'

'Yeah! Lerrim speak,' shouted a young voice this time. 'Aussie, aren't yer, mate?'

'My dad was Liverpudlian!'

A cheer went up which Lily joined in. She was enjoying herself.

'We have a hungry little girl,' said the preacher, his expressive eyes reaching out over the crowd. 'And what can I do about it?' He did not wait for them to answer but from the pocket of his habit took a brown paper packet. The crowd fell silent, watching him open it. 'Inside I have what I'm told is a genuine Scouser bacon buttie!' He flourished it in the air before stepping down from his soapbox and approaching May.

'Lil, I wanna go to the lav,' she whispered, jiggling from one foot to the other as he drew near.

'You started this,' said Lily, having a fair idea what was on the preacher's mind. 'You'll just have to wait.'

The Australian stopped in front of them and pulled away a piece of the sandwich and held it out to May. She hesitated.

'Take it,' murmured Lily, squeezing her hand. Her sister did as she was told. 'Eat it.' May obeyed.

'What about you?' said the preacher, whose grey eyes possessed a warmth and intensity that Lily had never seen before in a man.

'Thank you.' She smiled and took a piece. 'Not quite how Jesus did it but I think I get the point.'

'I'm glad I'm not wasting my time.' He smiled and they continued to stare at one another. Roman Catholic, thought Lily, what a waste of a man.

He moved on to the next person. 'Got me own butties, mate,' Lily heard the man say, and took them out of a pocket and opened them, offering half of one to the person next to him.

May tugged on her hand. 'Lil, I really do want to go to the lav,' she whispered.

Reluctantly Lily moved away, but she was remembering how, when she was Ronnie's age, she had been fired to carry the gospel overseas to sunlit lands. Maybe living in Liverpool had a lot to do with it? The river and religion could not be ignored. People travelled to and from the port; some settled, bringing with them their own particular brand of faith, often challenging that of those whose families had lived in the port for generations. Her family had never been drawn into what her father's brother, William, called tribal warfare. He was a Nonconformist and worked hard and he and his sister Dora followed the faith in their own way. Her father, though, said all religion was airy-fairy and caused nothing but trouble. Her mother, who'd been Welsh and had once been strong Chapel, had hushed him, saying good-humouredly, 'Do you want to be hit by a thunderbolt?' 'I'd like to see it!' he had replied, but had not argued when his wife had the children baptised in the local parish church so they could go to its school just five minutes' walking distance from the dairy. After she died he never set foot in church again, however, but found his spiritual, and temporal, nourishment from a bottle.

Lily sighed as she considered her life. Sometimes she still dreamed about those faraway places, and of a man who could match up to a picture she carried in her head. Someone who was tall, dark and handsome, who could be gentle and strong, generous but sensible with money, with a sense of humour and no conceit, who knew exactly what he wanted out of life. She knew it was a tall order, especially as she was nearly twenty-five and still had responsibilities that tied her to the family, but she had not yet given up all hope.

# Chapter Two

Lily set fire to loosely balled newspaper, watching the flames sear a charred path through Herr Hitler's nose before the chipped firewood caught. Her gaze wandered to the rattling kitchen window, misted with condensation, and she imagined the sun blazing down on scorched earth and a man in a pith helmet, short-sleeved shirt and shorts that revealed sunburnt muscular legs. In an instant an image of the priest at the Pierhead flashed into her mind and she wondered what his legs were like under his billowing habit. She smiled wryly, shook her head and washed her hands before fastening a white apron over a hand-knitted blue jumper and tweed skirt. She dragged one of her brother Ben's caps over her dusky curls and pulled on an old mackintosh. Yesterday had been her birthday, and she was conscious of time running out.

'Lovely day, Lil,' said Ben as he slipped past her and opened the door. He was three years younger and possessed the same colouring as her but was burly and stocky.

'You need glasses.'

He grinned and side by side they raced down the wet, slippery length of the backyard, past the cool room to the shippon. Lily pressed the electric switch and light dazzled on whitewashed walls, revealing the cows tethered in the stalls. Brother and sister began to shovel grain into the feed boxes.

'What d'you think of some Methodist leaving £60,000 to the Anglican Cathedral fund and his wife only £520 a year?' said Ben, glancing at her.

'Strange! Perhaps he's trying to buy his way into Heaven like some used to hundreds of years ago?' Lily put down the shovel and tied the cow's tail to its leg before turning her cap back to front. 'Doesn't say much for his wife, though.'

'She said that she's going to have to give up the chauffeur,' he said with plums in his mouth. 'Doesn't know how she'll manage!'

Lily grinned. 'Something must have sure gone wrong with their marriage, just like Mrs Simpson's former two.' Lily sat on a three-legged stool. Her strong fingers gently massaged and warmed the teats to 'let down' the milk. 'I remember reading about her first husband. He was a naval officer called Spencer. He said that their marriage failed because he was away at sea and she got lonely.' She frowned. 'Half the women in Liverpool could say the same thing but you don't see them rushing to the divorce courts.'

'Anyway there's the coronation of George and Lizzie to look forward to in a couple of months,' said Ben.

'Should be fun.'

'As long as Dad doesn't get too drunk.'

They exchanged grimaces. 'He was in late last night,' said Lily. 'I gave up waiting and went to bed.'

For a while there was just the noise of milk squirting against metal and the shifting and gentle breathing of the cows. In the entry the other side of the wall the sound of booted feet drawing near caused brother and sister to glance at each other. Through slats in the wall, the cows could gaze out on the outside world. 'If that paperboy dares,' whispered Lily, 'I'll have him.' She glanced at the cane which rested against the wall, but the footsteps did not pause. 'It's good job for him he didn't try it again.'

'He's only a kid,' said Ben, grinning.

'It's not funny for the cows having peas shot up their noses and in their ears!' A dusky curl escaped from Lily's cap, brushing the Friesian's flank as she checked the milk in the pail. She rose from the stool. 'This cow's almost dry.'

'I'll tell Uncle William,' responded Ben. After their grandfather had died, their uncle inherited the family farm out Knowsley way on the outskirts of Liverpool and provided the cows for their dairy in the middle of a street of terraced houses not far from Tuebrook.

Lily got up and went into the adjoining cool room and poured milk into the container on top of the chiller. She did it automatically. It was part of her daily routine. As soon as the milking was over she would start breakfast for the family.

'Any more bacon, Lil?' said Daisy.

Lily glanced across the table, conscious of her own untidiness. Her sister Daisy's brown hair was Eugene permed, which cost a fortune but considered worth the money, although at the moment she might as well not have bothered because it was hidden beneath a white turban. 'I'm saving the last slice for Dad,' murmured Lily, 'but I'll be going to the farm tomorrow so you could have some the day after. I need more provisions for the shop.'

'I fancy it now. Dad mightn't be up to eating. Let me have it, Lil.' Her sister's voice was persuasive. 'You can give him porridge or toast.'

'He needs meat. You know how thin he's gone.'

Daisy's blue eyes widened. 'It doesn't stop him drinking our money away! Why should I have to do without? I'm the one making sweets in Barker's most of the hours God sends!'

'Try and be a little more understanding,' said Lily coaxingly. 'I know he drives us mad but he has only got one leg.'

Daisy muttered, 'And he never lets us forget how he lost it.'

'The Great War was no joke!'

'OK! OK! Save the lecture,' groaned Daisy. 'I'm sorry I spoke.'

A bell jangled and Lily hurried down the lobby into the shop. On the other side of the wooden counter stood little Mrs Draper holding a jug with a beaded muslin cloth over it. 'Good morning, dear!' She beamed at Lily. 'Are you well?'

'Very well, thank you.' She dipped the measure into the churn standing on a marble slab and steadily poured milk into the jug.

'And your dear father?'

Lily had known Mrs Draper all her life and knew that her sympathetic manner was genuine. 'Just the same. How about you?'

'Mustn't grumble, dear. There's always someone worse off.' She leaned across the counter. 'We've got a visiting missionary. A really unusual young man with a voice like an angel.' Her bright eyes twinkled. 'Not that I've ever heard an angel but you know what I mean. He's showing slides of India at the mission hall. Perhaps you can bring the children along?'

Lily hesitated, not wanting to hurt the old woman's feelings. 'It depends on how Dad is. You know what he's like.'

Mrs Draper patted her hand. 'Of course I do, dear. But do try. You need to get out of this place and have some life of your own now and then.'

Lily could not agree more but she would have preferred to do something different from listening to a missionary; she didn't have anything against them but she preferred a more exciting prospect, not that any looked like coming her way. 'I'll try,' she promised nonetheless, taking the tuppence and dropping it into a small wicker basket on a ledge under the counter.

A boy in patched short trousers and a shrunken grey jacket held the door open for Mrs Draper. One of his stockings was already creeping down his leg.

'The usual, Johnny?' said Lily, taking the large chipped jug he held up.

'And Mam said, can she have two eggs?' He stood on tiptoe to lean on the counter.

'Your dad's home, is he?'

'Came back last night. He's been to Ceylon and was telling me and me bruvvers all about it in bed. I'm goin' ta sea when I grows up.'

'That'll be nice,' said Lily, carefully wrapping the eggs in tissue paper before coming round the counter and placing one in each pocket of his jacket. She gave him his change and opened the door, thinking that May and Ronnie should be up by now if they were to get to school on time.

May was already awake, lying on her back with the patchwork quilt worked by her maternal grandmother up to her chin. Her long flaxen hair, freed from its plaits, spread like crinkled paper on the pillow. Since she was a tot she had refused to set foot in the shippon. She hated dirt and dust and the smells that issued from the bottom of the yard. 'I don't think I'll go to school today,' she declared gruffly. 'I think I'm getting a chest.'

'You're going,' said Lily determinedly.

'But I don't learn anything!'

'You know it all? You know the capital of Spain and your five times table?' Lily wrenched the quilt from her grasp and the rest of the covers followed.

'Two fives are ten and Madrid's the captial of Spain,' chanted her sister, hunching her knees inside her nightie.

'The capital of Australia?'

'Sydney!'

'No. Canberra.'

'Why do I have to know?' grumbled May. 'I'm never going to go there. Now if you'd asked me the name of a

Red Indian tribe I could have told you the Sioux. They were in a cowboy film at the matinee.'

'Sorry, no go.' Lily hid a smile as she dragged her struggling sister off the bed.

She left May dressing and went into the bedroom her brothers shared. The room was a mess but that was because she had been asked to leave everything where it was. Recently Ronnie had taken up whittling and was forever making whistles and selling them to anyone who had a halfpenny. He was also football mad as were most boys in Liverpool. He was up now and kicking a football around the double bed that had come from their uncle's farm.

'Dad'll have you if he hears you.' Her face softened as she watched him.

'He won't hear me, though, will he?' His expression was far from childlike in his thin face. 'He's drunk and snoring like a pig.'

'That's enough of that!' She kicked the ball from beneath his foot and under the bed. 'I just hope he's put his leg in a safe place.'

'His leg was on the landing.' Ronnie licked the palms of his hands and smoothed his hair back with them. 'I thought he might fall over it so I hung it by its straps on the door. It'll make a lovely noise when he opens it.' He grinned as he bounced out of the room. 'I'll make me own toast,' he shouted from halfway down the stairs.

'Thanks a lot, and use a comb for your hair in future,' called Lily, going along the landing to her father's bedroom.

A pink-painted wooden leg dangled from the brass door knob. She opened the door and immediately the smell of rum mingled with the stale tang of tobacco to assail her nostrils. Her father had told her soldiers had been given rum sometimes before going over the top. She placed the heavy leg on a chair by his bed and picked up the trousers flung on the floor, glancing at the tuft of white hair showing above the old army blankets. There was no sign of him stirring. She left the room, convinced that it would be hours yet before he made an appearance downstairs.

It was three hours later that Albert Thorpe entered the kitchen. Lily was ironing and dreaming of her tall, dark and handsome hero who would take her away from it all, and didn't really want to be disturbed, but she put down the flat iron and stared at her father. If the photograph in a drawer was anything to go by he had been handsome once. It was hard to imagine now. Only forty-seven, he looked much older. His rumpled clothes clung to his gaunt frame and his cheeks were the colour of his tobacco-tinged moustache. The pale blue eyes seemed to be saying they wished they had not bothered to open that morning.

'I don't know why you do it to yourself, Dad,' she said, putting on the kettle and reaching for a packet of Golden Stream tea. 'Where did you go this time?'

'Only Bootle.' He sat at the table and wiped his hands over his face. 'Fred would have been forty-four. Sometimes I see him dying over and over in my mind.' His eyes filled with tears. 'I spoke to his widow. Nice woman.'

Lily shook her head. 'You can't go on torturing your-self for ever.'

'Lest we forget, girl.'

She experienced a mixture of irritation and pity. 'Why can't you remember the good things?' She picked up a loaf and pot of home-made rhubarb and ginger jam; the bacon had vanished and she guessed where. Still, her mother had always said when someone was low give them something sweet to eat. She placed a steaming mug of tea and a plate of bread and jam in front of him and considered how best to cheer him up.

'Nothing to eat, girl.' Albert cradled the hot mug in his hands.

'Tell me what it was like when you met Mam,' said Lily, hoping to change the direction of his thoughts. She sat opposite him and reached for a slice of bread and jam.

'What's the point in remembering? It just makes me sad thinking of the way she went.' His tone was glum.

Lily persisted. 'It was at a fair, wasn't it?'

He groaned and put a hand to his head. 'Aye! But it was a long time ago now.'

'So was the war but you haven't forgotten that! Don't you think you owe it to Mam to keep her memory alive as much as that of those soldier friends of yours?'

He made no reply and she felt angry and irritated. She stood and placed the flat iron on the fire. She felt like a bottle of fizzy pop about to explode. He would mope around the house all day. There would be no escaping him. She needed something different and suddenly remembered Mrs Draper's words about the missionary and India. Perhaps it wouldn't be so bad? She was interested in India. It was better than nothing and cheaper than going to the pictures.

May wriggled free of Lily's hold and unbuttoned the top of her coat. 'That's too tight and you scratched me!'

'If you'd kept still I wouldn't have,' she retorted, glancing at her own reflection in the lobby mirror as she dragged on gloves. The dark curly hair which she considered her best feature was crammed beneath a snappily brimmed blue velour hat trimmed with a feather. Her eyebrows were sooty arches. She raised them and smiled, wishing she had Carole Lombard's looks for her own mouth was too large – and as for her chin! It was much too determined-looking in shape to be thought delicately pretty. She pulled a face and caught sight of Ronnie in the mirror. 'Don't forget your balaclava. You don't want Jack Frost freezing your ears. And, May, wear your bonnet.'

'I will! I like this bonnet,' said her sister, fastening the pink plaited ties. 'It's better than Betty West's new one.'

'I'm glad something pleases you.' Lily gave her reflection one last scrutiny before hurrying the children out of the house.

She ran them down the street until they came to one of the wide entries that divided the long rows of terraced houses into three blocks, enabling them to take a short cut into the next street. Lights blazed from the begrimed red-bricked mission hall squeezed between houses which had been built during the last century like so many others in the city.

Inside all was bustle and the rows of folding wooden chairs divided by an aisle up the middle were filling quickly. On stage a large screen had been set up. Centre back there was a table on which stood a lantern slide machine, near which several men were grouped in discussion.

As Lily brushed past them, holding the children's hands, one of them looked up. She did not immediately recognise him until their eyes met and held. Then she tore her gaze away and passed swiftly by despite the fluttering somewhere beneath her ribs. She led the children to seats next to the inner aisle and sat between them.

'I'd like to sit at the front,' said May, getting up almost as soon as she sat down.

'You can't.'

'I'm not going to see anything here.'

'Sit down, May, or I'll take you home again,' said Lily.

May sat but in such a way that the seat tipped up and her behind got wedged in the space at the back. 'Help!' she yelled.

'Trust her,' groaned Ronnie, ducking his head and glancing about furtively. 'Always having to make people notice us.'

'I've a good mind to leave you there, causing trouble when we've only been here two minutes,' hissed Lily, standing up.

'Need a hand?'

She would have recognised the voice anywhere and felt the colour rise in her cheeks. 'Thanks a lot.'

They tugged and May was free. She looked mournfully up at her rescuer and said, 'I didn't mean to do it. It really was an accident.'

He raised one eyebrow. 'Are you sure?'

She gave him a puzzled look. 'I've seen you before.'

'That's right.' His gaze shifted to Lily's face and he held out a hand. 'I'm Brother Matthew of the brotherhood of St Barnabas. I'm an Anglican priest.' There was laughter in his eyes. 'I know for sure we've met before! Something to do with a kipper.'

Lily smiled. 'You look different without the habit.'

'So I keep getting told but it's too Catholic for a meeting like this,' he said ruefully. 'You'd be surprised, though, how warm and comfortable it is for outdoor work.' He released her hand. 'I'll have to go. I hope to see you later.'

Lily murmured agreement and watched his black-clad figure go to the front of the hall. There was nothing tall, dark and handsome about him but he definitely had something and she could agree with Mrs Draper about the voice. She was looking forward to hearing him speak.

First, though, they had to suffer the singing. A woman began to bash out music on an upright piano. 'Jesus died for all the children, all the children of the world, red and yellow, black and white . . .' Several sang louder than the preacher but Lily could pick his voice out. There were two more hymns and then Richard, the curate from the mother church, welcomed them all before introducing their visitor as a man who had been doing God's work in southern India. There was an expectant hush.

Matt Gibson stood on stage and opened a black leather-covered Bible. 'Though I speak with the tongues of men and angels and have not charity, I am become as sounding brass, or a tinkling cymbal. And though I have the gift of prophecy, and understand all mysteries, and all knowledge; and though I have all faith, so that I could remove mountains and have not charity, I am nothing . . .'

His voice had risen and Lily felt a delicious shiver run through her. This was sheer poetry! 'And though I bestow all my goods to feed the poor – and give my body to be burned, and have not charity, it profiteth me nothing . . .' His tone was impassioned and had speeded up. 'Charity suffereth long, and is kind, it beareth all things, believeth all things, hopeth all things.' His voice dropped to a silken whisper. 'Faith, hope, charity . . . but the greatest of these is charity.'

His reading had set the mood and there was a breathless silence as he closed the Bible.

'Is your neighbour hard to love?'

'Not 'arf!' exclaimed someone. 'Him and her are always going at each other, fist and tongue!'

'Shush!' said several people.

Matthew smiled. 'Well, sister, if you can't love them I'm wasting my time here because you won't be able to care for those in India.' He paused. 'India is a vast, beautiful country which has a population that runs into many millions. Many are poorer than any you might meet in the filthiest court in Liverpool. There are actually people called the Untouchables.' He paused. 'These are as much your neighbours as the person living next to you.' His gaze reached out, seeming to touch them all, met Lily's. She smiled without thinking and one corner of his mouth lifted. 'Our Lord Jesus would touch them just as He did the lepers in with rags and sores. But He has passed into the heavens

and we are his hands and feet on earth. It is our duty and
privilege to take hope to others.' His voice softened. 'Which
is why I am here to tell you how the church is doing just
that in India.' He jumped off stage. The lights dimmed.

He talked of the past and the Syrian church taking
the gospel to India hundreds of years ago, just as the
Jews took Judaism – and of the present, of Indian
Christians taking over the leadership of the churches as
the country strove for independence. His enthusiasm and
knowledge stimulated interest and excitement but he did
not forget the children and slotted in slides of monkeys,
tigers, and elephants bathing. He spoke of Rudyard
Kipling, telling funny stories that not only made the
children laugh but the adults too. There was information
about Hindu and Moslem ways of birth, marriage and
death. It was all highly entertaining and when the collection plate came round it was obvious he had not wasted
his time. He was thanked and clapped and it was over.

Lily did not move. Here was a different world, a
different man. She glanced in his direction. He was
surrounded by people. There seemed little chance of the
pair of them getting to speak.

'Well?' Mrs Draper popped up beside Lily, her eyes
sparkling beneath the brim of a black straw hat. 'Wasn't
he wonderful? Didn't he bring India alive? I could almost
feel the heat and the flies!'

May opened her mouth but Lily clapped a hand over
it. 'I don't want you saying anything about flies and dirt.
You and Ronnnie go and wait by the door.' For a moment
she watched them dart among groups of chattering people

before turning to the old lady. 'Where is he staying? Will he be preaching on Sunday?'

'He's in great demand and so is off somewhere else. It's not often you manage to get a speaker from India. Africa, now, that's more common.'

Lily tried to conceal her disappointment. 'I would have liked to hear him speak again.'

'A treat, my dear. What a pity you missed him in church last Sunday.' Mrs Draper moved towards the exit and Lily had no choice but to follow if she was not to appear rude. 'He could be back,' added the old lady. 'His father was from Liverpool and he wants to trace an aunt.'

'Can Anglican brothers marry?'

'I think they can, my dear. Although most choose celibacy and dedicate themselves to God.'

Lily glanced over in Brother Matthew's direction but there was a number of women crowded round him. No hope for her, she thought wryly, and made for the door where May was hopping about just inside and people were having to dodge around her.

'Can't you behave for five minutes?' Lily seized hold of her and cast a last glance the preacher's way.

Mrs Draper chattered all the way to her front door but Lily hardly heard a word. Her thoughts were in India. The sight of Daisy dancing in the street with a young man brought her back to the present. 'What d'you think you're doing?' She eyed the young man who hastily removed his cloth cap.

'We haven't been here long, Lil,' said Daisy. 'Cyril just brought me home from dancing class and we were practising the foxtrot.'

'This isn't the Grafton, you know,' she said with mock severity to the young man. 'Don't keep her out here long or she'll catch her death.'

As Lily and the children entered the kitchen Ben lifted his dark head from a book. 'Dad's gone out. Frank Jones came to see you and they went out together.'

The magic of the evening evaporated and Lily slammed her handbag on the table, her mouth tightening. 'If he comes in drunk, I'll have Frank! If I've told him once I've told him a dozen times that getting round Dad won't make a pennyworth of difference to me! I'm not at my last prayers and I'd rather go out with a toad than him!' She shrugged off her coat, put on the kettle and took a nightdress and a pair of pyjamas from the cupboard next to the fireplace, hanging them over the fireguard. 'You didn't tell him where we'd gone?'

'Dad did and they both agreed they didn't want to go and listen to any prissy-voiced missionary.' Ben yawned. 'Their words, Lil. Was he any good?'

'You'd have found it interesting,' she said blandly.

'We saw elephants,' said Ronnie, rubbing his hands on the warm fireguard. 'They were spouting water from their trunks. He's ridden on one.'

'What's prissy?' asked May, pushing Ben's book aside and climbing on his knee.

'Hard to explain, Maysie. Your face is cold.' He hugged her to him. 'Did you like the elephants?'

'I liked him. His voice was nice. Sometimes it reminded me of bells and sometimes water. It rose and fell and sometimes stayed in one line.'

Ben caught Lily's glance as she spooned cocoa into a jug. 'He's made a convert.'

'Probably made more than one.' Her voice was offhand. 'He's been shot at, caught up in a riot and nearly trampled to death.'

'Sounds an adventurous life for a missionary.'

Lily caught the envy in his voice and she said hurriedly, 'You wouldn't go off like some and fight in Spain just for a bit of adventure, would you, Ben? Thousands have died out there.'

He yawned. 'Not on your life! I get all my excitement in the Territorials. Besides, how would you cope without me?'

'I couldn't!' Lily kissed the top of his head, wondering if he ever resented taking on the job that had been their father's. Albert was still supposed to handle the reins for Ben, making the job of carting foodstuffs for cattle and horses easier, but too often he was left alone to cope. 'What did Uncle William say about Dad not turning up again?'

'Made allowances for him as usual.' He put on a deep voice. 'Can't be much fun having one leg, lad. Tell him the horse is missing him and that should get him here.'

'And did you?'

'He brought out a photo of a horse and cart all decked up for the May Day celebrations. Quite cheerful for him for once. Not that it lasted. Next moment he's going on about this horse he'd seen drown in mud at Passchendaele.'

'I hate mud,' chipped in May, her voice drowsy. 'And sand down me drawers.'

'Shush,' said Lily, easing her sister to her feet. 'Ben, did you put the oven shelf in?'

He nodded as the door opened and Daisy entered, bringing a breath of cold air with her. 'He's gone.'

'I didn't think he'd still be hanging about outside,' said Lily. 'Where did you find him?'

Daisy grinned. 'I know he's not much to look at but he really can dance.' She placed a cup next to the ones Ronnie was filling with cocoa and sighed soulfully. 'He's got this brother who's an absolute dream but can't dance for toffee. He's asked me out to see Freddie Bartholomew at the Hippodrome. What am I do do, Lil?'

'Don't ask me!' Lily smiled. 'It's obvious you can't prefer one over the other or you wouldn't be asking such a question. I'd find someone else.'

Daisy sat near the fire. 'How did your evening go? Was the preacherman worth listening to?'

'You missed a treat.'

'You're having me on.'

Lily smiled and folded May's clothes. Then she remembered her father and went through into the street but there was no sign of him.

No sooner had they drunk their cocoa and Ben had vanished upstairs with the younger children than there was a commotion outside. The sisters hurried to the door.

'Pack up yer troubles in yer old kit bag,' mumbled Albert from a sprawling position on the pavement.

Frank tried to lift him but to no avail. There was an apprehensive smile on his moonlike face as he relinquished his hold on Albert and gazed at Lily. 'You're looking pretty tonight, Lil.'

She felt irritated. 'I don't need any flannel from you,' she hissed. 'And keep your voice down or you'll have the neighbours out!'

'His leg just slid out from underneath him,' he whispered. 'It's not my fault!'

'Of course it's your fault! What were you thinking of, taking him out? You've got more money than sense!' She bent over her father.

'I felt sorry for him,' he said placatingly. 'But I bought him only one drink. It was some of the others who got him legless. Ooops! Sorry, Lil.'

She bit back a fiery retort. 'His artificial knee's probably locked. You get his legs. Me and Daisy'll take his head and shoulders . . . and don't drop him!'

Frank complied quickly. 'No, Lil. I only had a couple of halves.'

'You don't have to go on making excuses. Just lift.'

'Up and over. Keep yer head down,' mumbled Albert, sagging heavily in their grasp.

They carried him inside and set him down on the sofa. Lily straightened. 'Thanks, Frank. But if you ever get him drunk again, don't dare put your head through our door. Now out!'

'Not even a cup of tea, Lil?' He twisted his trilby nervously between his hands. 'I did want to speak to you.'

'I'll make a cuppa,' offered Daisy.

Lily frowned at her sister. 'We've got to see to Dad.'

'Sorry.' Daisy smiled at Frank to soften the blow. 'I'll see you to the door.'

He sighed, placed the trilby on his thinning mousy hair and followed her out.

Lily turned to her father and experienced an unfamiliar sense of helplessness. If only her mother had lived, she just knew he would never have got into this state. She began to unbutton his trousers.

Daisy re-entered the room. 'You are cruel to Frank. I'm sure he wants to marry you.'

'So he does but I don't want to marry him. Besides his mother would never allow it while she's alive. She'd sell the fruit shop first so he wouldn't have a penny to bless himself with.'

'She's an old bitch. I feel sorry for him.'

'He should stand up for himself,' said Lily firmly, undoing the straps around her father's shoulder and waist that held the artificial leg in place. Blood showed through the sock on his stump. 'Poor ol' thing,' she said softly. 'He's been going it too much.' Removing the sock she ordered her sister to get the medicine box. 'He'll have to leave his leg off.'

'At least it'll stop him wandering.'

Lily chafed her father's cold hands. 'Here we go round the mulberry bush, the mulberry bush, the mulberry bush,' he mumbled.

The two sisters exchanged looks. 'You wonder what's going on inside his head,' said Daisy, opening the box.

'Nothing that does him any good. Once I've put something on that sore we'll leave him here. I'm not struggling upstairs and I don't want to disturb Ben.'

Daisy fetched a couple of blankets. Lily sprinkled boracic powder on the sore and bandaged it before covering her father with a blanket and making sure the fireguard was secure.

As Lily said her prayers Brother Matthew was in her thoughts. If they met again she would have to make him sit up and take more notice of her. She snuggled up to May and when she fell asleep, dreamed of riding a bejewelled elephant with her arm around the preacher's waist.

# Chapter Three

Albert was driving Lily mad. His sore stump was taking its time healing because he had defied her more than once by strapping on his leg and going to the pub. Even with only a few pence in his pocket he managed to get drunk. While the effects of the drink were on him the pain did not seem to bother him but the next day he was full of moans. Last night she had hidden his leg.

'Where is it?' Albert banged his fist on the shop counter.

'Where's what?' said Lily, wide-eyed and innocent-looking. She removed a tray half-filled with eggs from near his hand.

'My leg, damn you! Don't come that with me, girl. I'm still your father and I'll have some respect!'

'I'm not telling you. If you haven't got the sense to leave it off just a few days longer, then I'll have to have the sense for both of us. You'll have an accident one of these days and then you'll be even worse off. It's you I'm thinking of, Dad. I don't want you suffering any more than you are already.'

Some of the anger left his face and there was a placating note in his voice when he spoke. 'Well, where's me crutches then? I can use them, can't I? I promised I'd meet someone in the cocoa house in Christian Street. That's if you can lend your old father half a crown?'

She looked at him cynically. 'Sure you don't want ten bob?' His face brightened. 'If you've got it, girl.'

'I was joking, Dad.'

'A florin then,' he pleaded.

'Sixpence.'

'A shilling. You've got the money here.' He clutched at the counter and reached for the small basket on the ledge under the counter but she moved swiftly and grabbed it at the same time as he did. There was a wobbly tussle.

The doorbell jangled.

'Give it me here,' yelled Albert.

'Not on your life!'

'Is this man bothering you, Miss Thorpe?'

The basket slipped from Lily's fingers but she had no time to reply before Matthew had moved and seized hold of the back of her father's jacket.

'Get your bloody hands off me,' gasped Albert, hopping around. 'This is me daughter and I'll thank you to mind your own bloody business!'

'Is this true?' Matthew stared at Lily with a rueful gleam in his eyes.

'I'm afraid so,' she said, wishing her father to Timbuctoo. 'But thank you, anyway.' She took the basket from Albert.

Matthew carefully released him. 'I'm sorry, mate. My mistake.'

Lily said, 'Dad, this is the preacher I told you about, so watch your language.'

'I'll say what I bloody like!' Albert shook himself like a terrier that had been out in the rain. 'He's no better than me! A Holy Joe who knows nothing about real life and suffering. I've met your kind before,' he muttered, glowering at him and rubbing his neck. 'Live in the clouds, you lot do.'

'Dad, shut up!' Lily opened his hand and pressed a shilling into it. 'Your crutches are behind the sofa. Watch you don't break your neck,' she whispered, opening the door to the living quarters. Albert arrowed Matthew a withering look before leaving the shop.

'You'll have to excuse him,' said Lily, facing the preacher. 'He says he doesn't believe in God but blames Him for losing his leg.'

'You don't have to apologise. There's a lot of people like that.'

Her mouth curved into a smile. 'There's another kind. Those who won't have anything to do with the church but who behave as if they believe everything it stands for.'

He smiled. 'I'm sorry I antagonised your father.'

'Dad would be prickly with God himself. He was bad enough after the war but when Mam died that was the finish. Now he can't settle to anything and drinks.'

'It can't be an easy life for you.'

'If he could forget the war it would be easier.'

His smile faded. 'It wrecked a lot of lives in Australia.'

Lily leaned forward over the counter. 'I suppose you're used to dealing with men with problems like Dad's.'

'Most men prefer to keep their pain inside them where I come from. They consider it more manly.' He took an egg from the tray on the counter and rolled it between his hands. 'My own father never spoke of his feelings after my mother died or of his pain when he was dying himself. Stiff upper lip and all that.'

She was interested in this information which stirred her compassion. 'Any brothers and sisters?'

Matthew shook his head. 'Mum went when I was three and Dad died a few years ago. It was when he was dying he told me more about his past than he had ever done before. He never stopped talking about Liverpool, where he was born, or India and China where he went with the British Army. He brought those places alive to me. So much so I wanted to see them for myself.'

'Liverpool must seem strange and drab after India and Australia?'

He placed the egg back on the tray and smiled. 'I enjoy the difference. I like the people and the bustle of the place. Besides I'm convinced it was God's will that I came.'

'Are you?' Lily had never met anyone who spoke so openly about God's will in the scheme of things. 'How do you know?'

'You just know,' he drawled. 'He won't leave you alone.'

There was a silence and she hesitated before saying, 'I believe you have an aunt over here? Have you found her yet?'

'To tell you the truth I haven't looked. Haven't had time.' He rested his arms on the counter and the action brought his face close to hers. 'Is it possible you might have time to help me?'

She could hardly believe he was asking her but did not hesitate. 'I can make time. Have you an address?'

Matt took a slip of paper from his pocket and handed it over. 'I know I could get a street map but it's more fun having someone explaining what's which.'

Lily looked at the address and said ruefully, 'I don't know it. I can tell you Seiont is the name of a Welsh river. A lot of the housing in Liverpool was built by Welshmen. Any clues to its whereabouts from your father?'

'He said Steble Street public baths was not far away.'

Lily was surprised. 'It's Toxteth way – not far from Park Road if I remember. My brother delivers in that area. There's several streets not far away named after characters out of Dickens's novels.'

He smiled, showing white teeth. 'I remember Dad read Dickens, Kipling and the Bible. He believed the British Army and the Church of England would stand for ever. The house is three storeys high and there were no windows at the back.'

'It must be from the times when the government levied a tax on windows,' she said thoughtfully, folding the paper between her fingers. 'Shall we go and find it?' She whipped off her apron. 'I'll have to be back for the second milking about threeish. If you don't mind waiting while I get a coat?'

'Of course not.'

Lily left him to run a comb swiftly through her hair. She pressed the back of her hands to hot cheeks and wondered how he had known where to find her. He must have asked, which meant he was interested. Which was all to the good because she was more than just interested in him! She found her best hat and turned the shop sign to CLOSED.

They caught a tram in West Derby Road and she pointed out the tobacco factory, the ice-cream parlour, the cinema and the home-made sweet shop. 'Terrible for the teeth but fascinating watching them being made.'

He looked amused. 'Dad mentioned Everton toffee.'

'Striped sugar coating with toffee inside. Daisy, my sister, helps to make them. They originated in a little toffee shop in Everton which used to be a township all of its own over a hundred years ago. Liverpool grew and gobbled it up.' She waved her right arm as they passed the Hippodrome theatre and cinema. 'It's thataway! You get a marvellous view of the river and the Wirral peninsula from up on the Brow. If you'd like to see it, I could show you one day.'

'I'd like that.' They were silent a moment, then he murmured, 'Dad mentioned a Princes Road. Said he remembered wealthy merchants riding in their carriages. It was tree-lined and more like one of those boulevards in Paris.'

She smiled. 'It's still there but past its heyday. There's not so many wealthy merchants these days. More Irish, I'd say. They flooded in after the potato famine in the last century. Liverpool was first port of call for those who couldn't afford America or Australia.'

'Bishop Dr David says there's a quarter of a million Irish living in the city right now.'

'I'm not surprised. Some would send them all back to Ireland now they want to be a real republic but most of us just accept them as part of the scenery. Anyway I've no call to speak against them. My grandparents were not native Liverpudlians.' She paused, suddenly aware of his clear steady gaze and she blushed. 'I'm sorry. I'm babbling on. I enjoyed your talk and the slides the other evening. I've always wanted to travel.'

'Where would you go, Miss Thorpe?'

'Where else but those far flung corners of the British Empire?' she said with enthusiasm. 'Those pink bits sprinkled all over the map of the world.'

'Not for much longer. The world's changing.' He looked grim for a moment.

'You're talking about India?' she said tentatively.

'Not just India. Germany is rearming and Japan is touchy about what's happening in China. They say they won't stand for communism.'

She was interested. 'I hardly know anything about Japan.'

'It probably doesn't seem a threat to Britain, that's why, but it could be to those far-flung corners of the Empire.'

It was as if a shadow crossed the sun and she said slowly, 'You make it sound as if what Japan does is serious?'

He hesitated. 'Forget I said it. Tell me about yourself, Miss Thorpe.'

'I'd rather you told me more about the places you've been,' she responded. 'And my friends call me Lily.'

He smiled. 'I'd rather hear about you, Lily.'

'Please! I've talked enough. You'll be sick of my voice.'

'Never,' he said softly. 'But we'll take turns or you'll be sick of mine.'

She could barely believe he had paid her such a nice compliment, and after that it was only by the sheerest fluke Lily noticed they had reached Lord Street because the conversation was so interesting. They shot off the tram just in time to change on to the next at the Victoria monument and headed in the direction of the Custom's House and then Park Road. It was not long before they were in Seiont Terrace.

The houses were tall and narrow, as he'd said, with steps leading up to the front door. Matthew knocked and a few moments later the door opened. An old woman with pipecleaners in her white hair, a clay pipe in her mouth and a pair of men's boots on her feet stood before them. She had both hands tucked into the massive bosom of her flowered pinny.

Lily glanced at Matthew's face but could not read his expression. Could this really be his aunt?

'Mrs Rowlands?' he enquired.

She removed the pipe and poked him with it. 'Yer aren't from roundabouts here, are yer, lad?'

He smiled. 'Australia! I wrote to you.'

'Can't read. Yer shouldn't be writing letters to them's can't read.'

'I didn't know you couldn't read.'

'Well, I can't. So what are you going to do about it?' The pipe came into play again.

'He could always read them to you,' interposed Lily, who was struggling not to laugh.

Bright brown eyes inspected her. 'He could. Will I like what's in them, though? Because if it's bad news I don't want to know.'

Matthew looked at Lily, who said in a quivering voice, 'You'll have to tell her.'

He nodded. 'Davy's dead. I'm sorry, Aunt Jane, but he's been gone years.'

'That's a shame. Nice funeral, was it?' She placed the pipe back in her mouth and sucked on it.

At that moment a voice called from inside, 'Who is it, Mam?'

The pipe was removed and she called, 'It's a man from some place or other and Davy's dead.'

There was silence before a woman of fortyish came into view. 'Who's Davy?' She stared at Matt and Lily. 'And who are you two? We don't know any Davys.'

Lily couldn't control herself any longer and shot down the steps and round the corner into the next street. Matthew joined her a few minutes later where she was laughing helplessly.

He stared at her with mock severity. 'You ought to be ashamed of yourself, laughing at the poor old woman.'

'She's not your aunt then?' Lily's voice wobbled as she wiped her eyes with the back of her hand.

'No.' He grinned. 'She's moved to some place called Bootle by a toffee works. Can't get away from sweets today.'

Lily gazed at him and thought, he's much nicer-looking than nice and he's got a sense of humour and he doesn't preach all the time. I could really get to like him . . . 'What do you want to do?' she said. 'Bootle's the other side of Liverpool and I don't know how long it'd take us to get there. I'm presuming you managed to get an address?'

'The daughter gave me it and she had the letters I'd written, having meant to take them to Aunt Jane when she got round to it.' He hesitated. 'As much as I'd like your company, you've got the milking to do. I think we'd best separate after you've pointed me in the direction of the right tram.'

'You should get one at the Pierhead. You will let me know if you find her?'

He nodded. 'I'll call later and tell you how I got on, if you don't mind? I'd like to meet Ben. If he knows Liverpool as well as you say he does, maybe he wouldn't mind taking me on his rounds? I'm thinking of doing for Liverpool in Australia what I did for India here. Hands across the oceans and all that.'

'Come to tea,' she said rashly, hoping for once her father would stay out late.

When Lily arrived back at the dairy there was no sign of Albert. She looked inside the larder and took out cocoa, flour, sugar and butter. She switched on the wireless and a failing voice came over the air, signalling that the accumulator needed changing. It would have to wait until tomorrow. There was no time if she was to bake a cake. She sang as she worked.

Ben came in smelling strongly of horses and sunflower seed cattlecake, which caused Lily to wrinkle her nose. 'You've been to the docks. We'll have to get on with the milking and then you can get washed and changed.'

He raised his eyebrows. 'I always do.'

'You'll have to do it quicker this time. We've got a visitor coming.'

'Not Aunt Dora?' he groaned, washing his hands.

'Don't be daft! You know she swore never to set foot inside this house until Dad's off the drink.'

'He should never have told her she looked like a crow.'

'It's a bit late now. Where's my apron?'

'Where you always put it.' He lifted it from its hook. 'What's up with you?'

Lily's eyes sparkled as she tied her apron. 'I don't want you making any smart remarks, little brother. It's the preacher, and he's coming to tea.'

'Thanks a lot!' He looked disgrunted. 'I like to relax when I come home. What'll we talk about?' He ran a hand through his hair. 'He'll go on about God and I'll have to watch what I say.'

'You'll have plenty to talk about.' She pushed him out of the house. 'You like reading about foreign countries and he's been everywhere. And he hardly mentioned God when we were talking. It was me that brought Him up because of Dad.'

'He's met Dad?'

'Not the most auspicious of meetings.' She told him what happened.

Ben grinned. 'Let's hope Dad doesn't come in while he's here.'

'He'll just have to lump it if he does.' Lily hummed an Ivor Novello tune as she switched on the shippon light and passed a shovel to Ben. 'Now let's get done quickly. I want to be ready when he comes.'

They were in the cool room when Ronnie entered. 'There's someone wanting you, Lil.'

Her eyes lifted from the milk filtering through into the churn. 'I hope it's not him, already! I look a mess.'

'It could be someone from the farm,' said Ben soothingly. 'I told Uncle William about the cow.'

'Not a cow today, please God!' The last thing she needed was the rigmarole of unloading and loading a cow. She hurried into the house with Ben behind her.

Immediately Lily set eyes on Matthew she snatched the cap from her head and said accusingly, 'You're early!'

'Sorry. I came straight from Bootle. If you want me to go out again . . .?' There was a twinkle in his eyes.

'Of course not!' She could not but respond with a smile, although she wished he had not discovered her in her working clothes.

She pushed her brother forward. 'This is Ben.'

Ben wiped his hands on the back of his pants before shaking hands. The preacher did not look as expected, dressed in dark trousers and a navy blue fisherman's jumper with no dog collar. 'Welcome to Liverpool.'

'Thanks. Has Lily explained?'

Ben nodded. 'It's not wildly interesting, vicar.'

Matthew smiled. 'I'm not a vicar and let me be the judge of what's interesting. I'll pay you, by the way, for your trouble.'

'You will?' Ben cast a swift glance at Lily before staring Matthew squarely in the face. 'I'd take you for nothing but if I'm honest some extra money would come in handy. But if you're short – if you're one of them that lives by faith?'

'I've got the money,' said Matthew gravely. 'How are you fixed tonight, by the way? Doing anything?'

'Nothing special,' said Ben warily. 'What's on your mind?'

'I'd like to take shots of Liverpool by night.'

'But it'll be dark!' exclaimed Lily, deciding to take part in the conversation. 'You can't be taking pictures then.'

'Of course I can!' Matthew stared at her. 'Night is a good time to get the atmosphere of a city. Don't you go out much nights, Lily?'

'Chance would be a fine thing,' she said lightly, a little hurt that he had asked Ben to go and not her. 'I suppose you won't want tea if you're going gallivanting?'

'Tea would be fair dinkum.' There was a quiver in his voice.

'Ronnie, put the kettle on,' she ordered, unfastening her apron and hurrying out of the room.

Lily washed speedily, considering he might just ask her to go if she was changed. She flung open a cupboard and looked through her scanty wardrobe. Nothing outstanding! She scowled and turned to Daisy's clothes, fingering several dresses before removing the latest her sister had made. It was blue rayon with a rounded neck and a flared skirt. She pulled it over her head, brushed her hair vigorously, outlined her mouth slightly with lipstick and raced downstairs.

Ronnie was carefully slicing the chocolate cake she had made and May was playing with the cat. There was no sign of Ben or Matthew.

'They can't have gone already?' she gasped.

'He asked to see the cows and the dairy,' said Ronnie.

'Blast! Why does he have to be interested in everything? I needn't have hurried!' She collapsed into a chair but immediately rose as the doorbell jangled.

When she returned Matthew was sitting at the laden tea table, eating her cake. 'It's good.'

'I do my best.' She had regained some of her composure.

He smiled and surprised her by saying, 'You look lovely.'

'Something I ran up myself.' She smiled sweetly at her brothers and sister, daring them to deny it. Sewing was her pet hate.

'I don't know how you fit it all in,' said Matthew. 'You women amaze me.'

'She amazes Frank,' said Ben, eyeing them both.

'Who's Frank?' Matthew stared at Lily but it was May who answered.

'Lily's beau! He drools over her.'

'He's a mummy's boy,' said Lily, wishing they had not mentioned Frank. 'He won't stand up for himself.'

Matt raised his eyebrows but did not say anything.

She thought his expression said enough. 'I need a man who's tough,' she said firmly. 'You've seen Dad. I can't always be the strong one.'

'We like Tarzan,' interrupted Ronnie enthusiastically. 'Our Lil says he's some hero but his conversation leaves much to be desired. Have you heard of him?'

A slight smile played round Matthew's mouth. 'I believe he was brought up by apes.'

'They did a better job than some mothers,' Lily could not resist saying as she reached for a potted salmon paste sandwich. She bit into it, aware that he was staring at her. She finished the sandwich and removed the tea cosy from the pot. 'More tea. Brother Matthew?'

'Thank you.' Their hands brushed as he handed her his cup and she was very conscious of that brief contact. She asked him if he had ever seen Mount Everest. He answered in the affirmative and talked about Nepal and the Ghurkas. 'My father said he never saw a soldier who was as efficient with a knife.'

Ben asked him about the troubles on the North West Frontier and they were soon into a discussion.

Soon after the table was cleared and Ben fetched a coat. Matthew said a warm goodbye but Lily's response was cool. Why couldn't he have asked her as well? Perhaps he didn't like her as much as she had hoped he did?

She did her chores. Everything felt flat. She saw the younger two to bed and switched on the wireless, irritated when hardly any sound issued from it. She reached for one of Ben's books. It was written by H. Rider Haggard, called *Montezuma's Daughter*, and was set in South America. She began to read but found it difficult to concentrate, wondering where Ben and Matt would go on a tour of Liverpool by night and whether he would return with her brother.

A hammering on the door caused Lily to fly to open it. Albert was outside, not alone but escorted by two policemen. 'He was found talking to one of the horse statues on St George's Plateau by the Cenotaph, Lil. He's getting worse,' said the younger one.

She managed to control her disappointment and embarrassment. 'Thanks, Wilf. I don't know where he finds the money to get into this state.' She stepped aside to allow the two men to half-carry her father inside. They placed him on the sofa and she offered them tea.

'Only if it's already made, luv,' said the older one she did not know so well. He rubbed his hands and held them towards the fire.

'I'll fetch his crutches,' said Wilf.

Lily put on the kettle and chattered with the two men. She gave them the last of the chocolate cake before seeing them out. Then she turned to the slumbering Albert. When would he learn sense? And where did he get the money from? She picked up the crutches and threw them down the steps into the coal cellar in temper. She covered him with a couple of blankets, cast a frowning glance at the clock and picked up *Montezuma's Daughter*. She continued to read until the print blurred before her eyes but when there was still no sign of Ben or Matt she went to bed in a bad mood.

Ben was lighting the fire when Lily entered the kitchen the next morning. 'What time did you come in?' she demanded.

He stretched and yawned. 'Late. I tell you, Lil, he's the strangest priest! Could be him being an Aussie.'

'I didn't know you'd met many,' she said frostily.

'Vexed, are you?' He took her apron from its hook and threw it at her. 'We went to some right dives, I can tell you.'

'I didn't know you knew any dives.'

He stared at a point somewhere over her shoulder and said vaguely. 'Oh, I'd heard of a few. Matt drinks, you know. Not a lot, just enough to be one of the boys.'

'Matt!' she said.

'He told me to call him that.' Suddenly Ben's expression changed and his voice was grim. 'By the way I saw Dad while we were out. You're not going to like this, Lil, but he was begging! He had this notice: OLD SOLDIER – FIVE KIDS TO FEED.'

'What!' Lily paled. 'Did the preacher recognise him?'

'How should I know?' He shrugged his shoulders. 'I could have died with shame. I walked right past him but Matt dropped money in his cap. I felt even worse then. I didn't know whether to say anything.'

'So you didn't?'

'He didn't mention it so I kept my mouth shut.'

Ben opened the back door. 'What are we going to do about him, Lil? It's not that I don't feel sorry for him at times but why could he never try harder for our sakes to face up to his life as it is? Look at Paddy Kelly who I see up Cranmer Street way. He lost both legs yet he always has a cheery word and makes jokes about skipping lorries to Southport.'

She sighed. 'People are just different. Does the preacher want to go on the rounds with you today?'

'Nope! He said tomorrow.' Ben grinned. 'He's a human kind of bloke.'

She gazed at him suspiciously, wondering if there was a double meaning to the remark, but she did not pursue it. 'Getting back to Dad . . . perhaps you could call here with the cart before you go to the docks and take him with you?'

'Oh, fine! Just what I'd like!' Ben slammed open the door to the shippon then hesitated before saying, 'But then if it's giving you a break, I suppose I can put up with him.'

'Thanks, Ben.' She hugged him.

He disentangled himself and smoothed his clothes. 'That's enough, Lil. Now let's get down to work if I'm going to be making an extra journey.'

Lily watched the horse and cart until it was out of sight. Albert was looking slightly the worse for wear but there had been a brightness in his eyes that had not been there yesterday. She had made no mention of his begging in the streets but determined it was not going to happen again. She was still smarting from the very idea that the preacher should have seen him doing such a thing.

She turned the sign to CLOSED, and with two shopping baskets on her arm, walked up the street, not pausing to say more than hello to neighbours scrubbing their steps or the tiled area behind the railings in front of their bay windows. She made her way to the tram stop near the huddle of the parish church, its walls and tall steeple blackened by the smoke from hundreds of chimneys.

She stood eavesdropping on a conversation about a lost pawn ticket and a husband's Sunday suit.

'Good morning, Lily. Going anywhere interesting?'

She whirled round. Matt had his camera held up to his face and she heard a click. 'You didn't give me time to smile,' she said.

'I wasn't sure if you'd have a smile for me.'

She pretended to have no idea what he was talking about. 'I'm going to my uncle's farm. Do you want to come?'

He nodded. 'Thanks for asking me. Last night we went to places which weren't suitable for a lady.'

'Why did you go?'

'Jesus didn't come to call the righteous. He ate with tax collectors and prostitutes.'

'None of us are righteous, though.'

He said lightly, 'There's plenty that believe they are. How's your father, by the way?'

She hesitated, not sure how to take his remark after her brother's words about Albert's begging. 'He's with Ben.'

'Ben's a good bloke.' His voice was quiet but obviously sincere. 'I'm sure your father will benefit from being in his company.'

'Dad used to ride years ago and he misses it. He'd go round to all the horse fairs. That's how he met Mam.' She found herself considering that her father had lost more than a leg because of the Great War.

Matt's voice broke into her thoughts. 'Here's a tram, Lily. Is it the one we want?'

'Yes.' She smiled at him and accepted his hand to help her up on to the tram. He also insisted on paying her fare. Then he asked her to tell him how her family came to Liverpool.

'My grandparents came by horse and cart all the way from Wensleydale in the late 1800s,' she said with pride. 'They started a dairy just like ours except it was closer to the city centre. They were hard workers and Grandfather had a passion for horses, much more than he did for cows. He had three sons and a daughter. One was killed in the war. Uncle William never went because he was that little bit older, and besides he was needed on the farm. But Grandfather didn't stop at dairying and horse-dealing. He went into buying and selling feed for animals all over Liverpool. It was years before he could afford the farm and a heap of land to go with it, but it came. Not so long ago Uncle William sold a field to a developer for a lot of money and there's houses now where I remember cows grazing.'

'You're fortunate, knowing so much about your grandparents,' murmured Matt, a distant expression on his face. 'My mother was a child immigrant and Dad said she'd never talk about the past.'

'What about your aunt?'

'I didn't see her. An old biddy stared at me through the window but didn't answer the door. A neighbour told me Aunt Jane has a job in that toffee factory they mentioned. The old biddy is her dead husband's sister.'

They reached the terminus and walked along a country lane hedged with hawthorn. Soon they came to red gates and went up a drive, approaching the farm from the side. There was a long shippon with dozens of doors, a smell of washed metal and milk and manure. In the distance there was shouting, grunting and squealing. The next moment a huge pig came in sight, pursued by several men.

Matt seized Lily's hand and they ran. Both were laughing as they entered the house. She opened a door which led into one of the back kitchens. Eggs were piled on a table as well as scoured bowls. There was a smell of baking and a woman's large rear could be seen as she stooped before an oven door. Lily coughed.

'You need your chest rubbing,' said the woman without turning.

'It's me, Aunt Dora, and I've brought you a visitor. I've told him you make the best scones in the country.'

The woman turned with a hot pie-plate held in her white apron and gingerly rose to set it on the table. 'Well, he's unlucky because I haven't made scones today,' she said tartly. 'It's apple pies but if I say so myself, they're just as good as my scones.' She stared at them and Lily hurriedly freed her fingers from Matt's grasp. 'Who's he?' demanded her aunt.

'Matt Gibson.' He smiled and held out a hand. 'I'm please to meet you, Mrs Thorpe.'

She wiped her hands on her apron. 'Miss Thorpe. And you're not from hereabouts.'

'My father was.'

'But you?' Her eyes were hard and inquisitive as they shook hands.

'Australia.'

She sniffed. 'What about your mother?'

'She was British.'

Dora sniffed again. 'At least you're not one of them that's run off with the King. Married twice! You'd think she'd learnt sense. Take him into the kitchen, Lily. I'll put the kettle on and bring tea in.'

Lily exchanged glances with Matt, who raised his eyebrows. She smiled, glad that he was not the type to be intimidated by her aunt. She led him along a stone-flagged passage and into the large living room which her aunt still insisted on calling a kitchen. In front of a black and silver old-fashioned fireplace lay a marmalade cat on a beautiful clip-rug. A clock ticked sweetly on the wall next to a large window.

'She'll have you, cat,' said Lily, scooping up the indolent creature.

'What's its name?' Matt stroked the cat's head and it purred.

'Aunt Dora doesn't believe in giving animals names,' she said in a mock-severe voice. 'Uncle William, on the other hand, says you've got to have names if there's more than one of anything. All the cows have names, even if it's Buttercup or Daisy.'

'No Lilies?' His eyes twinkled down at her. 'Do you know that passage: "Consider the lily how it grows? It toils not neither does it spin. Yet Solomon in all his glory was not arrayed like one of these."'

'Nice,' she murmured, trying not to show how much the words affected her. 'But this lily has to toil.'

'You're as refreshing as a flower of the field, though, Lily,' he said softly.

Before she had time to digest the compliment, a voice said, 'You'll be turning her head, young man.' They had not heard Dora enter and turned to look at her. 'You know your Bible then?' She placed a tray on a drop-leaf table. Her apron had been removed, showing the fancy tucking on a long black-velvet dress. 'What are you, young man? Not a papist, I hope. I won't have any of them here. Ungodly lot them Irish.'

'I'm an Anglican,' he said calmly.

Dora sniffed. 'They're almost as bad. Give me religion plain and simple. I don't know what made our Lily stay with your lot. I'm just glad Mother and Father know nowt of it. Otherwise they'd be spinning in their graves.' She left the room.

'She means it,' whispered Lily, sitting on the leather sofa by the window. 'You'll be glad to get out after half an hour. She'll be winkling every bit of information out of you she can.'

'Where does your father fit into all this?' said Matt, seating himself next to her and staring round the enormous room.

'He doesn't. He insulted Aunt Dora when he was drunk. It was a fool thing to do because she can be very generous when she wants.'

'And when she doesn't her brother begs on the street?'

Lily reddened. 'Ben wasn't sure you'd noticed. I don't know what to do about him,' she said in a rush. 'I give him very little money because we can't afford to waste it.

He was left hardly anything when Grandfather died because of his drinking.'

'No wonder you dream of faraway places,' said Matt, his eyes gazing straight into hers.

She felt a warmth inside her. 'Is it so obvious?'

'To me it is.' He leaned forward and although his lips barely brushed hers, she had time to notice how firm they were and would have liked to prolong the experience.

A loud sniff startled them apart. 'I won't have any canoodling here, young man. And, Lily, you should know better at your age.' Dora began to pour tea.

With a glint in his eyes, Matt said to Lily, 'How old are you?'

'Twenty-five.'

'I'd say that's old enough to canoodle.'

Dora frowned. 'What are you, young man? How do you earn your brass?'

'I'm a preacher and missionary, Miss Thorpe.'

Dora sat down abruptly on a straight-backed chair. 'Eh, now, young man! I hope you're not serious about our Lily? She can't be waltzing off here and there. It's her duty to look after our Albert and that's all there is to it. You being a clergyman you'll understand about duty and leave her alone now, won't you?'

'My intentions aren't important,' said Matt, looking amused. 'But if it's God's will Lily's future lies with me, then that's another matter.'

For once Dora Thorpe was flabbergasted and so was Lily. What could he mean? Did he mean what it sounded like? Whatever he meant, his words had brought alive the memory of that never quite forgotten dream of travel and adventure and her thoughts and emotions were in utter turmoil.

It was not until they were walking up the lane to the tram stop that Lily felt able to say to Matt, 'Did you mean what you said to my aunt?'

He gazed down at her with an expression she could not quite read. 'Which what? You mean about God's will?'

'Yes!' That would do for starters. She felt excitement surging inside her. 'Believe it or not, Matt, I wanted to be a missionary once but Mam died and I thought it only right to take her place.'

'And now?'

'I'd like to go before it's too late. There's Ronnie and May and Dad, of course, and I'm not qualified for anything but milking cows.'

'I think you're qualified in a lot more than that, Lily, You're a carer, and caring about people is the important thing in my kind of work. It's not an easy life. You have to be certain that it's really God's will and that keeps you going. Are you sure about this, Lily?'

She did not even pause to think again. 'Oh, I'm sure about it!' Her eyes looked up into his and she heard his quick intake of breath. The next moment he had lowered his head and their lips met. He removed the basket containing the eggs from her gloved fingers and placed it on the ground, bringing her against him. This time he made a thorough job of kissing her and she responded wholeheartedly.

Eventually he lifted his mouth and said against her ear, 'I've never felt like this about a woman before. Never thought I could demand the sacrifice living my kind of life involves. But it's different with you. I feel you could cope with anything. You're wonderful, Lily.'

She was trembling after his kiss but tried to calm herself, though desire to have him repeat the performance was like a plant inside her putting out leaves. 'There's nothing so marvellous about me,' she murmured. 'God made me the way I am.'

'He knew what he was doing.' He brushed her cheek with the back of his hand. 'Don't let life ever sour you.'

'I'll try not to.' A small laugh escape her. 'I can't believe the way you make me feel!'

'Perhaps it's love? Marry me, Lily.' He lifted her chin and kissed her again.

She felt as if she'd stopped breathing. Marry him! Leave Liverpool and go to Australia! She remembered her dream of those faraway places and without a second thought, as soon as she had breath, said yes.

# Chapter Four

'I don't know if I'm going to enjoy today,' said Ben, shrugging on an old tweed overcoat.

'Why? What's different about today?' asked Daisy, lifting her gaze from the *Red Star* propped against the teapot.

He ignored the question and nudged Lily, who was staring into space. 'What time did he say he'd get here?'

'What?' Lily's eyes slowly focused on her brother's face. She was wondering what had come over her yesterday. Was she in love with Matt? Did he love her? Neither of them had actually said the words: I love you.

'Matt! You saw him last. What time's he coming?'

'Half-eight. Is that all right?'

'It's fine by me. I don't know how Dad'll feel. Despite the cold he wants to come with me again.' He pulled on his cap. 'By the way, was anything said about the replacement cow? Bluebell's running dry now.'

'Sorry, I forgot to ask.'

'You forgot! That's not like you.' He groaned. 'I'll mention it to Uncle William again.'

'She forgot to wash my best blouse, too,' said Daisy, shaking her head. 'I don't know what's got into her.'

Lily came completely down to earth and said crossly, 'I do have a lot on my plate! I can't be remembering everything!'

'All right, all right! Keep you hair on,' said Daisy, folding her women's magazine and shoving it in her bag. 'It's not like you to lose your rag. You're not sickening for something, are you? Because I can't afford to stay off work.'

'You might have to if I wasn't here,' said Lily, placing the porridge pan on the stove as she heard Ronnie's feet thudding down the stairs.

Brother and sister stared at her. 'Where were you planning on going?' they said in unison.

Immediately Lily wished the words back. 'Nowhere! I was just thinking you should never take people for granted.'

'Ahhh! You poor thing.' Daisy placed an arm around her. 'You mustn't let Dad or the weather get you down. If only wishes had wings we could fly off to the sun.'

'Don't talk so daft,' said Ben, raising his eyes ceilingwards. 'She fancies herself in love! That's what's wrong with her.'

Lily's nerves jumped. If it was so obvious to Ben, it must be love but she was not ready to admit it. 'I do not!'

'Yes, you do! You've got your best dress on under your pinnie because Matt's coming.'

Before she could give a different reason for wearing her best frock, Ben had opened the door and closed it again.

Daisy stared at Lily, her expression lively and curious. 'Who's Matt?'

'He's someone connected with the church,' she said coolly, turning her back on her sister so she could not see her expression. She poured cream into the porridge as Ronnie came into the kitchen.

'Poor Frank,' said Daisy, reaching for her coat. 'How is this Matt connected, and what's he to do with Ben?'

'Mind your own business,' said Lily, wondering why she could not just come out with it and say, he's that missionary I mentioned but you were out when he called and now he's asked me to marry him and I've said yes. But she could not say it because Daisy would think she'd run mad, and perhaps she had, and she was thinking that she and Matt hardly knew each other and Australia was a long way from Liverpool and her family.

Daisy shrugged on her coat and said sniffily, 'When you condescend to tell me who he is, I'd like to meet him. I am your sister after all.'

'You'll meet him sooner or later.' Lily stirred the porridge with unusual vigor. 'Now are you going to work or not?'

'Of course I am. Although I still can't make out what he's got to do with Ben who hardly ever sets foot inside the church.'

Lily decided a little bit of information would not hurt and might sweeten her sister. 'He's showing him Liverpool. Now go to work. I've got to get Dad up.'

'Meanie, not telling me any more.' Daisy blew a kiss and went out.

Lily breathed easier and placed a bowl in front of Ronnie. 'Where's our May?'

'She said she's dying.'

'Oh, aye!' she said drily and left the room.

Not even a curl showed above the bedcovers. 'What have you got this time?'

May coughed. 'Double pewmonia.'

'Trust you. I might have believed it if you'd said ordinary pneumonia.' Lily was amused but she did not allow it to show as she dragged off the covers. 'Now up! Tomorrow's Saturday and you can have an extra half-hour then.' May groaned but rolled out of bed.

Lily was halfway along the landing to Albert's room when it struck her if she left him sleeping he might not wake up in time to go with Ben. It could save the family more embarrassment because there was no doubt he'd have a face on him when he set eyes on Matt. She crept downstairs but halfway recalled Matthew glancing round Aunt Dora's posh kitchen and saying, 'Where does your father fit into all this?' She remembered all the nice things he had said about her, and suffused by guilt she went and shook Albert awake.

By the time her father came sliding on his bottom downstairs it was twenty-five to nine and Lily had been to the shop door six times to glance up and down the street. Still Matt had not come.

'Porridge, Dad?' She tried to sound cheerful.

'No thanks, girl. Just a mug of tea, good and strong, and maybe an egg with a piece of fried bread.'

Lily put the frying pan on, broke an egg into it and hurried Ronnie and May out of the house. She stood a moment, keyed up for that first glimpse of Matt, but there

was still no sign of him. Perhaps he was regretting what
he had said and wasn't coming? She realised how much
she did want to see him.

It was as the clock stood at quarter past nine and Albert
was draining his mug for the second time that Ben entered
the house. He glanced at his father, then Lily. 'Where is
he?'

'I don't know.' She tried to sound casual as if Matt's
non-arrival was of no importance.

He rasped his chin with a fingernail. 'I can't hang
around, Lil.'

'Where's who?' said Albert.

'Nobody,' said Lily, giving her brother a look that dared
him to say anything about Matt. Ben got the message and
was silent.

'The invisible man, is it?' said Albert sarcastically,
lifting himself onto his crutches. He sniffed and stumped
out.

Where was Matt? pondered Lily as she watched them
go up the street. A sigh escaped her but there was no use
moping about so she removed her best dress, put on a
working one and wellies and went to muck out the shippon.

She was washing her hands when there was a banging
on the door and a voice shouted through the letter box,
'Are yer there, lass?'

'Hello, Uncle William.' She smiled up at the large red-
faced man in well-worn, thick worsted check trousers and
a jacket that almost matched. 'I wondered if you'd come.'

'Well, wonder no more, I'm here, lass.' He grinned,
revealing a mouthful of teeth as large as his smile, and

placed a heavy brown paper parcel in her arms. 'Dora said you might be feeling the strain of looking after our Albert and the youngsters. There's a couple of her lamb hotpot pies in there as well as apple and plum tarts. You're to bring the family for Easter dinner, as well.'

Lily had given little thought to Easter which was weeks away, and was a little suspicious as to why her aunt should be planning a family get-together. Was it to do with what Matt had said? 'Dad too?' she enquired.

William pushed his trilby to the back of his head. 'Dora didn't say not, lass. Perhaps she's thinking it's time to make up their quarrel.' He winked. 'Now open the back gate and you can give me a hand with them cows.'

'Will you be staying for a cuppa?'

'No, lass. I've got a man coming to see a horse so I can't be wasting time.'

She paused only to place the heavy parcel on the kitchen table and hurried through to the back, cheered by her uncle's arrival. Moving cows was always a performance when William came instead of the herdsman because he refused to use an halter, believing his voice had the same power over cows that the Pied Piper's had had over children and rats.

'Mind that tail!' he roared, waving his blackthorn stick over the backside of one replacement cow. Its hooves clattered and slipped on the damp cobbles and its thickly fringed eyes were nervous as Lily dodged out of the way past the brick-built midden. William herded it into an empty stall, singing a Tex Ritter song, and Lily gave the cow a pat.

'Now for the difficult part,' she said, her eyes gleaming as she closed the door.

'Nothing to it, lass.' He winked and turned to Bluebell. 'Come on, me beautiful girl.'

Bluebell responded to the touch of his stick on her rump. Lily swiftly slipped a rope halter over the other cow's head and headed for the open gate. Bluebell slowly followed Lily and the other cow along the back entry and into the street but she baulked at climbing the ramp into the lorry. She stood scenting the air. Perhaps it was the grass in Sheil Park situated across the road from the top of the street she could smell, because the next moment she was off, trotting in that direction.

Swiftly Lily unlooped the halter from the other cow and gave chase, watched by several interested neighbours as she swung the rope around her head and lassooed the cow. It was a skill which William had taught her and Ben. She panted and heaved on the rope. Then she heard her name called and, turning, saw Matt standing next to William. Her heart jolted but she waved matter-of-factly. He came strolling towards her, dressed in clerical black, his sunburnt face split by a smile. Instantly she was conscious of the dirt on her cheek and her working clothes, but his grey eyes were warm, and almost appreciative, she thought with relief, as if he was really pleased to see her.

The recalcitrant cow was led on to the lorry. William lifted up the tailboard and shot the bolts. 'I'll have to be going.' He squeezed Lily's shoulder and whispered in her ear, 'I like him but we need you here. You're a good sensible lass, see you stay that way.' For a moment she could not think what he meant. He turned to Matt. 'Nice meeting you, parson.'

Matt cocked an eyebrow. 'I wish you meant that, Mr Thorpe.' He held out a hand. William hesitated a second then shook it heartily before climbing into the cab and driving off.

Apprehensively Lily turned to Matt. Had he told William about his proposal of marriage? She hoped not. William might tell her father and Albert would be furious at not being told first. He would be furious anyway, she thought.

Matt smiled down at her and from a pocket took out a handkerchief. 'You've a smudge on your cheek.'

'I'm a mess,' she said ruefully. 'If you'd come when I expected—'

'You look fine.' He took her chin in his hand and wiped the dirt from her cheek. 'Shall we have a cup of tea? I'm desperate for a drink.'

'What made you late?' She could feel the heat rising in her face and wondered if any of the neighbours were watching. She cleared her throat. 'I'm sorry, Ben had to go without you.'

'It was unavoidable.' He went to pocket his handkerchief but she took it from him. 'Let me wash it.'

His fingers folded over hers and he said wryly, 'I can only stay ten minutes, then I'll have to be off.'

She wondered what had gone wrong but asked him to excuse her and to make the ten minutes a quarter of an hour, please, before running upstairs.

Lily stared at her reflection, wanting to look her best for him. How could he bear looking at her in this state?

It would be a wonder if he didn't change his mind. Apprehension gripped her and she knew then how strong was the attraction between them. She undressed and washed sketchily. She put on her best dress and dragged a comb through her dishevelled curls. Now her eyes were all sparkly. Alive! Is this how they had looked to Uncle William after Matthew had come? He had been warning her. 'You're a sensible lass,' she whispered to her reflection. 'Don't forget, and keep your feet firmly on the ground.' But hadn't she been doing that all her life?

She walked sedately downstairs, remembering Daisy saying that morning 'If wishes had wings.' There was a part of her that was soaring up and away, part that wanted to stay put.

Matt was standing in front of the fire, but turned as Lily entered and came towards her. She realised he looked weary as well as sombre. 'What is it? What's happened?' Without a second thought she went into his arms.

He said against her ear, 'The vicar had a heart attack during the night. He died a couple of hours ago.'

'How awful! What about his wife? Is someone with her?'

'The curate's wife.' He rubbed his cheek against her hair and kissed her left eyebrow. 'Poor Richard! He doesn't know if he's coming or going. He's having to see to all the arrangements so I've volunteered to do some of his sick calls.'

'Do you know your way around?'

'Not well enough.' He hesitated. 'I've offered to stay on for a while and help Richard until a new incumbent is found.'

She felt a kind of relief but wondered how he really felt about staying. Her eyes searched his face. 'Will you like that?'

'It'll be a new experience. Don't go away.' He drew her back into his arms with a sigh. 'It's comforting like this and I feel like being comforted. I've never worked as a parish priest before.'

'A different thing altogether, I should imagine.'

'Yes. I've never stayed in one place long. Only when Dad was ill and I stuck with him in Sydney. After he died I had to get away. A year ago I came in contact with the bush brothers for the first time in years. Their lifestyle drew me. I'm still only with them on approval, you might say, and I don't always behave the way I should. Perhaps through all this God could be saying it's time for something different again?'

'In what way different?' she said cautiously, wondering what it might mean to her.

'I can't say. I've learnt that sometimes you're only shown one step at a time.' He released her abruptly and ran a hand over his hair, his grey eyes uncertain. 'How about that cup of tea?'

'Are you hungry?'

'I haven't eaten since last night.'

'Then you must make time to eat.'

'Yes, Lily,' he said meekly.

She laughed, stopped worrying, cut the string on the parcel William had brought and lit the oven.

'Would you like me to show you the parish?' she asked ten minutes later as she poured tea. 'It'll help you to make up for the time you've spent here.'

'I thought you'd never offer.' His tanned face was suddenly alight with laughter and she felt a queer catch at her heart.

'I want to be of help to you,' she said slowly, putting the teapot on its stand.

He caught hold of her hand and kissed it. 'The first visit is to a Miss Fletcher.'

'Her father's the cobbler. They live over the shop. No problem there, except—'

'Except what?'

Lily frowned. 'Miss Fletcher loves nothing better than other people's business. If I go in with you she'll gossip.'

He stopped nibbling her fingers. 'Did I stampede you last night? Have you had second thoughts?'

'I wasn't sure if you'd changed your mind.' She felt unusually shy. 'We haven't known each other long.'

'How long does it take to know something feels right?' He pressed her hand between both of his. 'I felt something there between us the moment I first saw you.'

'I was attracted to your voice even before I set eyes on you.' She hesitated. 'Then when you took what I said about the kipper in the right spirit, I liked you a lot.' Her voice trailed away at the pleasure in his eyes and suddenly she knew it was all right.

'There's no need for us to rush into marriage,' he said.

'No.' She was relieved he understood and impulsively leaned forward and brushed his lips with hers. He caught her to him and kissed her deeply. Eventually they drew apart and she said unsteadily, 'Best eat your pie or we'll never get round the parish, and I've got to be back for the milking.'

He smiled and did as he was told.

By the time Lily arrived back Albert and Ben were home. 'Where've you been?' grunted her father. 'No cup of tea waiting for us and it's been a lousy day. Mrs Jones told us you went off with the preacher.'

'Stop moaning, Dad!' Ben glanced up from the newspaper. 'Our Lil's entitled to see who she likes.'

'I want to know why she was with him?' muttered Albert, draining his cup. 'She knows my feelings about his sort.'

'You're narrow-minded, Dad,' she murmured. 'And Ben's right, I can see who I like. But if you must know, the vicar dropped dead and Matt came to tell me. He's staying on at the church to help.'

'I'm not happy about him calling here,' said Albert, scowling.

'Be unhappy then,' said Lily, catching hold of her apron and pulling it off its hook. She opened the back door and walked out, wanting to slam it, but Ben was right behind her.

He waited until they were halfway down the yard before saying, 'You're made up he's staying, aren't you?'

She hesitated, wondering whether to tell him of Matt's proposal but decided it could wait. 'I suppose I am,' she murmured. 'I like him a lot.'

'It's more than that you feel.' He looked slightly unhappy. 'But he's educated, Lil. Think what you're doing.'

She was irritated by his drawing her attention to something she knew but did not want to think about. 'I am bright enough to have noticed that,' she flashed back. 'And to know men don't like women who are too clever! I'm also smart enough to have kept this dairy and household going for years. I read about things! We can communicate.'

'I didn't mean you were stupid,' said Ben, flushing. 'I'm just saying he's used to a different way of living than ours.'

'Thank God,' she muttered. 'I could do with a change.'

Ben's expression was suddenly gloomy. 'There's no talking to you.'

'No, there isn't! Now let's get on with the milking and don't say a word to Daisy about Matt or bring him up while Dad's there. I can do without his remarks at the moment.'

Lily need not have worried about her father. When they went back inside the house he had vanished and so had a large portion of one of the hotpot pies.

'He might have waited till Saturday to get drunk,' said Ben, slumping wearily into a chair.

Lily tapped her fingers on the table. 'You don't sound surprised. Has he got money?'

'Uncle William gave him two days' pay.'

'Damn him! He could have handed some of it over.' She felt angry, considering the way she had to be careful with every farthing if she was to save for a rainy day.

'Too late now,' muttered Ben, yawning. 'Better not tell our Daisy or she'll hit the roof.'

But Daisy had other things on her mind when she arrived home. 'The King and Queen are coming to Liverpool for the Grand National.' Her heart-shaped face was alive with excitement. 'Not that I'll get to see them. Now there's a man who knows his duty to his country, not like old Eddie with his fancy woman.'

'I suppose Eddie really loves her?' murmured Lily, adding thoughtfully, 'Which would you choose if you had to? Duty or love.'

Her sister hesitated. 'I suppose love, if I'm honest.'

'Aye. You'd leave the duty to me,' said Lily drily.

'You are the eldest,' said Daisy, frowning.

'So was Eddie.'

Daisy shrugged, took off her scarf and sat down. 'Let's forget it. What's for tea?'

Lily put a plate of pie in front of her and said no more, but she did not forget the conversation. There were times when she really did get fed up with being taken for granted.

On Sunday Lily and the two younger Thorpes were late getting to church because Daisy had decided to come, having discovered Matt's identity from her younger sister.

'Will the vicar be in Heaven by now?' whispered May as they crept into church, sketchily crossing themselves before sitting in a back pew.

'Shush,' hissed Lily, kneeling and burying her face in her hands so she wouldn't have to answer more questions. She was irritated, having determined to be early so as to sit at the front for a better view of Matt. Trust Daisy to think choosing the right hat was more important than getting to church on time.

She sat back and gazed down the long length of the aisle through a haze of incense. Hadn't she known it would be crowded with the vicar dying? Strange that. It wasn't as if they'd be seeing him. Morale booster for the curate, she supposed.

Richard was reading the lesson and Matt was sitting in a great carved chair in the chancel between the choir stalls. He looked distant, apart, and Lily's heart misgave her. She did not know that man. How could she have said she would marry him? She kept glancing at him as she went through the ritual of singing, praying, chanting. Then it was time for him to ascend into the pulpit. He stood there, his eyes reaching out over the congregation, searching, seeking, and suddenly she knew he was looking for her. Perhaps he was nervous? What had he said the day the vicar had died? 'I feel like being comforted.' He must have had quite a lonely life, wandering from place to place.

Matt began to speak in that powerful voice that sent delicious shivers down her spine. He spoke of Jesus turning his face resolutely towards Jerusalem. He spoke of a chosen destiny and yet of God being a God of surprises. 'Some of us like to know more or less what we'll be doing this time next week – next month. We like our lives to run like clockwork. We prefer things to happen the way we want, but it's God who is the initiator and we who are the followers.' A pause and Lily held her breath, not caring that May was scuffing her best shoes on the pew in front but Daisy did and kicked her feet down. Then she nudged Lily. 'Nice voice. No wonder you're struck.'

'Shut up,' she hissed, aware of several heads turning.

'Not bad-looking either,' whispered Daisy, taking out a packet of chewing gum.

Lily groaned but after that her sister did not say another word.

When the service was over, Lily sat for several seconds, wondering what her family would do and say when she upped and left. She did not dwell on the thought for long, preferring instead to think of a sunlit future in foreign lands. She had not told the family but she had asked Matt to Sunday dinner. Albert had gone out so there should be no trouble.

She caught up with Daisy, and her sister glanced sidelong at her and said with a grin, 'Not bad. But can he dance?'

'You can ask him. He's coming round in an hour,' she said nonchalantly.

'To see you, I suppose?'

'It could be that he just wants a pint of milk.'

'Like hell you believe that!' said Daisy, her smile vanishing. 'What's going on in your mind, Lil?'

'Thoughts. What goes on in yours?'

'I don't fancy no vicar.'

'He's not a vicar. He's a travelling preacher,' said Lily, her eyes dreamy as she imagined the future.

'So he's travelled and you find that dead romantic?'

'He's also got that lovely voice and gorgeous eyes.'

'You're besotted.'

Lily realised her sister was worried and slipped a hand through her arm. 'Yes.'

'Frank's a safer bet and he only lives down the road,' she said unhappily.

'I don't respect Frank. I respect and admire Matt,' Lily replied.

Her sister stared at her. 'But that's all it is, isn't it?'

Lily barely hesitated. 'We're going to get married.'

Daisy stopped in her tracks. 'Oh, come on, Lil! He's not going to marry you! You're different people from different backgrounds.'

Any doubt Lily might have had herself about their varying backgrounds vanished and she gave her sister a dagger-like look. 'He thinks I'm wonderful!'

'He doesn't know you!'

'What's that supposed to mean?' Lily was hurt and her temper rose even further. 'When I think of the way I cook and clean for you lot, it makes me mad your saying that!' She stormed away from her sister, past the wireless shop on the corner and up the street.

Daisy raced after her. 'Be sensible, Lil,' she panted. 'Let's pretend we're out when he comes.'

'Not on your nelly! Me and him are for each other, so you might as well get used to the idea now!' She burst into the house and went immediately to the kitchen and set about getting the dinner ready. Her father had not returned, thank goodness, and Ben was out with a mate from the Territorials.

She glanced about the kitchen with its well-worn furniture, deciding the best that could be said of it was that it was solidly made and comfortable. Her surroundings had never bothered her before but now she tried to see the room with Matt's eyes. It badly needed decorating. She glanced round at her family, at May playing with a doll, Ronnie sorting out cigarette cards and Daisy pretending to ignore her by twiddling with the knobs on the wireless set. Then she remembered Matt had seen the room before and had not been put off. Squaring her shoulders, she set the table with the best damask linen cloth and the heavy silver cutlery her mother had brought from Wrexham, and awaited Matt's coming.

'Yes, I can dance. You had to in Simla,' replied Matt in response to Daisy's question, his eyes glinting as he gazed across at her. 'Would you like a demonstration? Charleston? Foxtrot? Tango?' He glanced over at Lily who was clearing the table.

She smiled. 'Can you really dance the tango?'

'I'll prove it to you one day.'

'Never mind dancing,' said Ronnie from his perch on the stool at Matthew's knee. 'Is Simla in India?'

'Yes. It's in the Himalayan foothills.'

'Was your father stationed there?' asked Lily, drawing closer as she folded the tablecloth.

'He mentioned it as having the reputation of the live-liest place in India.'

'Did it have elephants walking in the streets?' demanded May, looking up from playing with a doll.

'Most of the streets are steep. You walk or go by rick-shaw. And talking about walking . . .' He looked up at Lily. 'If you've finished, perhaps we could go for a walk?'

'We could all go,' said May swiftly.

'You weren't asked,' said Lily firmly. 'You can help Daisy with the dishes.'

'Thanks a lot,' murmured Daisy, following her into the lobby. 'I was going out.'

Lily raised her eyebrows. 'You didn't mention it before. Anyway you can go out later. If I'm not back, you and Ronnie will have to do the milking.'

'I hate that! What'll I tell Dad when he comes in?'

'Tell him the truth.' Lily gazed at her pink cheeks in the mirror, tucked a curl behind an ear and fixed her hat at a jaunty angle.

Daisy scowled. 'I don't like the way you're behaving. It's not you.'

Lily whirled round. 'Perhaps this is the real me? The me that's been squashed down for years.'

'You're probably reading more into what he's said than there is.'

'He asked me to marry him! How can I read more into that?' She felt angry again as she drew on her gloves. 'Now if you don't mind, I want to enjoy his company.'

'Oh, Lil,' cried Daisy. 'Can't you see he's in a different class?'

Lily was still a moment, then she said in a seething voice, 'His father was a soldier in the British Army, so was ours.'

'His was probably an officer. What was Dad?'

'Unlucky!' snapped Lily. 'We come from good stock. Our ancestors worked for everything they had.'

'Shall we go, Lily?' It was Matt's voice.

They both turned. A tide of scarlet crept over Daisy's face and without a word she walked past him.

Lily realised she was trembling and took a deep breath but could not think what to say so remained silent and went out ahead of him.

'I thought we'd go to Bootle,' said Matt, taking her hand. 'It would be proper, don't you think, to meet my only living relative and invite her to the wedding?'

'I'm sorry about mine,' she said roughly. 'Daisy's only saying what Ben's said and probably what everybody else will think.'

Matt's expression was rueful. 'Your uncle warned me off. If my intentions weren't so honourable I'd find it funny. I never thought I was such a disreputable character.'

A smile vanquished Lily's cloudy expression. 'He warned me, too . . . said I had to be sensible.'

'He told me he was leaving you money and that you wouldn't get a penny if you didn't do your duty by your father.'

Her eyes widened with shock. 'He what?'

'It's true.'

She stopped in her tracks. 'I'm surprised at him saying such a thing to you. How dare he threaten you?'

'I don't think it was so much a threat as a plea. He's got a high opinion of you. I wondered if he'd once been in love with your mother.'

Lily stared at him. 'My mother?'

'He said you're alike and seemed to have had a great admiration for her. He had quite a talk with me before I called you.'

They started walking again with Lily deep in thought. 'Maybe he did love her,' she said softly. 'She told me that when Dad was away at the Front, Uncle William was a great help to her. She spoke of how difficult it was being parted for months and months on end.' She glanced up at him. 'He intended you telling me, of course.'

'I think so.'

'He should know me better than to believe money would make any difference but . . .' She hesitated. Perhaps it would make a difference to Matt? Put them more on a level.

'He doesn't want you leaving Liverpool. You mightn't have to, of course. We'll just have to wait and see.' He caught hold of her hand. 'Now let's get to Byrom Street. We can catch a tram there to Bootle.'

So he really was thinking that he might be staying put, thought Lily, not sure whether she was pleased or not. It didn't somehow match up to her dream but it might make her family happier. Hand in hand they strolled up the street, oblivious of the movement of net curtains in front windows as they passed.

They left the 23 tram at Boots corner in Stanley Road and walked up little Strand Road. Lily wondered how Matt was feeling, seeing the only living member of his family. She tried to imagine what it must be like not to have any kith or kin, and could not.

The gasworks were in the near distance to the left and as they went over the road bridge that crossed the Leeds-Liverpool canal, they could see a tall blackened chimney with the words WILLIAMS emblazoned on it. They paused to watch a barge being towed by a horse on the tow path and Lily was reminded that this canal went all the way to the county of her ancestors. 'I wonder how your aunt will feel?' she murmured.

'Pleased, I hope.' He squeezed her hand and his grey eyes were shadowed. 'Dad sent for her to come out to Australia but she must never have got the letters. It could have made a difference.'

She wondered in what way but did not like to ask. They began to walk again and talked about the canal and how long the life of the bargee would last. They turned into a street of small terraced houses and Lily wondered if his aunt had lost money in the Wall Street crash. Some lads were doing something with a set of pram wheels, a rope and a plank of wood, and they had to detour round them. They stopped in front of a green-painted door, but before Matt could knock, the door was opened by a woman.

She was tall and angular with a bony face which wore a welcoming expression. Her hair must once have been a rich auburn because there were still traces of colour in the thick greying single plait that hung over one shoulder. She wore a spotless flowered pinafore and there were slippers on her feet.

'I didn't believe her!' she cried, stretching out a hand and clutching the front of Matt's coat. 'I mean, the tales she tells you wouldn't believe half of them. But you're the dead spit of our Davy so it wasn't one of her stories! And besides, her next door told me as well,' she said with an air that was almost confidential. 'Come in, lad! Come in and tell me all there is to know about our Davy and Australia.'

Matt's expression was one of relief and warmth as he hugged her to him and it was several seconds before he held her off and said, 'I'm sorry, Aunt Jane, but Dad died a few years back. I've written several times but my letters were never passed on.'

Her smile faded. 'Oh dear, that is sad. I always hoped he might come back one day. He was good to me . . . so much older but he treated me like a little pet, God rest his soul.' There was a pause while she dabbed at her eyes. Then she smiled brightly and looked at Lily. 'Is this your young lady?'

'Yes. This is Lily,' he said with a hint of pride in his voice.

'How do you do, Lily?' Jane's head bobbed in her direction. 'You'll come in and have a cup of tea?'

They followed her inside.

'I won't take you into Amelia,' she said, bypassing a door. 'She's crippled with rheumatism but can talk the hind leg off a donkey and I want you all to myself.' She ushered them into the kitchen and ordered Matt into the easy chair in front of a glowing fire before placing an upright chair alongside it and telling Lily to sit herself down. They could see she was excited as she placed a kettle on the fire and turned back to Matt. 'I'm glad to see you, lad, but what made you come all this way from the other side of the world?'

He was silent a moment, watching her carefully as he murmured, 'Dad's fortune.'

A bark of laughter escaped her. 'You're having me on! Our Davy never had two ha'pennies to rub together.'

Matt glanced briefly at Lily and instantly she wondered what he was about. Could it be true his father had had no money when he left Liverpool? It would explain a few things.

'You've heard of the Boxer Rising?' said Matt. Both women nodded, all ears. 'After it was over the ordinary British tommies were allowed to loot the Summer Palace in Peking. Dad told me the empress wasn't a nice lady, being suspected of having poisoned a few people to get where she was. Anyway, he took some blue-coloured beads . . .' He paused.

Both women, who were hanging on to his words, chorused, 'Go on!'

'They turned out to be sapphires.'

There was a hush. Then Jane laughed and laughed, rocking herself back and forth, slapping her knee. 'Well, who'd have believed it! Just like Aladdin finding the magic lamp in a cave.'

'It was stealing really,' murmured Matt, his eyes bright.

'Spoils of war! And I'm not grieving for that empress!' Jane clapped her hands in delight. 'I bet the money did more good in our Davy's pocket than it would have in hers.'

'It could get you out of here if you wanted, Aunt Jane,' said Matt seriously, leaning towards her.

She looked at him in astonishment. 'I wouldn't move from here! I've made a niche for meself.' She made a movement with her head. 'And her in there needs me. But if you could spare a bob or two, it would be nice to have a bit put by for me old age.'

Matt's face creased into a smile. 'A bob or two it is then, with interest . . . and you can buy yourself a new frock for the wedding. Lily and I are going to be married.'

Jane's face lit up. 'I love a wedding. When's it to be?'

Matt exchanged a rueful glance with Lily, who had not got as far as thinking of a when or a where. She did not know what to reply. She thought of brides and honeymoons, of moons in June. 'June?' she croaked.

Jane laced her hands together and pressed them against her thin chest, her expression radiant. 'I'll have something to look forward to after the Coronation. Who'd have believed when I woke up this morning it would turn out to be such a lovely day?'

Matt and Lily were silent as they left the house and it was not until they were nearing the bridge that Lily, who had been busy thinking, said, 'Was all that true about your father finding the sapphires?'

Matt scrutinised her face, his expression amused. 'You can't believe I'd lie about such things?'

'You might,' she said, adding hastily as his eyebrows shot up, 'from the best of motives! Your aunt might not have been prepared to take money from you otherwise, and you probably want to help her.'

'And where do you think I'd find the money to help her if it wasn't true?'

'You'd eat less or something. You're the self-sacrificial type.' She smiled. 'It just seems so fantastic!'

'It's true!' He smiled. 'I don't lie, Lily, and don't make me out a saint. I'm not. My father sold the sapphires in Sydney. Then he met my mother and married her. I think he would have settled down for good then but she died and he couldn't rest. For years I had no idea he had so much money, and I know the difference having some can make,' he said drily. 'Look at those men over there all trying to get rich quick.'

Lily's gaze followed his to the pub set back from the road on the opposite side. There was a crowd of cloth-capped men gathered in a muttering circle, then there was a shout and a cap flew up into the air. 'Don't tell me,' she murmured. 'They play pigeon toss in Australia, too.

'Sure they do.' His eyes narrowed. 'Gambling, drinking . . . it's what a lot of men do when there's no women around to stop them.'

'If a scuffer catches them, they'll be for it,' said Lily, frowning. 'I wonder where their lookout is . . . that must be him leaning against—'

'What is it?' Matt's voice was sharp.

Lily made no answer but fled across the road in a fury. 'Dad! What on earth are you doing here?'

Albert lifted his head. 'Lily! It's our Lily!' The words were slurred. 'What are you doing here, girl? Spying on me, are yer?'

'You flatter yourself that I'd be bothered,' she snapped. 'You're a fool, Dad. The drink'll kill you one of these days, and it'll be all your own fault.'

'I'm not drunk.' He rubbed a sleeve across a dripping nose. 'Got a cold and the drink's pure-ly me-medic-medicinal.'

'I don't believe it!' Her eyes glinted frostily. 'But if it's true you can come home with us.' She seized hold of his arm as Matt drew near.

Albert shook off her hand, and noticing Matt, eyed him balefully. 'That's that preacher bloke. What are you doing here with him?'

'My aunt lives around here,' said Matt, giving him a nod. 'Great to see you again, Mr Thorpe.'

'An' I bet!' Albert sniffed. 'What are you doing with my daughter? She don't need no religion and should be home looking after the kids.'

Lily felt like screaming. 'That's all you think I'm here for, isn't it, Dad? To look after your kids while you go to the devil as quickly as you can! Well, I'm going to marry this preacher bloke and you'd better get used to the idea!'

Albert's face turned the colour of putty. 'You wouldn't do that, girl?' he gasped. 'We won't be good enough for the likes of him. He'll make you cut us off.'

'Matt's not like that!' She looked at him scornfully. 'As for you, you're a disgrace to the family and if you don't buck up your ideas you won't be giving me away.'

Some of the colour came back into Albert's face and he bristled. 'Don't want to give you away to him! You're my daughter and we need you.'

Matt said coolly, 'You've other daughters.'

'Not like Lily.' He looked miserable. 'She was happy till you came along.'

Lily felt a familiar pity. 'I wasn't unhappy.' Her tone held a little more warmth. 'I love all of you but there's been times when I've wanted to do something different.'

Albert shook his head dolefully. 'It hurts me to hear you say that. If I'd known we were all such a burden to you, I'd have finished meself off years ago.'

'Oh shut up, Dad! Stop feeling sorry for yourself and think of me for a change,' she said, exasperated once again. 'I've spent years thinking of you lot.'

'It's your duty! But I suppose whatever I say you'll marry him?'

'Yes! Yes! Yes!' she cried, irritated by that word 'duty'.

He glared at her, then his expression changed and he sniffed. 'I suppose there's nothing I can say then, and at least with him working at the church you won't be far away.'

Lily glanced at Matt, half-opened her mouth but he shook his head. 'Who told you that?' she demanded.

'One of the gossiping old biddies from the church.' He looked aggrieved. 'Told me it'd do me good to go, but don't you be thinking you'll get me to church, the pair of you.'

'Perish the thought,' murmured Lily and exchanged a smile with Matt. Telling her father she was marrying him could have been a lot worse.

Lily called at the farm a couple of days later, knowing that Ben had already broken the news to her uncle and aunt.

'We'll come to the wedding, lass,' said William, his expression dour. 'But I won't say we're pleased about it. I can't see Daisy doing half what you do or staying at home for long. She'll be off, and little May's too young to cope with housework.'

'They could all come and live here,' said Lily boldly.

'Our Dora wouldn't have it.' He hesitated. 'I'll give you a lump sum when you get married as it's likely you'll be needing it. I wasn't going to but Ben says your man's staying put at the moment and helping out at the church you go to.'

Lily thought, how do I break it to him that I could be going to Australia? She hesitated further before saying, 'We mightn't be staying in Liverpool, Uncle William.'

He stared at her hard. 'A church in Lancashire then? I'm sure he can swing it, lass, so you don't have to go too far. I'll miss you dropping in regular-like, but if you can come now and again it won't be so bad. I understand a woman has to go where her man's work takes him.'

Lily murmured agreement, deciding to say no more until she knew for certain what Matt's plans were.

'Don't forget to remind our Albert and Ben it's National day on Friday. We'll have a day off and I'll take them to Aintree so we can watch the race,' said William, smiling and rubbing his hands. 'I'll pick them up earlier tell them.'

Lily promised that she would. Although no gambler, she took an interest in the Grand National herself and always had a flutter. She'd won a few times and there was this dream of a wedding dress in Owen Owens . . .

Uncle William arrived early and she asked him to put a bet on for her. He smiled good-humouredly. 'What have you in mind, lass?'

'Royal Mail,' she said, having scanned the list of runners in the *Daily Post* already.

'It's a good horse,' said Albert, happy for once. 'Welsh-owned. Be a good little runner. You must have inherited your taste in horseflesh from me, girl.'

Perhaps she had? thought Lily, and handed over the pound of change she had taken from her cocoa tin before caution took over and she changed her mind.

It was a nailbiting few hours but to Lily's delight Royal Mail passed the winning post first at a 100-6.

'We'll go shopping tomorrow,' she said to May, turning down the volume on Jessie Matthews who was singing songs from the films. 'I'll buy you new shoes for the wedding.'

'Can we go and see the King and Queen, as well?' asked May, who had taken the news of her sister's forth-coming nuptials with aplomb, only wanting to know whether she would be a bridesmaid and have a new dress. 'We can wave them off at Lime Street.'

'OK!' said Lily, thinking if she and Matt did go to Australia it could be the last chance she would get of seeing royalty.

Early Saturday morning Lily and May purchased a couple of Union Jacks and managed to squeeze on to the Plateau at St George's Hall right opposite the grand North Western Hotel decorated with flags and bunting. The crowd was in a good mood; most professed admiration and liking for the former Duke and Duchess of York, and more than a couple had a few malicious things to say about Mrs Simpson, whose divorce action against Mr Simpson on the grounds of his adultery had gone to court the day before. There came a groundswell of noise and

cheering which grew louder and louder as a shiny limou-
sine came into sight. The royal couple alighted from the
car, pausing for a moment outside the entrance of the
hotel.

Lily and May cheered like mad, caught up in the mood
of the moment as Queen Elizabeth waved shyly at the
crowd before vanishing inside the hotel.

Exhilarated by the moment, and with May's hand
clasped firmly in hers, Lily forced her way out of the
crowd. Any doubts she might still have about marrying a
man she had known less than a month were put aside. It
was fun and exciting buying her trousseau. She had never
spent so much money on herself. First they went to
Blackler's where Lily purchased rayon satin underwear,
stockings and a full-length silk nightdress. Then to Lewis's
for a couple of floral silk crépe-de-chîne gowns at ten
shillings and sixpence each. The necklines were finished
with a jabot effect and the bodice and sleeves had pleated
frills. For her going away outfit she bought a box jacket
and a blouse with puffed sleeves, as well as a sailor hat
of pale blue straw with a wreath of pink flowers round
its brim. Then they hurried to Clayton Square and into
Owen Owens. She bought shoes, calf and glacé ones with
a full Spanish heel for herself, and strapped ones for May,
before dashing to the floor where the wedding dresses
were displayed.

Lily stared at the gown which had caught her eye. It
was made of lustrous white satin with rows of piping on
the bodice and a large circular train. As she tried it on
she glanced at her sister for approval.

'You look like a princess,' breathed May, her eyes shining. 'I can't wait for mine to be made.'

Lily smiled. 'I'll get Daisy to make you two dresses. One for the wedding and one for Coronation Day, and you'll look just like a princess too.'

It seemed to Lily looking back on that spring it was a happy time, spoilt only by her father having a few drams with William in the stables where his brother was showing off the new black stallion he had bought. He ended up falling in the garden where he crushed an old and much revered rosemary bush. Instantly Dora boxed his ears and banished him from the house again.

The month of May heralded in Coronation fever. Decorations began to appear in shops, on buildings and across streets. The sisters made crepe paper roses in red, white and blue and decorated the dairy window. There were to be parties in the streets, trees planted, fireworks and a flotilla of illuminated ships on the River Mersey. There was even to be a King's Champion ceremony outside the cathedral.

It was Ben who pointed out from an article in the local paper that there was a Liverpool in Australia. A bishop who had been ordained in their Liverpool, and had spent time being an army chaplain in the other one, had recently died. 'Perhaps Matt knows of him?' he said.

Matt did. The much smaller Australian Liverpool was not really that far from the centre of Sydney.

Matt was busy during this time. A new incumbent had been found for the church but would not be arriving until after the Coronation. Lily wished she could see more of Matt. When they were together she wanted no more out of life than to be with him, but when they were apart sometimes the odd doubt would creep into her mind. Was she fitted for his kind of life and how would her family cope without her?

The newspapers were filled with news of personages heading for London. There was a united service of thanksgiving in the Great Synagogue in London where the chief rabbi spoke of Britain and its daughter nations being the strongest hope against the moral barbarism in the world. It made Lily proud to be British, but it made it harder to forget Hitler's claim that France and Britain's seizure of certain colonies after the Great War was robbery and they should be returned to Germany.

'There's going to be trouble,' said Albert grimly. 'You can take my word for it, girl. The Lord Mayor of Liverpool's right in preparing people for the possibility of air raids as they've had in Spain. And God help us if they come! Gas attacks . . . I'll never forget the way they scared the hell out of us.' His hands shook as he pulled on fingerless gloves.

'Stop worrying, Dad,' said Ben. 'Hitler's bluffing. You just make sure you can handle the reins. I don't want any runaway horses while I'm loading.'

Lily pushed Germany to the back of her mind and got on with enjoying the Coronation celebrations.

On Coronation Day the family listened to the ceremony on the wireless before going to the street party. Daisy flirted with Frank, who had been looking miserable since the news of Lily's forthcoming marriage, but as soon as it was dark and people were dancing in the street, she told Lily she was going into town to meet Ted, the brother of her erstwhile dancing partner.

Matt managed to get away later in the day and swept Lily into his arms to the sound of Frank's tinkling piano. 'Let's dance.'

'I can't dance,' she said, smiling up at him. 'I've never learnt. You need Daisy.'

'I don't want Daisy. I want you.' His voice was intense and his eyes had an expression in them which caused a thrill to pass through her. 'Just follow my feet.'

Lily did as she was told and soon was giving herself up to the pleasure of being in his arms. After a while he danced her to the corner of the street away from the crowd where they stood swaying to the rhythm of the music for a moment. Then he kissed her with that fierce passion that sent waves of longing through her. 'Lily, I want you,' he groaned, burying his face against the curve of her neck. 'Thank God, it won't be much longer before we're married and we can sleep together.'

He had never spoken of bed before and she felt her cheeks going hot. 'I never thought you'd say such things,' she whispered. 'The church always seems against sex.'

A chuckle sounded in his throat. 'The church knows the power of sex, that's why. St Paul certainly did. Otherwise he wouldn't have told Christians that if they couldn't control their lust, they must marry.' He lifted his head and gazed into her shadowy face, and the tone of his voice changed. 'I've informed the brotherhood about our marriage and that I'll be leaving them, and I've had a letter from Joy, whose husband is an old school friend of mine. They rent part of my father's house in Sydney. Remember me telling you she deals with all my mail?'

'I'd forgotten. What do they have to say?'

'They enclosed a letter from a friend of mine in the ministry. I wrote to him about doing a preaching tour out there, including my impressions of the state of the faith in the north of England.' He paused.

'And?' prompted Lily, shifting in his arms as her heartbeat quickened again.

'He wants to know if he should go ahead and arrange it.' He paused and said seriously, 'I want to know if it's what you really want, Lily.'

She stared up at him. How could he doubt it after all she had said about her desire to travel. Go to Australia! She had almost stopped believing it would happen because of the way he had settled down in Liverpool. 'Of course it's what I want!' She hugged him convulsively. 'Wherever you are, I want to be.'

He looked at her, an almost uncertain expression on his face. Gently he ran a finger along the curve of her jaw. 'You really mean that? It won't be easy saying goodbye to your family. It'll hurt. You're going to the other side of the world.'

'I knew it might come to it.'

'But you haven't felt the pain of parting yet.' She almost did not catch the words.

'I know it'll hurt but none of us can have it both ways in this world,' she said with assurance.

'As long as you're sure.'

The note in his voice made her question why was he so insistent. 'We must do as you think right, but I'm all for it,' she said, placing the decision in his hands.

'Then we go.' He kissed her with an aching restraint and she wondered suddenly if he had ever been with a woman before becoming a priest or if he had always been celibate. There was still so much she did not know about him but it was a question she felt unable to ask.

Eventually they drew apart and began to walk back up the street. Lily caught sight of her father and felt the muscles in her stomach tighten. 'We'll keep quiet about Australia until after the wedding if you don't mind,' she said slowly.

'Don't you think it would be better to warn them?' said Matt, his brows drawing together over the nose that was almost perfectly straight.

Lily imagined the fuss Albert would kick up, and was filled with apprehension. 'Believe me, it's better to do it my way,' she said firmly. 'That way nothing can spoil our special day.'

# Chapter Five

On the morning of the wedding Lily drew back the curtains to allow the sunlight to flood into the bedroom and thought with a grimace, happy the bride that the sun shines on! She knew now they would be leaving for Australia ten days after the wedding, and for three of those days she and Matt would be away on honeymoon at a destination he was keeping to himself. She was filled with painful and conflicting emotions.

'Can I be first for the bathroom?' said Daisy, scrambling out of bed, her nightdress riding up about her thighs. 'You'll have things to do, Lil. You won't want to get smelly all over again.'

'You've got things to do, too,' she said quietly, facing her sister. 'What about the flowers? You said you'd pick them up.'

'I will! But I've time to get bathed first,' she said, smiling. 'I don't want the rest of them pinching all the hot water while I'm at the hairdresser's.'

'We'll keep the fire going all morning,' said Lily, picking up a nail file and toying with it.

'Excited?' said Daisy, glancing over her shoulder at her as she fingered the pink taffeta bridesmaid's dress hanging from the picture rail.

'What do you think?' Lily felt sick with sudden nervousness and hoped her sister would understand and not be awkward when she told her about their imminent departure for the other side of the world. 'You will manage while we're on our honeymoon? We'll be back Tuesday.'

Daisy sighed and picked a loose thread from the skirt. 'I'll have to, won't I? Do you know yet where you and Matt will be going when you come back?'

Lily came to a decision. 'I wasn't going to tell anyone yet, but perhaps you should know. Matt and I are going to Australia.'

A stunned expression fixed on Daisy's face and several seconds passed before she said, 'You can't mean it! What about Dad? How will I cope without you near at hand?'

'You'll cope! And lower your voice,' whispered Lily. 'I don't want Dad knowing yet. I've told you the first because you're my sister and,' she added in a rush, knowing suddenly she could not cope with telling the others, 'I want you to tell the rest of them after we've left on our honeymoon.'

Daisy collapsed on to the bed and May stirred and mumbled indistinctly. 'I thought it could happen but I hoped it wouldn't! Why do you have to go so far away? Surely Matt could find other work over here? There's loads of churches.'

'Don't blame Matt, blame God,' said Lily lightly.

'God! He's making you holy like him,' moaned Daisy.

Her holy! She must be joking, thought Lily, but she felt she had to get out of the room before her sister said anything else that might unsettle her. 'Where He calls we have to go,' she said, in that still flippant tone that disguised her

real feelings. 'Just think of it, Dais! Sun, sea, exotic sights –
and the company of a man who thinks I'm wonderful.'

'You've forgotten all the smelly sheep!' called Daisy
crossly.

Lily ignored the comment, keeping her mind on the
vision her own words had created. She went to wake her
father but he was not there and his bed had not been slept
in. She ran downstairs and out into the yard to the shippon.
Her brother had said he would do the milking single-
handed that morning. She flung open the door. 'Ben! Do
you know where Dad is?'

He presented her with an unshaven face. 'Isn't he in
his bed?'

'Would I be asking if he was?' she said impatiently.
'It hasn't been slept in. Didn't you wait up for him?'

Ben scratched his chin. 'It got late. I needed an early
start on the day.'

Lily pressed a hand against her forehead and thought,
everything is starting to go wrong. 'If he's drunk somewhere, I'll kill him!'

'He wouldn't,' said Ben stoutly. 'Not on your wedding
day. Deep down he cares about you, whatever he might
feel about your marrying Matt.'

'Sez you!' said Lily, pulling a face. 'Do you think he's
got cold feet?'

Ben hesitated. 'No.' He squared his shoulders. 'I
shouldn't really tell you this because he wanted to surprise
you . . . but if you're going to be thinking the worse, I
suppose I better had.'

'Tell me what?' she said, her curiosity aroused.

'He aims taking you to church in Grandma's old carriage. You know, the one in the stables at the farm?' Lily stared at him, utterly taken aback. Her brother grinned. 'He's done it up. He was planning on decorating it last night.'

Lily was overcome by a rush of emotion. 'I never thought he'd do such a thing for me,' she said unevenly, tears starting in her eyes.

'Goes to show, doesn't it?' said Ben. 'He does have his thoughtful side.'

She nodded, feeling terrible about leaving them all, but she had to put on a happy face. 'And there was me believing I was going in Uncle William's posh car,' she said with a smile. 'So you think he's at the farm?'

'It's a strong possibility. What are you going to do?'

'I haven't got time to do anything. I can only hope if he is there, he and Uncle William haven't shared too many drams, otherwise he'll be late.' She brushed away the sudden tears with the back of a hand and took a deep breath. 'Anyway, it's no use me standing here. I'll never get anything done and I'm expecting Mrs Jacobs and her sister soon. She said she would take care of everything while I'm in church.'

'Get going then,' urged Ben. 'You don't want our Ronnie messing up the place after you've tidied up.'

Lily nodded and ran up the yard.

Albert turned up a few hours later. His clothes were rumpled, his hair was unruly and there was stubble on his chin but he seemed sober enough as he pulled on the reins outside the dairy, watched by a group of admiring children. A couple shouted, 'Give us a ride, mister!'

'Where the heck did you spend the night, Dad?' said Ben, coming out of the dairy where he had been serving a customer.

'I slept in the stables. I missed the tram and our Dora got all toffee-nosed and wouldn't let me into the house because I'd had a couple of drinks.'

'She'll come round.' Ben's eyes narrowed as they ran over the black horse between the shafts. 'Isn't that Uncle William's pride and joy?'

'He's a beauty, isn't he?' said Albert, beaming as he eased himself down on to the pavement. 'I asked William if I could borrow him to pull our Lily's carriage.'

'And he said yes?' Ben was incredulous. Such horse-flesh didn't come cheap.

'Don't sound so surprised,' said his father huffily. 'I was used to dealing with horses like this in my day. Now get him some oats and give him a drink. I'll wait till yer come back, then I'll get meself ready.'

'OK.' Ben went and did as he was told.

'Thank God, you're here, Dad,' said Lily, placing the jar of Pond's Vanishing Cream on the dressing table as Albert entered the bedroom. She had seen his arrival from the window and was thrilled by the thought of travelling to her wedding in such style, but guilt over the secret she was carrying almost suffocated her. 'Why didn't you let me know where you were?'

'I wanted it to be a surprise. Our William and Dora are going straight to church like everybody else to save you work.' He grinned. 'He's a beauty, isn't he?'

'A real highstepper,' said Lily, peeping out of the window, not wanting him to know how moved she was. 'You can control him?'

'Give me some credit, girl.'

'Sorry. It's just so unexpected.' She leaned forward and kissed him. 'I thought you'd been and got drunk because of the wedding.'

'Only a couple.' There was a flush on his face. 'I'll save me real drinking till later.' He sighed heavily. 'I never thought I'd be losing me little girl.'

Lily smiled. 'Don't get maudlin, Dad. It's a long time since I was a little girl.'

'Aye! Your mam was alive then. If only she were here now.' He paused and toyed with a ribbon dangling from the bouquet of roses, carnations and gypsy grass on the dressing table. 'She was religious, you know? Believed in a heaven and all that – then to go the way she did. Didn't make sense to me.'

'I know, Dad,' she said, thinking, this is terrible! He'll have me in tears again if he goes on. 'I miss her, too.'

'Aye.' He sniffed and wiped his sleeve across his eyes. There was silence and Lily felt she was going to burst and almost told him about Australia but was too cowardly.

'I'd best get ready,' said Albert, rousing himself at last from whatever thoughts gripped him. 'The preacher won't like being kept waiting.' He left the room.

Lily closed her eyes and thought of Matt. Then she started counting, anything to keep her mind off her family. She lifted the white satin dream of a gown from the hanger on the picture rail. It was time she was getting ready too.

Oohs and ahhs rippled through the crowd of women outside the church as Lily carefully descended from the ribbon-and-flower-bedecked carriage in a cloud of white. Daisy came forward to help her with her train. 'I'm glad it's not raining,' she muttered, 'or this would get in a right mess. I want it to stay nice for when I get married – that's if you'll let me have it?'

Lily stared at her. 'What do you mean, you get married? Are you trying to spoil my day? They'll need you at home for a while.'

Daisy tossed her head and gave a harsh laugh. 'I'm not going to rush into anything, unlike you! But don't you worry over anything I do. You've made it plain that you no longer regard any of us as your problem by going to Australia.'

'That's not fair!'

'What's not fair about it? You know you've been like a mother to the younger two.' Daisy straightened and glanced at May, who was waving to a friend in the crowd. 'I'll have to sort that little madam out now.'

'Daisy, please will you stop it?' commanded Lily. 'You're spoiling my day!'

'I don't want you to go.' Her sister's voice wobbled as she fluffed out the misty silver veil screening Lily's worried eyes.

'Please, don't upset me now. Please, please! You know I don't really want to leave you all.'

'But you are and you look so beautiful,' sniffed Daisy. 'Not a bit like my sister at all.'

'Thanks!' Lily's sense of humour suddenly asserted itself. 'Am I the duckling that's suddenly become a swan?'

'I feel you're a stranger and I've lost you already.' Daisy swallowed hard.

'Here's Dad. Stop crying or you'll ruin your mascara. Think of wearing this dress yourself one day.'

'But you won't be here to see me.' Her voice wobbled and she turned away.

Lily had never been so glad that she was wearing a veil as when her father approached. She forced her lips into a smile.

'You really want to go through with this, girl?' he said, looking grim.

'Yes, Dad,' she whispered.

'Let's get it over with then.' He crooked his arm. Lily placed her hand inside it and determined not to allow anything to spoil the precious moments ahead.

'Lily Gwynneth, wilt thou have this man to thy wedded husband, to live together after God's ordinance in the holy estate of Matrimony? Wilt thou obey him, and serve him, love, honour and keep him in sickness and in health; and forsaking all other, keep thee only unto him, so long as ye both shall live?'

'I will.' Lily's voice was quiet but steady as her gaze shifted from the new minister, clad in gold and cream robes, to Matt who looked austere but undeniably attractive in a pristine white shirt and charcoal-coloured lounge suit. Their eyes met and she felt warmth flood her, although into her mind popped the thought that he only fulfilled some of the traits she had sought in her perfect hero. Why was she marrying him? she thought with unexpected panic.

'Who giveth this woman to be married to this man?'
said the vicar and the panic receded.

Albert cleared his throat but no words came out. There
was no need for them but he should have taken Lily's
right hand to give it to Matthew. She sensed the struggle
inside him and did not hesitate but grasped her father's
hand and did the job for him.

Afterwards, with Matt's ring on her finger while a
friend snapped their pictures, Lily was convinced she had
done the right thing in marrying him. He was her present
and future and life promised to be exciting with him. As
for her family, they would manage fine without her.

Aunt Dora did not believe so and came into the bedroom
as Lily was changing into her going away outfift. 'I don't
know how you can do it! Our poor Albert and those poor
children! Your Daisy won't do her duty by them for long
and what will happen to them then? It wouldn't be so bad
if you weren't going to the other end of the earth but—'

Lily whirled round the from mirror. 'How did you find
out about Australia?'

'From that woman!' Her black silk-clad bosom swelled.

'What woman?' said Lily, frowning.

'That aunt of that husband of yours.' Dora's eyes
glinted. 'How was it she knew and we didn't? It's a
disgrace, Lily! She thinks it's wonderful. Two young
people in love sailing off into the blue to a new life in a
new country. What's wrong with the old one? That's what
I say.'

'Plenty where some are concerned,' said Lily, her heart
beating heavily. 'But that's not the reason why we're

leaving.' She slipped on her snuff-coloured jacket and put the blame on God for her actions. 'I don't suppose you remember but Matt told you the first day you met him that he has to go when and where God calls him. It's His will that matters.'

'I can't believe it's God's will that you're deserting your family,' she snapped. 'As for not telling us – I think it's a disgrace!'

Lily's temper rose. 'It is my life! If you're so concerned, you could volunteer to look after them.'

'Me!' Her outrage was plain to see. 'Young people need young folk and I'm no spring chicken.'

'Neither am I,' said Lily, her expression mutinous as she took her new hat from a box. 'I'm twenty-five and I've reared May from a baby. I've well done my duty! You could be a bit more understanding. It's going to be painful parting from her and Ronnie.'

'Not painful enough it seems,' sniffed Dora, watching her set the hat at a flattering angle.

Lily turned on her. 'What do you want me to do? Cry blood?'

'Don't be silly,' said Dora, bristling. 'I've said my piece. I'll be going.' She marched to the door, only to pause as she opened it. 'I just hope you don't live to regret this day.'

Lily's eyes sparkled. 'Goodbye, Aunt Dora. Watch you don't fall down the stairs.'

'You'd like me to do that, wouldn't you?' said her aunt and slammed the door.

Lily was trembling and several minutes passed before she was composed enough to pick up her suitcase.

She met Matt on the stairs. 'Your Aunt Dora's left.'

'Uncle William as well?' Her voice was dismayed.

'Him too.' His eyes were hard as he took the suitcase from her. 'I'm the world's worst for taking you away. I'm selfish and utterly unchristian, according to your aunt. William didn't say a word.'

'Damn!' She squeezed his hand. 'Sorry. But why did you have to tell your Aunt Jane?'

'Because she asked me. I couldn't lie! I feel bad enough leaving when we're only just getting to know each other.'

She could understand that. 'You could have not told her the truth!'

'Lily, we should have told them all earlier,' he said with a touch of impatience. 'But you didn't want any upset.'

'I wasn't thinking of myself,' she countered swiftly.

'Did I say you were?'

'No, but—' A hand went to her head. 'I'd better go and see Dad.'

'He knows.'

'Aunt Dora told him?'

'Who else?'

Lily's spirits plummeted further and she said through dry lips, 'How did he take it?'

'She told me he was going to get the horse ready to take the carriage back to the farm. Shall we see him together before we go?'

Lily hesitated then shook her head. 'I'll go on my own, if you don't mind?'

He raised his eyebrows. 'Why should I mind? I don't doubt it'll be less difficult for you both without me there.'

She nodded and left him.

Lily found Albert still in the backyard, unplaiting the horses's tail. There was a handful of ribbons on the ground. She watched him a moment before approaching, noticing he was slightly unsteady on his feet. 'We'll be leaving soon, Dad. I just came to say tarrah.'

'Nice of you to bother, girl.' The words were barely slurred.

She took a deep breath. 'I know I should have told you about Australia but it was so difficult. I didn't want to spoil the wedding for you all.'

'Hah!' He did not look at her, which hurt more than if he had hurled abuse at her and looked at her with hate.

'I'll be back on Tuesday. We'll have some time together then.'

Still he did not look at her. 'And how long after that before you go travelling with him?' he snarled.

'A week,' she burst out. 'I was going to tell you!'

'Aye, sometime never! Perhaps you'd have written a letter to me from the ship!' He turned and looked at her.

'That's not true! I'm not that thoughtless.' She searched for a way to appease him and picked up one of the blue ribbons, twisting it round her finger. 'It was lovely of you to have done this for me.'

'You're my eldest daughter.' His voice was low and uneven.

Her heart sank. 'I knew you'd be upset.'

'Upset!' A sharp laugh broke from him. 'I lost your mother and now I'm losing you.'

'We can write to each other.' She touched his shoulder but he jerked away.

'Don't, girl. Go to him. He's what you wanted.'

'Yes. But that doesn't mean I don't care about you.'

'Not enough.' He turned back to the horse, resting his head against its flank. 'Don't let me keep you.'

She was hurting in a way she had never thought she could. There had been times in the past when he had seemed as much of a child to her as her brothers and sisters and now it was as if he had grown up and away from her. It seemed unfair after all she had done for him. 'Dad, be reasonable!'

'Tarrah, girl.' His voice was harsh.

Lily gave up. 'Have it your way.' Without another word she went back inside the house. Her eyes were damp and it hurt to swallow.

A crowd waved Lily and Matt off, and May and Ronnie ran alongside the hired car for a short way before falling back. Tears blurred Lily's vision because it was the first time she had ever been parted from them. They had been silent on the subject of Australia so she presumed they did not know yet about her leaving. How would they react? With his gaze still on the road Matt took one of her hands and clasped it firmly. He did not say a word but she was comforted. After a few minutes she reached inside her handbag and fingered the envelope her sister had handed to her saying it was from Uncle William. It felt thin and looked like it had been opened and resealed. Inside was a five-pound note. So much for her inheritance.

Matt said, 'We can manage without his money.'

'It's not the money.' She cleared her throat. 'He always seemed to understand – was always kind.'

'He's had a shock. Give him time.'

She attempted a smile. 'Dad's in shock, too. He'll probably get falling-down drunk and I won't be there to pick him up.'

'Try and put him out of your mind. We've got the honeymoon to look forward to. Don't let's allow worrying about your father to spoil it.'

She squeezed his hand and tried to stop thinking of herself. 'I bet you're wishing now you'd never married into my family?'

'I've no regrets.'

'Really?' That pleased her. She smiled and stretched. 'At least I had my wedding with no real bother, but I hope May and Ronnie will be all right when they get to know about Australia.'

'Our wedding,' he corrected, glancing at her. 'As for May and Ronnie, forget them too. It's just us for the next few days. Get some rest now.'

Lily settled herself more comfortably in the seat and closed her eyes. She set about trying to blank out the nagging worry for her family. She slept for a while but eventually began to drift into a level of consciousness where snatches of conversation came and went in her mind, mingling with odd thoughts. Just us, just us. No longer six to think of, just two. Him and her, her and him, till death us do part.

'I lost your mother, now I'm losing you. You won't be there to see me. I feel like I've lost you already.'

'You really want to go through with this, girl?'

'Yes,' she'd replied, impatient to get on with the act that would part her from her family. Aunt Dora ranting at her and her hitting back. 'I've well done my duty! It's going to be painful parting from May and Ronnie.' 'Not painful enough!' 'What do you want me to do? Cry blood?'

Blood! Blood! A feeling of horror swept over her and she tried to shake it off. Parting is such sweet sorrow . . . There were tears. What was sweet about parting? It hurt. Was there always some loss in gain? My wedding. Our wedding. Of course, our wedding, just the two of us.

'We've got the honeymoon to look forward to, don't let worrying about your father spoil it.'

Lily's eyelids flickered open and she sat up abruptly, filled with a strange panic. There were unfamiliar green fields and hedges on either side of the road and the smell of elder blossom mingling with the scent of grass and clover came through the open window. 'We've got to go back!' she cried.

'Relax, Lily,' said Matt, his voice concerned. 'We're in Wales and haven't far to go now.'

She stared at him and slowly did as he said, thinking how relaxed he looked. He had changed into beige slacks, an oatmeal and brown sports jacket, and his cream shirt was open at the neck. 'I think I was dreaming,' she murmured.

'You've been sighing and grunting.'

'Like a pig, I suppose?' Her voice was rueful. The panic evaporated utterly.

He responded to her remark with that smile which warmed his eyes and created tiny dimples at the corners of his mouth. It had the power to make her heart flip over in her breast. 'A fair dinkum, teeny weeny piglet,' he teased. 'Unlike that bristly monster that chased us at your uncle's farm.'

He reached out a hand and she clasped it, enjoying the smooth feel of his skin as his fingers entwined with hers. Unexpectedly she was aware of a strong sense of belonging that had never been there before and tried to picture what it would be like when they reached their destination. She was inexperienced in matters of love but Mrs Draper had invited her to have a cup of tea with her a couple of days ago and given her a heart to heart, presuming that Matt was as innocent as Lily was about such things. She only hoped the advice would come in handy. It had been a real revelation!

An hour or so before dinner they reached the Elsinore Hotel, enlarged, redecorated and refurnished earlier that year. It was situated on the Grand Promenade in Llandudno, which had blossomed from a small mining and fishing village during the Victorian era into a successful and popular holiday resort.

Lily laid out one of the new floral silk crépe-de-chîne frocks over a chair and glanced at Matt, who was placing a suit on a hanger. Of course, he would be used to looking after himself and did not need her help. She dabbed a touch of Evening in Paris perfume behind her ears and on the pulses beating heavily at her wrists, then she wandered over to the sash window overlooking the sea, aware of the positive ache in the pit of her stomach. Despite Mrs Draper's words she wondered if it would be better to wait for Matt to make the first move. To be deliberately planning to seduce her husband somehow seemed shocking. How long would it take? How long to dinner? Perhaps she should change now? Should she start at the top or the bottom?

Having barely noticed the long curving stretch of the promenade, or the pier a couple of minutes' walk away, she turned from the window and kicked off her shoes. Matt looked in her direction and she just knew his thoughts must be travelling along the same lines as hers. With her heart beating heavily, she sat on the side of the bed and dragged up her skirts.

He moved to slip a hand inside her stocking top, and with slow deliberation undid a suspender button and rolled down her stocking while watching her expression. He kissed her bare toes and she smiled and undid her other suspender. He took the stocking from her and tossed it over his shoulder. 'I hope there's more coming off?' he murmured, a warm sparkle in his eyes.

Her cheeks were rosy as her fingers found the button on her skirt almost the instant he did. 'Allow me, Mrs Gibson,' he said, his voice husky. She guessed hers would have sounded funny if she could speak but for the moment emotion had taken away her voice. His eyes held hers as he pulled down her skirts. The breath caught in her throat as he pulled her to her feet and pressed her against him, kissing her passionately.

Remembering Mrs Draper's advice, her fingers found his trouser buttons, carefully trying not to arouse him so soon. His mouth lifted and his hands dropped to his sides. He stared down at her as she undid the buttons.

He cleared his throat as he stilled her hand. 'Do you know what you're doing to me, Lily?'

'I have a good idea,' she stammered. 'Mrs Draper told me what to watch out for.' She blushed.

'Mrs Draper?' He shook his head in disbelief and sat on the bed, pulling her on to his knee. She could feel the outline through the fabric of his underwear against her bare thigh and felt excitement and an inexplicable yearning swell inside her. He was roused. There was no doubt about it but it could all be over too swiftly if she did not slow him down.

She jumped up and his eyes followed her. 'What is it, sweetheart? Are you scared?'

'No!' She wasn't, not really. Her face burned. 'It's just that I don't want to rush things.'

'I see.' His tone was wooden.

Did he really? Lily considered how she would like to be swept off her feet to wherever making love would take them and not have to think about delaying tactics to make it more enjoyable for her as Mrs Draper had said. 'I haven't a mother to tell me,' she said, taking a deep breath, 'and I've never done this before.'

'I should hope not.' He smiled and folded his arms across his chest. 'But I presume Mrs Draper told you what to expect?'

'Yes. Do you know what to expect, Matt?' she blurted out.

He grinned. 'I've a fair idea. I haven't always been a priest and a lad can learn a lot in a mining town.' His grey eyes met and held hers and he added softly, 'I have been celibate but I coped because I never met anyone I wanted to share my life with the way I do you.'

His words affected her to the core of her being and she went to him. Her arms went round him and she buried her head against his chest. He kissed the side of her neck and licked her bare shoulder. She lifted her head and their lips met and she stopped thinking and allowed her own physical desire to have its way with her. He strained her against him but there was still clothing in the way. With their eyes shut and their lips still fastened together, they removed their other garments. It was all right, she told herself, they were married! Married for better, for worse! She could feel him rigid against her stomach and wondered if he would be able to hold out. She pinched its end with a thumb and a finger and brought his head down between her breasts with her free hand. Mrs Draper had told her to do that. She hoped it worked. Who'd have believed Mrs Draper would know so much? But she hadn't always been a churchgoer and her mother had been well acquainted with certain activities in Lime Street.

Matt removed her hand and kissed her with such force that she could not think of anything else but the two of them. She moaned as his mouth found her breast and he caressed it with his tongue. Doing what comes naturally is a marvellous thing. She felt as if her whole body was a balloon about to float off. His mouth moved down over the rest of her, slowly, deliberately, as if he was finding pleasure in discovering every inch of her body. She stroked the bony outline of his hip and his buttocks, until suddenly neither of them could bear to be apart any longer. It hurt her a little but she could bear a bit of pain and wanted to enfold him inside her. But strangely, as she did so, it seemed he was unfolding bursts of pleasure inside her, just like a chrysanthemum exploding into a mass of petals, bringing sheer delight.

'What are you thinking?' Matt's arm went round her waist, pulling her close.

Lily turned in his embrace and snuggled up to him, feeling safe and warm, and cossetted. 'A mining town, you say?'

'I'll tell you another time but right now I'd rather tell you I love you.' His voice contained an emotion that sent tingles down her spine. 'I could easily forget the whole world and just go on making love to you over and over again. I forgot to say the evening offices. I do that every evening normally.'

'I'm sorry,' she said meekly. 'I didn't intend coming between you and God. But it was nice, wasn't it?'

'Nice!' He laughed and outlined her mouth with a finger.

She kissed his hand. 'I suppose we'd better get dressed or we'll miss dinner.'

He nodded but the only move he made was to kiss her and bring her hard against him and they began to make love all over again.

Afterwards, when they felt really hungry, they went outside and into the street behind the hotel and bought fish and chips. They ate them out of the paper as they walked by the shushing sea in perfect peace.

It seemed strange to Lily when she woke next morning that there were no cows for her to milk, no Ben to exchange news with, no children to rouse and feed, no sister to squabble with, no father to chide. She sighed, remembering their quarrel. Then she determined not to think about it or worry about them. Hours stretched before her waiting to be claimed in a completely different way. She felt Matt move beside her and his leg slid over hers. Desire stirred inside her and she smiled as she turned towards him. Later there would be breakfast cooked by someone else.

They went to Holy Trinity church and afterwards took the zigzag path up the Great Orme, a massive limestone headland on one side of the bay.

'Lewis Carroll is said to be have been inspired to write *Alice in Wonderland* somewhere round here,' said Lily, sitting on Matt's black mackintosh, looking over the sea towards Anglesey as he took a photograph of her.

'Fascinating,' he said, his eyes twinkling. 'We clergy are not without our talents. If it wasn't for the hotel and the golf course, I could have made love to you all over again up here.'

'You wouldn't, out in the open?' She smiled up at him. 'Is that all you have on your mind?'

'We are on our honeymoon.' He leaned over and kissed the top of her head. 'Tomorrow we'll go somewhere quieter.'

He sat beside her and they talked. He told her about his life after the death of the mother he could barely remember. 'Dad had a yen to dig for gold so he went to the goldfields north of Brisbane. I was placed in a kind of Anglican orphanage-cum-school but during the holidays Dad would come for me.' She watched his face as he talked, trying to read his expression. It must have been lonely for the small boy he had been. 'The men were really tough on the fields. They had to be, and most knew nothing of organised religion,' he said, chewing on a grass stem. 'Only that brought to them by the bush brothers. I was impresssed by them even at an early age and they brought balance to my life.' He paused and smiled. 'Now your childhood.'

Lily would rather have heard more about him but she spoke of her life when her father was away at the Front and how she had never had a holiday before. 'There was always the milking, you see. I remember Mam's mother and sister coming to visit us. I didn't understand a word they said to me because they spoke in Welsh and they chided Mam for not teaching me it.' She sighed, her fingers twisting a tussock of grass. 'I never saw them again after Mam's funeral. Dad never encouraged them to call.'

'So this is the first time you've visited the land of your mother?' said Matt, stretching out flat and pulling her down beside him.

'Yes,' she murmured, feeling like she was making a momentous statement. 'And it's probably the last with us going to Australia next week.' For a moment she felt as if a cloud had crossed the sun. Then she remembered how much she wanted to go.

The next day they went to Conway Castle. 'We have nothing as old as this in Australia, except the landscape,' said Matt, pressing a hand against a grey stone wall.

Lily placed her hand alongside his and closed her eyes. 'It was built by Edward the First's men to keep the unruly Welsh led by Llewelyn under control,' she said in a sing-song voice. 'Until then the Welsh had always defeated the English in the mountains. Edward was crafty. He gathered a fleet and crossed the Menai Straits and burnt the harvest on Anglesey, where it's better for growing grain. Grain which would have fed Llewelyn's hungry men during the winter. They had no choice but to pay homage to Edward or starve.'

Matt's voice was amused. 'I take it your mother told you all that.'

She opened her eyes and grinned. 'In that exact way. Wales is full of true stories as well as legends. There's a sad one about a lord who had a hunting dog that was more pet than killer. He left him one day guarding his son. A wolf entered the hall and made for the baby but the dog wouldn't let him near.'

'I suppose there was a fight?' said Matt, twisting his fingers through hers.

'A real bloody one. When the lord returned the dog limped over to welcome him – only to have a sword stuck through him because his master thought he'd killed the baby.'

'He hadn't, of course.'

'Of course not,' she said approvingly. 'The lord was heartbroken when he found the dead wolf.'

'And the moral of the story is?'

'Could be, act in haste, repent in leisure? But I prefer, don't always presume something until you know for sure.'

Matt's eyes smiled into hers. 'I prefer that, too. Now let's go somewhere quieter.' He caught hold of her fingers and led her to the car.

They drove up into the green rolling hills along narrow winding lanes bordered by high hedges of hazel, honey-suckle and hawthorn. It was a perfect day. The sun was warm and as they got higher the scenery was breathtaking. Even when the car got a puncture it did not spoil the day. Lily sat on a grassy bank among purple, blue and yellow tiny wild flowers, drinking in the view across a valley to a line of partly forested hills, the tops of which were plum-coloured in the late afternoon sun.

'It's awesome, isn't it?' said Matt, glancing up at her.

'Yes.' Lily rose and kissed the back of his neck. 'Your changing a wheel is a sight I never thought to see either. I didn't think you were so practical.'

He tightened a final nut and straightened. 'Another part of my life story. When I was about sixteen Dad struck it rich again and gave up the gold digging and we went walk-about. Only we didn't walk, we had a truck. When you're stuck in the middle of the bush or the desert you have to be your own mechanic. I helped Dad out loads of times.'

She smiled and handed him a rag. 'Next?'

'Sydney.' He wiped his hands on the rag. 'Dad bought a beaut house overlooking the harbour. He didn't have long enough there. Pity for him to die when as an adult I knew him well enough to understand why he did things the way he did when I was a lad. He never got over my mother's death.' He tossed the rag into the boot, his head bent, but Lily caught sight of his expression and was aware that her husband was a man of different facets, seemingly so confident and yet with an unmistakable vulnerability which was probably due to the kind of upbringing he had had.

'Why didn't you ever settle in the house in Sydney?'

'It's as I told you,' he said, flashing her a brief smile. 'I went where I believed God called me.'

'Why didn't you sell the house?' She moved closer, putting her arms round him.

'Its links with Dad, I suppose.' His voice was muffled against her hair.

'Haven't you ever felt that God might be calling you to settle there?'

'No. I knew coming to Liverpool was right. I'm not so sure about leaving it.'

'Aren't you?' Her emotions were suddenly confused. It would be easier on the family if she stayed but she did want to go to Australia. 'But everything's arranged,' she murmured. 'You said your friend—'

'It is!' He lifted his head and looked suddenly weary. 'Don't worry, Lil, you'll see all those sights you've set your heart on.'

'I wasn't worrying.' She felt uncomfortable because he made it sound as if he only wanted to go to please her. 'I said wherever you were I want to be, and I meant it,' she said slowly.

'I'm glad to hear it.' He bent his head and kissed her.

She knew she had said the right thing but still experienced a sort of guilt.

That evening they went to the New Prince's Theatre in Mostyn Street to be entertained by Ambrose and his Orchestra in 'Calling all Stars'. Elizabeth Welch sang, Larry Adler played his harmonica, and Flotsam and Jetsam made them laugh. Afterwards they walked along the promenade as the stars pricked on in the sky. The air was fresh and moist with the tang of the sea and the greenery of the hills behind. This Wales was where her mother had been born and where her parents had met. Lily recalled Matt's words about the heat and the dryness of the outback and realised as if for the first time she was travelling to a foreign land. How different her life would be. None of the familiar sounds and sights. No Ben or Daisy, no Father, or Ronnie and May whom she had reared as if they were her own. She felt a constriction in her throat and could not get rid of it.

That night Lily clung to Matt after they had made love. 'You do really love me, don't you?' she demanded. 'And you'd forgive me if I did anything you didn't like?' She had no idea what made her speak in such a way.

He said drowsily, 'What were you planning on doing? Running away with the milkman?'

'Very funny.' She could not prevent a laugh. 'It's just that people do hurt each other without intending to. Say you love me.'

'How can you doubt it?' His tone was surprised as he held her tighter.

'I just want to hear you say it,' she murmured, resting her head on his bare shoulder.

'I love you. I'll always love you.' He kissed the hollow of her throat and her upper breast. 'I believe we were meant for each other from the beginning of time.'

A relieved sigh escaped her. His way with words was a balm, soothing emotions which had momentarily become too much for her. Tomorrow they would return to Liverpool and her family. Soon she would be saying goodbye to the world she had known all her life and sailing off to a completely new one.

# Chapter Six

'I hope Dad isn't going to cut off his nose to spite his face and tell me never to darken his doors again,' said Lily, as they drove up Islington past the toy wholesaler's.

Matt smiled. 'It'd be a bit of a waste when we're leaving the country in a week's time.'

She frowned. 'That'd be Dad all over, though.'

'Stop worrying. Could be he's seeing things differently now.'

Lily hoped so but could feel the tension building up inside her. Ben should have finished the second milking and would be home, so that should make matters easier between her father, herself and Matt.

The car drew up outside the dairy and she stepped out. Immediately she noticed the curtains were drawn upstairs. Daisy must have forgotten to open them. One of the neighbours was sandstoning the front step. She looked their way.

'Hello, Mrs Day,' said Lily, smiling.

The woman gave a solemn nod, half opened her mouth, then shut it again and wielded the sandstone with more vigour.

Lily hurried ahead of Matt into the shop. The bell jangled and immediately May came through from the back premises, a buttie in her hand. She flung herself on Lily. 'Gosh, am I glad to see you! It's been terrible here and our Daisy's been driving me mad! She expected me to fetch coal! Me!'

'Is that all?' Lily hugged her. 'Where's Dad? I thought he'd be here.'

May threw back her head and said in an awed voice: 'You still don't know? Dad's dead! They put out a bulletin on the wireless to try and get in touch with you.'

'Dead!' Lily could not believe it. She gazed over May's head at Matt imploringly.

He moved to put an arm around her. 'How?' he said succinctly.

'It was Uncle William who found him,' said May, talking rapidly. 'His head was all kicked in and there was blood splattered everywhere. I heard him telling our Ben.'

Blood! thought Lily dazedly, vaguely remembering some kind of dream she had had. 'Where's Ben?'

'In the cool room. He went to see the body and came back as white as a sheet. I heard him telling our Daisy that he hardly recognised Dad. He thinks he tried to mount the horse and it panicked.'

'The fool, the fool!' cried Lily, her hand going to her mouth. She could picture her father's death vividly. Blood! Cry blood! She should have realised he'd do something stupid! She felt dizzy and clung to Matt. He led her over to the fireplace where a fire was laid and sat her on a chair and told May to make tea while he found the matches.

He set light to the kindling before kneeling in front of Lily.

He took one of her hands between both of his. 'Your father was a grown man, not a child. He was responsible for his own actions. Don't be blaming yourself.'

The world steadied but it took a great effort for Lily to speak. 'How did you know I was blaming myself?'

'People often do in such circumstances.'

'But it was my fault! If I hadn't—'

'No, it wasn't!' It was Ben's voice. He had entered the room.

Lily looked up and felt a rush of sympathy and affection for him. His face was drawn with weariness. 'I'm sorry, Ben, you've had to cope with everything. It must have been terrible.'

'Better me than you,' he said in clipped tones. 'I don't know what he was thinking about. If he was thinking! He'd had a skinful, otherwise he'd have known better, but he never looked further than his own nose. I wish it hadn't happened but . . .' He ran a hand over his face. 'Lousy homecoming for you. Did you have a nice honeymoon?'

The question seemed so incongruous and she was so relieved he was not blaming her for her father's death that a laugh burst from her. 'Oh, Ben! What a question to ask!'

'We had a beaut time, thanks,' said Matt, smiling.

Ben said, 'If the truth's known we're going to miss our Lil more than him. I can't help thinking Dad's better out of it.' He reddened and glanced at Matt. 'I know that's not very tactful but he would have only got worse without Lil around.'

There was an uncomfortable silence, broken by May holding out a cup to Lily. 'Let's all have a nice cup of sweet tea!' she beamed. 'Everyone says it's good for shock.'

Lily managed a smile and sipped the tea. It was weak and too milky but at least it eased her dry throat.

Matt asked Ben when the funeral was to be. He said there was to be an inquest and they discussed the arrangements which would have to be made afterwards. Lily felt as if it was unreal. Were they really talking about her father? What should she do? Matt said he would go with Ben to see William. She offered to go with them but he said they would have to take May if she went and they'd rather not. Besides she would be better resting. She agreed because her legs still felt weak. Then she suddenly remembered her younger brother and asked where he was.

'He came in at lunchtime complaining of not feeling well so I told him he was best in bed,' said Ben, running a hand through his dark hair. 'I was surprised when he agreed.'

Lily's brows knitted. 'In what way not well?'

'He couldn't say.'

'It's probably shock,' said Matt.

Without another word Lily forced herself to her feet and up the stairs.

Ronnie was in bed, a *Dandy* in front of him on the blue and white cotton cover but he was not reading. His eyes flickered over her. 'I thought I heard you coming in.'

She sat on the side of the bed. 'What's up, Ron?'

'Don't feel well.'

'Is it Dad dying?' He shook his head and immediately winced. 'Your head hurts?'

'Yeah. And me throat, and I feel sick.'

'Oh dear!' She would have smiled at his woebegone face if she had not been feeling so miserable herself. 'Is it my leaving? You do know I'm going to Australia?'

'I don't want you to leave.' His voice was hoarse. 'But it's not that. I really don't feel well.'

'Shock can make you feel odd,' she said soothingly.

'It doesn't make your throat sore,' he rasped, frowning.

'It could if you've been crying over Dad.'

'I wouldn't cry over him!' His tone was scornful. 'He never had any time for me, only himself!'

Lily decided to ignore that comment. 'Let's have a look at that throat.'

Obediently he opened his mouth. Even if his throat had not been red and sore-looking, the sight of his furry tongue was enough to convince her something was seriously wrong. She said that she would fetch him a drink and some aspirin and went downstairs to discover Matt and Ben had left.

'They said they'd be back as quickly as they could,' said May, the tip of her tongue protruding as she struggled with a piece of knitting.

'Fine,' said Lily absently, and made a fresh cup of tea, only to discover when she reached her brother's room that he had been sick all over the linoleum. She had just cleaned up the mess and was washing her hands when Daisy arrived in from work, bringing fish and chips from the chippie.

'So you're back,' said her sister, a relieved expression on her face. 'What do you think? A right turn up for the book, hey?'

Lily had to bite on her tongue to stop herself speaking her mind. She wondered how Daisy could sound so uncaring. 'Do you think like Ben that it'll make life easier for you?' she asked, resting both hands on the table.

Some of the brightness died in Daisy's face and she was silent as she unwrapped the food. 'At least he won't be drinking our money away.'

Lily sighed. 'I suppose you're right. But you've another problem. Ronnie's not well. If he's not improved by morning, I think you'll have to get the doctor out.'

'Me!' She stared at Lily in dismay. 'Can't you do it now you're home? You will be postponing going to Australia? I mean, we need you with all this upset!'

Lily felt as if her heart plummeted into her stomach, and her fingers gripped the table convulsively. 'Everything's arranged! We've our tickets and Matt's itinerary is all worked out!'

'Matt could still go,' said Daisy hopefully, beginning to unwrap the fish and chips. 'I mean, I'm hopeless when people are sick.'

'Ronnie is not people,' said Lily irritably. 'He's your brother! And I'm sure you can cope perfectly well if you want to.'

'Sure! I'll give up work!' said Daisy sarcastically. There was a silence. She sighed. 'Sorry. But we'll need my money, things aren't going to be easy for us.'

Lily thought swiftly. 'I suppose I could call the doctor and stay round here tomorrow if necessary, but I won't be stopping so don't depend on my doing so. You might have to give up work whatever you say. How are you going to manage everything otherwise?'

Daisy shrugged. 'Ben'll manage the milking without me and our May'll be here before and after school for people who want milk.'

'She's only ten!'

'She's older in the head,' retorted Daisy. 'And if you're so worried about her being too young, you shouldn't be leaving her.'

Lily's own head began to ache. 'Listen, Daisy,' she said strongly, 'the last words Dad spoke to me were angry ones, so try and imagine what it's like for me coming back to find him dead. The last thing I need is you trying to make me feel guilty about leaving you all. You are nineteen! I was only fourteen when I took over from Mam and I had May as a baby to look after – and Ronnie was only a year older. You should count yourself lucky.'

'All right, all right. Keep your hair on. I didn't mean to sound unfeeling. It's just that everything's been so terrible and confused!' She bit savagely into a couple of chips.

'You coped, though?'

Daisy sighed. 'It was only three days but it felt longer. I haven't done any proper washing. God knows when I'll manage to change the sheets. Will you be staying in Dad's room?'

'We planned on a bed and breakfast.' Lily took knives and forks from a drawer in the sideboard.

'You mean you vant to be alone?' said Daisy, raising her eyebrows expressively.

'We have only just got married,' murmured Lily, just about hanging on to her temper.

'But you'll be here tomorrow? What about the day after?'

'I don't know,' said Lily, through her teeth. 'Let's just take one day at a time. I'll be here tomorrow with Ronnie, packing my few belongings while Matt gathers his things from the vicarage.'

Daisy said moodily, 'It'd be better if you were staying here.'

'Well, we're not!' The last thing Lily wanted was to come back to the dairy and her old way of life. She had begun a new one and was determined to continue it.

She called May over to the table and put the men's plates in the oven. Daisy asked where they had spent their honeymoon and Lily told them about Wales and the variety show they had seen at the theatre.

Ronnie thumped on the ceiling and automatically Lily flew upstairs, to discover he had been sick again, this time over the bedcover. She stripped it off with the blanket underneath and dumped them in the bath, running water on to them. She was beginning to feel more tired than if she had done a full day's work. That was the shock, she guessed.

Hesitantly she went into her father's room and sat on the edge of the bed, thinking about him and trying to pray, remembering how he had been missing on her wedding morning. The sheets on the bed were still clean because he had spent the night at the farm. She and Matt could sleep here, she thought, plagued by guilt again. Only it might be better if Ben did. She found herself worrying about Ronnie once more. Then, hearing Matt's voice, she left the room.

'What did Uncle William have to say?' she said, going over to him.

'Not much,' he replied, his expression softening as he took both her hands in his. 'Are you all right?'

She nodded. 'Ronnie isn't, though. What about Aunt Dora?'

'Her usual self.' There was a sudden shadow in his eyes and Lily wondered what her aunt had said to him. Probably she had blamed the pair of them for her father's death. Matt added, 'There's to be an inquest tomorrow. Ben and I will go. There's no point in you upsetting yourself.'

'We're hoping the funeral can be on Friday,' said Ben, dropping his head on his hand as he leaned on the table. He looked really tired.

'Good.' She wanted it over with as soon as possible. The mixture of unreality, horror and guilt were still with her. She needed something to do, so she made tea and took their dinners out of the oven. 'I'll do the second milking for you tomorrow, Ben,' she said, considering it was the least she could do if her brother was going to the inquest and would probably have to do deliveries.

'Thanks. I've got a lot to fit in.' He yawned. 'As soon as I've finished this I'll get to bed. The last few days have been a bit of a nightmare.'

She rumpled his hair affectionately, then remembering Ronnie, told them about the vomiting. 'It might be better, Ben, if you slept in Dad's room, if you don't mind? The sheets are clean.'

He groaned. 'You think it might be something catching?'

'You can't take chances, not with you doing the milking. Get Daisy or May to check how he is.'

'Do I have to touch him?' said Daisy in alarm, looking up from her magazine. 'I don't want to catch anything.'

Matt gave her a frowning glance but it was Lily who said impatiently, 'Would you rather May, a ten-year-old, saw to him? Anyway, I'll be round in the morning. I'll see to him then.' She stood, needing to get away. 'We'll have to be going.'

Ben smiled and held up a hand. 'See you then.'

Lily blew him a kiss and she and Matt left the room.

They found a suitable guest house in Lord Nelson Street by Lime Street station. Lily sank flat on the bed as soon as they entered the room, closed her eyes and freed a deep sigh. 'Thank God! I feel like I've been through the mangle. Our Daisy was going on about us postponing our voyage.'

'And you think that would be wrong?' said Matt, opening a suitcase and taking out his Book of Common Prayer. He sat on the bed beside her with it unopened on his knee.

She opened her eyes. 'Our berths are booked and every-thing's planned. You'd be letting people down if we postpone,' she said. 'You couldn't get a letter to them quickly enough.'

'That's true,' murmured Matt, opening the prayer book. 'Let's hope the funeral can be on Friday and that Ronnie is going to be all right.'

'Yes!' She sat up, hunching her knees and putting her arms round them.

There was a furrow between his brows. 'How worried about him are you?'

Lily bit her lower lip then said lightly, 'Worry worried.'

'And you're happy to leave him to Daisy's unloving mercy?'

'Not happy.' She pulled a face. 'I just hope I'm wrong and it isn't anything catching.'

'I hope so too.' He put down his prayer book and reached for her. She shuffled across the bed and they wrapped their arms around each other. 'I told you it wouldn't be easy, sweetheart.'

'I hurt –' she took his hand and placed it firmly in the region of her heart '– right there.'

'I'll kiss it better.'

'Can you?' A small sad smile curved her mouth.

'I can try.'

He undid her brassiere, kissing her neck and throat as he did so before reaching her breast. She reached out for him, holding him close, but a moment later the worry, the guilt and the grief were back, like lead weights in her mind and her heart. 'Matt.'

He raised his head. 'Don't think about it.'

A laugh escaped her. 'How is it you always know what's going on in my mind?'

'Easy in this case. You're thinking of your father, and should we be doing this?'

'And should we?'

He cuddled her. 'If it comforts you I don't see why not. Should you stop eating and having cups of tea?'

'I need to drink and eat to live.'

'And you don't need this?' He gazed into her face, then pushed her gently down on to the bed and slid on top of her. He kissed her with a melting tenderness which brought unexpected tears to her eyes. They made love very slowly, which she found infinitely comforting.

The noise of a train huffing and puffing and rattling the sash window woke Lily next morning. She discovered Matt already dressed. 'The inquest is at ten,' he said, coming over to her. He planted a kiss on her mouth. 'I thought I'd pick up Ben and afterwards return the car to the hire place. You can sleep a little longer if you want.'

'No!' She scrambled out of bed. 'Wait for me. I might as well go to the house now. I can get some shopping on the way and prepare something for tea for the whole family. There's also that bedding to do.'

Matt shook his head at her. 'If you must, you must, but they're going to have to learn to look after themselves.'

'It'll only be a few more days.' She reached up and kissed him before getting ready with a speed that caused him to comment drily that she was definitely the woman to have with him on the move.

'How is he?' Lily asked Ben as soon as she stepped out of the car.

'He says he's hot and has been sick again.' He ran a hand over his face. 'And he's got a rash. I think we'll have to get the doctor. I've kept our May away from school in case it is something catching.'

'You haven't been in to him?' she said swiftly.

'I stood at the door.' Ben dug into his pocket. 'I've got some money—'

'No! You might need it,' said Lily, pushing him towards the door. 'You go off to the inquest with Matt.'

She found May washing doll's clothes in a bowl in the kitchen. 'Are you feeling all right?'

May nodded absently. 'Can I mangle these?' she asked, holding up a hand-knitted bonnet and coat.

Lily answered in the affirmative and ran upstairs.

Ronnie's neck and arms were covered in a rash which seemed to be spreading to his chest. He'd already had chickenpox and measles, so she was certain this was something different. 'How d'you feel, love?'

'Awful,' he croaked. 'Me throat's terrible.'

She placed the back of her hand to his forehead and found it burning hot. She made him as comfortable as possible and went to see Mrs Draper.

'Of course I'll stay in the house with them, dear,' said the old lady, patting Lily's arm. 'Not a nice homecoming for you. So sorry about your father.'

Lily thanked her and hurried to the doctor's surgery to receive a promise that he would call later. She did some shopping on the way home and was relieved when Mrs Draper offered to take May to the park.

The doctor closed his black bag and gazed over his spectacles. 'The boy has scarlet fever, Mrs Gibson.'

Lily's hopes took a nosedive. She laced her fingers tightly together in front of her and cleared her throat. 'He'll need careful nursing then?'

'You can't possibly nurse him here,' he said firmly. 'I'm afraid I'll have to insist on his going to the fever hospital, and everything in this room will have to be fumigated. Has he been anywhere near the cows or in the dairy?'

Lily shook her head and said proudly, 'It's spotless in there. Everything is scrubbed and scalded twice daily.'

'I see.' He allowed himself a pinched smile. 'You'll have to have a word with the men when they arrive about whether it needs doing again and if you can sell the milk.'

She nodded, resigned to that possibility. 'How long will Ronnie need to be in hospital?'

'It depends on how well the disease progresses. If we're lucky the fever will abate within three days. I'll arrange for the boy to be taken to hospital today. You can visit him in a couple of days and see how he is.' He wrote out a bill and handed it to her. She glanced at it briefly, glad she had not touched Uncle William's five-pound note, and handed him his fee, wondering what she would do if Ronnie didn't start to improve in three days. It made her heart ache seeing him so poorly.

Matt came in shortly after Lily had done the second milking. Everything in the coolroom and dairy had been washed and scrubbed meticulously. An ambulance, which she had to pay for, had taken her brother to hospital. The fumigating van had called and the strong smell of disinfectant hung over the whole house.

He wrinkled his nose, watching her put on the kettle. 'What is it?'

'Scarlet fever. He could be a lot better by Monday.' She forced a smile and changed the subject swiftly. 'What happened at the inquest?'

'Death by misadventure,' he said carefully. 'It's OK for us to have the funeral on Friday. Your aunt and uncle were there. Ben said your Aunt Dora asked him if she could have Albert's body taken back to the farm.'

'Cheek!' exclaimed Lily, anger flaring up inside her. 'After the way she wouldn't let him in the house, she thinks she can take over now!'

'She said she'll have someone lay him out properly, and buy the coffin.'

Lily stiffened. 'What did Ben say?'

A slight smile lightened Matt's finely boned face. 'He agreed. He could hardly have the body brought back here with the way things are.'

Her anger faded. 'Aunt Dora just wants to look good.'

'Probably. But it could be that she wants to make amends.'

'Hmmph!' Lily folded her arms and strolled over to the fireplace. She rested her head against the mantelshelf, gazing into the fire's glowing heart. 'I suppose I should be grateful. People can get funny about dead bodies. It's bad enough with Ronnie having the fever. Some'll go elsewhere for their milk.' She turned to face him, her blue eyes thoughtful. 'What about a service, Matt? He was an unbeliever.'

He raised his eyebrows. 'You don't consider we've an understanding, merciful God?'

'Of course!' she said impatiently, waving an arm. 'But Dad wasn't exactly a friend of his.'

Matt took her hand. 'It's your decision,' he said softly. 'We can just dig a hole and put him in it if you feel it's more honest.'

A small laugh escaped her. 'If he'd gone first, there'd be no doubt about what Mam would have done. She'd have had a service whether he'd have liked it or not. So we will and he'll lie beside her.'

'Do you want me to arrange it? I've got to visit the vicarage.'

Lily nodded and wondered what to arrange for Ronnie when he left hospital. She broached the matter with Daisy when she arrived home, hoping her sister had a few more caring thoughts about her brother.

'Ask Aunt Dora if he can stay with them. They've plenty of bedrooms, good food and lots of country air,' said Daisy, picking up her knife and fork. 'This looks good, Lil,' she said of the breast of lamb hotpot. 'You're a much better cook than I am.'

'I'm not asking Aunt Dora,' said Lily, her expression determined. 'You'll have to ask her when Ronnie comes out if you can't be bothered to look after your own brother.'

'I'm not giving up my job.' There were two spots of colour high on Daisy's cheekbones. 'I told you we need the money.'

'You mean you *like* the money!'

Daisy made an exasperated noise. 'What if I do? It's none of your business if you're going to Australia. You just go and leave us to muddle through. We'll survive somehow! As it is I'll have to take time off for the funeral. When is it?'

'Friday.'

Daisy nodded. 'I've mentioned it to Mavis in work. She said she can lend me something black.'

Lily held her temper. Perhaps Ronnie would be all right and Aunt Dora would have him to stay?

Despite the short time they had to prepare, the funeral went off without a hitch. There were plenty of people there, and whether this was due to her father's popularity as a character in the area, or people's sympathy for the family, it did not matter to Lily. She was just glad he had a decent send-off. She and Dora were coolly polite to each other. William still seemed in shock and there were tears in his eyes as the coffin was lowered into the grave. He gave Lily an unexpected hug and said he was sorry about everything and asked after Ronnie.

'I'm seeing him tomorrow. I'll let you know,' she said, relieved that all was well between them again.

The next day, because she was the only one allowed in to see Ronnie, Lily went alone to the fever hospital in Grafton Street, not far the from the Brunswick Dock. She hated the Victorian atmosphere of some hospitals, possibly

because some had once been workhouses and she associ-
ated them with poor people's misery. She was shown to
where Ronnie lay in lonely isolation.

'You mustn't go near him,' said a rustling, bestarched
nurse. 'Speak to him through the curtain.'

'Why?' said Lily bluntly, touching the damp heavy
material which smelt overwhelmingly of disinfectant. 'I
touched him when he must have been contagious!'

The nurse strugged. 'Those are the rules, duck.' She
stepped in a tray of disinfectant and vanished through the
doorway before Lily could say more.

She parted the curtains and gazed at the figure in the
high metal-framed bed. 'How are you, love?' she
whispered.

Ronnie's head turned slowly in her direction and immediately she noticed one side of his face was swollen.
'Terrible,' he answered in a faint, sad voice which wrung
her heart. 'I've got nothing to do but lie here and I'm still
too hot and me ear's killing me.'

'Have you told the nurse?'

'Yeah! But she hasn't done anything much,' he said
fretfully. 'Did you bring me any comics?'

'Yes. And some orange juice. I'll have a word with the
nurse about your ear.'

'Not now! I want to know when you're going to
Australia.'

Lily hesitated. It was easy to say to Matt they had to
go and to tell Daisy she was old enough to cope, but now
she felt a whole storm of conflicting emotions welling up
inside her. She cleared her throat. 'Tuesday.'

His eyes seemed larger and darker in his spotty face. 'Will you still go if I'm dying?'

She forced a laugh. 'If you can make jokes you must be getting better.'

He groaned and his thin face twisted. 'I feel terrible, Lil! I tell yer, I hope our May catches this. She's always going on about having something but never gets anything. It would serve her right!'

'That's not a nice thing to say about your sister,' said Lily, a quiver in her voice.

Ronnie sighed heavily. 'It's not fair!'

There was another silence.

'Will you go to Australia?' he asked earnestly. 'I know you're married now but you could always go a bit later. Matt would let you. I know he would if I'm really ill.'

Lily sighed. 'He wants me with him, Ron.'

'You could ask him.' Her brother looked at her mournfully. 'I really feel ill.'

Lily was swamped with guilt. It wasn't like her younger brother to complain. 'We'll see.'

There was a pause. 'Is Dad buried now?'

'Yes. Hopefully he's with Mam.'

'I wonder if I'll go to Heaven and see her?'

'Of course you'll go to Heaven!' Then she added hastily, 'Although that won't be for ages yet.'

'I might die and you'll be in Australia.'

'You're not going to die,' she said emphatically, starting to feel haunted.

'I feel like I'm going to die.'

Lily took a deep breath and changed the subject.

Afterwards she spoke to the sister about Ronnie's ear.

'We're watching it. A suppuration of the ear happens in some of these cases.'

'What's that mean?' said Lily, staring at her across a desk. 'In plain English, please.'

'It means that the infection from the throat has spread to the ear and is affecting the Eustachian tube. It is painful because of the pressure on the eardrum, but one can only hope—'

Lily cut in ruthlessly, 'How long will it take for him to get better?'

'One cannot say for sure. It depends on how he fights the infection. Other complications can arise, of course.' She moved the open casebook on her desk an inch. 'Now if you'll excuse me, I have work to do.'

Lily stared at her, her temper rising. 'What do you mean, other complications? Are they dangerous? I'll be leaving for Australia soon and I must know.'

The woman, who must have been some ten years older than Lily, lifted her eyes from the book. 'It might never happen.'

'What might never happen?' Lily took a bottle of orange juice and several comics from her shopping bag and slammed them down on the desk.

The sister jumped. 'Really!' she said. 'There's no need to work yourself up, my dear. The hearing can be affected and in some cases the kidneys but there's no sign of that in your brother's case. Now if you really don't mind, my dear, I've a lot to get through.'

Lily took a deep breath and thought of telling this woman what she thought of her. Some nurses were worse dragons than Aunt Dora. 'Make sure my brother gets the comics and orange juice. Thank you for being so understanding and easing my mind.' She walked away. If it hadn't been for the risk of infecting others she would have liked to have carried her brother out of the hospital and taken him home.

On Sunday May's luck ran out when she came out in a rash and was taken to join her brother. The smell of disinfectant in the house was doubly overpowering and Lily's head ached unbearably.

'Two of them!' cried Daisy, covering her eyes with a hand as she rested one elbow on the table. 'How can I cope with two of them when they come out of hospital? Especially as from what you say our Ronnie might have problems! I just can't handle this, Lil! I'm not maternal like you!'

'You said you were going to ask Aunt Dora to have them,' said Lily, shooting Matt an uncertain glance. He was supposedly reading his Bible but she could tell he was listening.

'That was a joke,' groaned Daisy.

'Try her, anyway.'

'She'll say they're my responsibility!' She stared at Lily. 'Couldn't you just stay a bit longer – till they're both back at school? I mean, you said the nurse said our Ronnie could lose his hearing in that ear. How do I cope with that?'

'She needs sacking, that woman,' said Ben, who had remained silent so far. 'Worrying our Lil when there's nothing she can do about it.'

'I did ask,' she said ruefully.

'What are we going to do then?' said Daisy. 'What with having to pour milk away, we need my money more than ever!'

Matt stood up. 'I'm going to church,' he said shortly. 'I said I'd say a last Evensong.'

'I'll come with you,' said Lily, rising swiftly.

As soon as they were outside Matt said, 'Don't say it. Let's wait until after the service.'

Lily desperately wanted to talk about her feelings but knew, because he had told her in the past, that he needed an uncluttered mind before giving a service. She would have to keep quiet. Even so she could not resist saying, 'We mustn't let anything spoil the show! I have to put on a happy face even though I feel awful inside! It's like being on stage, being in the ministry.'

'You're not the first to draw that parallel,' he said quietly. 'Candles, costumes, words written centuries before.'

'All the world's a stage,' she said bleakly.

'And I wanted us to continue to be centre stage together.'

'Matt, please, listen.'

His mouth tightened. 'After, Lily. We'll go straight to the guesthouse and discuss it there.'

She fell silent, utterly miserable, wondering why God should want Ronnie partially deaf and had allowed May

to succumb to the fever when she had sailed through life
so far without even catching a cold.

Lily found no peace in church, her body was too restless, her emotions in turmoil, her mind buzzing with words
she wanted to say. Instead she had to keep them in until
they reached the guesthouse.

Then they burst out of her. 'I can't go, Matt!' Lily
paced the bedroom, her arms folded tightly across her
chest.

He stood in front of her and prised her arms apart
before gripping her hands tightly. 'I told you it would be
difficult when it actually came down to it but you always
seemed so confident you could cope.'

'I didn't know my father would die and my brother
and sister would be dangerously ill,' she cried.

'Are they dangerously ill? Has the doctor said so?'

'They could be, if further complications set in.'

'You're looking on the black side. Let's pray about
this, Lil. Trust God.'

'I can't!' she said miserably. 'He might take them away
from me.'

'You were quite happy to leave them before,' he said
slowly, his eyes intent on her face. 'You might never have
seen them again.'

Lily bit her lip. 'It was different then. Now, seeing
them in pain and so vulnerable, it hurts me. What if
they die and I'm not there? I've always been there for
them.'

'You can't stop them dying. Death's the final enemy.
Beating it is what the Christian message is all about.'

'I know that! But I can't just walk away,' she whispered. 'I love them.'

'You love me, don't you?'

'Of course I love you,' she cried. 'But you can cope without me! You've done it for years.'

His grip tightened on her fingers. 'I've got used to coping with you. I can let my guard down with you. It's lonely sometimes in my position and I don't want to be without you.'

'I'll follow you out later.' She went into his arms. 'When Ronnie and May are better or . . .' Her voice trailed off.

He stroked her hair and she felt a sigh go through him. 'We could both stay here. Cancel all my engagements. Start a different kind of life with me as a curate somewhere in Liverpool.'

Her head lifted and she stared at him with moist eyes. 'You can't do that. Remember we said it would be letting people down? You go ahead and I'll follow.'

'I want us together,' he said firmly. 'I feel strongly it's what God wants.'

'It's what I want,' she replied swiftly, 'but—'

'Then stay with it!' Unexpectedly his grey eyes sparkled with anger. '"No man, having put his hand to the plough and looking back, is fit for the Kingdom of God!"'

Suddenly she was infuriated with him. 'Don't quote scripture at me, Matt! I haven't been committed as long and as wholly as you to the Christian cause. Don't expect me to run before I can walk, and don't blame me for being what you said I was. You said I had a great capacity to love. To care. Do you want me now to switch that off because it suits you?'

'Of course not! But isn't that what I'm saying? You're part of me now. I don't want to have to do without you.' He reached out for her but she backed away.

'You mean in bed?'

He stared at her. 'What's so terrible about that? It's a big part of being married. I thought you were happy with our lovemaking?'

'I was. I am,' she added in a quieter voice. 'Why are we arguing about it?'

'Because I said and you said—' He stopped. 'Don't let's go into it all again. I love you, Lily. I want us to be together. I want to show you Australia and show Australia you. Or stay here together.'

Stay here? thought Lily. When she had dreamed of faraway places half her life. He had to go or they might never escape. She reached up to press her lips against his and with her free hand undid his trouser buttons. 'Let's decide later,' she whispered, pulling out his shirt tails and stroking his stomach. Matt's throat moved but no words came out. He removed her hand and lifted her off her feet, to carry her over to the bed.

'You'll come as soon as you know for sure about May and Ronnie?' said Matt a couple of mornings later as he and Lily stood very close, looking out over the Mersey, the liner not far away.

'Yes,' she said, wishing even at this late stage God could perform a miracle and Ben would come running down the floating bridge to tell her that she could go to Australia with Matt after all, that the kids were better and they could manage fine without her. But she and Matt had called at the hospital and they were not better. 'I'll be with you in a month – six weeks at the latest.'

'Don't change your mind.' He gazed down into her face, his eyes the muted grey of a lowering sky.

'As if I would.' She laughed and hugged his arm tightly.

'Good girl.' He removed a curl which had blown against her mouth and kissed her passionately. She clung to him and as soon as his mouth lifted, said, 'I'll write often, care of the house in Sydney.'

'I'll try and get my first letters on a passing mail boat coming this way.'

She laughed unsteadily. 'Three weeks or so there, three weeks back. I could be getting there when your letter reaches here saying you've arrived.'

'I'll write to you anyway.' He held her close and she could feel him trembling with the same emotion she felt, but men did not cry and she mustn't.

He removed her arms from about his waist. 'Go!' he said huskily. 'I don't want you waving as the ship departs. Clean break now.'

She stared up into his face which was now so familiar that she knew exactly where the tiny bump was on the side of his otherwise straight nose, and the mole just beneath the line of his jaw. 'You do understand why?' she said impulsively, looking directly into his eyes.

'Yes. I can imagine how difficult it is for you.'

She knew it was true. His perception was something she had not reckoned on when she married him. He kissed her once more, long and deep, then tore his mouth from hers. 'God bless you, Lily. Pray for us.'

She nodded, unable to speak, then blew him a kiss before running blindly from him.

# Chapter Seven

Only three days after Matt departed, Lily was wishing herself on the briny with him. Instead she perched back to front on the outside bedroom windowsill, cleaning the windows. She was missing him far more than she had imagined and the hours lacked that edge of expectancy when she had known he would be there at the end of the day. But at least Ben looked less tired and Daisy had stopped moaning and she had the consolation of knowing if anything did go wrong with Ronnie and May, she was on hand. As well as that Uncle William had delivered several new cows in full milk and handed her five hundred pounds in a black velvet drawstring bag.

She had been incredulous as she fingered the notes. 'Are you sure? I'm still planning on leaving, you know?'

'Aye, I know, lass,' he said heavily. 'But our Albert should have had that and more years ago. Besides, I behaved unfairly to you. Duty always came first with you in the past, but now when duty decrees you should be with Matt, you're here because the family needs you. I respect you and Matt for making a hard decision and when you have to leave us I'll wish you the best of luck with my whole heart.'

She had been as grateful for his words as the money and only hoped Ronnie and May would get better so she could join Matt in the time promised.

Unfortunately when Lily went to fetch the children it was to be told Ronnie was still having trouble with his ear. The doctor made an appointment for him to attend the Eye, Ear, Nose and Throat Infirmary in Myrtle Street. May, on the other hand, suffered no complications but looked washed-out and was irritable because her skin was peeling off.

'I look terrible,' she wailed. 'I'm not going back to school till I look lovely again.'

'You've a fine opinion of yourself, my girl,' rebuked Lily, but she could not prevent a smile and was relieved to have her sister almost her normal self.

May's words reminded her it would soon be the school holidays and she wondered what to do. It would have been different if they had been well because they could have gone with Ben on his deliveries, but not the way they were. She felt dejected as she wrote to Matt, explaining the situation, but was certain he would understand.

It was the day after she sent the letter to Matt that Frank came into the dairy, looking slightly shamefaced. 'A pint of milk and four eggs, Lil.' He placed a bulky brown paper bag on the counter. 'That's for the kids. They are all right now, aren't they?'

'Not infectious, if that's what you mean,' she said, leaning towards him, her elbows on the counter. 'They're sitting out in the yard, getting some sunshine. You can tell your mam the risk of fever was over weeks ago. I always thought we were friends, Frank. I'm disappointed in you for not being in.'

'Now, Lil, don't be like that!' He thumped a jug down beside the brown bag. 'Mam's got to be careful with our being in the food business, you know.'

'You don't have to make excuses. You're not the only one who's been missing.' She flicked open the paper bag with a finger. Inside there were a couple of oranges, apples and bananas. 'Does your mam know you've taken these?'

He flushed. 'I can act off my own bat, Lil. You aren't half hard on me. Even so, I must admit to being glad you're still here.'

'Not for much longer. As soon as Ronnie's ear's sorted out and the school holidays have been and gone, I'll be off.'

'But not just yet!' He leaned forward across the counter. 'We could go to the pictures? It'd do you good to get out.'

She raised her eyebrows, wondering where he had got the courage to say such a thing. 'What would your mam say to your taking out a married woman? You do surprise me, Frank,' she said, filling his jug from the churn.

'Your Daisy thought it a good idea,' he said eagerly. 'She said you could do with a break, and with me being an old family friend nobody would see any harm in it.'

'And you believed her?' She did not wait for him to answer. 'I'd ruin your reputation, Frank. Thanks, but no thanks.' She felt really annoyed with Daisy. Her sister knew exactly what her feelings were towards Frank. Then she had a thought and, smiling at him, she said, 'Why don't you ask Daisy out instead? I'm not keen on that

Ted she's seeing. I've always thought she's got a soft spot for you but you've never looked her way.'

His round face went brick-red. 'You can't mean that, Lil? She's so young and pretty. She wouldn't want me.'

And I'm not so young and pretty, am I? thought Lily wryly, wondering if Frank realised what he had said. Even so she carried on smiling as she placed four eggs in a paper bag and handed them to him. 'You won't know until you try. Come to tea on Saturday and I'll make sure she's in.'

He stuttered his thanks and turned towards the door. 'You haven't paid me, Frank,' she called, a tremor in her voice. 'And you've forgotten your milk.'

'Sorry, sorry! I'm all of a doo dan!' He handed her some money without looking at how much, picked up the jug and walked out the shop.

Lily folded her arms and could not wait for her sister to come home.

'I've asked Frank to come to tea on Saturday.' Lily placed a plate of scouse in front of Daisy. The kitchen was quiet except for the ticking of the clock on the oak sideboard. She had sent May and Ronnie to bed early and Ben had gone out.

Her sister smiled. 'That'll be nice for both of you but what are you telling me for?'

'I want you here.'

'Want me?'

Lily nodded grimly. 'I'm a married woman now in case you've forgotten. I want a chaperone.'

Daisy put her tongue in her cheek. 'He told you, did he?'

'I don't know what was in your mind, but forget it.'

Her sister said lightly, 'There's such a thing as an annulment – or divorce on grounds of desertion.'

'You're mad!' said Lily incredulously. 'Annulments are granted only if the marriage hasn't been consummated. I can assure you ours has! And Matt has not deserted me.'

Her sister grinned suddenly. 'I suppose it was a daft thing to do. I just wanted to keep you here, that's all. But why ask Frank to tea?'

'For you!' Lily smiled sweetly. 'I know he's not most women's idea of a hero but he'd always be faithful and you could twist him round your little finger.'

Daisy laughed. 'You're as mad as I am! I'm in love with Ted.'

Lily buttered a slice of bread. 'It wouldn't do any harm to make him jealous. He's such a good-looking bloke he must have a big head.'

Her sister placed her elbow on the table and rested her chin in her palm. 'He let me down the other week. Perhaps it wouldn't do him any harm to discover I'm not always at his beck and call. He doesn't need to know Frank's no competition.'

'I'll do us something really tasty,' said Lily, considering how nice it would be if Frank married Daisy and moved into the dairy. Her sister would have to give up her job and she would be there for the kids and shop and she could go to Australia with a clear conscience. 'I'll ask Ben to cadge a chicken off Uncle William. It'll have to be plucked and drawn but it shouldn't be too much of a hardship if we share the work.'

Daisy shuddered but remained silent.

'These are for you!' Frank thrust the sweet peas and a box of Cadbury's Milk Tray at Daisy as he entered the kitchen in Lily's wake.

Her lightly powdered face lit up. 'Why thanks, Frank!'

Ten out of ten, Frank, thought Lily approvingly. You've done the right thing for all you look a dafty. Now Ted's never brought her a thing. I suppose the trouble with some handsome men is they believe they're God's gift to women and their looks are enough.

Frank flushed. 'I've always been fond of you, Daisy.'

Her smile became fixed. 'I am courting, you know,' she said softly. 'But you don't have to let that put you off. Nothing's settled.'

He said earnestly, 'Then I'm in with a chance?'

'You could say that.' Her eyes danced and she touched his cheek with the flowers. 'I appreciate these anyway, and I'll go and put them in some water.'

'Something smells nice.' Frank followed her over to the sink.

'It's chicken.' She smiled at Lily. 'We both thought nothing's too good for you, Frank. You're such an old friend.'

'Less of the old,' he said, grinning at her. 'I'm only twenty-six. It's not so old.'

Lily, pulling out a dining chair for him, thought, please, please, don't say he looks older, Dais! Use a bit of tact!

'It must be because you seem so – so mature,' said Daisy, placing the vase of sweet peas in the centre of the table.

'It's probably because there's been just me and Mam since the war and she always treated me like the man of the house,' said Frank.

Lily bit her lip to control her merriment and mused, so *that's* how his mother treated him – and there was us thinking *she* was the man of the house!

'You have such a confident air, Frank,' murmured Daisy, a quiver in her voice. He pulled out a chair for her. 'And you're such a gentleman. There's not so many of them around these days.'

Lily smiled and ordered Ronnie to stop tormenting May with the chicken's claw, wash his hands and come to the table.

Despite Ronnie and May only picking at their food, the meal went off well. Daisy talked about music and dancing and Frank was surprisingly well informed. After the meal he offered to play the piano.

'It hasn't been played for a long time,' said Lily, collecting dirty dishes. 'But see what you can do with it. Our Daisy can turn the pages for you.' She smiled encouragingly at them both.

Frank ran his fingers over the keys with a confidence generally lacking in most things he did. 'It needs tuning but it's not too bad.'

Daisy lifted the lid of the stool and took out a sheet of music. 'Play this,' she challeneged, placing it in front of him and just managing to avoid the old-fashioned candle holders on the upright part of the piano.

He looked up at her with a besotted grin, before lowering his eyes to the music and launching into 'When

They Begin the Beguine', playing with lots of little flour-
ishes and definite talent.

'You're good!' Daisy's surprise was obvious. 'Let's
find something else.' He rose from the stool and lifted its
top and together they searched through the sheet music
inside and came up with 'Roses of Picardy' and 'Ain't
We Got Fun!' among others.

Lily left them to it, pulling May away from the piano
and telling Ronnie, who was sorting out cigarette cards
depicting scenes from the British Empire, it was time for
bed. Her hopes were high that in music Daisy and Frank
had found common ground.

Ronnie's appointment for the clinic came round and the
news was not good. He was deaf in one ear. Lily had
suspected as much from the habit he had developed of
holding his head on one side when people were talking
or he was listening to the wireless, and she hoped he
would cope when he went back to school. She prayed
that by then Frank and Daisy's relationship might be
closer.

She scanned the shipping columns in the *Weekly Post*
which told of arrivals and departures in Liverpool and
other far-flung ports of the world and learnt of Matt's
ship's safe docking in Sydney. The next day, to her relief
and pleasure, she received a letter from him. She opened
it eagerly and read:

Darling Lily,
I am missing you unbearably but hopefully by the time
you receive this, you will already have booked your

berth and will be on your way to join me in a couple
of days. I managed to get this on a mail boat heading
for Liverpool when we were going through Suez. I wish
you could have been with me. You'd have enjoyed the
sounds and smells and sights of Egypt – not that I saw
much of them. So far I haven't mentioned May and
Ronnie but that's because I'm certain they are all right.
We always think the worst where people we love are
concerned.

It's lonely nights but I'm filling my time sorting
out slides, I've got a beaut one of you outside the
church the day I asked you to marry me. It was the
most impulsive action I ever took but it was the right
one. Have you remembered to pick up the photographs
I took on our honeymoon, and could you possibly pay
Aunt Jane a visit before you leave? She's going to
miss us. I am also writing rough drafts of talks, leaving
spaces where perhaps you could put a word in. I really
believe you and I sharing some of the talking can
work.

I'll be staying in the Sydney area a week or so. That
way you can have a rest before we go travelling. I love
you very much and can't wait to see you again. God
bless.
Your loving husband,
Matt

Lily read the letter again and then carefully folded it and
put it away. It had brought Matt closer and she determined
to book her passage as soon as May's birthday was over.

But now the holidays were here she decided to take the children to places they had never had the time or the money to visit. She paid a widow woman to do the housework and another to take her washing to the washhouse and prepared to cram in as much as she could in the short time left to her.

Their first port of call was Liverpool Zoo at Otterspool so that Ronnie could see a real elephant, lions, and the infamous Mickey the chimp. He had a deadly aim with a football and was known to have bitten a few people, but this only served to enhance his reputation. Ronnie was fascinated by the zoo but May was not so struck. 'They all smell,' she said, turning up her dainty nose.

The next outing was to Southport Pleasureland where for tuppence a ride they scared themselves to death on the newly opened big dipper. They came home on the train, tired and happy despite its having rained, and Lily felt certain that her brother and sister were well on their way to recovery. She planned another treat but they said they'd rather play out in the street with their friends.

Lily decided she would go and see Jane.

'I've had a letter from our Matt,' she said, waving the paper in the air. 'Sez something about going to a place called Adelaide that's known as the city of churches,' she murmured, reading it out carefully. 'Then to a silver mining town called Broken Hill, and then into sheep country.' She turned the letter over between her hands and smiled up at Lily from her chair in the backyard. 'He writes a real good letter does that nephew of mine, and even sez he hopes to see me. Perhaps you'll come back here one day?' Her words startled Lily. She knew working in Liverpool was something Matt had said he'd considered but he couldn't have really meant it, could he?

She pondered that question over the coming days as she filled her free hours with wandering round Liverpool. She took a trip on the ferry to New Brighton, her eyes drinking in the views of the docks and the Wirral coast. She realised she was going to miss the old place but told herself she was going somewhere more exotic and beautiful.

She received another letter from Matt, saying he understood about Ronnie's ear but please to come soon. He would write to her care of his address in Sydney as he would be travelling about now. She thought fondly how she could trust him to understand and wrote back saying she would be with him soon.

May had decided what kind of birthday party she wanted. 'It's not going to be a kids' party because I'm entering my second decade,' she said proudly, her eyes shining. 'Frank can come because he's useful for the entertainment. He and our Daisy can do a duet and he can play while I dance – although I could do it better if I had a pair of taps.' She winked at Lily. 'Uncle William can tell jokes and our Ronnie can do a tune on one of his whistles.'

'And what do I do?' said Lily good-humouredly. 'Make a birthday cake, I suppose?'

She nodded. 'A proper one with candles.'

May's birthday was on a Sunday. After the milking Lily iced the cake she had made the day before and took breakfast up to her sister with her present on a tray. May went for the present first, tearing the brown paper open. Her face lit up and she immediately put the red tap shoes on and scrambled out of bed to dance around the room. Then she dressed and it was out into the street to show off to all her friends, a much happier little girl than the one who had been so mopey after her bout of scarlet fever.

That afternoon Lily set the table and put the cake in pride of place in the centre. A car tooting its horn drew the whole family outside on to the pavement. All their eyes widened at the sight of the enormous, spanking new car drawn up at the kerb. William descended from it with great aplomb and helped Dora down. 'What do you think, Ben?' He waved a proud hand over the vehicle. 'It's an Armstrong Siddeley – a car of quality and high performance.'

Ben strolled over to the automobile and stroked its bonnet.

Lily said with a smile, 'You say that like a salesman, Uncle William. She must have cost you a pretty penny.'

'Enough, lass,' he said briefly. 'Sold another field.'

May pushed forward. 'Can I have a ride round the block in her, Uncle William?'

'Jump in, lass.' His ruddy face broke into a smile. 'Anyone else for the Skylark?' Ronnie, Frank, Daisy and Ben climbed into the car with alacrity and were off.

Lily turned to Dora, who as usual was wearing a long black dress. On her head she had an enormous black hat which consisted mainly of a glossy-winged bird. 'A cup of tea, Aunt Dora?' she asked, trying to sound friendly.

'Aye, I suppose so. Got more money than sense that brother of mine. Cars!' She sniffed. 'Legs are good enough for me. Let's get inside, Lily, and you can tell me what you're up to.'

'If you mean when am I leaving, I book my passage tomorrow.' She led the way inside.

Aunt Dora sniffed. 'I suppose you've got to go.'

'There's no suppose about it! I have a husband. My place is beside him.'

'I suppose you've done your best,' said Dora grudgingly, gazing around the room. Her eyes lighted on the open paino. 'It's getting used, I see. Polished for once, and you've put candles in the holders.'

Lily allowed the insult to her housewifely skills to pass, and murmured, 'Daisy did it. She's learning to play. Frank's teaching her.'

Dora's eyes almost popped out of her head. 'Isn't he the one who once had an eye to you?'

Lily removed a teacloth from a plate of sandwiches. 'He's got his eye on Daisy now but I don't know if it's going to work.' She sighed. 'Irritatingly, she still fancies Ted's handsome face.'

'Well, I suppose you can't make people have the ones you'd like them to.' Dora fidgeted and glanced round the room again. 'It's dark in that corner. You should light the candles.'

'You do it if you want them lit. There's matches on the mantelpiece.' Lily whisked out of the room to fetch a bottle of Full Swing lemonade from the cool room.

The clock ticked loudly in the silence as Dora lit the candles but it was broken a moment later by the return of the others.

Lily ordered them to sit at the table. They obeyed, still talking about the car. She hushed them and put her hands together and closed her eyes. Silence fell and with the slightest quiver in her voice she thanked God for all the family being together and especially asked Him to bless May who was eleven that day. She prayed for Matt and the peace of the world, thanked him for the food, and said a quick amen.

There was a chorus of amens and the noise level rose. Lily wondered if it was only she who was experiencing a dreamlike feeling, thinking of Matt and her father and that soon she would be leaving them all.

Ben talked to Frank, May chattered to Uncle William, Daisy was forced into a stilted exchange of questions and answers with Dora. They all seemed happy enough. Lily smiled at Ronnie but he did not smile back and she wondered if her departure was on his mind. The candles on the cake were lit and May managed to blow them all out in one go to the cheers of everyone.

Frank took up a position on the piano stool, the glow of the candles lighting his face. On May's orders he began to play 'The Good Ship Lollipop'. She sang and danced and they all cheered. Then May ordered Daisy to play a duet with Frank.

'Yes, birthday girl,' said Daisy, laughing as Frank went to fetch a chair.

Lily smiled and thought, perhaps they will get on after all when I'm gone. She watched as Daisy took a sheet of music from the stool and set it on the piano stand. It slipped and her sister leaned forward.

Afterwards the next few seconds seemed unreal to Lily because one moment all was well and the next Daisy's hair had caught fire in the candle's flame.

'Your hair!' shouted Lily, and catching up a chairback cover flew across the room the second Daisy realised what was happening and screamed. Frank dropped the chair but seemed frozen where he was. Half of Daisy's head was fizzling and in flames. Lily brought the cover down, swathing her hair in it. The next moment Daisy slumped against her.

Suddenly Ben was beside Lily, taking their sister's weight. 'Hell, Lil! Look at her face,' he whispered.

'I know,' she said, feeling peculiarly calm as she lifted the cover to see that the flames were extinguished.

'Is she badly burnt?' said Dora, hurrying over.

'Put her on the sofa, Ben,' murmured Lily.

'Can I help?' It was an ashen-faced Frank.

She thought, he's better off out of the way. 'I don't think so.' She smiled to soften the words.

'But . . .'

'Please,' she said quietly. 'Come back later, Frank.'

He stared down at Daisy and left without another word.

A shocked-looking William said, 'Shouldn't we take her to the hospital, Lily, lass?'

She passed a hand over her eyes. 'What can they do? I remember Wilf the policeman's daughter was burnt and they couldn't prevent the scarring.'

'You can put butter on burns,' said Dora, shaking her head. 'Or flour.'

'I know what I'd want if I was burnt,' said Ronnie, whose head had been turning as they talked. 'Something cool. Milk!'

'Cold milk,' said May, nodding sagely, 'straight from the cooler.'

Daisy's eyelids fluttered open and she stared up at them. Her hands went to her cheek and the side of her head and she moaned, 'Oh God, it bloody hurts! It's burning, burning!'

'Daisy!' came her aunt's shocked voice.

'Cold milk,' said Ben, heading for the coolroom.

'A doctor! I know someone,' said William, making for the door.

Lily put on the kettle, found the medicine box and took out a couple of aspirin, her eyes on her sister's face.

Daisy's terrified gaze met hers. 'What must I look like? I could be scarred for life!' Tears trickled down her nose.

'You'll be all right,' said Lily gently, taking hold of her hand. 'Do lie down.'

Ben entered the room with a jug of milk. He hesitated. 'Lil, get her over to the sink.'

Daisy looked at him. 'What are you going to do?'

'It'll cool it down, Daisy,' said Ronnie and May, nodding in unison.

'Butter's what she needs,' said Dora positively.

Ben and Lily exchanged looks and she knew which she'd prefer. 'Over to the sink, Dais.'

Her sister did as she was told, moaning as she walked like a zombie across the room. Slowly Ben trickled the milk over her hair and down the side of her face where the flame had reached her cheek.

'Does it feel worse or better?' asked Lily, staring anxiously into her sister's eyes.

'Not worse but I'm cold.' She shivered.

Ben didn't need asking again to get more milk, and Lily sent Ronnie to fetch a blanket.

By the time William and the doctor arrived Daisy was in less pain and the blistering on her face had been arrested but she was still shivering despite the blanket.

'So you used cold milk,' said the doctor, who was the son of a farmer friend of William's. 'My gran used to swear by a poultice made up from chopped carrot, cabbage and ivy leaf with nettle juice. Others say butter does the job.' His eyes twinkled.

'Did your gran's remedy work?' asked Lily, reasssured that they had not done her sister any harm.

'She said it did.' He smiled at Daisy. 'I can send you to hospital if you wish but it is only a relatively small area of skin you've lost. You'll need to have a dressing on it and to keep quiet for a couple of days. I'll give you some tablets.'

'Will I be scarred, doctor?' she asked in a trembling voice.

He hesitated. 'There will be some scarring but a bit of face powder will hide it and your hair will grow.'

'My hair,' moaned Daisy, her hands going to her head. 'The money I paid for that perm!'

'It could have been worse.' Lily's voice was relieved.

Over the next few days it was obvious Daisy did not share Lily's opinion and when Ted and Frank called she refused to see either of them. 'I look a sight! A fright!' she wailed. 'I look like a scarecrow struck by lightning!'

Lily laughed. 'If they love you, they won't care!'

'I care,' cried Daisy, and burst into tears.

'Give it another week then,' said Lily, worried about her. She wrote to Matt, hoping he would continue to be understanding where her family's needs were concerned. There was a limit to a man's patience, she thought anxiously. There had been no more letters from him and she hated not knowing where he was or what he was doing.

Daisy felt no different a week later. 'You'll be wanting to go back to work, though,' said Lily, irritated.

'Work!' Daisy's expression was horrified. 'I couldn't go to work.'

'Stay at home then,' said Lily, pleased. 'You can do my job, ready for when I leave.'

Her sister winced. 'I'm not going to work in the shop. They'll all look at me.'

'So what? It's never bothered you before.'

'It bothers me now!'

'I'm leaving next week, Daisy.' Her tone was firm. 'Tomorrow we'll go for a walk. It's time your face had some fresh air on it.'

'No, Lil,' she said, paling.

'Yes,' said Lily, and went into town and booked her passage.

The next day she told her sister to get ready to go out.

'Can we go the back way?' said Daisy, looking nervous.

'Sure.'

Daisy went upstairs and came down wearing a veiled hat. 'Don't mock, Lil,' she said, placing a hand in the crook of her arm and gripping hard. 'You don't know what it's like to be ugly.'

'Frank doesn't think you're ugly,' said Lily. 'He'd probably marry you if you'd have him.'

'I'm not having a man who's sorry for me. I want one who admires me,' said Daisy, her bottom lip trembling.

'Frank does! Now forget men for the moment and just relax.'

But Daisy seemed unable to and every time anyone approached she darted behind Lily, who at first was amused but soon begin to feel irritated. Just a few more days, she told herself, and insisted her sister went out alone the next day.

'I can't,' said Daisy in a trembling voice.

'Of course you can!' She handed her some money. 'I need some potatoes.' She pushed her sister out of the door and slammed it, hoping Frank could do something with her.

She might as well have saved her breath. Her sister arrived home on the run minus the greengroceries. 'I couldn't do it,' she gasped, sucking in air. 'I couldn't breathe. I felt I would die if I went inside.'

'You need your head examining,' said Ben in disgust, who had entered behind her. 'Come on, Lil. It's time for milking.' He opened the back door. 'By the way, Uncle William's bringing a couple more cows. Soon there'll be lots more lovely milk for our Daisy to sell after you've gone.'

'You and your stupid cows!' she yelled. 'You don't care about me!' She burst into tears.

'Oh, hell!' said Ben, and dived through the doorway.

Lily followed him. What was she to do about Daisy? She looked down the yard and longed for Matt. He might have had an answer. She hardened her resolve. Daisy was going to have to cope. Come what may, Lily was definitely going to Australia next week.

'I don't want any of you to come with me,' said Lily, placing her suitcase on the floor by the door.

'You don't mean it,' said Dora, the blackbird in her hat swaying sidewards. 'William's brought the car specially.'

'Don't make this any more difficult for me, please.' Lily's voice held a slight tremor as she avoided looking at the family ranged in front of her. She pulled on a beige kid glove. 'I – I don't want to stand on the ship, watching you all getting smaller and smaller.' A tear rolled down her cheek and she brushed it away. 'I don't want you missing me. I just want you all happy.'

'Oh, shut up, Lil!' said Ben in a choked voice. 'You know damn' well we'll miss you!'

She lifted her head. 'Shut up yourself, Ben Thorpe!' A sob shook her body. He threw his arms round her, kissed her cheek, then thrust her away and blundered out of the kitchen into the backyard.

Lily wiped the tears from her cheeks and attempted a smile for her younger brother and sister. Ronnie looked away but May smiled, 'Bye, Lil. Perhaps we can come and see you one day?'

She nodded. Perhaps it was possible, when she and Matt were settled somewhere. She would not mind settling in Sydney. She looked at Daisy, who was gazing down at her hands. 'Bye, Dais,' she whispered. 'Keep the home fires burning.'

'Sure.' Daisy did not lift her eyes and her voice was barely audible. 'I hope you'll be happy.'

Lily turned to William. 'Thank you,' was all she could manage, and she blindly reached for her suitcase. His hand got there first.

'Come on, lass,' he rasped. 'D'you think I'd let you be going on the tram? I'll drive you to the Pierhead and you can sail off just how you want it.'

She nodded, took one last look at them all. Her arms ached to hug Ronnie but he would not even look at her. Without another word she walked out of the kitchen, trying not to think she might never see any of them again.

# Chapter Eight

'It's a beaut, isn't it?' drawled a voice with an Aussie twang from behind Lily. 'Only opened five years ago.'

Lily glanced up at the massive skeletal arch of Sydney Harbour Bridge and then at the plump woman in the pink frock. 'It must take some painting.'

'Sure, but it'll keep some men in work and that's what's needed these days.'

'You are Joy? said Lily, smiling and holding out a hand.

The woman's slightly pouting lips eased slightly. 'You are Matt's wife?'

'Yes, I'm Lily.' She picked up her suitcase. 'You must have thought I'd never get here. I did as your husband told me on the telephone and stayed put. I had thought of walking but—'

'It's more confusing than you thought.'

'The distances are greater than they appear on the map and I wasn't sure if I was on the right side of the harbour.' Lily found herself almost babbling but why she should feel she had to make excuses she did not know.

'Kirribilli is north side. You could have taken the ferry, but knowing you had luggage, I brought the car.' She began to walk. 'You were lucky to catch us in. Pete's leave is nearly up. I don't know if Matt told you he's in the Australian Navy?'

Lily fell in step beside her. 'Yes. And that they've known each other since schooldays.' She hesitated. 'He said you haven't heard from Matt?'

Joy did not answer immediately but paused to open the car door. 'Not recently, and I'm not sure where he is. Last time we spoke he talked of taking a break and coming home but when I told him about Pete's leave he said he'd give us some time on our own. Of course, he didn't know you were on your way.'

'But he should have known!' exploded Lily, feeling near to tears. She shaded her eyes from the glare of sun on water. 'You did send my letters on?'

'Sure, I did,' said Joy, reddening. 'But he's been moving on and God only knows when they'll reach him. He does have a habit of getting sidetracked sometimes. He could have met some swaggie on the road. I take it you know what Matt's like for talking to all and sundry?'

'Yes.' She got into the car, trying to conceal her acute disappointment. 'What's a swaggie?'

'You'd call them tramps. Some are misfits from the war who've never been able to feel comfortable in society again. The depression didn't improve their situation.' She pursed her lips. 'Lots of men went walkabout in search of work which was almost impossible to find. When did you last hear from Matt?'

'Not for a couple of months.' Her mouth drooped. 'He said he'd write to me care of his Sydney address.' Her spirits lifted. 'Of course! There'll be letters from him which'll tell me where he is.'

'Had no letters,' said Joy, starting the car.

Lily stared at her. 'You're joking!'

Joy turned pale blue eyes on her. 'Don't see any reason to make a joke about it,' she said in a toneless voice. 'He phoned a couple of weeks ago to see if you were here. Pete said no and that was the last we've heard from him. Have to tell you he didn't sound pleased that you weren't here.'

Lily could not think of an answer to that. Of course Matt wasn't pleased if he hadn't received her letters.

Joy slanted her a glance. 'What kept you so long? Matt said something about a younger brother and sister being sick but seemed to think they were getting better.' She paused. 'You're not having a baby, are you?'

'No!' Lily was startled. She hadn't even thought of a baby being the possible consequence of the nights of love with Matt. Probably because there had been so much else to think about.

'I am,' said Joy with a proud air. 'But don't mention it to Pete. It's early days and I just know he'll fuss and worry about going back to his ship if he finds out, and I don't want that.'

'I wouldn't dream of saying anything,' murmured Lily, gazing at the scenery as they crossed the bridge. What kind of person did Joy think she was to discuss other people's private business?

'That's OK then.' Joy hummed beneath her breath as she drove onto the bridge. 'Try not to worry about Matt,

He'll turn up. Take a look at the scenery . . . have you ever seen any better?'

Lily looked out of the window at the panorama surrounding her. It was different from Liverpool, was all she could think. The water was blue instead of khaki green, the roofs were red, and lots of houses were painted in pastel shades. Here was a lovely sunlit city but she was too overwhelmed by homesickness and worry about Matt to appreciate it.

On the other side of the harbour Joy brought the car to a halt outside a house halfway up a street which ran up from the harbourside. The walls were painted pink and the upper windows were fronted by balconies protected by lacy wrought-iron railings.

Joy opened the door into Matt's part of the house and showed Lily to his bedroom and left her. She sank on to the bed and dropped her head into her hands and let the tears trickle through her fingers. She had been so looking forward to seeing him and felt lost and alone in this strange house. She lifted her head and looked about her, trying to see his personality imprinted on the room, but there was nothing that spoke of Matt to her. It was well furnished in light oak and the double bedstead was made of solid brass. Curtains and coverings were pale green and there was a crucifix on the wall behind the bed. Perhaps it was so impersonal, thought Lily, because he spent so much time travelling?

She rose and wandered out on to the balcony outside and looked towards the harbour, busy with small craft. She felt lonelier than ever, imagining Matt gazing out at this same view. If only he would walk through the door, now, today, tonight, she could bear anything.

But Matt did not come home that night. Neither did he phone and there was no mail from him over the next few days.

On the Sunday after Lily had attended the service in St Andrew's Cathedral on George Street and prayed to hear something from Matt, Joy invited her to have dinner with her and Pete and Lily accepted hoping to learn something more about Matt and this couple who rented part of his house.

Their floor was very different to Matt's, more lived in. The furniture was not so solid, fabrics were bright yellows, reds and oranges. There were pictures of flowers and seascapes, and little space that was not taken over by clutter.

She waited until after dinner to speak of her concern about there still being no word from Matt. Pete was a stocky, brown-haired, laconic man.

'The car could have gone crook,' he said.

'Matt knows something about cars,' said Lily earnestly. 'Surely he would have been able to sort it out by now?'

'Depends where it happened and whether he had spares. Wouldn't you agree, love?' He glanced up from the newspaper at his wife.

'Sure. If it was something Matt couldn't fix he'd have started walking,' drawled Joy, placing a cup of tea on a table near Lily's hand. 'And he'd make sure he had plenty of water with him. So I wouldn't worry about him dying of thirst!'

Lily let out a strained laugh and ran a hand over her hair. 'Having just come from England, thinking of someone dying of thirst doesn't immediately spring to mind. So what can we do?'

Pete folded the Sunday newspaper, dropped it on the floor and stretched out his legs. 'What about that Fraser family Matt mentioned?'

Joy frowned. 'What about them?'

'Who are the Fraser family?' demanded Lily.

Pete's expression was thoughtful. 'It might be worth getting in touch with the Harringtons in Bourke after I've gone and asking their address, love.'

Lily clenched her fists in her lap. 'Why can't we get in touch with them now?'

'Probably no need,' Pete told her. 'Matt won't thank you for fussing. He'll turn up sooner or later. It's not the first time he's done something like this.'

Lily gave up in frustration. They just weren't concerned but she was madly worried. If Matt did not arrive in the next couple of days she determined to do something, whatever Pete said.

Pete returned to shipboard duty and Joy, prodded on by Lily, got in touch with the Reverend J. Harrington in Bourke who told her that Matt had left weeks ago but, yes, he had mentioned dropping in at the Frasers' place for a couple of days.

'See! Pete was right,' said Joy, yawning as she placed the receiver back on its hook. 'The trouble with these outback stations is it can be so lonely and boring out there they hang on to visitors. He's probably stayed more than a couple of days but is on his way home now.'

'You think so?' said Lily, getting to her feet and pacing the floor. 'So you don't believe he could have broken down?'

'I don't think there's any need to worry,' said Joy comfortably, picking up a skein of cream wool. 'Give it a couple more days and if he's not back by then we could write to the Frasers.'

Lily stared at her. 'A couple of days! And then how many more for a letter to reach them? Isn't there a train or a bus to Bourke I could take?'

'Sure! Bourke is a big wool port. Once you could only get there cross-country by horse and then up the Darling by paddle steamer.' She held out the skein of wool to Lily. 'Hold this for me while I wind it.'

Lily felt like screaming with frustration but instead placed the skein about her wrists. Joy seemed to be unable to concentrate on anything but the baby. 'You say I can catch a train to Bourke now?' she said patiently.

Joy nodded. 'You'll have to go on your own. I can't risk losing this baby. And don't forget it'll be further than you think. This isn't little old England, you know.'

'Tell me another,' said Lily drily, and made up her mind if Matt did not return in the morning she would pack a bag and go and buy a train ticket. If she had not been so anxious she would have been furious with him for putting her through all this worry.

Matt did not come home so Lily boarded a train destined for Bourke with the name of the Frasers' station in her purse. She was determined to find Matt whatever it took.

# Chapter Nine

Lily dropped the rucksack Joy had lent her on the gravel and eased her shoulders as she gazed at the sprawling single-storeyed house fronted by a verandah which was broken by a flight of steps leading to the front door. Beyond it she could make out several large outhouses. A sigh escaped her. She was stiff and sore from riding motorbike pillion and being bumped over dirt roads. Twice she had been flung off but fortunately had landed on grass. The bike belonged to a parishioner of the Harringtons' who just happened to be passing the Frasers' place. He had dropped her at the gates, telling her she could walk the rest of the way. She only hoped she wasn't wasting her time as she did not want to do that walk again. Evening was coming on, she was hot, hungry, utterly worn out, and dying for a cup of tea.

She took a deep breath and approached the door, only to stop on hearing a vehicle drawing up. Her pulses raced but soon settled when she saw the man climbing out of the truck was not Matt.

'Where did you spring from?' He was tall and the rolled-up shirt sleeves of his blue cotton shirt showed tanned, muscular arms.

'Are you one of the Frasers?' She walked over to him.
'You're a Pom.'

'I'm Liverpudlian.'

'Can you cook?' he drawled. 'I did ask them to send
a woman who can cook.'

'Of course I can cook!' She was startled by his remarks.
'What's that to do with anything?'

'Plenty. You're hired. Go round the back. You'll find
Doreen there. She'll show you what's needed before she
goes.' He walked away from her towards a paddock where
several cattle grazed.

'Hey, hold on!' cried Lily, running after him. 'I'm no
hired help, mate! I've come to find my husband. I was
assured I'd get a warm welcome. The Frasers like visitors,
I was told.'

He turned, gazing down at her from eyes she could not
tell the colour of because the brim of his hat cast a shadow
over the top half of his face. 'I'll pay you what you ask
as long as you don't flirt with the men.'

'Didn't you hear what I said?' Lily drew herself up to
her full height of five feet, four inches. 'I'm a married
woman!'

'So? The shearers haven't arrived yet. You can work
in the house until your husband turns up with them.'

She took a deep breath and said emphatically, 'My
husband does not shear sheep. He's a preacher and I was
informed I'd find him here.'

His expression changed and then he swore profusely.

Lily frowned. 'Do you mind? I'm not used to that kind
of language.'

'Used to sweet talk, are you, lady?' His tone was as chill as hers. 'Well, I'm telling you now – your husband has gone off with my sister and I'll knock his block off when I see him!'

Lily stared at him in disbelief. 'You're a liar!'

'He's the bloody liar. Never a word about a wife! Abby probably thinks—' He stopped, his mouth tightening. 'We were all taken in, not just her. He was a mate! We never thought a preacher –' He paused and breathed deeply. 'But you don't have to worry. A couple of my brothers have gone after them and you can have him back. He mightn't be in one piece but you can try putting him together if you care that much about him!'

Lily went hot and cold, and sky and grass shifted unpleasantly. Reaching out, she gripped the nearby fencing to steady herself. She swallowed the bile in her throat and forced down the panic his words had roused. 'You're making a big mistake, Mr Fraser,' she whispered. 'Matt wouldn't. He's not that kind of man.'

'Isn't he now?' he drawled. 'Abby left a note. She says she's gone off with him and that they're lovers. Do you hear that, Mrs Gibson?' he shouted. 'She wrote it in black and white! The news caused Ma to have one of her turns and she's taken to her bed.'

'I don't believe it!' cried Lily, getting a grip on herself. 'Did you see them go?'

'Of course I bloody didn't or I would have stopped them!' His tone was exasperated.

'Then we only have your sister's word that she's with him,' said Lily strenuously, relief flooding her.

'They're both missing so don't kid yourself, lady.'

'I'm not kidding myself.' She stared at him with loathing. 'How old is your sister? Mrs Harrington said she was quite young.'

'Sixteen. What's that got to do with anything?' His expression tightened.

'Plenty! She's at that age.'

'And what does that mean?'

'Oh come on, Mr Fraser.' Her laugh held a hint of scorn. 'How often does a young girl out here set eyes on a presentable man? She probably threw herself at Matt and scared the life out of him. He's run!'

A flush darkened his cheekbones. 'My sister had plenty of real men interested in her. She didn't need no silver-tongued preacher.'

'I'm glad to hear it because she's not getting him,' Lily exclaimed hotly. He was silent. 'Well? Realise your mistake?' she said, her eyes glinting.

'I'm not mistaken. They've gone together, believe me.' He paused. 'How did you get here?'

'I was dropped off at your gates by motorbike. Why?'

'How are you going to get back to Bourke, Mrs Gibson?' A taunting grin twisted his tanned face. 'You've got a long walk. G'day.' He touched his hat and strode away.

Swine! Lily was infuriated. Forgetting her sore feet, she walked over to where her rucksack lay and swung it over her shoulder. So he was an example of that Australian manhood she had heard of – the hard kind who didn't know how to treat a woman. Alternately cursing him and telling herself Matt must be in Sydney by now, she forced her legs to carry her back up the long drive.

She was within sight of the gates when a car came through them. She did not move over but carried on walking. 'You get out of the way,' she muttered, gritting her teeth against the pain in her heel. But the car slowed. A head poked out of the window as she passed but the man only gazed at her without speaking. She felt certain he was another Fraser. She glanced at the back seat and saw it was unoccupied and felt satisfaction. So much for that Fraser man's conviction that his brothers would bring Matt back in pieces. The other brother had closed the gate and was now eyeing her dishevelled figure in a way that irritated her. He nodded but she ignored him, limping past him and on up the dirt road in what she believed was the right direction.

Half an hour later it was definitely cooler. Lily's mood had changed and she was no longer just angry but worried. The land on either side seemed to stretch to infinity and was flat and featureless but for the odd group of what she presumed were gum trees. The silence felt eerie to her city ears and she longed for the security which Matt's presence had always provided. She was undecided what to do. If she carried on walking when darkness fell she might wander off the road and get lost. She remembered what Matt had told her about the fate of Australian explorers Burke and Wills. Don't be stupid, she chided herself, that had been in the 1800s and in the real outback. People travelled this road. Still, as she carried on walking her thoughts were occupied with pictures of snakes, spiders and nasty horrible bulldog ants creeping up on her in the dark.

Suddenly she heard the noise of a vehicle behind her and immediately felt better. She stood in the middle of the road, waving her arms, waiting to be noticed. It was not until the truck stopped a few feet from her that she realised the first Mr Fraser was the driver.

'Well?' she said coolly as he slid his long legs out on to the road. 'Your brothers didn't find him, I see.'

He stared at her, his annoyance obvious. 'I thought I might catch you up. They weren't where Abby said they would be.'

Lily smiled. 'Surprise, surprise! Perhaps she sent you on a wild goose chase and doesn't want to be found? It can't be much fun having three older brothers bossing a girl about all the time.'

'There's five of us and she needs looking after,' he said harshly. 'Her going off with your husband proves it. What are you going to do about finding him?'

Her backbone stiffened and she tilted her chin. 'Why should I tell you, Mr Fraser? You want to knock his block off and I object to that. I love my husband.'

He pushed back his hat and his eyes narrowed. 'More fool you. Were you scared?'

'Of what?' she said, surprised by the question.

'Of the idea of being out here on your own at night.'

She stared at him, her expression pensive. 'That was your intention, was it? Frighten the city woman out of her wits for calling you a liar. You're not nice, Mr Fraser.'

Slowly his mouth eased into a grin. 'The name's Rob. I'll give you a lift into Bourke.'

'That's big of you.'

'Take it or leave it.'

She did not hesitate. Little as she wanted his company it would be stupid to turn the offer down. 'OK. I reckon you owe me a favour for making me walk this far with sore feet.'

He said nothing, only signalling with his head for her to get in.

Lily climbed into the cab and within seconds the truck was bucking and swaying along the earth road. She gripped the side of the seat but made no complaint, only praying they would arrive in one piece.

He dropped her off outside the railway station after a journey during which neither of them spoke. She thanked him, adding that if they ever met again it would be too soon. He grinned and drove off.

She limped inside the station to enquire when the next train left in the morning, believing she would see Matt when she arrived back at the house in Sydney.

The pink-washed house with the sun on it in Kirribilli was a welcome sight and so was the cool sparkling water of the harbour. Lily ran up the steps, imagining Matt's face when he saw her.

Joy opened the door and looked beyond her. 'Where's Matt?'

'Isn't he here?'

'No. I thought he'd be with you.'

Lily felt like weeping and sank on to the top step, gazing unseeingly across the street. 'He'd been there and gone. They didn't know where,' she said wearily, thinking that really wasn't a lie because Matt hadn't been where they believed.

Joy frowned. 'It's not like him to leave it so long without letting us know where he is.'

Lily rested her damp forehead against the palm of her hand. 'I take it there's been no letters or anything?'

'There's one from England for you. I'll brew up and you can read it while you wait.'

Lily forced herself up and followed Joy through into the backyard where there was a paved area with trees and a lawn. She sat in a cushioned cane chair and Joy dropped a bulky envelope on her lap. Numbly Lily picked it up. It would be from the family.

'Here, drink this. I've put plenty of sugar in it.'

'Thanks.'

Joy squeezed her shoulder. 'He'll be all right.'

Lily smiled unconvincingly and tried not to worry as she drank the tea and forced a couple of beef sandwiches down her. Then she picked up the envelope and slit it with a knife, hoping at least the news from Liverpool would be good. They must have written the instant she had left. Inside was another envelope addressed to her in Matt's writing. Her spirits rose as she tore it open and unfolded the single sheet, only to see it was dated more than three months ago.

Dearest Lily,

Why don't you come? Aren't I as important as your family? You say Ronnie's ear's not right yet but it probably will never be right and there's nothing you can do about that. Dear God, I need you right now!

The meetings haven't been going as well as I expected. Perhaps that's down to me? My heart's not in what I'm doing and I question if this is really what God wants me for now. I need some guidance so I'm going to see a brother friend of mine up in Queensland. If you do come, Joy will be able to tell you where to find me. I still love you but do you love me? Have you ever or was it just the lure of those faraway places which maybe now don't seem so attractive?

Love,

Matt

She dropped the letter on her lap as if it had burnt her. How could he doubt her? She felt hurt, angry.

'Bad news?' said Joy, leaning forward and replenishing her teacup.

'It's from Matt but it was written three months ago.' She gazed unseeing across the garden, repeating, Queensland, Queensland, stupidly inside her head.

'What's he say?' Joy's voice was unemotional as she refilled Lily's cup before seating herself comfortably on the other cane chair.

Lily focused on Joy's chubby face. 'He says he's going to Queensland to talk to some brother friend. He said you could tell me where to find him.'

Enlightenment brightened Joy's pale blue eyes. 'He'll be up Cairns way, near Atherton, on the edge of the Northern Great Dividing Range. Are you going to write and let him know you're here?'

Lily tapped the letter against her teeth and came to a decision. 'No. I don't trust the post. This has taken three months to reach me. I'll go there.'

Joy stared at her and then said with almost reluctant admiration, or so it seemed to Lily, 'I'll say this for you, you're not afraid to do what you think. Have you got enough money? Cairns is at least three times as far as Bourke – and it could be dangerous your travelling all the way up there on your own. The men don't get to see so many women and it's untamed country in some places, and can be hotter and clammier than down here.'

Lily forced a laugh. 'Are you trying to put me off?'

Joy shook her head. 'I was just thinking too that Matt wrote that three months ago and he phoned us only a few weeks ago. He might have changed his mind. It could be better to wait and see if he turns up here in the next few days.'

'You've said that before,' said Lily impatiently.

Joy chose to ignore that comment. 'Men are so thoughtless, and too often men like Matt are elsewhere in the realms of the spirit. He's not used to considering anyone else but himself normally.'

'I wouldn't agree with that,' disputed Lily. 'Matt has his feet firmly on the ground. He cares about other people. You said yourself he'd speak to anyone.'

Joy flushed. 'I wasn't meaning that exactly. I meant his having a wife. He'd need to give thought to your needs and he must find that difficult after being on his own for years.'

Lily thought about that but found herself defending Matt. 'He was prepared to stay in Liverpool with me,' she said strongly. 'Although I wouldn't argue with some of

what you say.' She folded the letter between her fingers.
'Anyway, can you tell me where to find this brother friend
of his?'

Joy nodded. 'I'll go and find the address and a map.
Give you an idea of the place names up in Queensland.'

While she was gone Lily opened the other letter. It
seemed the family was well. Ronnie was helping Ben out
with the milking. May was serving in the shop after school,
and Daisy was just about managing to face people,
although she sometimes came over all queer. Her hair was
still too short to perm and she hated herself. They were
all missing her and hoped she and Matt were happy. Love
and kisses from them all. Lily experienced that terrible
homesickness again but told herself she would be cured
of it when she found Matt.

As soon as Joy handed her the map, Lily spread it on
the floor and knelt on the rug. Joy stabbed at the map
with a finger. 'It's round about there! Herberton is a
mining town. There's an Anglican school and the church
and the building where the brothers live. Brother Antony
is Matt's particular mate. You'll have to get to Cairns
first and then take a smaller train. It's quite a journey.
There's lots of ravines and the train goes over spider-
webby bridges as it climbs to the plateau. I'd come with
you only . . .'

'You look after that baby,' said Lily firmly, staring at
the map. A large reef was shown as a jagged line running
beside most of the east coast of Queensland. She could
imagine the sea, a deep turquoise blue, and could almost
feel the hot sun on her back. She prayed fervently Matt

was up there. Maybe they could have a second honey-moon by the Coral Sea? She thought how romantic that sounded.

She rose, her face alight with determination. 'I'm defin-itely going! I feel right about this which must mean God wants me there.' She thought wryly she was getting into Matt's habit of thinking about God's part in things now. Was he turning her holy?

'I wouldn't want to do it,' said Joy, twitching her nose. 'But if you're so sure then perhaps you should go.' She slapped at a fly. 'Do watch out for anything that flies or crawls, mosquitoes, crocodiles – and don't forget Corron oil for sunburn, and your sunhat.'

Lily smiled. 'I won't. Neither will I forget a good strong pair of shoes.'

'That's if Matt doesn't come home tomorrow.'

'I'll give him to the weekend,' said Lily.

'We'll go shopping tomorrow then,' said Joy happily. 'I'll take you to DJs. You should be able to get a decent pair of jungle boots there.' Lily thought she had to be joking!

It was the next day when they were returning from the David Jones departmental store that Lily saw Rob Fraser standing opposite the house. She did not say anything to Joy but made the excuse she had forgotten something and told her to go on ahead.

As soon as Joy was inside Lily went over to him. 'Bit far from home, aren't you, Mr Fraser?' she murmured, wondering when he had last shaved.

'I got to thinking,' he drawled.

'Congratulations! You've realised how wrong you are about Matt at last.'

'Nope. I realised I should have stuck with you. If you think that much of your husband, you'll find him for me.'

A disbelieving laugh escaped her. 'You mean you're going to tail me?'

He grinned. 'You've got it! You're smart for a Pom.'

Her faced stiffened. 'And you're stupid. I'll have the police on you if you start harassing me.'

His eyes hardened. 'You do that and I'll tell them and a certain Sydney journalist I know just why I'm here. Married preacher runs off with sixteen-year-old should make a bonzer headlines.'

Fury surged inside her. 'You snake!' she said explosively.

His expression hardened. 'He's with her. You just don't want to see it.'

Lily controlled her anger and smiled sweetly. 'Matt is in North Queensland. He's up there visiting a friend. I received a letter from him yesterday. Go home, Mr Fraser, and look after your sheep. You won't find your sister in my husband's company.' His jaw dropped and she found great satisfaction in knowing she had taken the wind out of his sails. 'G'day, Mr Fraser,' she said in a mocking voice, and walked across the street, convinced it was the last she would see of him.

A couple of days later he was back. Lily could scarcely believe her eyes. What the hell was he playing at? Why couldn't he go away? She tried to ignore him but could not. So when Joy was resting in the backyard she went out to him. 'Why are you here?'

'Abby's not back and I got to thinking . . .'

'Again?'

'Sure, why not? It keeps the brain ticking over,' he drawled. 'If he's in Queensland, why haven't you joined him? What are you doing here in Sydney? If you love him so much, you'd be up there with him.'

'I plan to join him as soon as I can arrange it.'

'I don't believe he's in Queensland.' His eyes were a hard blue.

'Tough luck!' she said softly, controlling her anger and leaving him.

For the rest of the day Lily could not get Rob Fraser's words out of her mind. Perhaps she shouldn't wait for the weekend but leave for Queensland right away? She would sleep on it.

That night she dreamed of Matt fighting with a crocodile in a mangrove swamp. She woke in a sweat and prayed, please God, let him come tomorrow! But Matt did not come.

The next day Rob Fraser returned, knocking on the front door to Lily's annoyance. The last thing she wanted was him accosting Joy and telling her his lies about Matt. 'Will you go away?' She made to close the door but he wedged it open with his foot and took something out of his shirt pocket and waved it under her nose.

'I've got two tickets here that'll take us to Cairns tomorrow morning, Mrs Gibson. How about it?'

'Are you crazy?' She almost laughed in his face.

'More than crazy, I reckon, but there you are. I want to find my sister. You say you love that husband of yours. What say we go looking for them together? I want to see your face when I'm proved right.'

Lily's hands curled into fists. She would have enjoyed punching him on the nose. 'I'll buy my own ticket, thank you.'

'I did think you'd pay me for this one.' His weathered face was unsmiling.

But he had made Lily's mind up for her. 'I'll get you some money.'

'Good. We could travel up on the same train but we don't have to stay in each other's company.'

'That suits me fine. I can't wait to see you proved wrong, Mr Fraser.' She gave herself no chance for second thoughts but paid for the ticket and hoped she could avoid seeing him the next day.

Joy helped her pack but after looking in her wardrobe, said, 'You'd best buy a waterproof. Matt said when it rains, it really can rain up there.'

So Lily bought a mackintosh, as well as a book by Australian author Arthur Hoey Davis who had lived in Queensland. With another couple of novels she had brought from England, it should do to pass the time on the long journey ahead. She packed Carron oil, face cream, iodine, plasters, writing paper, envelopes, and the silk nightdress she had bought for her honeymoon, as well as several dresses, underwear, and the jungle boots she had purchased. She believed, physically and mentally, she was prepared for all eventualities. Emotionally, she was a little mixed up. Rob Fraser's persistence worried her, and yet she would not believe Matt had betrayed her and was hopeful that time would prove her right.

There was no sign of Rob Fraser as Lily boarded the train and it was her hope he would not appear until they reached Cairns over a thousand miles away. Then she caught a glimpse of him while changing trains at the Queensland border and hurried into a carriage, hoping he had not seen her.

They were well past Brisbane when Lily saw him again. Weary, but unable to sleep because she was too keyed up with not knowing what lay ahead, she was gazing out of the window at the slow brown waters of a river when the corridor door opened and he entered. Without speaking he sat opposite her.

'Do you know Rockhampton is almost directly on the Tropic of Capricorn?' he drawled.

'Is that information supposed to excite me?' she said, gazing at him from beneath drooping eyelids.

'I thought you might be interested – you being from England.'

'Why?'

He shrugged. 'You wouldn't cross the Tropic of Capricorn in England.'

'No.' She was not going to encourage him.

He clasped his hands loosely between his knees and leaned closer. 'Money from the goldfields further inland helped to build Rockhampton and Cairns. Can you picture it, only sixty, seventy years ago, men coping with heat, dust, thirst, plagued by mosquitoes, but driven on by the desire to strike it rich?'

'I'm not without imagination,' she said drily. 'And besides Matt told me about such things. He lived among the miners for a while, although not as far back as that in time, of course.'

His face set in moody lines. 'Hard to believe that of the preacher.'

'You don't really know him, though, do you?' she said softly.

'I reckon I'm a good judge of character.'

'Oh? Then why did you say you liked Matt at first – that he was a mate?'

He frowned. 'That's beside the point. Let's get back to what I was saying. Now my Scottish grandfather was a miner. He married a girl from over the border in New South Wales. It was her father who built the house I was brought up in and his great-grandmother came over with the First Fleet when she was only a child. It was 1787 and they were bringing the first convicts over.'

Lily was interested despite herself. 'You're proud of your ancestors?'

'They fought with the land, the climate, starvation and disease. A lot died, some went mad. It made men out of those that survived.'

'Even the women, I suppose?' she said lightly.

He wasn't amused. 'They couldn't keep up with the men but those that worked alongside them had to be tough! Soft city women like you would have gone under.'

Her temper rose and she closed her eyes to shut him out while she thought of a way to get back. When she spoke her voice was harsh, 'My paternal grandfather was a farmer in Yorkshire. They breed men and women like granite up there to cope with wild moorland and weather to match. Then things got bad moneywise and he moved to Liverpool, which is a huge port built on trade in slaves, tobacco, cotton and sugar. It's a mean place for some and you need a sense of humour and a certain toughness to cope with it. Our family business was dairying. From childhood I milked cows every day. Mam died when I was fourteen and I had to be mother to the younger ones.' She opened her eyes. 'So don't go telling me I'm a soft city woman, Mister Fraser.'

She had silenced him but only for a moment. 'I suppose you married the preacher to escape.'

'I did not!'

'You mightn't believe it but you did.' A smile played round his mouth as he leaned back. 'I reckon his coming from Australia had a lot do to with it. You should have come over as a single women, lady.'

'Don't call me lady! I'm not one.' A frown clouded her features, 'Just lose yourself, I want to read.'

'Sure you do.' His grin widened but he stood up. 'I'll see you in Cairns.'

'Not if I see you first,' she said under her breath, picking up her book and determinedly ignoring him as he went out, but she could not help thinking there were some women who would have gone for his dark good looks.


'I'll carry that.'

Lily shifted her gaze from the swinging baskets of tropical ferns which decorated Cairns station to Rob Fraser's face. Her weariness was overlaid by a mixture of excitement and homesickness. She felt as if she was in a world far removed not only from Liverpool but Sydney as well. The atmosphere was more than just warm, it was humid, and there was a sweet smell in the air mingling with the salty tang of the sea and other odours that were alien to her. A short while ago the train had passed through bright green fields which Rob had told her were of sugar cane. There were houses riding high on stilts, built, he said, to keep termites at bay. In the near distance she could see jungle-clad cliffs and a mountain which was shaped rather like a pyramid. Now she could understand why Joy had recommended jungle boots. It was all so foreign! Suddenly she was relieved to have Rob's company and without a word handed her suitcase to him.

They did not speak as she quickened her pace to keep up with his long stride. The white sandy street reflected the bright tropical sunlight, hurting her eyes. It was flanked by huge fig trees where people walked slowly in the shade. The buildings were of wood, metal-roofed, and some had latticework verandahs with stairways leading down to the ground. She paused to put on sunglasses, the heat sapping her energy. 'Do you know where you're going?'

'I stayed in a hotel along here once with some cousins from Rockhampton,' he drawled. 'They have a cattle station.' He tipped his hat to the back of his head as he halted in front of one of those wooden buildings with verandahs. 'This'll do us. Spend a night here then catch the train in the morning.'

Lily decided not to argue, it would be good to have a break from travelling. She was shown to a room overlooking a garden, bright with flowers and patchy with shade from a tree which had showered petals on the lawn. She dropped her suitcase, stripped off and washed all over. Then she stretched out on the bed which had a cloud of mosquito netting above it and pulled it down. For a moment her mind was filled with thoughts of Matt and she ached for his arms around her. Then she drifted into sleep.

The room was full of shadows when she woke and someone was hammering on the door. 'Hang on, hang on,' she muttered. 'Give me a minute.'

'It's Rob Fraser,' called a voice. 'You sure can sleep, lady. It's tucker in half an hour. I'm going for a beer.'

Damn him! she thought. Who did he think he was, hammering on her door? Even so she called, 'OK! I'll see you downstairs.' She yawned, stretched, and reached for her suitcase. After another wash, she donned one of the floral crépe-de-chîne frocks bought for her trousseau, dragged a comb through tangled brown curls, outlined her mouth with lipstick and went downstairs.

In the dining room the tables were spread with damask cloths and places were set with cutlery and serviettes in glasses. There were already people seated, including Rob Fraser. Even from the doorway she could see he had made an effort. She hesitated a moment then went over to him.

'You've shaved,' she murmured, sitting opposite him.

'Thought I should.'

She could see the admiration in his blue eyes as they inspected her and wished it did not give her pleasure. It

seemed an age since Matt had looked at her in such a
way. Inwardly she cried, where are you now when I need
you?

Rob's foot touched hers under the table. 'It's fish. Coral
cod or king snapper. Do you like fish? And would you
care for a drink?'

'I like fish. I don't like beer but I am thirsty.' She drew
her legs in and thought how a tan became a man. His shirt
was spotlessly white and beneath the fabric she could see
the bulge of muscle in his upper arms. There was a virility
about him which she could not help but admire.

'You could have pineapple juice with a drop of rum
in it?'

'Not too much rum.'

'I'll tell him just a splash.' The warmth of his smile
took her by surprise and she had to remind herself that
he was only here because he wanted to knock Matt's block
off. She looked away and round the room. A middle-aged
woman at the next table smiled tentatively. She returned
the smile before shifting her gaze to a nearby wall where
there were photographs of men with beards, looking
eminently respectable, with gold chains and watches
across waistcoated fronts.

Rob placed a glass in front of her and sat down.

'Thanks.' She sipped the drink cautiously and found it
to her liking. Their meal came and they ate in silence. He
fetched a couple more drinks and she offered to pay but
he shook his head.

'Keep your money in your purse, lady, you might
need it.'

'The name's Lily.' She pushed away the pudding plate with a satisfied sigh and leaned back in the chair. 'That was good but I feel full up now.'

'Perhaps you'd like to stretch your legs? We could go along the Esplanade.'

She hesitated, wondering if it was wise.

He drained his glass and stood up. 'Please yourself.'

She finished her drink and rose to her feet. 'I suppose a walk would be sensible. It'll help me to sleep.' His eyes glinted and immediately she questioned what was going on in his mind but it was too late now to change hers. She wondered what Matt would think of her being in his company and felt a spurt of anger at his doing a vanishing trick. Then she reminded herself that he had wanted them to be together, had even offered to stay behind in Liverpool so that they could do that very thing. It really was partly her fault they had lost touch with each other.

Perhaps to salve her conscience Lily walked a few paces behind Rob and it was not until he stopped and stared out over the moonlit water that she came alongside him. She felt more relaxed. He had not made a wrong move and she hoped it would continue that way. 'I love the smell of the sea,' she murmured, breathing deeply of the salt-laden air.

'Probably reminds you of home if you lived in a port.' His arm brushed hers and she was tempted to move away but thought he might believe he was having an effect on her.

'Maybe.'

'You never mentioned a father when you spoke of your family.'

'He died while Matt and I were on our honeymoon.' She experienced afresh the grief she had felt then and her eyes filled with tears. Despite all her father's faults she had cared for him.

'That must have been rough.' He reached out and touched her hair.

'An understatement,' she retorted, aware of a need to be comforted.

'So what happened?'

'Dad had his head kicked in by a horse. It was a difficult time because we were due to leave for Australia within the week and had to arrange the funeral. At the same time my younger brother fell sick and then my sister. There was nothing for it but for Matt to come on ahead. He didn't want to leave me but I insisted.' She looked out over the sea, remembering the moments before his departure. Could Matt really have believed that she saw him only as a passport to Australia? she thought uneasily. How could he doubt her love for him? Then suddenly she remembered his last letter and how there had been no mention of Daisy's accident. Had he received any of her letters since then? She knew he had been travelling around but even so surely one of them should have caught up with him?

Rob Fraser's arm slipped round her waist and he kissed her neck. 'No!' She pulled away, impatient with herself for letting him believe he could take liberties with her. 'You're forgetting something, Mr Fraser.'

'Not me! For a moment you did, though.' His smile was smug.

'You're wrong! I was remembering,' she said emphatically. Without waiting for him to reply she walked away, telling herself she must keep him at a distance in future.

Rob did not follow her and it was not until the next morning that Lily saw him again. It was early and wisps of mist still clung to tree tops on the slopes of the mountains as the train began its ascent. Neither of them spoke, only nodding in recognition. Lily was glad to see the woman who had been seated at the next table in the hotel and instantly started up a conversation, telling her where she was going and why.

The woman showed interest and said her name was Kate Moffat, and yes, she knew of the bush brothers, having lived up on the Herberton ranges for more years than she cared to remember. She talked about the building that housed the headquarters of the Brothers of St Barnabas, the centre for the travelling High Anglican priests, some of whom had come from Oxbridge universities years ago, spurred on by the first Bishop of North Queensland on a visit to England. 'It's a hard life up here,' she murmured. 'There's a greater need for them to practise self-denial – to live rough and to preach to those who are more interested in bodily survival and the material world than the other.' She went on to tell her more about the area and asked Lily about England, listening with interest before offering an invitation to drop in at her place anytime.

Lily spent some of that long journey writing a letter to her family, telling them of places and people she had met but she made no mention of Rob Fraser or of Matt's being missing.

To her immense disappointment she did not find Matt in Herberton, only the information that a group of brothers had gone west towards the Gulf of Carpentaria, taking with them a couple of visiting missionaries, the names of which the elderly priest could not remember.

'One of them must be Matt,' said Lily positively as she posted her letter in Herberton post office near the cenotaph.

'You hope it's him but you've no proof,' said Rob shortly. 'Admit it, you've come up here on a fool's errand.'

She glanced up at him and her jaw set stubbornly. 'I don't believe I have. In fact I'm so sure he's with them that I intend staying up here until he returns.'

There was a puzzled expression on his handsome face. 'It could be months. Do you really care for him that much?'

'Yes, Mr Fraser, I do.' She smiled. 'There's no sense in your hanging around waiting for him, though, so goodbye.'

He did not move. 'Have you got enough money to stay for months?'

'You don't have to worry about me. I'll manage.'

'I believe you will.' He frowned and rubbed his chin with the brim of his hat. 'There's a few places I think they might be but I'll be back whether I find them or not.'

She felt a familiar irritation at his presumption that Matt was with his sister. 'What about your sheep? Won't they be missing you?' she said sarcastically.

His eyes narrowed. 'I'll be calling in at home, I am needed there, but we all want Abby found. You take that Mrs Moffat up on her offer. She might be able to help you out.'

'I've already thought of that,' she said. 'I can think for myself! Goodbye, Mr Fraser.'

He stared down at her. 'I don't suppose you'll miss me, Lily?'

'I don't suppose I will,' she said blithely, and walked away, pausing to gaze in the Mining Assay Office before entering a cafe to have a welcome cup of tea.

She stayed out of his way for the rest of the day and was still in bed when the train left early the following morning. Despite his saying he would return she hoped it was the last she would see of him. He was much too arrogant for her liking.

When Lily told Kate Moffat she intended staying for a while and would need a job, Kate informed her there were several families on farms around Atherton who would welcome some help in the house. They mightn't be able to pay much but they would feed her and provide a roof over her head.

So a week or so later Lily found herself living with the Newman family, whose wooden-walled home with a verandah was pretty basic. The water closet was outside and there was no plentiful supply of running water, which she missed. Still she was prepared to live anywhere and do anything in order to stay close to the headquarters of the brotherhood.

She contemplated Matt's surprise when he discovered she had been working up here just so she could be near to him. Her job was not difficult, being not so different to that which she had done at home. She looked after the younger children (the older ones were away at school), milked cows, washed, sewed, and was general dogsbody.

She admired the Newman parents who were hard-working, proud, uncomplaining folk, if lacking in humour. She soon realised this could be down to the dividing line between surviving and going under being narrow and ever with them.

As well as the farm Mr Newman had a timber mill, and the rainforest giants were constantly being chopped down to be sold, as well as to clear the rich red earth for more farming.

Mrs Newman, a work-worn wisp of a woman, told Lily how the Aborigines believed the trees had souls and would cry out when axed. Lily found herself sympathising with that belief. Often she felt dwarfed and nervous when walking with the children between the enormous trunks in the forest. It was a completely different but exotic world to the one she had been accustomed to and it was not always pleasant. She received warnings about this plant and that, which flowers and berries were deadly, and once in the garden saw a snake, beautifully patterned, coiled on the grass in the sun after a sudden shower of rain.

Often she was swamped by homesickness. Christmas came and went and the weather was hot and humid. Lily longed for England and the cold feel of sleet on her face. There was still no news of the missionaries returning and she wondered desperately how long she might have to wait and felt that maybe she was mistaken in her conviction that Matt was with them. She knew for definite he was not in Sydney because Joy had written at Christmas, forwarding a couple of letters from the family. Lily devoured every word written but there was never enough of them for her liking. Her family were not at home with pen and paper. Daisy was just about coping but all of them had been relieved when Aunt Dora had invited them to the farm for Christmas dinner.

February brought drenching rain showers and mist and a short note from Rob Fraser, forwarded by Kate Moffat, asking if she was still there and informing her that his sister was still missing, which caused her sudden unease. What if Matt wasn't with the brothers? What if—? She shunted the thoughts to the back of her mind. She was miserable and lonely, far from home and those she loved, and that's why she was doubting him.

A few days later the brothers returned and Matt was not with them. Lily's disappointment overwhelmed her and she just did not know what to do next. Where was he? She could not believe he had run off with that girl. Would not believe it. Perhaps he was dead? Surely he would have written to her if all was well? But then all hadn't been well with him. He had believed she did not love him. She remembered him saying something about his rushing her into marriage. Perhaps they had rushed into it without proper thought to how different their lives had been and the kind of people they were? But they had been happy during the short time they had had together, she told herself fiercely. They had laughed and loved and they had needed and wanted each other madly.

Suddenly she felt sick. Maybe that's what Matt had missed? After years of celibacy suddenly to have sex and then to do without it. She faced the thought squarely but did not want to believe it. He had a strong will and had done without before and could do so again. Perhaps there was a letter from him in Sydney? It was some time since she had heard from Joy. She told the Newmans she was leaving, packed her suitcase and caught the next train to the coast.

# Chapter Ten

It was on alighting at Cairns that Lily saw Rob Fraser. The wind was getting up and it was raining and she was in no mood for any smart remarks from him about Matt.

'Don't say it!' she said, making to walk past him.

'It wasn't him?' He flung his sodden hat into the air.

She wanted to burst into tears but gritted her teeth instead. 'What are you doing here?'

'I said I'd come back. You've saved me a journey. Although I've have had a lousy one so far. There's floods further south and the train was delayed. If this keeps up we'll be stuck here.'

'God forbid. I never thought of rain like this in connection with Australia.' She lowered her head against a sudden squall.

'It's the rainy season.' He grinned. 'You should have done your homework before coming.'

'Oh shut up!' she said sourly.

'Be thankful it's not cold.' He plucked the suitcase from her hand and walked off with it. She made no haste to catch up with him, having a fair idea where he was going. She was deathly tired and needed a rest.

Lily booked in at the same hotel as Rob, seeing no reason to look elsewhere. She refused his invitation to dine but when she came down later he was alone in the dining room and the wind was rattling the windows and bending the trees. It was scary and she did not feel like being alone. Besides, if they were the only two in the place, they would spend the whole time either glancing at each other or trying to avoid doing so. She sat opposite him.

'I thought you'd change your mind.' His face wore that smug expression that irritated her.

'I might change it again if you start making smart remarks.' She sought for something to say and came up with the banal comment: 'I've never known such wind.'

His dark eyebrows rose. 'They have cyclones up here. Drink?'

'You mean this could be the start of a cyclone?' Her voice rose in alarm.

He placed a hand on her shoulder and his mouth against her ear. 'Eat, drink and be merry, for tomorrow we die,' he shouted.

She pushed his hand off her shoulder. 'You're really cheerful.'

He grinned inanely and went in the direction of the bar and she wondered why she put up with his company. She thought of Matt and hoped there would be plenty of rum in the drink. There had been little rest for her since the return of the brothers and she was tired of the thoughts going round and round in her head and could do with a good night's sleep.

The waiter brought some kind of mutton stew. 'What do you think of this wind?' she shouted.

'Known worse,' he said laconically and left her.

Rob came back with their drinks. 'This weather could take the roof off.'

'The waiter said it could be worse,' she murmured, not looking up from her plate.

'He's trying not to worry you.' He raised his glass. 'Here's to tomorrow and that we're still here.'

She gulped down half her drink. 'I'm leaving for Sydney tomorrow.'

'That's if we're still alive, Lil.' His eyes slid down over her face and the outline of her breasts in the close-fitting frock. Lily chose to ignore the look and his comment.

The wind continued to howl like a thousand banshees. She glanced at a window. The rain had stopped for a short while but now it was coming down in sheets. She thought of sailors at sea and felt overwhelmingly sorry for them. She thought of Matt and fumbled for her drink and drained the glass.

'Another, please,' she said loudly, pushing the glass towards Rob. 'And when you come back, you can tell me all about your sister. I want to know exactly what she's like.'

Rob stared at her and opened his mouth but no words came out because at that moment there was a sound like an express train approaching and the whole building shook.

Lily sprang to her feet in alarm. There was almighty bang as several windows shattered. Rob flung her to the floor, rolling her under the table as flying glass, debris and rain were blown across the room. She clung to him in terror, believing her last hour had come and wishing she was with Matt. The wind having found an entry sent pictures and cutlery crashing, whirled cloths from tables and bowled over chairs and tables. Rob hooked his arms round a leg of their table and, realising why, she did likewise with another leg. It seemed the sensible thing to do when at any moment the roof might fall in.

They remained under the table for what seemed like hours. Several times it shifted and they with it, but after a while their particular gust of wind seemed to lose impetus while elsewhere others were wreaking havoc.

Inside the room it went quiet and they released their hold on the table and crawled from beneath it. Still on her knees, Lily gazed round the wrecked dining room. 'Oh God,' she said unsteadily, 'I don't think I can stand up.'

'I thought you were tough,' said Rob, getting to his feet and offering her a hand.

'We don't have cyclones in Liverpool.' She took his hand, only to have him catapult her against him. His arms went round her. 'What are you doing?' she said in a flat voice, knowing now it had been a definite mistake staying in his company.

That grin she was getting to know so well came into play. 'I thought you might still want to hold on to me. You were like a limpet before.'

'I'd have hung on to the waiter and he's fat and forty,' she said drily.

'I don't believe you. I think you like me.'

He tilted her chin and his mouth came down over hers in a manner that was as determined as it was ruthless. She responded without intending to, although in no way was there a sense of drowning in pleasure as with Matt's first kisses. When Rob lifted his head to draw breath, she said, 'That's enough.'

'No, it's not. You kissed me back.' He said it with that confident smugness that was beginning to drive her mad.

'Don't read anything into that,' she said firmly. 'And you're wrong, Mr Fraser, I don't like you.'

He smiled. 'Like too bland a word? Shall we say we find each other attractive?'

Lily thought about that, leaning back against his arm so she could watch his face. Perhaps if she had not had a couple of drinks she might not have been so honest. 'I'm not sure what I feel about you. I feel something but it's a far cry from what I feel for my husband. I happen still to love him.'

Rob frowned. 'How do we know he is your husband? If he's done the dirty on you and run off with my sister, he could have other women in different places.'

Lily was utterly taken aback. 'That's a lousy thing to say!'

'How long have you known him?'

'What's that got to do with anything?'

'So you haven't known him long?'

She felt like hitting him but was stopped by someone clearing their throat and saying, 'You two all right?'

Lily jumped and pushed Rob away. She picked up a fallen chair and then looked at the staff gathered there. 'Do you want a hand clearing up?'

'It mightn't have finished with us yet.' The receptionist's face was glum as, wielding a brush on a table, she sent glass splintering to the floor.

'We could make a start, though,' said Lily, considering she would be glad to do anything to keep her out of the arms of Rob Fraser, whom she could sense was glowering at her.

'OK.' The woman smiled and handed the sweeping brush to her. 'I'll get another – and thanks.'

'I think I'll have a drink,' drawled Rob, and skirting the debris on the floor, left the clearing up to Lily and the others.

When she went to bed, despite the rum she could not sleep because she was wondering what to do about Rob. She had spoken the truth about what she felt about him but his words about Matt had hit their target. Not that she believed for one minute Matt could be a bigamist but maybe she was making a mistake in expecting such high standards from him, just because he was a man of God. She remembered Ben saying how human he was and Matt himself saying he was no saint, but if it was true and he was with this girl – she felt terribly hurt and depressed by the thought – where were they?

The thought continued to taunt her until the wind began to drop about six in the morning and she fell into a doze. When she woke it was to sun climbing in a blue shiny bowl of sky, painted with a few rosy-edged ragged clouds.

The air was warm, clammy and sweet with the scent of rain-sodden petals.

Lily packed her suitcase but left it in the bedroom until she found out when the train going south was leaving. She went out into the debris-strewn street and walked in the direction of the station. Half a roof was missing from a building and several trees had been uprooted. The sea roared loudly and she guessed it would take a little longer for the waves to calm down.

Rob was already at the station. 'The train'll be an hour or so late. There's an obstruction on the line.'

'As long as it's leaving,' she said quietly.

He scrutinised her face as he walked alongside her back up the street. 'Have you any idea now where to look for the preacher?'

She forced a smile. 'Do you think I'd tell you if I did?'

'If you want to prove to me he's your husband, I reckon you would.'

'Why should I want to prove anything to you?' she said, exasperated. 'You don't think I believe he's like some sailor with so-called wives in every port?' He was silent. 'You can't,' she said with a laugh. 'It's stupid! I know him. He's an honest man.'

'They why didn't he tell us he was married?'

'Did you ask him whether he was?'

'No, but—'

'There you are then!'

A scowl crossed his face. 'My sister was hooked on him. He must have seen that. I reckon she had it so bad he'd be able to make her do anything.'

Lily felt a cold sensation in the pit of her stomach. His conviction was hard to cope with. 'I've had enough of this,' she said tersely. 'I think it's best if we say goodbye right now and don't have anything more to do with each other.'

Rob's mouth set stubbornly. 'I'm not saying goodbye until one of them turns up. You should feel the same.'

She held on to her temper. 'Matt could be in Sydney now! Your sister could be at home. I suggest we go our separate ways to see if that's so. We write and let the other know if it is or isn't. Will that suit you?'

He shook his head. 'We go to my place first and if we draw a blank there we go to Sydney.'

Lily felt a moment's helplessness. 'Rob, can't you understand, I don't want your company!'

A slow smile lit his face. 'That's the first time you've called me by my first name.'

'So?' She laughed. 'I thought Australians were famous for being matey and you've called me Lil several times.'

'That's got nothing to do with it, I reckon. I think you're softening towards me and that's why you're scared of being with me.'

She shook her head, confounded by his determination. But she could be just as determined. 'I'm not going to your place. I'm tired of the pioneer spirit. It's the city for me.'

'We have an electric generator.'

'No!' she said firmly, and walked away, praying he would stay out of her life.

It appeared Lily's prayer was answered because there was no sign of Rob after she boarded the train. She had bought Marcus Clarke's *For the Term of His Natural Life* in an attempt to understand the Australian mentality, but found it difficult to become completely caught up in the book, though it did leave her wondering if Matt had broken down after all, and whether he had perished of thirst or starvation in the grey hostile bush as so many escaped convicts had in the early days. She did not want to believe it but it was another thought to go round and round in her tired brain.

When she left the train in Sydney, she found Rob waiting for her at the barrier. Her nerves, already fraught due to uncertainty and worry, caused her to snap at him: 'Can't you take no for an answer?'

'I got to thinking.'

'You'll be putting a strain on your brain.'

His smile faded. 'That's not funny.'

'It wasn't meant to be. I'm just not pleased to see you.'

'That's because you're scared of the truth about you and me and that so-called husband of yours.'

'You're fooling yourself!' Lily pushed past him and ran. She'd had enough.

Sydney looked wonderful. The sun shone on sandstone buildings, turning them golden, while water from sprinklers glistened on the hairy stems of giant tree ferns. The temperature was what Lily, having been in the north, would now call pleasant and if she could find Matt at the house with a reasonable explanation for his absence she would be deliriously happy. She just wanted to see him. Lugging her suitcase, she caught a ferry across the harbour.

Joy opened the door but did not look overwhelmingly pleased to see her. 'I didn't expect you! I've got some friends here,' she said hurriedly.

A sigh escaped Lily. 'I take it there's no news of Matt?'

'None. I presume you haven't heard anything either?' she said in rapid tones.

'Would I be asking if I had?' Lily's voice was sarcastic. She did not feel like being nice to anyone now.

There was a long silence while she waited for Joy to move out of the way so she could step inside, but the other woman just stood there, not looking at her.

'The thing is,' said Joy, 'it's not unknown for men to take off into the bush if there's something they want to get away from. It's easy to disappear here.'

Lily could hardly believe what she had said. 'Are you suggesting Matt wanted to get away from me?'

'I wasn't saying that exactly!' Joy flushed. 'I mean, I don't know what I meant,' she said unhappily. 'I just don't know what to say. I can't understand what's happened to Matt.'

'Do you think he's dead?' said Lily bluntly.

'Dead?' Joy's eyes met hers briefly. 'I suppose it's possible. What do you think?'

'I don't know what to think. I was convinced he was up in Queensland but I was wrong.'

'What are you going to do?'

A harsh laugh escaped Lily. 'Right now I'd like to get into my husband's part of the house, Joy. I've been travelling for days and I'm desperate for a cup of tea. So if you could let me pass, I'd appreciate it.'

'Of course!' She turned pink. 'I wasn't thinking! Come in and meet the girls. I'll make the tea.' She led the way into the backyard where a couple of heavily pregnant women were sitting in the shade, sewing tiny garments. 'Patsy, Nita, this is Lily. She's from England.

They chimed hello in unison then resumed their conversation, which appeared to be about swollen ankles, heartburn, a strange ache under the bump and the peculiar movements of their expected offspring.

Lily sat on a patch of grass in the sun, feeling excluded, but after a minute or so she stopped listening to a conversation which she found boring and thought of Matt. What else could she do to find him? Should she get in touch with the police? After what Joy had said about people disappearing it seemed pointless. Did she really believe Matt wanted to get away from Lily? The thought made her feel wretched.

A cup of tea was placed on the grass in front of her. 'You aren't hungry, are you?' asked Joy.

Lily was but the way the question was asked caused her to answer in the negative. She could not understand Joy's changed attitude to her. Maybe it was because of the baby? Or possibly she found Lily's presence an embarrassment in the circumstances? It had not slipped her notice that Joy had not introduced her as Matt's wife to the other women. She looked at them, immersed in their gossip, and was irritated. This was her husband's house and garden and she might as well not have been there. She drained her cup and rose to her feet.

Joy looked across at her. 'Where are you going?'

'A walk.'

Joy looked relieved. 'A walk'll do you good. I'll do us some supper later.'

'I can do it myself, thanks. I don't want to cause you any bother.' She nodded to the other women and left them to their baby talk.

As Lily walked along the harbourside she gave serious thought to the possibility of Matt's having gone walkabout to get away from her but came to the conclusion it did not make sense. He had wanted her with him. She found herself going over and over the same ground she had covered that night in Cairns. Could he have gone off with Rob's sister? If he had, then he was a hypocrite and not the man she had believed him but what her Aunt Dora might have called 'A right swine!' Can a person be two different people? Can they change that much? She closed her eyes and relived moments she and Matt had spent together, remembering him saying, 'You're wonderful, Lily, don't ever let life sour you.' Had life suddenly turned sour on him when she had not turned up? She gazed over the harbour and remembered the last time she had seen his aunt. There had been no doubt in Jane's mind that her nephew was as special as her brother Davy had been. Matt had been so good with her, kind and generous. Something stirred in the recesses of her mind.

'Lily!'

Her thoughts had been so fixed on Matt that for a moment she was convinced it was his voice she heard but when she turned it was Rob Fraser. A sigh escaped her. 'How did you find me? I hoped I'd seen the last of you.'

He grinned. 'Honest to God?' It was an expression the children had used in Liverpool and suddenly she was overwhelmed by that painful longing to be with her family. Tears filled her eyes.

'What is it, mate? Are you feeling crook?' His expression was sympathetic for once.

'I want to go home,' she whispered.

'You mean England?'

'Yes! I want my family.' There was a catch in her voice. 'I've still got money my uncle gave me, it'll get me home.'

He shook his head. 'You can't do that, mate. You're not a quitter. We'll find them and then I'll sort him out. You'll be better rid of him.'

Something snapped inside her. 'You still believe you're bloody right, don't you? Matt wouldn't! He couldn't!'

Rob's expression hardened. 'If you believe that, what are you getting so worked up about? But let's try proving you're right and carry on looking for him. We could try where my brothers looked in the first place.'

Lily pulled herself together. 'And where's that?'

'Broken Hill.'

She stared at him. 'Isn't that a silver-mining town?'

'Sure is! Stuck flat bang in the middle of nowhere. It's rugged, hard country and it'll take us days getting there.'

'Hot and dry, I suppose?'

'You've got it.'

Lily frowned. The thought of being stuck on a train, travelling through flat, featureless scenery that seemed to go on for ever and ever, in the heat depressed her, but the name Broken Hill had struck a chord. 'Are you thinking of going straight away?'

'You aiming on coming with me?'

She did not hesitate. 'No. I'll make my own way.'

He pursed his mouth and shook his dark head. 'You're better having company. A woman alone is fair game.'

'I already know that,' she said with a touch of acid.

A grin widened his mouth. 'I'd be a perfect gentleman.'

She looked disbelieving. 'I need time to think about it and I could also do with a few nights' sleep in a proper bed.'

'I don't want to hang around the city too long,' he said, hands in pockets. 'Makes me feel hemmed in.

'You don't have to. As I said, I can go it alone.' She walked away.

It was not until Lily arrived back at the house that she remembered Joy's unwelcoming attitude, but the other woman was all smiles when she opened the door and had supper ready. When Lily mentioned she was thinking of going to Broken Hill, having remembered Matt speaking of the place in a letter, Joy could not have been more helpful. When Lily mentioned not fancying a long journey by train again, she said in the nicest possible way, 'You don't have to go all that way by train. By far the easiest way would be by coastal steamer to Adelaide and up by train from there. It might take you longer but it would be a nice break. You're looking tired and you could stay there a few days. Pete and Matt have this elderly lady they keep in touch with who now lives in Adelaide. She was the school matron or some such thing. She'd probably be happy to put you up for a couple of nights. I'll give you her address.'

Lily had the feeling she was being got rid off but she was glad to go. This way it would be easier going it alone and she would tell Rob so if he was still in Sydney.

He was. She discovered him standing across the street from the house the next morning, and when told of her plan, he said, 'Never been on a seagoing ship before, only on a paddle steamer up the Darling.'

'You're not coming with me,' she said firmly.

'Be an experience.' He smiled.

Lily hoped he didn't have shipboard romance on his mind. They left a week or so later on a cargo boat. Rob was having to work his passage, much to Lily's relief. She guessed he would be hard to handle if he had too much time on his hands. As it was she saw nothing of him for days because she was terribly seasick. The much smaller cargo boat rode the waves very differently from a large liner and it wasn't until they had entered the Bass Strait that Lily begin to feel her normal self again.

The ship carried two other passengers, a retired British couple who had lived on a tea plantation in Ceylon and loved to travel. They were standing at the rail with Lily and Rob, telling them they had been informed they might see whales as the ship forged along the south coast of Australia.

'My brother once went aboard a whaling factory ship in Liverpool,' said Lily, grimacing. 'He said it smelt awful.'

'Killing the southern right whale has been outlawed now,' said the husband, nodding ponderously. 'The female used to come into the bays to calve and too many of them have been killed off.'

'Easy pickings,' said Rob, and, before anyone could say another word, seized Lily's hand and dragged her away. 'Let's walk along the decks I scrubbed this morning.'

'That was rude,' she hissed. 'They're nice people. Interesting.'

'They're bores.' He frowned. 'And I don't aim on being stuck with them every evening when I can spend time alone with you.'

She smiled. 'You're getting bored? Isn't being a sailor to your taste? You shouldn't have come.'

He pulled her close. 'I wouldn't be bored if you weren't so standoffish.'

Lily was aware of the strength in the arms around her. 'I need a strong man!' said a voice in her head. She remembered saying that to Matt, who seemd to believe there were different kinds of strength. She attempted to push Rob away. 'You're forgetting why we're here – and you never did tell me much about this sister of yours. What's her name? I've forgotten it.'

'Liar! It's Abby and she's now seventeen. Her birthday was a month ago. She's tall, brown-haired, and I suppose you could say nice-looking.' He pulled Lily back against him so that her nose was pressed into the hollow of his collarbone and her breasts were squashed against his chest.

'You're holding me too tight,' she said, struggling.

'Can't be tight enough for me but you can wriggle as much as you like, I enjoy it.' He grinned down at her.

She controlled her impatience. 'Rob, you're hurting me. Let me go!'

'Say please.'

'Please let me go.'

He released her, only to slip an arm round her shoulders. 'You wanted to know about Abby.'

'Yes.' She breathed a sigh of relief. 'I suppose she was spoilt, the only girl after five boys?'

'Naw! Ma wanted a girl but that's because she wanted help in the house.'

'Figures,' murmured Lily.

He smiled. 'You said you could cook. Come and stay with us if we don't find them. Best time of year outback, not blistering hot and I can show you all over our place. We could camp out, be all alone.'

Lily laughed. He really was quite blatant. 'You mean be a domestic slave like your sister was? No thanks! And besides, I don't think camping out would be very sensible – like your putting your arm round me isn't.'

'Look at that sunset, Lily, and don't talk to me about what's sensible.' He drew her against him and this time he kissed her with that same determination he had shown in Cairns. She stiffened, just as determined not to respond. When he did eventually release her she left him without a word and went to her cabin. It had been a mistake travelling with him and from now on she was going to stay out of his way.

It proved difficult, because whenever their paths crossed he told her she was fighting a losing battle and forced her into his arms. Why not give in and admit the attraction between them? Matt had done the dirty on her, shouldn't she do the same? She told him to go to hell which did not amuse him.

Lily determined when she left the ship and Adelaide it would definitely not be in his company. It should be easy enough. She had not told him about Miss Morell so reckoned he would look for her in the hotels and guesthouses and, drawing a blank, hopefully go on his way without her.

Adelaide felt English in a way that Sydney did not. It was smaller and lacked the hustle-bustle feel of a big city. The streets were neatly laid out and the buildings had a gracious air to them, being built solidly of stone. Miss Morell lived in North Adelaide. On asking a passer-by the way, Lily was directed to go through the park and told she couldn't miss it.

Miss Morell turned out to be a tall, well-padded woman of sixty with a definitely maternal air about her. So much so that Lily told her Matt was missing and it was months since she had heard from him. Had she any idea where he could be? Miss Morell was to prove more informative than Lily had reckoned on.

'Matt was here a while ago. Told me he had an English wife.'

Lily leaned forward eagerly, placing her teacup on an occasional table. 'I take it he was alone?'

'Certainly he was alone . . . said he was missing you.'

'Did he say where he was going next?'

'Broken Hill. Always had a soft spot for miners did Matt. Then he was going to sheep country. He was hoping you'd join him there.' She stared pensively at Lily. 'We also talked about New Guinea?'

'New Guinea?' Lily was confounded as well as confused. 'Isn't that an island up off the north-west coast of Queensland?'

'That's right. One of the brothers is doing missionary work in Papua. We were discussing it.'

Lily was silent, wondering if that information meant anything.

Miss Morell eyed her keenly. 'Letters do go missing and take so damn' well long getting places,' she murmured. 'What are you going to do?'

'I was going to go to Broken Hill but if he was on his way there when he called here, it's unlikely he'd still be there.' She frowned. 'You've known Matt longer than I have. What do you think could have happened to him?' Even to this woman who knew Matt well, she could not mention Abby.

Miss Morell filled their teacups. 'If something was bothering him he would want to be alone to think and pray. Marriage, I believe, makes new demands on people.'

'You mean he really could have gone walkabout?' she said stiffly.

Miss Morell smiled. 'He could have. But why don't you try the missionary society he was with when he went to India? He has married friends there he might have spoken to.'

Lily nodded but was remembering only too well the dash up to Queensland where Matt had supposedly gone to see a friend and talk. She just did not want to explain to someone else she was seeking the husband she had travelled across half the world to join and who seemingly had deserted her. She had some pride. Pain, razor sharp, cut into her. How could Matt do this to her? She thanked Miss Morell for her help and left.

It was not until Lily was walking through the park that she remembered she had planned on asking Miss Morell if she could stay but going back was the last thing she wanted to do now. There seemed little point. She would find somewhere else.

She had only been registered at the small hotel not far from King William Street a short while when Rob found her. 'You could have waited for me,' he murmured as he sat across the table from her.

'I was trying to get rid of you,' she said, moodily stirring her soup.

He did not appear to have heard her. 'You look crook. What's happened?'

'Matt's been here and probably went to Broken Hill months ago. I don't believe he was ever with your sister. I think he's gone off somewhere alone.'

Rob pursed his mouth. 'I don't believe that!'

'I knew you wouldn't.' She glanced at him from beneath her eyelashes and broke a bread roll in half. 'I think you've got to accept you've made a mistake. Your sister probably left to see a bit more of life than that found on a sheep station.'

'She had a good life at home!' His tone was sullen. 'Never wanted for anything. She and Ma only had to ask for a new stove, new dishes, new frock, anything, and it was theirs whatever the cost of having it delivered. She'd have had to find herself a paid job in the city and from what I've heard they ain't that easy to come by.'

'I'll have to get one myself.'

His blue eyes fixed on her drooping mouth. 'I've offered you one. No need to go looking elsewhere.'

She shook her head. 'I'm a city girl. Besides I suspect the job you're offering me might get me into trouble,' she said drily.

He grinned. 'I must admit me and you in the sack together is something I can't get out of my mind.'

She felt inestimably weary. 'Forget it, Mr Fraser, and drink your soup.'

His expression changed and he stretched a hand across the table to cover hers. 'Forget him, Lily. I've really got a fancy for you.'

'Fancy! Thanks for the offer but I have to refuse. I'm going to stay here a few days, then go back to Sydney by train.' Her voice was expressionless.

'So no Broken Hill together?' His grip on her fingers tightened so much it hurt.

'No. And you're hurting me.'

He slackened his hold. 'You're going home to England then?'

She hesitated, and experienced a strong conviction that Matt would eventually get in touch with her and when he did she wanted to be around. 'I'll give it a bit longer.'

'Then I won't give up.'

'You're wasting your time.'

Rob smiled, dropped her hand and commenced to dunk bread into his soup.

He left the next day, saying he would see her in Sydney before the month was out. She told him not to bother.


Joy was really put out when Lily turned up again so soon. 'I thought you'd be away ages. What happened?'

Lily decided that it was really none of her business. 'I changed my mind. All this going from one place to another is tiring me out. I'm staying put for a while. That way Matt's got a better chance of finding me.'

Joy said slowly, 'You mean stay in this house?'

'Definitely stay in this house,' said Lily firmly, stretching out her legs and holding her face up to the sun. 'It does belong to Matt and I am his wife. When he turns up it might be that we'll settle here. He talked about being a parish priest when we were in Liverpool. He'd have to do a curacy somewhere first but perhaps he could eventually get a parish in Sydney and we could live here.'

Joy cleared her throat. 'What if he doesn't turn up? How long will you stay?'

Lily opened her eyes and stared at her. 'As long as it takes. I'll find myself a job and I'll try not to get in your way. I think this house is big enough for both of us.'

Joy flushed. 'You do what you want – but when the baby comes you might find it inconvenient.'

Lily smiled. 'I shouldn't think so. I'm quite good with babies. You might actually be glad to have me around.' On that note she left the house and went for a walk in the Royal Botanic Gardens where she wrote a letter to her family, making out everything was wonderful.

Lily managed to land a job as a waitress in one of the harbourside cafes. It did not pay much but not having rent to pay, her wages with tips were enough for her to live on and she still had a good bit of Uncle William's money tucked away. She was unhappy but tried not to let it show.

Her first wedding anniversary came round and she thought there just might have been something from Matt, but there wasn't.

Joy gave birth to a son after a long drawn-out labour. Pete came home and had a fraught conversation with Lily about the Japanese getting above themselves and believing they could conquer the southern hemisphere. He told her not to say a word to Joy about it.

The days passed slowly and still there was no sign of Matt. Ben wrote telling her Herr Hitler had rung alarm bells by invading Czechoslovakia. The Prime Minister had met with him and gained an agreement to what was said to be peace in our time!!! The exclamation marks gave her cause for thought and she put the peace of Europe back on her prayer list.

Joy's baby cried a lot and she was slow to recover after the birth. Lily felt it was ages since she had passed an undisturbed night. Still there was no news from Matt and she despaired. Christmas approached and the temperature soared. She longed for her family. Australia, despite its beauty and sunshine, had stopped being her Shangri-La. Feeling lost and lonely, she was starting to believe there was really no place like home but had not quite given up hope of Matt returning.

It was in such a mood that Rob Fraser found Lily when he arrived in the city four days into the new year of nineteen thirty-nine. After being on her feet all day she was too tired to argue when he suggested they go for a drive, look at the ocean and have a picnic. He was surprisingly silent and they reached the almost deserted Bondi Beath without either of them having said a word. He spread a rug on the sand and told her to make herself comfortable. She sat watching the surf roll in, half mesmerised by it, as he unpacked a picnic basket. She continued to gaze at the ocean as she ate cold mutton sandwiches and drank a glass of Aussie white wine.

It was Rob who broke the silence. 'I went to Broken Hill.'

There was something in his voice that roused a submerged fear. 'And?'

'They'd been there.'

She put down the half-eaten sandwich in the sand. 'You're making it up!'

Instantly he was angry. 'They stayed in Argent Street at the same hotel, for God's sake! When are you going to accept he's a louse?'

She felt sick to the stomach but still she refused to accept what he said. 'When he tells me to my face he ran off with your sister, that's when!' she yelled.

'And what if that's never? Are you still going to stay true to him?' He seized her upper arms and forced her flat on her back. 'Lily, I want you! Forget about him and come home with me.'

'Be your fancy woman, you mean? No thanks!' She averted her face. 'I made vows which I intend to keep. You still haven't found them together.'

'Lily, don't be like that.' He sounded quite desperate. 'He's an adulterous, betraying dingo. Think of it, Lily. He's betrayed you and you're staying faithful like a fool.' He pressed kisses on her face and neck.

She felt as if an iron hand gripped her heart. 'Is that supposed to make me feel better about what you're suggesting?'

He made no reply, his hands moving over her body. He kissed her unresponsive mouth and undid the top four buttons of the prim white blouse. She felt numb, as if none of it was really happening. Matt with that girl! Matt with that girl! The words repeated themselves over and over in her head like some dreadful manta. Rob eased the blouse off her shoulders but it was not until he dropped on to her and bit the peak of an exposed nipple that she came alive. 'Get off me, Rob,' she snapped. 'What the hell do you think you're doing? I didn't ask for any of this.'

'It's what you need, though,' he mumbled.

'You're wrong!' She struggled to bring up her knees to force him off but he was too heavy. 'Rob, will you get off!' One of his hands slid up her bare leg and slapped her thigh. The surf crashed on the beach a few feet from them. 'Our shoes'll get wet if we don't move!' she said desperately. 'Rob, will you behave yourself, please!'

He shifted and gazed down into her face. 'How can
you care about getting wet at a moment like this?'

'What moment?' she demanded. 'The moment when
you force me into doing something against my will? It's
not you I'm married to! If I was maybe I'd think this was
real romantic, but as it is, it's wrong. So will you move
your carcase before I start screaming?'

'You wouldn't,' he muttered.

'Wouldn't I?' She opened her mouth wide.

Swiftly he placed a hand over it. 'All right! But I don't
know why you should be so moral when that louse of a
husband of yours has deserted you for my sister.'

She pushed away his hand. 'Because that's the way I
am!' There was a catch in her voice. 'And maybe you
wouldn't fancy me so much if I was easy.'

'Maybe I wouldn't.' His hand stroked her bare
shoulder. 'OK! One kiss as if *he* didn't exist and then
I'll move.'

She stared up at him and sighed. He really did have
film star looks so why couldn't she feel more for him?
Her arms went up about his neck and brought his head
down. She kissed him with Matt in her thoughts. A kiss
which seem to go on for ever though it was not as good
as some kisses can be. She dropped her arms and pushed
him away. 'Take me home, Rob, and maybe if you behave
I'll see you tomorrow evening.'

'Take a day off. I've got to go back in the afternoon.'

She shook her head and could see he was annoyed.

All the way home they were both silent. She was trying
to think sensibly with a clamp on her emotions. What was

the truth about Matt and his sister staying in the same hotel in Broken Hill? If it was true, she thought suddenly, it could not have been long after Matt had seen Miss Morell and told her he was married and missing Lily. What if Rob was lying about them being booked in the same hotel to gain his own way?

He drew up outside the house. 'So I won't see you tomorrow?' he said stiffly, his hands gripping the steering wheel.

'Sorry, Rob.' She wondered if it was any use asking if he was telling the truth but decided it was not. He was a stubborn man. 'Have a safe journey.' She kissed his cheek.

He stared at her, that mulish expression back on his face. 'I haven't given up. I'll be back.'

She smiled and shut the car door, convinced he would falsify information for his own ends, as they said on the movies. Without looking back she went into the house, having decided if Matt was not with Abby, then she would do what Miss Morell had suggested and write a letter to the Anglican Melanesian Mission.

As she waited for an answer Lily was tormented by bad dreams. Perhaps Matt was dead, had been so all this time.

Three weeks later she received an answer from the Melanesian Mission: Matt had volunteered for missionary work in Papua months ago. He was working in a remote village from which they received little news. As far as they knew he was safe and well.

Lily could only believe Matt had changed his mind about marrying her and had gone back to following his

God. Maybe he had sinned with Abby and this was the
only way he could cope with his guilt? The information
put a seal on what she had almost decided. With her
dreams in shreds, she bought a ticket on a liner which
would take her home to Liverpool.

# Chapter Eleven

Lily glanced up the street of redbrick houses and then at the wording THORPE'S DIARY on the shop window, and considered how familiar, yet strange, it looked. Her homecoming had a peculiar feel to it. She had expected grey clouds and khaki-coloured waves but the surface of the Mersey had reflected the blue sky under a warming late March sun as vessels of all shapes and sizes went about their business, just as their forerunners had for hundreds of years. She had felt a strong sense of history going along Dale Street. The towering blackened Victorian buildings, guardians of commerce, had given her the same feeling as slipping on a comfortable well-worn shoe after wearing new high heels. This was home.

As the tram rattled its way up William Brown Street, past the reference library and museum on one side and St John's Gardens where daffodils bloomed on the other, she had experienced that inexplicable surge in her blood which she had never felt in Australia but which was somehow connected with the feel in the air of an English spring.

Until she stepped on to the landing stage she had been uncertain whether her actions had been right. As the ship surged into the northern hemisphere, she had been very conscious of turning her back on a dream New World and in so doing making it impossible to have a claim on such a dream in the future. God only knew if she and Matt would ever see each other again, and she was no longer exactly on speaking terms with God at the moment.

'Is it really you, Lily?'

She placed her suitcase on the sandstoned front step of the dairy and turned to see Mrs Draper, a half smile on her wrinkled face.

'Don't say it,' said Lily in a pleading voice, wondering if instead of Aunt Dora and Mrs Draper to give her advice, things would have been different if her mother had been there to turn to.

'Don't say what, my dear? It's lovely to see you.' She held out a hand and gripped her fingers. 'They've missed you! We've all missed you. Always a smile for people, not like—' She stopped abruptly, pursing her lips. 'No, I won't say it. You'll find out for yourself. Maybe when you've got a minute you can call in for a cup of tea and tell me all about your adventures and what your dear husband is up to? Could you do that, my dear?'

'I'll do my best,' said Lily, warmed by her words despite the sinking feeling in the pit of her stomach.

'I'll see you later then.' The old lady trotted off down the street.

Lily took a deep breath and pushed wide the shop door but no bell jangled and there was nobody behind the counter. She looked up and saw a piece of rag tied round the bell's clapper. A puzzled frown creased her tanned face and getting a stool from a corner she climbed up and tugged the rag free. Then she opened and closed the door several times, setting the bell jangling.

'Who's messing with my bell?' called Daisy irritably from the lobby. 'I'll have your life if it's one of you kids!'

'What'll you do to me, miss?' said Lily, mimicking a child's voice as her sister came through the door.

'Lil!' Daisy dropped the slipper she was carrying and put her hands to her face, her eyes filling with tears.

'I know it's a shock,' said Lily unsteadily. 'But there's no need to cry.'

'I can't believe it!' She dropped her hands and clutched the front of Lily's coat. 'Ben never said!'

'Ben didn't know.' She hugged her sister tightly. 'I hope you're pleased to see me and won't ask too many questions all at once?'

'Oh I won't ask anything.' Daisy stared at her. 'You don't know what it's been like. I haven't known what to do. I hate being at home. But I've done my best to do things the way you'd have done them.'

'Your heart's not in it.' Lily scrutinised her features, realising her sister had never become again the girl she had been before the accident. There was a discontented droop to her mouth and her hair was pulled back in a loose knot in the nape of her neck. She wore a flowered overall but no make-up. Fortunately the scar left by the burn had turned white and was barely noticeable.

'My heart's not in anything.' Daisy sighed. 'There's talk of there being another war. Our Ben was saying Britain and France have pledged to support Poland if Hitler

invades.' She spoke in a quick breathy voice. 'I don't
know what I'll do if we were to have air raids as they did
in Barcelona – but the Corpy are making all kinds of
preparations and going on about carrying gas masks and
I can't help thinking about what Dad told us about gas
attacks in the trenches.'

'It probably won't happen,' said Lily.

'You think not?' She nodded and Daisy appeared
reassured because she smiled. The smile altered her whole
face, making her appear more youthful. 'Anyway, what
about you?' she asked, obviously forgetting what she had
said about not asking questions. 'What are you doing here
from down under? You made it sound marvellous in your
letters.'

Lily picked up her suitcase and pushed Daisy in the
direction of the kitchen. She had done a lot of thinking
on the voyage home but only now did she made the decision what to tell her sister. 'Make us a cuppa and I'll tell
you all about it.'

The tea was duly made, accompanied by a shop-bought
scone spread thickly with farm butter. Lily did not speak
until the first cup of tea was drunk. 'Matt's in New Guinea
spreading the gospel to the headhunting natives. It's a
largish island up from the Queensland coast.'

Daisy's eyes widened. 'And you let him go?'

Lily brushed crumbs from her lap, and avoided looking
at her sister. 'You know Matt. If he believes that's where
God wants him, then nothing's going to put him off, not
even having a wife.' She tried to keep the bitterness out
of her voice but did not quite succeed.

Her sister shuddered. 'Isn't he brave!'

'Hmmph,' murmured Lily. 'But who wants a dead hero?'

'At least he had the sense not to order you to go with him.'

'Oh, yeah, he had that much sense,' murmured Lily, filling her cup again and wondering if she would have gone if the choice had arisen. It would have been a real test of love, she thought wryly, living like Jane and Tarzan in the jungle with the natives.

'Was it his idea that you came home to see us? Nice of him if it was.'

'He left that decision to me. He knew I still had some money left over from Uncle William's little nest egg.' She lied without flinching. 'How are Uncle William and Aunt Dora, by the way?'

'She's much the same as usual but he's not supposed to do as much . . . had some kind of funny turn. Ben says he's not very good at being told.'

'Tell me a man that is,' said Lily, leaning back in the chair and stretching her legs towards the fire.

'Ted's the same,' said Daisy bluntly. 'I never thought he'd be so persistent.' She glanced at the clock on the mantelpiece. 'Any minute now he'll come in the shop, suggesting we go for a walk. He lost his job a few months ago.'

'Poor Ted.'

Daisy nodded. 'It's hit him hard. I feel sorry for him.'

Lily smiled. 'Then you doll yourself up and go for your walk while I mind the fort.' She would be glad to have a few minutes to herself before Ben and the children came in.

Her sister hesitated. 'How long will you be staying, Lil?'

'I'll be here for a while,' she said evasively, leaning forward and poking the fire. 'If you can get a job, you go back to work.'

'Thanks!' Her sister hugged her and ran upstairs.

After Daisy left with Ted, Lily wandered round the house, looking in the bedrooms. It seemed Ben was still using her father's old room. He had put up a shelf for his collection of second-hand books and a faint scent of tobacco hung in the air; the once familiar smell of rum had seemingly gone for ever. She went into what had always been called the girls' room. Daisy had left her apron on the floor and there was face powder on the dressing table. Lily looked at the double bed and could not fancy sleeping three in it again. She decided she would buy a single. For a moment she remembered how comforting, as well as exciting, it had been sleeping with Matt, and felt a familiar ache. The medicine for that kind of pain was work, she told herself, and went downstairs.

She found her old pinafore, still on its hook, and walked down the yard to the shippon. She sniffed the familiar smell of straw, metal and manure. There was a reassuring sense of belonging as she moved among the cows, recognising several old friends and talking to them softly. Then she heard footsteps coming down the yard and hurried to the door to fling it open.

Ben stared at her before a slow smile eased his face and she realised he was not surprised to see her. 'How?' she demanded.

'How what?' he said.

'How did you know?' It was almost as if the last seventeen months had never happened.

'It was the way you wrote. I knew something was up. What went wrong?'

'I don't know if it was me that went wrong,' she said slowly. 'I'll tell you while we do the milking.'

Lily told him everything and afterwards he was silent for a long time. 'Well?' she demanded at last. 'What do you believe is the truth?'

Dark blue eyes met dark blue. 'You say you never received a letter from Matt after that first one we sent you?' said Ben.

Lily caught on quickly and her heart begun to beat with thick heavy strokes. 'You mean there was a second?'

He nodded. 'It was months after. I was surprised when it came but thought maybe it was something to do with the post. It's a long way between here and Australia. Anyway I sent it to you in Sydney.'

'When did it come?' Her voice was breathless. 'Can you remember the time of year if not the month?'

'Summer!' he said without hesitation. 'It was when it didn't get dark till after ten.'

Lily pressed a hand against her lips. Their first wedding anniversary. It had to be then. But what had Matt written, and why send the letter to Liverpool, and why had she not received it when Ben sent it to her? How different everything would have been if she had received that letter. It might have said much that would have helped her understand his actions and she could not help wondering if there had been others that had gone missing.

'I don't believe Matt ran off with any sixteen-year-old,' murmured Ben.

She looked across at him. 'So I've only God to contend with then,' she said with a slight laugh.

'Matt never pretended his work wasn't important to him,' said Ben slowly. 'But it sounds to me as if he doesn't know you went to join him. Perhaps he believed you'd had second thoughts about marrying him.'

'I didn't. Ever.'

He raised his eyebrows. 'Even when this Rob bloke came on the scene?'

'I was flattered. He's so different to Matt . . . full of himself.' She stood, not sure how she felt now, and carried the pail of milk into the cool room.

Ben followed her. 'Are you going to write to Matt and tell him you've been and gone and come back from Australia, then?'

Lily hesitated, then shook her head. 'What would be the point? He's in a village miles from anywhere. Perhaps that's the way he wants it?' She attempted a smile. 'I've made a right mess of things, haven't I?'

He shrugged. 'Things happened that you couldn't have foreseen. If you'd gone with him straight away . . .' They were both silent. Then he smiled. 'Anyway, I'm thankful for small mercies. You're here now and I'm glad of it. Our Daisy's been a right misery guts. She's not cut out to stay at home. Now she can find herself a job.'

Lily agreed. She'd had enough at the moment of slaving for someone else for a pittance. At least here in the dairy and the house she was mistress of all she surveyed and could pick her own hours.

At that moment the door bust open and May entered the cool room. Her cheeks were flushed and her hair hung down her back in a thick plait. 'It's true!' she cried. 'I didn't believe it when Mrs Draper said you were home. Now we might have something decent to eat. You wouldn't believe the meals our Daisy dishes up!'

'They couldn't have been that bad because you've grown,' said Lily with a smile in her voice.

'I know,' said May, thrusting out her burgeoning breasts. 'Jean McGuire's only got a couple of pimples and she's dead jealous. Can I have a bra? Our Daisy said no, all the lads'll come after me, that I've got to carry on wearing me liberty bodice and keep it flat. You don't think that, do you, Lil?'

Before Lily could open her mouth, Ben grunted, 'Heaven help the lads in a year or so with you around,' and left the room.

'What's wrong with old narky? I thought he'd be glad to see you back,' said May, hoisting herself up on to a table and swinging her legs. 'Have you come home for a holiday? I'd have thought you wouldn't ever come back here.'

'Then you're wrong, aren't you?' said Lily, seizing her arm and dragging her off the table. 'Hygiene, May.'

May stuck out her tongue and then hugged her. 'I know it's too late now but do a lamb hotpot tomorrow.' Her voice was muffled against Lily's shoulder. 'I always loved your hotpot.'

'I'm glad I was good for something.'

May pulled away, her eyes bright. 'I'm going to run and meet our Ronnie so I can be the first to tell him you're here!' She raced out of the room.

Lily thought how she would have liked to run to meet her younger brother but felt certain a fourteen-year-lad would not like it. So instead she peeled potatoes and put them on to boil. There was liver in the meat safe so she fried it with onions, made gravy and opened a tin of peas. Ben came downstairs with his hair damp. 'That smells good. You could sole shoes with our Daisy's liver.'

'Poor Daisy,' said Lily in a mock severe voice. 'You're an ungrateful lot.'

'That's what Ted kept saying. He wants to marry her despite her treating him terrible.'

'Well, that's no good if he hasn't got a job.'

'That's what she told him the other day. I heard them arguing.'

Lily wondered if Frank still had any part in her sister's life but kept quiet.

She had just switched the potatoes off when she heard voices in the yard, then something crashed against the wall. She hurried over to the door and opened it. 'Hello, love,' she said.

Ronnie straightened up, bicycle clips in hand, head held on one side. His face had changed, was longer, angular, and the sleeves of his blazer and shirt exposed bony wrists. 'It is you!' His voice broke, deepened mannishly. 'I wasn't sure if our May was having me on.'

'No, it's really me.' She smiled, touched him, was reassured as to his well-being. 'Tea'll be ready in a minute.'

Over tea they talked and talked, until Ronnie remembered he had Scouts that evening, changed and dashed out. May also vanished, saying she was just nipping up to Jean McGuire's house. They were going to have to go at doing each other's hair differently.

Lily looked across at Ben, feeling like a spare part with the rest of the family out on this her first evening home. 'What about you? Haven't you got somewhere to go?'

'Later,' he said, a slight pucker between his dark brows. He lit a cigarette. His smoking was something new but she kept quiet. 'Lil, you do realise there could be a war?'

She paused in mid-stitch. 'Daisy said something about Poland but surely the Germans have got more sense than to push their luck?'

'Hitler thinks we won't fight because nobody's stopped him so far – but we're going to have to if he invades Poland.'

'Why are you telling me this now?' she said lightly.

'You know I'm in the Territorials – so it's likely I'll be among the first lot to be called up. In fact, I might volunteer.'

She was stunned for a moment, and when she did speak, her voice was a harsh whisper. 'After all what Dad said about the Great War I never did understand why you joined the Territorials.'

'Didn't you?' He drew on his cigarette and a veil of smoke drifted in the air between them. 'It was because of what happened to Dad. I didn't want to end up in the army knowing nothing. I wanted to make sure I knew more about staying in one piece than Dad did. I remember Mam telling us how thousands volunteered in the last war, thinking it was something noble and that they'd easily thrash the life out of Jerry. I don't think like that . . . but I'd enjoy having a go at the Nazis because I can't stand the way they think they're so perfect.' His eyes met hers. 'And as well as that, a German shell destroyed the man Dad could have been as surely as that horse killed him when it kicked his head in.'

Lily nodded. 'OK, I understand. It's just that—'

'I know. It's just that you're a woman and you want me safe.' He raised his shoulders, then let them drop. 'Forget about it for now. I was just warning you if you were planning on staying that it's not going to be a picnic.' He picked up a book, opened it, slammed it shut and stared at her, his eyes concerned. 'It won't be like the last war, Lil. Liverpool will be a prime target for the bombers. Lloyd George realised that back in '37. Hitler will try and destroy our ships and the docks. We're an island race.'

Tentacles of fear gripped her stomach. 'Are you trying to frighten me into going back to Australia?' She forced a laugh. 'I've burnt my boats, Ben! I've some money left from what Uncle William gave me but that's for a rainy day. Besides is Australia that safe? Pete, Joy's husband, said something about the Japs. I'd just as soon take my chances over here. This is my country.'

Unexpectedly he smiled. 'You still feel like that? You made Australia sound pretty special to the kids.'

'Even the Garden of Eden must have had its drawbacks or Eve wouldn't have listened to the serpent,' she said lightly, switching on the wireless. 'How about a cuppa before you go out?'

'I won't bother, thanks.' He squeezed her shoulder and left the room.

A thoughtful Lily had just finished scalding the milking pails when Daisy came in. She stood in the doorway, watching Lily dry her hands before bursting out, 'I wouldn't have said yes if you hadn't come home but seeing how you have I did and I think it's only right because he'll be leaving soon and I won't see him for ages and he wants me now.'

'What are you talking about?'

Lily stared at her sister's flushed face. Her eyes glistened and she gripped her handbag tightly. 'I'm going to marry Ted! It'll have to be a register office do. We haven't time for banns.'

With her mind still filled with all that Ben had said, Lily thought, not another blinkin' would-be hero! 'What's he gone and done?'

Daisy took a deep breath. 'Joined the navy. It's better than being on the dole. We'll just have a little party here and a night in Southport before he goes. I've saved a bit of money that'll help pay for it.'

Lily felt an almost hysterical laugh building up inside her. 'When?'

'Next week.' A shadow crossed her heart-shaped face. 'The only snag is getting a job if I'm married. I've got to save for when we get a place of our own.'

Lily almost said, you'll get one if there's going to be a war, but thought it wiser to keep quiet. 'You'll find something,' she murmured.

Daisy gave her a radiant smile before leaving the room and running upstairs.

It was not until Lily went to bed that she saw her wedding dress hanging from the picture rail. It caused her heart to turn over. 'You're going to wear my dress?' Her voice came out as a husky whisper.

Daisy turned from the mirror, her face covered with Pond's Cold Cream. She looked anxious. 'You did say I could, Lil. I know it's not going to be in church but I want to put on a good show.'

Lily smiled but considered had she known then how much it would hurt seeing it again, she would have buried it six foot under on the farm. She climbed into bed and closed her eyes on the dress but she could not shut out the memories.

The next evening her aunt and uncle called, Ben having informed them of Lily's return home. Dora parked herself on the most comfortable chair nearest the fire. 'Well, it's nice to see you, Lily, but why that husband of yours has to go headhunting when he has a wife to take care of, I don't know! I always thought he had no sense.'

'Perhaps he's really got a line to the Almighty and he knew we needed her here right now?' said William, beaming at Lily and squeezing her hand.

'That's as maybe,' retorted Dora. 'But what about Daisy? I suppose she's got herself in trouble and that's the reason for the rush?'

'You've got too much of a suspicious mind, Aunt Dora,' said Lily, controlling her temper and telling them about Ted joining the navy.

'I suppose she won't be the first if war comes,' said Dora, her cheeks wobbling slightly. 'You'd better get stocking the cupboards, Lily. There's bound to be short-ages. And I'll give you some chicks to rear and make sure you have a cockerel.'

'It hasn't happened yet,' growled William, his face a bright purplish-red. 'Don't be worrying the girl.'

'No, it mightn't happen,' said Lily cheerfully, not wanting her uncle to start worrying about Ben. She changed the subject quickly. 'You are coming to the wedding then?'

They nodded and asked her about Australia. She began to talk about Queensland. William's high colour subsided and she breathed easier.

As befitted her special day Daisy was having a lie-in with breakfast in bed on the morning of the wedding while Lily attended to the customers. It was barely eight o'clock when Frank Jones entered, an arm behind his back. It was the first time Lily had seen him since her return and she thought that despite his hair being thinner he looked better than when she had left. She smiled in a friendly fashion, wondering why he had come in today of all days. How did he feel about Daisy getting married? 'Hello, Frank. Long time no see.' She smiled warmly.

He flushed. 'It's good to see you, Lily.' He brought his hand from behind his back and flourished a bunch of pink tulips. 'These are to say welcome home. Mam got some from the market today. I don't know if they have them in Australia.'

Lily was touched by the gesture. 'They're lovely! That's really kind of you, Frank.' She placed the flowers on a stool. 'How are things with you? How's your mam?'

He rested his elbows on the counter and leaned towards her.

'I've joined the civil defence! Mam's not pleased because she thinks the Jerry planes won't be able to get over the Pennines, that it's just an excuse for me to get out of the house, but it isn't, Lily,' he said earnestly. 'If war comes civilians will be on the battle front as well as the soldiers. I'm training as an air raid warden. I want to do my bit here in Liverpool.'

'That's very worthy of you, Frank,' she said, thinking that in the Great War men of his age staying at home would probably have been given a white feather.

'I'm glad you think so.' He added hesitantly, 'I know I had hopes myself once but I don't begrudge Daisy her happiness. Tell her that and give her my best wishes.'

Her heart softened. 'That's real nice of you, Frank.' She covered his hand with hers. 'You're a nice man altogether.'

He reddened as he stared down at her hand. 'I'd better go. Mam'll be wondering where I am.'

'You don't want any milk?' She removed her hand.

'I'll come back later,' he said gruffly, turning to go. He stopped abruptly and gazed at her. 'They're saying Matt's been got at by headhunters. Is it true?'

Lily's heart flipped over painfully. 'No, Frank.' Her voice was firm. 'They're being got at by him. See you later.'

She felt sympathy as he went and for some inexplicable reason into her head came the words 'Always the bridesmaid never the blushing bride'. Because if Frank ever did get married he would blush and might not know what to do with his bits and pieces!

Thinking like that reminded her of her wedding night but she pulled herself up short. It was going to be an emotional day as it was, so she'd be better not go making herself miserable this early in the morning.

The rest of the day was certainly one of mixed feelings; seeing Daisy with her newly permed hair, wearing her wedding dress, caused Lily to wish she could turn the clock back but it was too late now, she told herself. Life had to be taken as it came.

As the year progressed Lily discovered it was impossible to pretend that there might not be war. Naval reservists were called up as well as other men of twenty and twenty-one for the forces. Ben broke the news that he was leaving.

'But war hasn't even been declared!' she cried, gripping the back of a chair. 'Can't they wait? Why the rush? It might never happen!'

'Of course it's going to happen and you know it,' he said, wandering round the room, picking up things and putting them down again. 'We've discussed it. Hitler has no sense of honour and you can't believe anything he has to say. He said he'd keep out of Spain and he didn't.'

Lily sank on to a chair, feeling as if a dark pit had opened beneath her. 'It's horrible!'

Ben looked uncomfortable. 'Yeah, but keep your chin up, Lil. It won't make me feel any better if I know you lot are all worrying about me. Pray for me and think the best.'

She nodded and asked if he had told Uncle William.

'I thought it best. He took the news better than I imagined. I think he was half expecting it, but Aunt Dora exploded and told me I should have said I worked on the farm and was indispensable.'

Lily wanted to say, I agree with her for once, but she didn't. 'I suppose Ronnie can help me with the milking, and during the school holidays he can help with your job.'

'That's what I said to Uncle William and I could see he was pleased with the idea. Ronnie's been helping me since Dad died, as you know, and he'll be fifteen at the end of the month. He could leave school now, really.'

'No!' said Lily, hitting the arm of the chair with the palm of her hand. 'He won that scholarship so he's staying on.'

'OK.' He juggled the change in his pocket. 'That's settled then. You can tell Ronnie after I've gone. I don't want any fuss.'

So Ben went off to prepare for war with no flags flying and no farewell party and Lily wondered what her father would have thought of his sons.

Ronnie was perfectly amenable to the idea of continuing to help with the milking, although he had not done the early one since Lily had come home and had trouble getting up, not always hearing her call. At first he was inclined to fall asleep, his head resting against the flank of a cow, but eventually his body clock got the hang of early rising again and they worked well as a team.

Lily gave herself no time to brood, filling her hours with work. Her chicks grew and her cockerel started to cause a disturbance in the neighbourhood. She joined the WVS and knitted blankets and socks and learnt first aid. She bought blackout material and despite her dislike of sewing, with Daisy's, and May's, help made curtains for all the windows.

They were just in time, for on the day the Orangemen marched it was announced in the *Liverpool Echo* that there was to be a blackout in the north-west as far as Chester and Northwich. It was to take place from midnight for four hours the following night to test the ARP machine. Wartime conditions would be simulated by having mock gas attacks and explosions, fires and rescues from collapsed buildings. The RAF would fly overhead to check the blackout, although Speke had been given permission to leave their lights on as the production of war planes was deemed more important than a blackout practice.

Lily allowed Ronnie and May to stay up to see what it would be like. It was a dark night with heavy cloud

and rain but they managed to catch a glimpse of the
odd plane's navigation light and heard a couple of explosions. It seemed unreal to Lily, as unreal as her dreams
of Matt and war-painted natives, of cooking pots and
Australian Aborigines, of sun and storm, mosquitoes
and Rob Fraser.

Bombs falling in Liverpool! It couldn't possibly
happen . . . but Frank assured her that it could.

Some in Liverpool thought the war had started when
a couple of pillar boxes were blown out at the corner of
Green Lane but it was not the Germans but the IRA, and
the man apprehended said he hadn't believed the bombs
would go off.

'And if you believe that, you'd believe anything,' said
Aunt Dora with a sniff.

Shortly afterwards the German High Command
declared there would be war over Germany's claim to
Danzig if the Führer said so; they had the best workers,
weapons and soldiers in the world now. It was sabre-
rattling at its worse and infuriated Lily for it was common
knowledge that thousands of German Jews and non-Aryans
had left Germany that year in fear of their lives.

To get away from the news she took May to Lewis's
where there were millions of flowers displayed as part of
the Liverpool Flower Show. It was a haven of fragrance
that soothed them, but they could not forget the possibility
of war for long. Remembering what Dora had said about
shortages to come, Lily bought May several frocks for
the autumn, a new suit for Ronnie, and some flannelette
sheets for 2/6 a pair.

Then everything seemed to gather momentum. British ships on the Yangtse River were bombed, allegedly by the Japanese. Germany made a non-intervention pact with Russia and Hitler was jubilant. Britain reaffirmed its agreement with Poland to fight if its interests were violated and British cities prepared to evacuate mothers and children.

May and Ronnie were determined not to go.

'You need me to help with the milking,' said Ronnie earnestly. 'And besides, I'm going to volunteer my services. I've been talking to Mr Jones and he says they'll need lads like me with a bike and knowledge of the city when the air raids happen.'

'I'll have him!' said Lily, infuriated. 'I don't want him filling your head with thoughts of heroics. You're going! You'll enjoy Wales. It's a lovely country.'

'I hate the country,' said May moodily, swinging her gas mask. 'Nothing happens there.'

'There won't be any bombs, that's the main thing,' said Lily.

Ronnie's head turned in her direction. 'Our May can go and stay at Uncle William's farm. It's in the country.'

'Only just,' said Lily.

'It's enough,' said May, her face brightening. 'Although there'll be Aunt Dora to put up with.'

A slight smile eased Lily's taut expression. 'I think it's more of a case of whether she'll put up with you.'

'I'll get round Uncle William,' said May positively. 'He likes me.'

Lily's eyes narrowed. Her sister was growing up too fast for her liking. Still, better for her to be closer to home under Dora's eye. 'All right. You can both go to the farm if they agree.'

'No!' said Ronnie, his jaw set determinedly as he stared at Lily. 'I'm not a kid. I'm fifteen. I don't have to go back to the grammar now there's going to be a war. I can stay here and look after you and Daisy and do Ben's job full-time.'

Lily's heart sank. 'Now, Ron . . .' she began.

He turned his head, presenting her with his deaf side. 'I'm not listening.'

May grinned. 'Let him stay. I'll get round Uncle William the better if he's not watching.'

'You'd better be on your best behaviour, my girl, that's all,' said Lily, agreeing reluctantly that Ronnie could stay.

Less than a month later Lily was regretting her decision and had spilled her first tears of the war. After Hitler's solemn assurance he wouldn't wage war on women and children, a refugee train in Poland had been bombed and the liner *Athenia* had been torpedoed in the Atlantic.

She had no doubt he would bomb British cities if he got the chance and wondered if Matt in his Papuan hideaway had any idea that Britain and its Empire were at war.

# Chapter Twelve

Lily went over to the half-open window and pulled aside the curtain but she could not see or hear any planes despite having heard the blood-freezing sound of the siren earlier. Ronnie was talking to Frank in the dark street below when suddenly the all-clear sounded.

A few minutes later her brother appeared in the bedroom and his expression was vaguely disappointed. 'Mr Jones said bombers were heard but they've gone away,' he murmured, scuffing the rug with the toe of his shoe.

'That's all right then!' Lily smiled her relief and climbed back into bed.

'He says they'll be back.'

'He would,' she said drily, considering how Frank had changed since he had been made air raid warden for their area. Some considered he had grown too big for his boots and few took his warnings seriously. It was nine months since war had been declared and no bombs had fallen so far on Liverpool, but that did not mean the port was not suffering. After the worse month for shipping casualties in the Atlantic families were reeling from the loss of so many of their menfolk. Sadly for Daisy, Ted had been killed in the first months of that year when his ship had been torpedoed. After weeks of weeping, a tight-lipped but vengeful widow had joined the WRNS and was somewhere in Scotland. Less than a month ago Ben had been evacuated from Dunkirk and was now at a camp in Wales.

Ronnie thrust his hands inside his pockets and now his voice contained a note of excitement. 'Mr Jones reckons this is the start of the beginning! We're going to be up against it like Winston Churchill said in his speech. We're really going to have to fight them on the streets.'

'But we're never going to surrender! I know,' said Lily, yawning. 'Go back to bed, Ron, before you wake May.' Her sister had returned to the city like so many others, lulled into a sense of false security when Hitler had not come straight after Britain but had been busy gobbling up most of Europe.

Ronnie gave up and did as he was told.

Several weeks later bombs were dropped on Birkenhead across the Mersey but by then everyone knew the battle for air supremacy was being fought in the south of England with London suffering all-night raids. After that for several nights running Merseyside received the attention of the Luftwaffe and part of the docks and the overhead railway were damaged.

Lily insisted on May's moving out to the farm again and she went without complaining, much to Lily's relief. She herself had no intention of leaving with having the dairy to run. Besides, she had volunteered as a driver for the WVS, having persuaded William to teach her earlier that year.

Ben came home on leave but was unwilling to talk about what had happened in France. There was a hardness in his eyes and a tension about his mouth which had not been there before, and Lily was reminded of her father. But Ben was more concerned for them than himself. 'You'll be sensible, won't you, Lil?' he said earnestly. 'I know what happened over Matt has hit you hard, but if danger threatens, head for the farm and stay there.'

'Yes, Ben,' she said meekly, having no intention of staying under Dora's roof.

At the end of August the bombs came closer to home when Mill Road hospital was hit and incendiaries were dropped in Everton. Two nights running, Lily was out with the WVS mobile canteen serving tea and soup to the firemen and those whose homes were burning. Some of them took their loss philosophically. 'Ah, well,' grunted one middle-aged woman, sitting on a chair she had managed to salvage and hugging a crocheted black shawl round her, 'it'll save me nagging at my fella to rewallpaper the bedroom. Although the plaster was crumbling to bits with the damp and he was always saying it was a waste of time! This is the warmest that house has been in ages!'

'Aye, it's a nice blaze, Maggie,' said one of her neighbours, puffing on a cigarette. 'Pity we haven't got any 'taters to cook on it or even ol' Hitler to be Guy Fawkes. You and Willie can sleep in our parlour if our house doesn't catch as well!' She held out her cup to Lily. 'Fill that up again, chuck, nectar it is. And while I can still have me cuppa, no blinkin' air raid is gonna get me down!'

Lily admired their attitude, and did as she was told.

A couple of evenings later when she was not on duty, the siren wailed its awful summons again. She had dozed off in front of the fire but woke with a start. She switched off the wireless and looked across at Ronnie, who was reading the newspaper. 'Time to go,' she said, picking up her knitting.

He dropped the paper and was halfway through the doorway when he turned and said, 'You'll be all right making your own way, won't you?'

She knew he could not wait to be off on his bike to the command post, so smiled and hugged her jacket round her. 'Of course I will.'

Lily walked slowly up the street through the darkness. Somewhere up near the other end she could hear Frank banging on a door. The next moment someone collided into her and she would have fallen if they had not clutched her shoulder.

'Sorry! It's so darned dark and I'm not used to the blackout. I didn't see you there.' Lily froze as the voice took her back to a different time and place. She cleared her throat but no words came out. He spoke again with concern, 'Are you all right? Did I frighten you?'

This time she managed a whisper. 'I never expected to hear your voice again, Matt.'

'Lily!' His hand slid over her shoulder and up her neck to caress her cheek, her nose, her mouth, and she was aware that his skin was rough where once it had been smooth. 'It's really you! Lord, who'd believe we would meet like this?' he said hoarsely.

Her heart was racing but she sought to make her voice sound cool, calm and collected though it came out as a croak. 'Who indeed?'

He fumbled for her hand and gripped it tightly. 'Lily, we've got to talk.'

'Not before time!' she exclaimed, trying to recapture the anger she had felt towards him during his absence. 'Perhaps you can explain why the hell you had to go off to New Guinea for the past two years? Not telling me beggars belief!'

'I wasn't there two years,' he said swiftly. 'If I had been, I would have been here sooner!'

'That doesn't make sense.' Her voiced sounded suddenly raw.

'It would if you'd let me explain.'

'Can you explain the letters you didn't write?' She had control of her voice now if not her hand.

'I wrote some all right,' he said grimly.

'But I never got them. I never knew where you were for over a year. That was cruel, Matt. Torture! I imagined all kinds of things happening to you.'

'I didn't hear from you for months either,' he retorted, his voice rising. 'Not after Ronnie's ear when I wrote two letters on the same day. Isn't that cruel?'

'You don't have to shout at me! I did write. You just never got my letters.'

They stared intently at each other through the darkness, each trying to make out the other's expression, though they could not. Then they heard as if for the first time the drone of bombers and the firing of ack-ack guns. They looked up and saw tracer patterns and parachute flares lighting the sky. There came the noise of explosions in the near distance. Without a word Lily pulled on Matt's hand and they raced down the street.

In the dim light of a couple of torches they saw anxious eyes turning in their direction as they dived into the air raid shelter and pulled the door shut behind them. One of the faces belonged to Mrs Draper, who was sitting on a lower bunk bed, turning a heel on a khaki sock. 'Evening, dear. Not the best kind of night for an evening stroll.'

'I could do without Hitler's hailstones,' gasped Lily, looking for a place to sit. There was a bunk bed free by the entrance.

Matt had already spotted it. He sat, pulling Lily down with him. They gazed at each other and she felt that once familiar fluttering under her ribs. She could hardly believe she could still feel the same about him after all that had happened, but she did and took in his appearance greedily. His face was browner than when last she had seen it, his cheeks leaner and his jaw more angular, but the bump on his nose was the same and his grey gaze still had the power to communicate with her in a way nobody else's could.

Mrs Draper spoke again. 'Are my eyes deceiving me or is that your dear husband I see, Lily?'

'Yes,' she said starkly. 'He's just arrived home.'

'Not an auspicious moment, Mr Gibson, but you're very welcome,' said the old lady.

'Thank you,' said Matt in a vague voice, still staring at Lily. 'I would have been here sooner but the ship on which I left India was torpedoed.'

India! thought Lily, astonished, but was silent, not wanting the neighbours to realise she had not known where he had been.

A tiny voice piped up: 'You're an Australian, though, aren't yer, mister? Me aunt lives in Brisbane. Perhaps yer knows her?'

'Shut up, Tommy, Australia's a big place,' said his mother.

Before Matt could speak again the all-clear sounded and with sighs of relief they all trailed out of the shelter.

'I didn't find out until a few months ago you'd been to Australia,' murmured Matt against Lily's ear as they crossed the road.

'How come?' she said with a touch of breathlessness. 'But then maybe that's not so surprising. If you'd stayed in one place long enough, you would have done.' She was suddenly angry again. 'When I think of the way I went looking for you, I could scream. And you've been in India of all places!' She almost choked on the words.

'Lily, I can explain.' There was a hint of desperation in his voice.

'I'm sure you can,' she hissed. 'God called you there! That's always your reason for doing anything, going anywhere.'

'You knew that,' he said. 'What I didn't realise was how loving and being married to you would tear me apart, cause me to have to make choices between Him and you! I never had to do that before, Lil. I had to think long and hard.' He was prevented from saying more because the siren sounded again and Mrs Draper, who was a few feet

in front of them, turned and shooed them in the direction
of the shelter. Automatically they obeyed.

'In and out like a blue-arsed fly,' muttered one woman,
seating herself before taking a small bottle from her pocket
and unscrewing the top. She took a swig from it and
offered it around. They all politely refused, although Lily
felt that she would have liked a drink.

'Tell us about Australia then,' said the woman, pock-
eting her bottle.

Matt looked at Lily. She stared back, raising her
eyebrows. 'Go on, tell them,' she said with a touch of
acid. 'You're the expert.'

'I'd prefer listening to your impressions,' he countered,
smiling.

She hesitated, realising how so many of her impressions
were tied up with Rob Fraser. Now hardly seemed the
time to bring up her reason for being in his company. 'I
don't want to talk about it,' she said in a low voice. 'It
hurts remembering. Besides, you know the country and
its people better, so you talk. It's what you do best. Sweet-
talk people.'

He winced and she realised she had used Rob's words
about him. How could she do that? She did not really
believe it. Her eyes went to his face and the word 'Sorry'
was on her lips, but he started to speak about the goldfields
and of Henry Lawson, a poet.

'He was more than just a poet, though,' Matt said,
warming to his theme. 'He was a campaigner for the
rights of the working classes. He was born in a tent in
the goldfields of New South Wales. His family was

poverty-stricken and he grew up despising those who exploited the poor.'

'Too right,' muttered several people. 'Give us some of his words then. Anything to stop us thinking of them bombs falling.'

Lily realised she had forgotten the air raid, having fallen under the spell of Matt's voice once again. She looked at him and their gazes locked. She felt heat rising in her body but could not look away.

Matt cleared his throat. 'This is taken from "Shearers" and catches the real feel of the outback.' He recited softly but with feeling:

'"No church-bell rings them from the Track,
No pulpit lights their blindness,
'Tis hardship, drought, and homelessness
that teach those Bushmen kindness;
The mateship born, in barren lands,
Of toil and thirst and danger.
The camp-fare for the wanderer set,
The first place to the stranger."'

He fell silent. Then said, 'That's what you could say Christianity's all about – mateship, giving the first place to the stranger, or to others, as Jesus said.'

Lily stared at the faces of those listening and was aware that Matt had really woven his magic again. Silver-tongued! 'Did he sweet-talk you?' Rob's words came into her head once again and she felt suddenly guilty. Her stomach churned.

Little Tommy piped up. 'What about "Waltzing Matilda" – do you know that?'

Matt rumpled his hair and said, 'What Australian doesn't? It's almost our national anthem.' He began to sing and they all joined in.

Mrs Draper, her small eyes bright, said, 'What about a hymn, Mr Gibson?'

Matt exchanged a wry smile with Lily and began to sing the Twenty-Third Psalm which was taken up by all of them. Then it was a rousing 'Jerusalem' and 'Onward Christian Soldiers'.

The all-clear sounded and they came out of the shelter, easing their backs and looking round. There was a blaze in the upper storey of a house near to the main road but it looked like Frank was on the scene, as were several firefighters. There was a chorus of goodnights and Lily and Matt walked back up the street, Mrs Draper trotting at his side, asking about Papua.

After the old lady left them Lily found herself wanting to ask questions but not knowing how to begin. Matt was silent as well, and she decided he was waiting until they were really alone. They went into the house and found Ronnie, asleep in a chair, smuts on his face, legs stretched out towards the cold cinders in the fireplace.

'Where's he been?' asked Matt, his face softening. 'Is he OK?'

Lily told him Ronnie was acting as messenger boy. She glanced at the clock which showed four-twenty. 'I'll fetch him a blanket. There's no point in waking him. We'll be doing the milking in an hour or so. You'll have tea?' she said politely.

'Lily!' Matt reached out for her but she backed away, knowing that once he touched her she would be unable to think sensibly, and she wanted to get a few things straight first.

'I have to get that blanket,' she said.

A small smile lifted his mouth. 'Still putting them first, Lily?'

She was unsure whether it was an accusation. 'What's that supposed to mean?'

He shrugged. 'Fetch the blanket. I'll put the kettle on.'

She hesitated before blurting out, 'I need a few moments to think!' Her hands gripped the back of the sofa. 'Your arrival is unexpected, Matt. I waited a long time. Joy must have told you.'

'Eventually!' He turned from the stove and threw the matches on the table. His eyes glinting, he said, 'We had a disagreement. It appears she kept back some of our letters. She'd grown used to thinking of my house as hers.'

Lily experienced a rush of emotion. 'I don't think I'm that surprised! She definitely acted as if I had no right to be there.'

They stared at each other, and Ronnie stirred. Matt seized hold of Lily's arm and drew her out into the lobby. 'It was the missionary society who told me you'd written but I found that out later rather than sooner. Communications aren't that good in New Guinea but I heard rumours about the war so I left for India where I had a couple of friends in the British Army who told me exactly what the situation was in Europe. I believed you to be still in Liverpool and I knew I had to get back to you. I told the Society I was leaving and it was then I discovered you'd come looking for me. Convinced you were in Sydney, I caught the first ship I could but it was torpedoed, as I said.' His hand had tightened on her arm but before she could comment, he continued, 'Fortunately we were picked up by our own side. When I eventually reached Sydney you'd well gone. You can guess the rest.'

Lily felt much better hearing all this but still had a question. 'But why did you go to New Guinea in the first place? Why didn't you stay in Queensland as you said in your last letter?' She saw a muscle in his jaw clench and carried on in a whisper: 'I know you were pretty fed up because I still hadn't joined you, but . . .'

'I was more than fed up!' he interrupted. 'I kept wondering if I'd made a mistake, given in to my carnal desires as the Bible says. I started thinking you didn't love me enough after all – that you were realising you'd made a mistake in marrying me. That I was a means to an end which now you did not want after all. I needed to get away – to be alone – to think and to pray. So like St Peter with his fishing, I went back to what I already knew. Being alone was the way I'd always dealt with problems in the past, but it didn't work this time because they weren't just my problems but ours and I should have considered beforehand the changes being married would make. Instead I rushed you into marriage because I wanted you. It was the wrong thing to do as time proved.'

'You were never just a means to an end,' said Lily tautly. 'And I don't believe our marrying was wrong, but we should have talked more as you said. I had guessed some of what you've said. Miss Morell told me you probably needed to be alone – that marriage must have been a big step for you.'

'She was right as usual. She's known me a long time – was like a mother to me. I was utterly selfish.'

'We can all be selfish,' said Lily quietly. 'But let's get back to what you did. You went to New Guinea where the natives have been known to eat people. It doesn't make sense!'

'I suppose it wouldn't make sense to most people but I needed isolation.' His eyes twinkled unexpectedly. 'You didn't think I'd really been eaten, did you? It's not quite like that any more in New Guinea. Most of the natives prefer roast pig.'

'I didn't know that!' She flushed. 'But truthfully I didn't think of you being eaten, only that you'd left me without a word, having realised your mistake in marrying me.'

He stared at her intently. 'And that mattered?'

'Of course it mattered! Why else would I have gone out to Australia? Why else would I have spent months going here, there and everywhere trying to find you?' There was anger in her voice as she remembered all the worry and pain of those months, and Rob Fraser. She wondered if now was the time to mention him but Matt had come back at her with more words.

'You wouldn't have had to do all that if you'd have done as I asked and gone out with me!' He drew a deep breath. 'Everything would have been all right! Neither of us would have been hurt! But if we both still care there's a chance to mend things. We are husband and wife for better, for worse. Do you still care?'

'Haven't you been listening to what I've said?' she whispered.

Matt did not hesitate but drew her into his arms and his mouth found hers unerringly. She stopped thinking and surrendered to the pleasure of the moment. With their mouths still locked, somehow they managed to climb the stairs. It was almost as if they were afraid to let go in case they lost each other again.

Inside the girls' bedroom they tumbled on to the bed and continued to kiss and hold each other. She knew she wanted him, could feel desire rising inside her, was aware he wanted her. Suddenly they could not hold off any longer. She watched as he undressed, her fingers trembling as she struggled with her suspender button, but she managed and when he turned to her, naked, she was ready. Her breasts brushed against his bare chest and his mouth sought hers blindly. She could not get it out of her mind that after being torpedoed, he had crossed the world to find her despite the continuing danger of U-boats. Her bare toes rubbed the inside of his calf as her fingers wandered slowly down his chest, stroking the hairs on it, attempting to twist them round her little finger, reassuring herself of the reality of his presence. He removed her hand and buried his head against her breasts. 'I've lived this moment over and over,' he said in a muffled voice, holding her tightly.

'Me too,' she whispered, her insides melting as his hand slid lower and she remembered what ecstasy making love with him could be. She wanted to cement their relationship quickly, to be joined to him. With part of her mind she was still afraid that something might go wrong to prevent them sharing that oneness they had known before he had left for Australia. For a flashing instant Rob and Abby surfaced in the front of her mind again but she dismissed them. It was God who had been her rival and Joy had played her part in keeping them from each other. Rob had lied to her. There was no need to mention Abby and spoil things.

She explored Matt's loins, enjoying knowing it gave him pleasure, but he removed her hand and rolled her on to her back, planting kisses all over her face. Then he ventured downwards, his mouth and fingers rediscovering her body in a way it had not forgotten, and then he took her and she surrendered everything to him.

The hammering on the bedroom door fortunately came after they had collapsed in a tangle of sweaty limbs. Yet they drew apart as if caught in some illicit act.

'Lil! Did you put the kettle on?' yelled Ronnie's exasperated voice. 'I heard it whistling just before it's bottom boiled out but I thought I must have put it on and forgotten. It's time to rise and shine. Are you getting up?'

She struggled to sit up but Matt's arm across her body held her down and his laughing eyes gazed into hers. 'I'll be with you in a minute,' she called to Ronnie.

'OK. But don't hang around. I'll do you some toast.'

'Thanks.'

Matt's head drew closer and their lips met in a long, leisurely kiss. 'Forgo the toast,' he murmured. 'Forget the cows. We've got three years to make up, Lil.'

She smiled and smoothed back a lock of tawny hair that had fallen into his eyes. 'How many nights is that?'

'More than a thousand.' He nuzzled her ear. 'We'd have to be at it day and night. We'd have no time for anything else. No eating, no sleeping, no praying.' His mouth lingered on hers. 'No parting, no war.'

'The war!' A sigh escaped her. 'Much as I'd like to stay, I have to leave you. The cows are calling as is the cockerel and there's only me and Ronnie to see to them.'

'Where's Ben?' he asked.

'With the army in Wales. He's seen action in France but thank God he got away.' Reluctantly she drew away from him.

'And Daisy?' He watched Lily as she reached for her clothes, unable to get enough of the sight of her.

She told him about Daisy and May as she dressed.

'Poor Daisy.' His eyes fixed on her face. 'Wouldn't you have been safer at the farm? Why stay here?'

'Ronnie was determined not to go. I couldn't leave him alone. Besides I felt I had a duty to keep the dairy going and help where I can. As well as that I've no desire to live under the same roof as Aunt Dora.'

'I'll have to find some war work here.' He lay with his arms folded behind his head, his eyes narrowed in thought. 'I've a feeling this is where the front line is going to be for some time.'

'That's what Ronnie says.' She sat on the bed and his arm slipped about her waist. He kissed her again and she realised there was a desperate anxiety behind the kiss and with a sense of shock she thought, this is wartime and on front lines people get killed! They had to snatch every moment together they could, but for now she had to milk the cows or people would not get their pinta.

Lily told Ronnie about Matt's return as they exchanged information about the raid.

Her brother was delighted. 'Mr Jones is the one Matt should speak to,' he said, forcing himself between two cows. 'He reckons we're in for it now good and proper, and every able-bodied man is going to be needed.'

She and Matt discussed what he was going to do over a breakfast of porridge and toast. She had offered him an egg but despite her saying they weren't short because her hens were laying he told her to give it to a child, that porridge would do nicely, adding that he would sort himself out concerning papers and war work and she was not to worry about him or change her day.

Matt did not come in for lunch. Officialdom being what it was he could be some time. There had been an appeal for blood donors so Lily went to the Royal Infirmary along with a stream of other people, some of whom could not stop talking about last night's raid. The Customs House had been set on fire and an air raid shelter in Cleveland Square had received a direct hit. It was depressing and upsetting and she did not want to think about it. Matt was back and making love had been wonderful. She did not want to let worry, jealousy or guilt cloud her happiness, although why she should feel guilty about Rob Fraser, she did not know. It was not as if they'd done more than kiss. Even so Matt might not see it in that light and she wanted nothing to spoil their life together from now on.

Lily had put a rabbit on to stew by the time Matt arrived home that evening. 'Did you get everything sorted out?' she asked.

He nodded, planting a kiss on the tip of her nose as he slid his arms around her waist. 'I managed to see the vicar. The curate's joined the army as a chaplain. It seems I might be of some use, organising a rest centre in the church hall for the homeless, keeping their spirits up and helping them to find other accommodation. He's already got a couple of homeless families in the curate's house. I said I'd be all right here. He's going to get in touch with Church House about paying me something.'

She realised he was happy. 'It seems as if you came at the right time.'

'So did I until I saw Frank,' he said ruefully. 'He was surprised to see me and doesn't seem to think I'm good for anything.'

'How does he make that out?'

'He says it's because I've had no civil defence training and that I'm not a practical man!'

'That's not true,' she said defensively. 'I've seen you change a wheel.'

'You tell him that, my sweet.' He hugged her against him and kissed her. 'I told him I was prepared to drive an ambulance but he said I don't know the city well enough.'

'The rat!' Her eyes sparkled. 'He *is* getting too big for his boots. You don't have to know the whole city and you wouldn't be on your own! I know of typists and house-wives who've volunteered to drive ambulances. I'll put you in touch with the right people. I'll show him he can't speak to my husband like that!'

'Thank you, Lily, but don't let's turn Frank into an enemy.' He rubbed his cheek against hers and his hands wandered over her body.

'You're too nice,' she said reprovingly, pressing against him. 'This is war.'

Matt smiled. 'But we're not at war with Frank.'

She nodded, thinking that Frank might have hoped Matt would never return but he had, thank God, and she hoped there would be no raid tonight. But why wait until tonight? 'How many nights did you say went into three years?' She began to untie her apron.

In his eyes there was a wakening response. 'We'll never get them back, Lil.'

'No?' She smiled.

He swept her off her feet and carried her upstairs and she felt overwhelmingly happy despite the unasked ques-tion about Abby still lurking in the dark recess of her mind.

# Chapter Thirteen

Lily felt nauseous as she slumped in a chair in front of the fire after doing the milking and serving in the shop. Just ten minutes' rest, she pleaded with God. At six that morning she had still been working with the mobile canteen, serving tea or soup and butties to the homeless, and nurses from the nearby nurses' home in Mill Road which had been bombed.

It was difficult to believe in a couple of days it would be the season of goodwill and peace to all men. For the last three nights wave after wave of aircraft had passed over the city, dropping incendiaries, parachute mines and high explosives. She wondered what Ben would make of so many familiar landmarks damaged or obliterated. He had managed to get leave for Christmas but Daisy had written to say she could not face the long journey home. Lily had hoped the family could all be together and with that thought in mind had asked Matt to get in touch with his Aunt Jane.

Lily need not have mentioned it to him because Matt had made up his mind to visit her, having heard that Bootle had been hit hard during last night's raid. It was not the first time it had suffered badly because of its docks and expanse of timber yards, some of which had caught fire last night. Jane did not live so close to the docks as to make it highly dangerous but the gasworks, easily recognisable from the air, was just a short distance away. An incendiary had dropped on it at the end of summer, causing little damage, and Matt had tried to persuade Jane to leave then but she had refused to go.

Lily worried about her husband. In the last couple of months she had discovered he had a fatalistic attitude to life and death which she was unsure whether to label heroic or foolhardy, because, despite Frank's words, Matt's offers of help to fight fires or rescue the buried had been received with gratitude from the often over-stretched services. She sometimes wondered if he enjoyed the danger because of the kind of life he had led, and part of her wished he was different. She wanted him home safe because there was something important to tell him. She tried to imagine what he would say, but it was something else they had not thought to discuss before they married. She grimaced, closed her eyes, and dozed off.

Matt came in just as Lily closed the door for lunch, but he was not alone. With him were a boy and a girl of about four years old. Their hair could have been blonde beneath the dust and tears had washed paths through the dirt on their chubby little faces. There was the acrid smell of smoke and plaster dust emanating from them and she could have wept for them, and herself. She had so wanted a few hours alone with her husband. It was three nights since they had slept together and she saw little of him during the day as he sought to comfort the bereaved and help the living. Her eyes met his above the children's heads. He looked tired, worried, and was as dirty and smelly as the children. It was not the first time he had brought the homeless home.

She forced a smile. 'What have you been up to? Did you find Jane?'

He shook his head. 'I'll tell you later.'

She felt a familiar rage and sadness, believing the worst. 'I'll run a bath and then I'll make you all something to eat.'

He shook his head. 'Food first, please, Lil, and a cup of tea. We're starving, aren't we, kids?'

They nodded dumbly, their eyes blank.

Lily made porridge despite the time, thinking they might not be able to manage heavier food. She wondered about their family as she half listened to Matt talking quietly. He would make a good father, she thought, as she poured cream over the porridge and spooned a dollop of Aunt Dora's home-made raspberry jam into each bowl.

'Now eat it all up,' she said, setting it on the table in front of them.

The children looked at each other as if for reassurance and sank their spoons into the porridge, forcing it into their mouths. A sob burst from the boy and he gagged on the food.

Lily moved quickly. 'Hush, hush now.' She put an arm round him.

'Mam used to say "Eat it all up",' stuttered the little girl, 'and we can't!'

'You must try because your mam would want you to,' she said gently. She glanced across the table at her husband. 'Speak to them, Matt. Take their minds off things.'

He stared at her from beneath drooping eyelids. 'I doubt if anything can do that. Their names are Joe and Josie, by the way.'

She smiled. 'Try, while I find them clean clothes.'

He nodded and covered her hand with his own a moment. Tears pricked her eyelids.

She left him with the children and went over to a cupboard where she kept clothing purchased at jumble sales for such moments. As she rummaged through it, she half listened to Matt's voice. There was something about the way he spoke of angels and heaven which was infinitely reassuring but she wondered if he still believed in what he said after the horrors seen in the aftermath of the raids.

Despite it being afternoon Lily decided a few hours' rest would do them all good so she found clean pyjamas and put hot water bottles in beds. After the children had managed to eat most of the porridge she dumped them in the bath together and anointed their scratches and cuts before dressing them in pyjamas slightly too large for them. Then she tucked them up in her father's old bed. She handed them a comic each and told them she'd be back soon.

After putting their clothes to soak in the sink, Lily went in search of Matt. He had bathed and was in bed, his hair curling damply on the pillow. 'That's probably the first sensible thing you've done in days,' she murmured, starting to undress.

'What are you doing?' Suddenly he looked less weary as he watched her strip in the darkened room.

'I thought you might need warming up and I want a cuddle and to talk.' She lifted the covers and her naked hip slid against his. He pulled her close and ran a finger slowly down her spine. 'I didn't find Aunt Jane.'

'You think she's dead?'

His brows drew together and his expression was pained as if to think hurt. 'I thought everything was all right because I could still see that toffee works chimney rearing up against the sky but nearly the whole of her street's gone and part of those next to it. It's a mess! I spoke to several people but nobody knew her. One ARP told me that whole areas of Bootle were evacuated weeks ago because of unexploded bombs but they were vague about exactly where which families have gone. Aunt Jane could have gone into Lancashire or she could be among the dead.'

Lily pressed against him, holding him tightly. Jane was his only blood relative and Lily could guess what the loss of her meant to him. They were silent, just comforting each other. Eventually Lily said, 'Where did you find the children?'

He sighed heavily and rubbed his face against her shoulder. 'They were sitting on the corner of a street just across from the toffee works with their sister. She'd been injured in the blast that killed their mother. The sister told me she went back for her handbag. Apparently she shielded them from the worst when they followed her and a land-mine went off right in front of the house.' He paused, frowning. 'They'd been told by a policeman to stay where they were, that someone would come for them. I think they'd been forgotten. Perhaps he was killed. The sister isn't badly hurt. A slight concussion and superficial injuries. She's in hospital and I promised I'd look after the kids until she gets out. Their father was killed at sea last June.'

'Poor loves,' said Lily, forcing down the lump in her throat. 'We'll have to do something for them. Although . . .' she hesitated. 'I don't know how much I'll be able to do, Matt. I'm having a baby!' she blurted out, without meaning to do so in that manner.

He stared at her and she wondered whether he had taken in what she had said because he looked stunned more than delighted.

'You're not pleased,' she murmured, pulling away from him.

He ran a hand through his hair. 'Of course I'm pleased you're having our child! It's just the timing!'

They were not the words Lily had wanted to hear but she forced herself to stay calm. 'There's nothing I can do about the timing, Matt!' A nervous laugh escaped her. 'It's God's!'

He sat up abruptly. 'You'll have to get out of Liverpool, stay at the farm.'

She frowned. 'I don't want to stay at the farm. I want to stay here.'

'You're not thinking sensibly. You'll be safe there.'

'Oh, yes! Bombs drop in the country, you know,' she said pettishly, not wanting to leave him.

'Not as often as they do in the city!' His grey eyes hardened. 'You'll obey me in this, Lily. I want you and the baby out of danger. We haven't suffered too much from the bombing around here but I've seen what a heavy raid can do and I don't think they've finished with us yet.'

She stared at him thoughtfully. 'You're inconsistent, Matt. You talk of God's will and His plan. Well, if it's God's will I and the baby survive then we'll survive just as well here as at the farm.'

He was silent a moment, then reached out and placed a hand on her belly. 'So I'm inconsistent where you and our baby are concerned,' he said quietly. 'Perhaps that's a lack of trust in me, but I was thinking I was being practical.'

Her heart softened and she covered his hand with hers. 'I want us to be with each other as much as we can, Matt. You'll have to come to the farm too. If anything were to happen to you, I don't know what I'd do.'

His fingers curled about hers. 'I can't sit on the sidelines out of danger. It's different with women and children.'

'Not any more, Matt,' she said firmly. 'What about Jane and those children in the other room? Their mother is dead! We're all in this together, and while I'm fit I'm staying with you.'

He shook his head. 'Lily—'

'No, Matt! I won't go!'

'You will!' His expression set mulishly. 'Once before I let you persuade me against my will to let you do what you wanted and it was one of the biggest mistakes I ever made.' He crushed her fingers and she winced.

'Matt, you're hurting me.'

He released her hand and kissed it. 'Sorry.' He moved away from her. 'Now I'm going to snatch an hour's sleep while you make up your mind you're going to do exactly what I say.' His expression was weary. 'Afterwards I've got to work out what I'm going to say in my sermon this evening.' He turned from her, pulling the covers over his head, effectively shutting her out.

Lily stared at the humped shape of him in the bed, feeling rejected and frustrated, struggling with the desire to continue arguing the point. Matt wasn't thinking straight. Who would take care of him and Ronnie, and serve in the shop, look after the hens and the cows? She knew her brother could do a lot and he had less delivering to do because there was less corn coming into the port because of ships and their cargoes being lost at sea, but he was beginning to help on the farm more because of the men being called up. There was also the fact that she had worked hard at making the dairy a going concern and liked earning some money she could call her own.

She would have to leave things for now, though. Matt surely wouldn't expect her to go to the farm immediately with Ben about to arrive. Besides there were the orphans to see to and Matt could not cope with them alone, she thought with a satisfied smile.

She found the children asleep and stayed awhile, gazing down on them, thinking of the baby inside her. Every now and again the twins' round little faces twitched, and Joe, who had his thumb in his mouth, would suck it vigorously. Poor mites! She would get Ronnie to explain about them to Uncle William, certain that he would manage to persuade Aunt Dora that two extra small mouths to fill on Christmas Day was not beyond her capabilities.

It was as Lily had thought and Matt did not insist on her going to the farm there and then. In truth he seemed to have forgotten what he had said and she was not going to bring the subject up.

On Christmas Eve, May arrived at the dairy with money to spend. She had grown taller and prettier and at fifteen had a curvaceous figure. 'I thought we could go shopping,' she said cheerfully, cutting a slice off the loaf she had baked herself and brought to impress her sister.

'That's fine with me. Although there mightn't be much in town after the raids,' said Lily cheerfully. She was feeling less nauseous and a little happier because the raids the night before had been less severe. Matt had taken the twins to the infirmary in Stanley Road. Being a clergyman had its uses in opening doors that were often closed to others, he'd said, determined the twins should be reassured about their sister's care.

Lily's mood soon changed on overhearing a conversation on the tram into town. Manchester had been heavily bombed and the centre was still burning with the Exchange and all Piccadilly down. It seemed that the Luftwaffe had only gone elsewhere for a night out. When would it all end? She felt a sudden fierce protectiveness towards her unborn child and decided Matt could be talking sense and perhaps she should stay at the farm for the sake of the baby. She felt better having made the decision.

Neither of the sisters had seen before the damage to Philip, Son and Nephew's bookshop or Russell's store on the corner of School Lane and Church Street. Its clock tower and the figures that used to come out when it chimed were gone for ever.

'It's horrible,' said May, her mouth drooping. 'It doesn't feel like Christmas with some of the buildings all blackened and broken down. It makes me realise you were right making me stay on the farm. Besides I'm getting to like it, although Aunt Dora has me working like a skivvy.' Her lovely eyes gleamed. 'She's teaching me to cook . . . says I've got a nice light touch with pastry.'

'Matt wants me to go and stay at the farm,' said Lily.

May looked startled. 'But you're not going to, are you? I thought you said nothing would ever separate you from him again.'

A shadow darkened Lily's eyes. 'I'm having a baby and that's a big something. Don't tell the others. I want to do that myself.'

Her sister was delighted. 'No wonder he wants you out of it! When's it due?'

'May. It's a long way off yet and I'm not going to be worrying about it.' She smiled and hugged her sister's arm. 'Now it's Christmas and ol' Hitler's not going to stop us enjoying it, so let's get spending.' She pushed open the door to Woolworth's and they went inside.

Matt had told Lily to buy something for the twins, saying it was important they had something to open on

Christmas morning. She bought some wooden blocks for Joe. Josie was having one of Mrs Draper's dolls, which she knitted and sold for the Seamen's Fund. Lily bought a couple of picture books and sweets and chocolate, and on the second-hand bookstall behind St John's Market in Williamson's Square she found several books which she thought her menfolk would enjoy.

Ben was not expected until evening because there were always delays when travelling these days so Lily told May not to wait around in case there was a raid.

Matt had found some coloured paper from somewhere and he and the children had made paper chains and were putting them up in the kitchen as Lily prepared an enormous pan of scouse. He told her about the twins' sister. 'She's all right – was able to talk to them and that's done them good. The nursing staff said if she had somewhere to go, someone to look after her, they'd let her out for Christmas.' He bit into a carrot, chewing absently. 'I'm going to have to try and find them somewhere they can be together.'

Lily's heart sank. 'Why you, Matt? We never seem to have a minute to ourselves. Surely someone else can do it?'

'Dealing with people's problems is what my job's about,' he said quietly. 'I was thinking—'

'No, Matt.' She just knew what he was thinking. 'She can come for Christmas but they can't stay indefinitely.'

He eyed her mournfully with the tiniest smile curling the corners of his mouth. She found herself weakening. 'You're not going to tell me how there was no room at the inn, are you?' she said with a laugh. 'Because honestly, Matt, if it isn't safe for me and the baby here, how can it be for those children and their sister?'

He hesitated. 'You're right. But what about the farm? There's a room above the stables not being used and space in the house. It's sinful when people are getting bombed out and are homeless. It won't be long before the authorities realise the space Dora's got and she gets landed with someone she'll fight with cat and dog.'

Lily laughed. 'You'll never persuade Aunt Dora,' she said positively. 'She'll hold out as long as she can. I've got to ask her about my staying there yet so don't upset her, Matt.'

His eyes brightened and he pulled her against him. 'So you're doing as you're told, woman?'

'Yes, man.' She rested her head against his shoulder. 'But only if the raids continue.'

'Agreed.'

'And I'll come here every day.'

'I should hope so! I'll need someone to wash my socks.'

'Is that all I'm good for?'

'You know you're good for lots more.' He nibbled her ear.

She pushed him away but her cheeks were pink and her expression warm. 'Not in front of the children. Now scoot! I want to make some mince pies before Ben arrives.'

Her brother turned up half an hour later. Lily flung her arms around him. 'I thought you'd never get here. I was worried.'

He dropped his tin hat, gas mask, kitbag, and held her off from him. 'I was more worried about you lot! We know Liverpool's been copping it.'

'We're surviving.' She smiled. 'How are you finding the land of your fathers?'

His expression brightened. 'Lovely country and the natives are friendly to us foreigners.'

'Foreigners? Our mam and grandparents were Welsh!'

'Well, there are foreigners among us. There's an RAF training base not far away with New Zealanders and Aussies.' He looked at Matt. 'You'd feel quite at home. And there's this nice old lady with this enormous house and gardens who throws it open to all and sundry. She thinks we're all heroes. We have a few friendly drinks and a few friendly fights.'

'Fights? Aren't the Jerries enough for you all?' said Lily.

He grinned. 'It's nothing serious. And I've told them we're just as friendly in Liverpool and to drop in any time they're over this way.'

'Thank you, Ben,' she said with mock severity. 'As if I didn't have enough visitors with Matt's waifs and strays.'

Ben pulled a face. 'And now there's me to feed. I've got a whole fortnight's leave.'

'Well, you can spend it at the farm,' she said promptly. 'Uncle William was saying he has a lot to discuss with you.'

He asked after his uncle and from then on the conversation was taken up with family and business matters.

That night there was only a light raid, much to their relief. On Christmas Day, William arrived in the Armstrong Siddeley to take them to the farm. They had made a promise not to talk about the war that day, but it was not easy considering the debris, bomb craters and unsafe buildings which needed to be avoided in order to collect the twins' sister.

'This is Vera,' introduced Matt.

She was a tall girl, with pale delicate features and waving brown hair fashioned peek-a-boo style, which did not quite conceal a black eye. The skirt of the navy blue suit she wore was a little on the short side, which was to her advantage, revealing long slim legs. Her shoes were well worn but highly polished. A bandage showed beneath the cuff of her left sleeve and she appeared nervous, biting on her bottom lip as she stood gazing at them.

Lily and William smiled and said hello. The twins chorused for her to come and sit by them, but Ben, who was sitting in the front seat and had been gazing wordlessly at her, scrambled out of the car and offered his seat. 'You'll be more comfortable here than squashed in the back,' he stammered.

'Thank you.' Her voice was just a thread of sound and she stared at him gratefully from elongated brown eyes.

Lily lifted one of the twins on to her knee and tried not to stare at Ben as he squeezed in next to her. It took some doing because to her knowledge it was the first time he had ever looked at a girl in such a way. She spoke to him and he answered as if in a dream. He's in love, smitten at first sight, she thought, wondering what that boded for the future.

Over dinner Lily watched Ben and Vera and it was obvious to her the girl was as smitten as her brother. It showed when he asked William and Dora could Vera and the twins board with them? Ronnie and May had taken the visitors to see the animals.

'She'll be able to help on the farm now most of the men have gone, Uncle William,' he insisted, his expression animated. 'I've got a fortnight, I can teach her quite a lot in that time.'

His uncle agreed and when Matt stressed the need for those who had to help those who had not, Aunt Dora also said yes, adding since she had been aiding William and May outside there had not been enough hours in the day and she was always tired. It was not like her aunt to show weakness and Lily felt concerned. Then she remembered the baby. The news brought a smile to Dora's face, although for a moment she reverted back to her old self and reminded Lily that her mother had died in childbirth and she would have to take care of herself and not do too much. Albert had been too wrapped up in himself to see what had been needed at the time, which was typical of men.

Matt said shortly, 'I have every intention of my wife having the best of care, Dora.' But instead of insisting Lily stayed safely at the farm that night they went home together.

Lily was quite happy to do so, although she would have liked to be on hand to see how the relationship between Ben and Vera progressed. She found out within the week when Ben announced he and Vera were getting married and asked Matt how he went about getting a special licence. She expected Matt to counsel him on the wisdom of not rushing into something so important as marriage but he did not.

'They're right for each other,' Matt said succinctly. 'You can see it just looking at their faces and they're always talking.' He officiated at the wedding which was attended only by the close family. The obviously happy newly-weds had a two-day honeymoon in Blackpool before Ben returned to his unit.

Matt tried to find out more about Jane but it was difficult with victims' bodies charred beyond recognition and survivors coming and going from the countryside. For the docks to keep working, the dockers had to stay alive, so it made sense for them to escape the bombing where they could.

There was a welcome lull in heavy bombing for a couple of months and Matt said no more about Lily moving out to the farm. Feeling well, and with the baby moving inside her, she got on with life. She tried not to worry about the war or Ben. Vera went to see him in Wales and soon after they heard he would be going abroad. He said they had not been told where for security reasons but he and Vera worked out a code so he could let her know when he was leaving and where he was going, but she received no letter or phone call and could only presume that they had whisked him away before he had a chance to get in touch.

With few raids life almost felt normal. Then halfway through March, Lily and Matt were having a welcome break at the pictures when the sirens started. They stayed where they were, enjoying the film and believing the raid would only be a light one, but an incendiary started a fire and they were told to leave. They came out of the cinema to the sound of machine-gun fire. Flares lit up the sky, enabling them to see the duel taking place between two planes. Mesmerised they watched as tracer bullets travelled along the plume of a Heinkel bomber with a Nightfighter in hot pursuit. The planes tore across the sky, then suddenly there came a tremendous explosion and they could see burning bits and pieces of aircraft plunging from the sky. There was a hush and then the crowd let out a cheer.

'Let's go,' said Matt grimly, seizing Lily's arm. 'Tomorrow you go to the farm.' She nodded, wishing the men had been able to parachute out. It did not matter than the slain were the enemy. They were someone's husband, son or brother.

Lily was to remember that aerial fight a couple of mornings later. She had just finished helping Uncle William and Vera with the milking, wanting to get away as soon as she could to see if Matt and Ronnie were all right, when the twins came into the house at a run.

'We've found a man,' they said breathlessly and in unison. 'He speaks funny English, not as good as Matt, and thinks he's broken his ankle.'

The three grown-ups exchanged glances. 'A Jerry, d'you think?' said William, reaching for the shotgun which had never been far from his hand since war was declared.

'Your guess is as good as mine,' murmured Lily.

Vera's mouth tightened. 'If he's one of theirs I know what I'd like to do with him.' She made a twisting gesture with her hands and strode out of the shippon accompanied by the twins.

Lily and William hurried after them to the field, where to their relief an airman in RAF blue was trying to fold his half-torn parachute, while propped up on one elbow among rows of early cabbages. There was a smear of mud and a long scratch down the side of his face but he grinned as they approached. 'Gidday sports!'

'You're an Aussie!' chorused the two women.

'You're quick. Name's Andy Gardner.'

Lily could not help a smile. He reminded her of Rob Fraser and suddenly she was remembering the sunshine and the flowers and life before the real gut-gripping fear that the bombing had brought to all their lives.

William cleared his throat. 'We should get his boot off if his ankle's broken.'

Lily roused herself. 'It'll hurt like hell and we've still to get him on his feet and we can't go lifting, Uncle William.'

Vera agreed and sent the twins to fetch May, and between them the two young women managed to get Andy into the house, where William phoned a doctor and the Australian asked if he could ring his base at Speke, a few miles away.

The women fussed around Andy who informed them he came from New South Wales, and soon he and Lily were talking of places she had visited and completely forgot the time. The doctor arrived and said Andy's ankle was only a bad sprain. He also had a talk with Lily and they discussed her coming confinement as she had decided it would take place at the farm. It came as a shock to her to realise it was well gone two before he left. She wondered if Matt was worried about her, then decided he could have phoned from the post office if he was concerned. She felt definitely annoyed about him not doing so.

Yesterday she had arrived home to find the house empty and had done most of the washing before he came in. He had been visiting the bereaved and seemed distracted. She had been feeling unusually vulnerable and anxious but had not liked bothering him with her feelings, especially when someone else had arrived, homeless and asking for his help. He had ended up offering her Albert's old room without consulting Lily, which she now remembered had annoyed her. She thought they should have discussed it. Afterwards there had been barely time to snatch a meal together before she had to leave to catch the tram. Thinking about it, Lily decided she would not rush into Liverpool and back to the farm again. The doctor had said her blood pressure was up and she should be resting more with the baby due in less than two months.

About six in the evening Matt phoned and it seemed to Lily that he did not care if he saw her or not when he said he hoped to get a good night's sleep for a change because he was not fire-watching that night. She felt undesirable and unwanted.

Dora, seeing her flushed face, suggested she had a bath and maybe an early night. Not accustomed to being fussed over by her aunt, Lily was touched by her solicitude and did as she suggested. She enjoyed a long soak with the new *Woman* magazine and was just rubbing her hair dry when she heard the sound of a vehicle drawing up. Her heart quickened its beat. Perhaps Matt had found transport and had come to spend the night with her?

She donned the satin dressing gown he had given her for Christmas and hurried downstairs. Then she stopped abruptly, her heart bumping heavily. In the hall stood two men in RAF uniform. One was a stranger but the other she knew. He was Rob Fraser.

# Chapter Fourteen

'Lily!' Rob bounded up the stairs.

She gazed into his face and thought, he looks just as young as ever and as attractive, whereas the war is ageing Matt and me before our time. 'Hello, Rob.' Her voice was quietly controlled. 'I never thought to see you here.'

'I always hoped I'd see you again,' he murmured. 'That's why I volunteered and came up here.'

'That was a daft thing to do!' She flushed. 'It was all a misunderstanding . . . Matt was in New Guinea. We're back together and I'm having his baby.'

He stared at her for what seemed a long time and his eyes were the hard blue of sapphires. 'Men get killed in wars. Perhaps Matt will?'

Lily could barely believe he had said such a thing but before she could comment. Vera, who had entered with the two men, called, 'Do you two know each other?'

'Sure do,' said Rob, switching on a smile. 'Small world, isn't it?' He clomped downstairs.

'We met briefly when I was in Australia,' said Lily, as she followed slowly in Rob's wake. She smiled at the other airman who was dark-haired and sallow-skinned. 'I presume you've come to collect Andy and you've got to rush off with him?'

'Not particularly, have we, mate?' Rob's eyes flashed a message to the other man. 'There's time for a cuppa if you're offering.'

'I wasn't,' said Lily, knowing it would not do to allow Rob into her life again.

Vera stared at her in surprise. 'But they've come so far, Lil. I thought—'

She laughed lightly. 'They haven't just flown in from Australia! They've only come from Speke, over the way.'

'Cruel, Lily, when I've got so much to tell you,' said Rob reprovingly. 'Abby turned up after you left. You remember her?'

Her stomach lurched and for a moment she could not speak. Then anger superseded the fear of what he might say and she murmured, 'Vera, perhaps I'm being a little unkind. Make the men a drink. I'm going to bed.'

She began to climb the stairs, heard a door open and the murmur of voices before they were shut off and thought, thank God! She jumped when Rob said, 'I'd still like to get to talk to Matt about other things besides Abby.'

She stared at him, suddenly convinced there was a hint of a threat in those words. She wished she had told Matt about Rob but it was too late now. She felt the blood drain from her face, and seizing hold of the polished oak knob at the top of the stairs she clung to it and took several deep breaths before turning and staring down at him. 'You're determined to cause trouble, aren't you?'

'Sure am. Told you I wanted to knock his block off.'

A tight smile pinched her mouth. 'You're out of luck! Matt isn't here. I've evacuated from Liverpool because of the bombing and the baby.'

He frowned. 'So where is he?'

'I'm not telling you.'

He shook his head as if in disbelief. 'Out of harm's way, I bet. Then I might as well tell you what Abby had to say.'

'No!' she blurted out. 'I don't want to know.'

His eyes glinted. 'Coward! You don't trust him, do you?'

'You're wrong.' She closed her eyes briefly. 'I'm tired. The doctor says I've got to rest. Another time, Rob.'

'When?' Lily shrugged and he added, 'Next time I have some time off we could meet – go somewhere and talk. This place has a phone, doesn't it?'

'I don't consider that a good idea.'

A laugh burst from him. 'Definitely not! But you'll come? We could have fun, baby or not.'

Lily could not believe he was still interested in her. She thought of Matt, who seemed to have little time for her these days, wrapped up as he was in dealing with other people's problems. Rob was certainly flattering her and it would be nice to have a bit of masculine attention, so it was almost on the tip of her tongue to say yes. Instead common sense asserted itself and she shook her head and moved as swiftly as she could into the bedroom she shared with May, closing the door firmly behind her.

As Lily climbed into bed she told herself it was the last she would see of him.

With a little difficulty she lay on her side, pulling the covers over her head to shut out any noise from below, but sleep evaded her because she could not get Rob out of her mind. Was it true he had really come all this way hoping to see her? Or was it purely chance they had met again? Did she believe in chance? Matt didn't. If it was not chance what part had Rob to play in their lives? With a sinking heart she thought of her husband and Abby. She did not believe Matt had seduced the girl, so why had she stopped Rob from speaking?

She turned on her back and stared up at the ceiling with its fancy scroll-like cornices and considered how she should have mentioned Rob and Abby to Matt instead of worrying about it complicating matters between them. What if Rob had not come hoping just to see her but to get revenge on Matt? If he had he had to have a strong reason to do so, and the only reason she could think of was that he had found out something more about his sister and Matt. She felt confused and scared at the thought, but could only hope she was wrong and it was chance that Rob had turned up here so unexpectedly. Even so, in case he tried to get in touch with Matt, she had better tell her husband what part Rob had played in her time in Australia as soon as she could.

When Lily arrived at the dairy the following day it was to find the lodger in the kitchen, frying sausages. Matt was nowhere to be seen and she was hurt and angry that he was not there to greet her. Why couldn't he be here when she wanted him?

'Hi, kid!' The woman's face was the colour of parchment and her eyes dark-ringed circles. 'You OK?'

Lily felt like biting her head off and saying, 'What the hell are you doing taking over my kitchen?' but she remembered in time that the woman's ten-year-old daughter had been killed and her son, who was seriously injured, was in hospital. She felt ashamed of herself. 'OK, thanks. Are you managing all right, Nora?'

'Fine. I hope yer don't mind me using yer stove?' Her tone was anxious. 'And I did a bit of washing and sold some milk.'

Lily felt redundant but smiled. 'You're welcome.'

Nora flicked the sausages on to a plate and said awkwardly, 'Yer man said he'd be in dinner time so I thought I'd cook him something. Always on the go, he is. I don't know how he keeps up.'

'On a wing and a prayer, I think,' said Lily drily, putting on the kettle.

At that moment there was the sound of a door opening and Matt entered. His face was drawn but his eyes lit up as Lily moved towards him. She realised she couldn't talk now about Abby and Rob. The timing was all wrong. She pushed Matt gently back into the lobby and closed the door. 'All quiet on the Western Front last night?'

'Yes, thank God! You could have stayed.'

'Perhaps I will tonight.' She kissed him. 'You look whacked. I've brought one of our May's home-made loaves for you to sample. With a couple of Nora's sausages, it'll put some meat on your ribs.'

He smiled and hugged her. 'There's nothing wrong with me that the sight of you can't cure.' His lips touched hers and any misgivings she might have had faded. Why spoil things? No need to mention Abby ever. Rob was just being his normal overriding self and calling her bluff. No man would fancy her in her condition. He was having her on and would probably never get in touch with her again.

'G'day, could you spare a pint of milk for a thirsty Aussie?'

Lily turned awkwardly, a bucket of bran in her hand, and was immediately angry. Men! They were always where you didn't want them to be! 'What are you doing here? I thought I told you—'

'You know why I'm here.' His voice cut ruthlessly through hers. 'I want you to listen to me. I don't want him having it all.' He took the bucket from her. 'You shouldn't be carrying this in your condition.'

'My condition's got nothing to do with you,' she retorted, placing her back against the sun-warmed wall of the shippon and hoping Vera would not choose this moment to come out.

'That's a pity. I think we'd have enjoyed making a baby together.'

'You flatter yourself! Anyway, you shouldn't be saying such things. Someone might hear you.' She wished she had stayed in town but there had been a bad raid a couple of nights ago during which Lister Drive power station, up past Donkey's Hill, had been hit. Matt had insisted on her leaving, just in case.

He smiled. 'So what if people hear us and believe there was something between us? It would be true.'

'It would *not* be true,' she said wearily, wishing he would go away. 'You can be a charmer, Rob, but there's no point in this conversation or my listening to you. I have a life here so please vamoose! Matt's a good man! You should see the way he helps people.'

'I've seen the way he helps people,' he sneered. 'Now my sister—'

'No, Rob!' She covered her ears but he dragged her hands away.

'You're going to listen to me.'

At that moment Vera came out of the shippon. 'Lily, where—' She paused as she caught sight of them. 'I didn't know Rob had come to see you.'

Her tone sounded suspicious to Lily and she felt sick as she pushed his hands away. 'I felt faint. You know how it is when you're having a baby.'

'I wish I did,' said Vera shyly, her expression changing.

'I'd give anything to be having Ben's baby. It's nice to see you again, Rob.'

He flashed her his most attractive smile. 'I've just dropped in with Andy. He wanted to say thanks again and I was just looking around. We have a place back home, although it's a bit bigger than this.'

'A bit!' Lily bit back a sharp laugh. 'It's enormous!'

'You've seen it?' asked Vera with obvious interest.

'Yes,' said Lily shortly, realising she would have to be careful where Vera was concerned. She turned to Rob. 'If you've seen enough, maybe you'd like a cup of tea?'

'Maybe I would.' He smiled at Vera and saluted, placed the bucket of bran on the ground and taking Lily's arm led her in the direction of the house. 'Nice girl.'

Lily shook off his hand. 'She's married to my brother so don't go turning your eyes in her direction.'

He stopped and stared at her reproachfully. 'How could you say such things when I only have eyes for you.'

She could not prevent a smile. 'In my condition? Ha!'

'I wish you weren't in that condition because of him – that's why I'd do anything to turn you against him.'

'Even to telling fibs, I suppose?'

He grinned. 'What d'you think I am? They slept together and that's the truth, but as soon as Abby discovered he was married she left him. Too ashamed to come home she found work in Broken Hill but eventually she had to come home to have the baby.'

Shock waves rippled through Lily's body and she stared at him. She had never thought of a baby. 'I don't believe it!' she cried.

'You don't want to believe it. You want to go on believing he's all those things he preaches.'

'Yes,' she said starkly. 'And more. He makes me feel on different levels in a way nobody else can. I love him! Can't you get that into your thick head?'

There was silence and Rob seemed shocked rigid by her words. Across the garden and a couple of fields away in the fresh spring green of a clump of trees a cuckoo called as if mocking her.

Rob eased his shoulders. 'He got her pregnant in a way nobody else could have. Give me your body and I'll save your soul – that was his promise.'

The way he said it took Lily's breath away. 'You're a pig,' she said explosively. 'He's not that kind of preacher! I'll call your bluff, Rob. I'll tell him what you said. Tonight! This afternoon! No, now!' She stormed away from him and went in search of William. When she found him she asked if there was any petrol in the Armstrong Siddeley and could she borrow the car?

He eyed her dubiously. 'Can you manage it, lass?'

'You mean can I get behind the steering wheel?' She made her tone light and amused to hide her pain.

William chuckled, asked no more questions, and Lily drove off without another word to anyone.

It was as she passed the church that she caught sight of Matt talking to a woman and fury surged through her. It did not matter that the woman was old enough to be his mother. It was enough that she was female and in his company. Matt's women. The words settled in her mind. Nora. Vera. This one and Mrs Draper. And there were others who all thought he was lovely and kind, a good listener, always there for them. But not for her, she thought. They never seemed to have enough time to talk.

She drew up alongside the kerb and called him. It was several seconds before he looked up and she drummed her fingers on the steering wheel as he excused himself and came over.

'What are you doing with your uncle's car? Is it an emergency?' Then in an alarmed voice: 'You're not about to have the baby, are you?'

'And if I was, could you spare me the time?' she demanded.

His brows drew together. 'What is this? Are you upset about something?'

'Too damn' right I am,' she muttered. 'Get in the car, Matt. I want to talk to you.'

His eyes narrowed. 'I don't take kindly to my wife swearing or to giving me orders.'

'Please, lord and master,' she muttered. 'But now is not the time to tell me that wives should be subject to their husbands! I need to talk to you and I want your full attention with no interruptions.'

'You are in a mood.' His expression was grim. 'What's got into you?' He climbed into the car and she drove off immediately along Belmont Road, past the Lido picture house. Through the open window came a mouth-watering smell from Barker and Dobson's sweet factory as they passed the top of Whitefield Road. Everton mints and chocolate dragees, she thought with part of her mind, wishing she had something to bite on. Where do I start asking about Abby? Do I creep up to it or plunge right in?

'What's on your mind, Lily?'

She glanced at him. 'Australia. You stayed on a sheep station near Bourke. There was a girl called Abby.' She felt rather than saw him tense, heard the hiss of his indrawn breath and felt a chill of fear. Earlier her uppermost feeling had been anger with Rob, then jealousy and hurt when she had caught sight of Matt unexpectedly with the other woman.

'It's one of those airmen at the farm Ronnie mentioned, isn't it?' he said quietly.

'Rob Fraser!' she spat out his name.

He surprised her by saying, 'I quite liked Rob . . . never satisfied with the answers I gave him. Always had another question to ask. But I never thought he'd turn up here.' He paused. 'But of course, he's not here by chance.'

'I knew you'd say that,' cried Lily, wishing she had not started this. 'All part of God's plan, I suppose?'

'For my punishment.'

'What?' She had not really expected that. For a moment she took her eyes off the road. He called a warning and she saw the crater just in time and turned the steering wheel frantically. The car swerved, missed the hole and narrowly avoided a cat, which shot through the doorway of a building with shattered windows on the other side of the road. She trod on the brake, the car skidded to a halt and she was flung against the steering wheel and all the breath seemed to be knocked out of her.

'Lily, are you all right?' Matt's arm went round her shoulders but she shook it off.

'Go on,' she gasped in a trembling voice, lifting her head. 'Why should God punish you?'

'Never mind that now! What about you? You look ashen.'

'Never mind . . . what I look like!' She felt as if her whole world was suddenly crumbling and had to force the words out. 'Why should . . . God punish you? What have you done?'

He stared at her, his eyes a cloudy grey. 'What did Rob say? What's he accused me of?'

'You ran off with his sister.' She moistened her lips. 'Made her pregnant. She left you when you told her you were married.'

A muscle tightened in his neck. 'And you believe him?'

'I'm telling you what he said!' She hammered her fist on the steering wheel. 'I'd like you to deny it.' Her voice was strained and she was feeling terribly sick.

'You can't believe it!' The skin around his mouth and nose was white and taut. 'I'll admit I behaved stupidly. I should have realised what was going on but lots of women and girls come to talk to me, appear fascinated by what I have to say and the life I've led. I'll admit to having been lonely and flattered when she hung on to my every word, but that's all there was to it!'

Lily was starting to feel more than sick. She was hot and cold and shivery and there was pain where she had been flung against the steering wheel but she could not let go. 'What about Broken Hill?' she managed to say.

'She asked me for a lift, said she had a friend there and her brothers were too busy to take her. I couldn't see how I could say no without appearing rude and ungrateful for their hospitality. I remember us setting out and her being a bit forward . . .' His voice trailed off.

'And?' She took several deep breaths in an attempt to ward off a sudden faintness.

His brows drew together. 'I don't remember getting to Broken Hill but we must have got there,' he said slowly. 'Because what I do remember is coming to on the floor of a hotel bedroom with the proprietor bending over me. Apparently I'd lain there all night. There was a vase beside me and my head had been cracked open.'

'I see.' She didn't really but she did not want to think any more about what was and wasn't the truth because she was scared. Something was going wrong inside her!

'Lily, are you all right?' Matt's arm went round her and this time she let it lie there.

'I feel terrible,' she whispered. 'You'd better drive.'

'Do you want to lie down?'

She nodded, heard him open the door, felt him lift and carry her, lay her down on the back seat and cover her with his jacket, and then she drifted into a strange world of increasing discomfort and pain in her belly which crept and retreated like waves lapping on a shore. Then it was as if the wind had risen and was smashing the waves on to the sand.

When the car stopped she felt herself being lifted, carried and placed in her bed. The pain now seemed an intrinsic part of the icy desolation which gripped her. She felt terribly alone, although she knew there were people about because there were voices.

'It's coming too soon,' said a voice she vaguely recognised. It had been there when Daisy had been burnt, soothing and sensible.

'Will my wife be all right?' The tone was urgent and pain-filled.

Matt! she cried inwardly. How could you hurt me like this? The tears welled in the inner corners of her eyes and trickled down her nose. The voices faded into the background as someone gently wiped her face. The pain steamrolled over her body again and she gritted her teeth.

'Don't fight it, dear.' It was a woman's voice. 'Go with it.'

Lily felt like laughing. Go with it! Where else can I go? Oh God, why are you doing this to me? My baby, my baby! She moaned and tried to turn over to escape the pain but there was no escape from its demands.

'Push now, breathe, push! Doctor, you'd better come!' called the woman's voice.

'Nearly there.' His voice was kind and encouraging.

She knew he was right and pushed with all her strength. Then she waited for the baby to cry but it never did.

# Chapter Fifteen

Lily woke from a doze and for a moment she thought all was well and then she remembered and was desolate. She stared at a blue bottle buzzing ineffectively against the window and thought, my baby would have been due this week. Instead it's a whole month since he died. Will I never stop hurting?

There were footsteps on the stairs and hurriedly she reached for the magazine May had brought and found herself reading about whether an unmarried girl should give herself to her soldier sweetheart when on leave. She was reminded of those times when she and Matt wanted each other madly and had had such hopes for the future, but everything had changed now. She had not spoken to him since the baby had died, blaming him for the loss of her child. Why could he have not told her about Abby before? Then it would not have come as such a shock. Being knocked on the head and losing part of your memory was something you would not easily dismiss, and yet he had never mentioned it. Why? Because he felt guilty about the whole episode! At least with Rob she knew for sure there had been little more than a few kisses.

Pain and a need to make Matt hurt even more swept through her as he entered the room. She pretended to be engrossed in the magazine.

'Lily, we've got to talk,' he said forcefully. 'It's wrong of you to shut me out. It hurts me as much as you that we've lost the baby, surely you must realise that?'

From beneath her lashes she saw his lean fingers grip the wooden board at the bottom of the bed but still she did not look up into his face, knowing if she did so he would see it as a response. She wanted to scream, how can it hurt you as much as me? You didn't live with him moving inside you day and night. But she remained silent, continuing to stare at the page as if absorbed by its contents, knowing it was infuriating him.

'For God's sake, say something!' he demanded, leaning forward and wrenching the magazine from her grasp. 'Your silence won't solve anything! If it's that girl Abby this is about and not the baby, have you thought we only have her word for it that I did anything? I don't remember and that's the gospel truth!'

How convenient, thought Lily, almost giving one of Aunt Dora's sniffs.

'If you really loved me you'd give me the benefit of the doubt,' said Matt desperately.

She considered how difficult it was to keep silent when all her instincts were saying, yell at him, hit him. She wanted to shout, you've admitted spending time in that girl's company, to being lonely, to giving her a lift! Your name and hers are in the hotel register. Why didn't you tell her you were married and she might have stayed away?

Did she hit you when she found out? Did you force your-self upon her? Rob said she has your baby alive and that hurts more than anything! But to say all that would be communicating with him, crossing a bridge, and she needed space around her which he could not penetrate while she nursed her grief.

She heard the rustle of pages being turned and then he said, 'Did May bring you this? Did you have a sisterly heart to heart? You can talk to your family but not to me, it seems.' There was a short silence then he added quietly, 'Remember us saying we had a thousand nights of love-making to catch up on? Now we might as well be a thousand miles apart.'

Lily felt the tears catch in her throat but still she was silent. She slumped lower in the bed and closed her eyes.

He was silent for a long time and she waited for him to leave, then he said, 'So you're carrying this on? It's going to be war without words between us?' There was a sound of tearing paper.

Her eyelids flew open. He smiled grimly at her, scat-tering magazine paper like confetti on the eiderdown before walking out of the room. She wanted to smash something but told herself that would be resorting to his tactics. Men are so childish, she thought, and toyed with the idea of leaving him and returning to the farm, but she did not want to chance meeting Rob and had told the family to tell him they had no idea where she was and let them make of that what they would. Besides this was her home. And who knows? Matt might go and bring another one of his homeless women into it if she was not there.

Suddenly she remembered that tomorrow Nora's son was coming out of hospital. Her heart sank. She did not want to cope with someone else's troubles. Perhaps it would be a good idea to get away from the strained atmosphere of the house for a day. Tomorrow was May the first. She would go and see if there was peace of mind to be found elsewhere, away from those who knew her.

But the best laid plans, never mind hastily decided ones, often don't work out, thought Lily the next morning as she faced a helpless and scarlet-faced William, who had a giggling twin swinging from each arm. 'It's just that we're calving, lass, as well as having a hundred other things to do,' he said in a flurried voice, 'and these two imps keep getting into mischief. If you could just take them out of our hair for the day, it'd be appreciated.'

She thought, why did it have to be today? The last thing I want is two kids hanging round my neck.

William stared at her anxiously. 'Of course, if it's too much trouble or you're not feeling well?'

'No, I'm fine,' she lied, seeing no way out of doing what he asked without worrying him. 'I was thinking of having a day out. I'll take them with me.'

His eyes brightened as he lowered first one twin to the floor and then the other. He delved into a pocket and produced a handful of silver. 'Buy yourselves some ice cream! Go to the pictures, lass! Anything! I'll come back for them this evening.'

She shook her head. 'Don't you be rushing yourself here, there and everywhere. You're supposed to be taking things easy. I'll bring them back on the tram.'

He looked relieved and kissed her fondly. 'You're a good lass. Always have been.'

'You've always been prejudiced in my favour,' she said, with an eye to Joe, who had just picked a couple of eggs from a basket on the counter. She took them from him and pushed him and Josie out of the shop so they could wave to William as he drove off.

Even before he was out of sight Josie had turned the full power of her limpid blue gaze on Lily. 'Can we go to the seaside?'

The sea! thought Lily with an almost feverish longing, imagining a gentle sea lapping on the sand, but of course the beach was out. There'd be barbed wire and it was no secret that many a ship had gone down due to floating mines. What if one swept ashore with the tide?

'I'd like to go on the ferry!' Joe jumped on and off the kerb, his eyes fixed on her face.

'Stop that!' Lily seized his arm. 'No way would I risk taking you two on a boat, unless you've come with your own built-in lifebelt, which I doubt.'

Joe pouted but Lily was unimpressed.

'Aren't we going anywhere then?' Josie's mouth turned down at the corners, reminding Lily of Orphan Annie.

'I said we would, didn't I?' she said severely. 'But only if you behave yourselves. If you don't, you can forget the ice cream.'

'We'll behave, Aunt Lily,' they chorused and smiled like newly created cherubs.

She was not fooled by such easy promises of good behaviour but told them to play outside while she fetched a jacket, made some sandwiches, found a bat and ball, discovered a couple of old fishing nets in the gas cupboard, and washed out jam jars which she tied string to. She called the children from out of the Morrison shelter in the cool room, handed them a fishing net each and told them to quick march.

It was green and fresh and peaceful in the park but high in the sky not so far away floated silvery sausage-shaped barrage balloons, reminding Lily that there was a war still going on despite there having been few raids that month.

She sat on her jacket, her eyes on the twins as they fished for tiddlers in the shallow, circular boating pond, and found herself remembering her childhood and that of her brothers and sisters after the death of their mother. There had been few times when she had been able to bring them to the park like this, but sometimes Uncle William had turned up and taken them out of her hair so she could get on with the housework. She wondered how people did without family and despite her determination not to feel sorry for Matt, found herself wondering about his child-hood. It must have been lonely and hard with little feminine influence to soften the edges.

He seems to have coped all right, said a voice inside her. He managed to catch you. You're not going to go soft on him now. There's plenty of women prepared to do that.

Look at the way Nora, even in the early days of her grief, mothered him. You've had no one to mother you in fifteen years!

Lily dropped her chin on her knees and stared stonily into space. Probably there'd been plenty of females interested in him. Women like Miss Morell and Abby. So harden your heart, girl. A deep sigh escaped her and she felt herself sinking into depression, only to be roused by a yell from Joe.

'Aunt Lily! I've caught a fish! What do I do with it?' He jiggled the net about in the water, his babyish features alight with mingled pleasure and anxiety.

She shoved her problems to the back of her mind and scrambled to her feet, dunking a jam jar in the water, half filling it. She showed him how to tip the fish out of the net and into the jar. He beamed at her and she forgot herself and gave the children all her attention.

After a while the twins had enough of fishing and played at bat and ball. They tired of that, too, but Lily felt a deep reluctance to go home on her first real day out in weeks. 'Where else would you like to go?' she said.

'Ice cream,' said Joe, turning his smutty face up to hers. 'Big dishes of it!' He held his arms out wide.

Why not? thought Lily, and seizing their hands, hurried them in the direction of the Capoldi Ice Cream Parlour.

With two small children, tired and stuffed to the gills with ice cream, Lily decided the cinema would be a waste and they caught the tram which would take them most of the way to the farm. Dora stated Lily looked worn out and suggested she stay the night. She agreed and went to bed early. For the first time in weeks she fell asleep within minutes of getting into bed.

It was not until after breakfast the next morning that Lily learnt there had been a short raid over Liverpool. Immediately she left to catch the tram, worried about what she might find at home.

She did not arrive at the dairy until midday and on entering the shop was confronted by a irate and filthy Matt. 'Where in God's name have you been? Nora's been hysterical and is in bed! A house the other side of the next street was hit by a landmine. Nobody in there, thank God, but the shippon and kitchen were damaged in the blast! Some of the cows have got out! Another was killed and Ronnie has had the butcher take it. Several more aren't giving milk. A couple of your hens are dead with shock, although fortunately your chicks were inside the house and are OK.' He drew breath. 'Why couldn't you have left me a note? Did you have to be so utterly selfish at a time like this and go off without a word? I've been worried sick!'

Immediately Lily, who had been worried sick herself and had come to the decision she would forgive him anything so long as he was safe, reversed her decision. Her selfish? When she had spent the day looking after two lively kids! How dare he? She walked past him into the kitchen. Every pane of glass was smashed in the window, a wall had cracked, the door frame looked crooked and there was a layer of soot over everything. Damn! she thought. It's going to take ages clearing this up.

Matt entered in her wake. 'Lily, now is not the time to keep up this stupid wall of silence. Where have you been?'

She did not answer but went out into the yard which was littered with bits of brick, plaster, slate and more glass. Inside the damaged shippon, there was an enormous hole. The house opposite them at the back was minus all its windows and its chimney had collapsed and damaged the roof. She stroked one of the remaining cows, noting there was a cut on its flank.

Matt was suddenly at her side. 'Ronnie got rid of most of the mess in here and has gone looking for the cows that escaped. He was worried about the cat but it's come back. I thought you'd be pleased about that.'

Lily nodded. Matt opened his mouth, then closed it and left her. A sob broke in her throat but she swallowed it, wiped her damp eyes and went back indoors. There was no sign of Matt. She donned a pinafore and set about clearing up the mess.

When the sirens sounded that evening a wild-eyed Nora and son shot into the iron Morrison shelter where Lily had placed a double mattress. She followed, knitting in hand, with Mrs Draper whom she had invited to share their shelter when necessary since several communal shelters had been hit in air raids. She had no idea where Matt was as he had not come in for tea. She determined not to worry about him. If he wanted to play the hero and get himself killed, let him! He was as bad as her brother. Why couldn't they just be cowards like some others? It was less worrying.

Ronnie had gone off on his bike to the command post after returning with three of the cows which he had found in Sheil Park. He and she had filled up the hole in the shippon wall with rubble which hopefully would keep the rest of the cows in.

That night was not one Lily wanted to remember. The next day a grim-faced Matt came in early afternoon, ate what she put before him without speaking, snatched a couple of hours' rest in bed and then went out again. When the sirens went it was back in the shelter for Lily and the others, but not to sleep.

That night it felt as if Hitler was throwing everything he had at Liverpool. Bombs screamed, machine-gun fire rattled, and there was the crump of falling masonry and explosion after explosion. Lily forced herself not to freeze at every sound but to talk about the radio, cinema, and ability of Gracie Fields and George Formby to make you laugh. Mrs Draper, who was with them again, and seemed to have a calming effect on the trembling Nora, talked about a trip to Blackpool as she knitted yet another man's stocking.

So the hours passed and still the raid went on and Lily's mind was like a dog chasing its tail, round and round, worrying, worrying about Matt and Ronnie. Even Mrs Draper had run out of conversation but Lily could see her lips moving in silent prayer. Well into the early hours there was an explosion which shook the house. They all clung to each other and Nora sobbed uncontrollably.

Lily could not bear it any longer. She crawled out of the shelter and ran upstairs to look out of the bedroom window. In the direction of the docks and the city centre the whole skyline was a fiery red with smoke billowing everywhere. It was as if Hell itself had reared up from the bowels of the earth to engulf the area. In contrast Lily felt as cold as ice. Liverpool was being destroyed! She had no idea how long she stood there, with her imagination running riot, praying feverishly, not knowing what words she used. Then suddenly she stopped, was no longer cold, only drained of emotion. She forced herself to move and go downstairs.

Nora's terrified eyes met hers. Lily forced a smile but found herself unable to answer the question in that look.

At last the all-clear sounded and they crawled out of the shelter. It seemed a miracle that the cows and Lily's remaining few hens were still alive and not a house down in the street. The acrid smell of burning was overpowering and there was a layer of ash over pavements, windowsills and steps. Several of the neighbours were out. Little Johnny, who still planned on going to sea but now to fight the Germans, waved to her and his mother said wryly, 'Still alive then, Lil?'

'Looks like it,' she retorted brightly.

Neither of them spoke their thoughts but Lily wondered how many people on Merseyside had not woken up that Sunday morning. She wanted to cry and cry but swallowed back tears and clenched her jaw and went back indoors.

'I'm going to make a proper cup of tea,' she said to Nora, whose teeth were chattering. 'Then I'm going for a walk after the milking and see what I can see.' Strangely she had stopped feeling sorry for herself during the night.

Her heart felt heavy but it was with a different kind of sadness to that which she had felt over losing the baby. She drank a couple of cups of tea but did not feel hungry.

'I can't stand another night of it,' whispered Nora, spreading dripping on a slice of toast and handing it to her son. 'Me and Pete are getting out, girl.'

'You can go to my uncle's farm,' offered Lily.

Nora shook her head. 'I'm going further than that. I was hearing the other day that one of me neighbours has gone to Ormskirk. She gave me her address. I'll be off in that direction as soon as it's light.'

Dawn was tardy in coming and when it did arrive it was a smoky, fiery, scarlet orange. Lily fed the cows and milked them single-handed, then served people their milk before going walkabout late morning.

It was a red-eyed, grey-faced Frank who told her that Mill Road Infirmary had been hit, with mothers and babies killed. Someone had said they'd seen Matt in that area. She felt an overwhelming relief that he was still alive. 'What about Ronnie?' she asked. He hesitated and her mouth went dry.

'Well?' she whispered.

'He hasn't reported back yet, Lil. Not that that means there's anything for you to worry about,' he said hurriedly. 'Lots of the streets are impassable and with his knowledge of the city he was sent to help guide some of the outside help in. There's that many fires our own men can't cope. The docks and the city centre are still burning and water and gas and telephone lines are disrupted. They've drafted troops in to help. It's chaotic.'

She cleared her throat. 'Do you know what that enormous explosion was early this morning?'

Frank looked even grimmer, if that was possible. 'Ammunition ship at Huskisson Dock – went up like a box of giant fireworks. There was also an ammunition train that blew in Lower Breck sidings. Frightened the life out of most of us, I can tell you,' he said, shaking his head. 'Thought our last hours had come.'

Lily nodded, her heart heavy, before walking swiftly in the direction of Mill Road Infirmary, trying to harden her heart against the sights she might see. There was still the sound of an explosion every now and again which caused passers-by to exchange glances. One man, clearing debris from a shop door, said in a jokey voice, 'The end could be nigh. You'd better get your haloes polished, girls, ready to meet St Peter.'

It was too close to the truth to be really funny but Lily forced a smile considering he was doing his best.

She would not have recognised her husband kneeling among the rubble if an exhausted-looking first aid man drinking a cup of tea from a WVS canteen had not pointed him out. Matt had a woman in his arms and Lily was aware of a familiar jealousy as she scrambled towards him. Then she saw him pass the nightgowned woman to a man next to him and realised she was dead. Tears pricked the back of her eyes and she scrubbed them away as she clambered over piles of bricks. When next she could see clearly her husband was cradling a baby in his arms and she could not mistake the anguish in his face.

'Matt!' she called.

He looked up but did not move as she approached.

She knelt in the rubble, barely feeling the pain inflicted on her knees, and stretched out her arms for the baby. He hesitated before handing the child to her. She gazed into the tiny, crushed and battered face, considering how the midwife had taken her own baby away without allowing her to see it, in the belief it would lessen her pain.

'Goodbye, baby,' she whispered. 'God bless.'

Suddenly she could no longer see the child's face for tears and sensed rather than saw the man who took the child from her.

'Lily, what are you doing here?' Matt's voice sounded raw, as if it hurt him to speak.

It probably does hurt, she thought, tasting the dust on her teeth and against her throat. 'Ronnie hasn't come home.'

'I see.' He laughed harshly. 'I should have known only concern for your family would make you speak to me!'

His words pained her. 'What about you?' she cried. 'You're here. I could have been killed in the raid for all you know. You're more concerned for other people than me!'

'That's not true. But would it be so surprising if it was, after the way you've behaved in the last weeks?'

'I was hurt! I'm still hurting.'

'Don't you think I am?'

'Not as much as me! I haven't betrayed you!' The words which she had not meant to say were out before she could prevent them.

He stared at her from eyes a steely-grey in his begrimed face. 'We don't know if I did.'

She hesitated. 'All right we don't,' she said roughly. 'But what about Ronnie?'

'I can't do anything about him. I've got a task to do here like all these men. They have families, too, but they can't walk away. We've got some people out alive and you're holding the work up. Go home. Ronnie could be there by now.'

She thought about that and nodded. 'I'll see you later.'

'Be careful where you walk,' he warned.

She rose carefully and left him. She would make chicken soup with the remains of the carcass of one of the dead hens. Matt would be hungry when he came in and, thinking positively, so would Ronnie.

Her brother arrived home late that afternoon. There was a bandage around his head and he looked at least three years older than last night. He was minus his bike. 'What happened?' She hugged him before pushing him into a chair.

'I was blown off my bike.' He rubbed his eyes. 'It's a wreck, Lil. I'm going to miss that bike. It was the first big present from Uncle William I ever had.'

'You won't be able to be a messenger now, will you?' She experienced a wave of relief.

'I'm of help to them. They said they'd find me another.' His expression was suddenly hopeful. 'But perhaps the bombers won't be back tonight. You want to see it in town, Lil. Lewis's is a mess and Blackler's is completely gutted. As for round Paradise Street and South Castle Street, the fires are still burning and men are still trying to get people out of the rubble. Half of the rescuers are asleep on their feet.'

Lily wanted to weep again, thinking of all the unsung heroes this war was creating. She made tea but when she went to hand it to her brother, he had fallen asleep. Finding a blanket, she covered him with it and drank the tea herself, wondering when Matt would come home.

He arrived at tea time but they had no chance to talk. He fell asleep at the table as he ate. Sunday, the day of rest, thought Lily wryly. But they were to get little rest that night or the next as the heart of Liverpool continued to burn, providing an illuminated target for the Luftwaffe.

Then just when it seemed it was going to go on for ever and they'd all collapse under the strain, the bombing stopped. At last Matt and Ronnie came home, went to bed and slept the clock around. She left them to it. She slept in the Morrison shelter, knowing that sooner or later she and Matt would have that talk, but for now it would have to wait.

At the farm they had a frantic phone call from Daisy, asking if they were all right. It was a relief to be able to reassure her, said Uncle William when he saw Lily.

'Any chance of her coming to see us?' she asked.

He pursed his lips. 'She was a bit cagey about that but let's hope there's a chance of her being drafted down here.'

When Lily told Matt of the conversation, he murmured, 'I suppose if she has to find digs you'll want her to come and live with us?'

There was something in his voice that caused her to say irritably, 'Would you object? Nora's gone so there's room. She is my sister after all.'

He riffled his fingers through his hair. 'She's sharp. She'll suspect there's something wrong between us.'

'Well, there is,' said Lily frankly. Now the danger had passed, all the pain over Abby and losing the baby returned in a painful surge. 'You fell in love with someone else.'

'I never feel in love with Abby,' he said stoutly. 'I told you what happened.'

'As you care to remember it.'

His mouth tightened. 'Are you saying I'm lying about not remembering?'

Was she saying that? 'I don't know,' she murmured. 'I only know it hurts me unbearably to think you might have a child somewhere to someone else.'

'I don't believe it!' He looked wretched but she hardened her heart.

'We both know the way some women react to you.'

'I can't help that.'

'Perhaps not, but you have to admit it's not impossible.' She cleared her throat. 'If you were lonely you could have slept with that girl.'

He stared at her then moved over to the window. 'I want to tell you to believe I wouldn't do it, but if you can't then what do we do? Can you forgive me? Perhaps you'd like me to serve some kind of penance?'

'A punishment to fit the crime,' she said, far calmer than she felt.

He turned and faced her but she could not make out his expression as he had moved out of the range of the lamp. 'You mean no sex?'

Was that what she meant? 'You said it.' Her voice was flippant but her heart was thudding in her breast.

Matt was so still it was as if he had stopped breathing. Then in weary tones he said, 'If that's what you want, Lily. You carry on sleeping in the shelter. I'll sleep upstairs.' Without another word he walked out of the kitchen.

She watched him go. In her mind she could see herself running after him and saying, 'That wasn't what I meant at all! I'm not sure what I want. I do want you to hurt like I'm hurting still. Call it tit for tat. Call it a shared experience if you like. We've shared so little lately. I need you to realise I'm your wife, but also not to bank on my accepting anything you do because of that.' But she did not put the thoughts into action. Her pride made her stay where she was and she forced herself to remember those years without him when she had had to do without the comfort of his arms around her and everything else that being married to a man meant because he had spent time with Abby and other people and with his God.

# Chapter Sixteen

'Good cup of tea that, girl.' The man shoved his filthy cap to the back of his head and lit a cigarette.

'Do you want another?' offered Lily, forcing a smile and determinedly trying to ignore the smothering sense of loss and hopelessness which still gripped her months after her baby's death, and had been made worse by the death and injury of so many others and the partial destruction of the heart of her proud city. The doctor had said she must rest but she could not keep still and wanted to help to bring some sense of order where there was desolation, while at the same time wanting to run from the sight of it – to find a green haven where there were comforting arms and her mother's lilting Welsh voice telling her that all would be well in the end. She knew the space which she had enforced between her and Matt was disastrous to her own well-being but seemed powerless to do anything about it.

As for Matt, he had involved himself even more in helping others while she put hours in with the mobile canteen, supplying tea, soup and sandwiches to the men demolishing buildings and clearing away rubble. All her days were filled with some kind of work, anything to stop her thinking, but the thought of Abby having Matt's baby alive somewhere still tormented her.

The workman spoke again, rousing her from her thoughts. 'I don't know what we'd do without you, luv. You and our boys in blue still managing against the odds to get through with our tea.' His teeth showed nicotine yellow in his mucky face as she filled his thick white cup with the amber-coloured tea.

'We've all got to do our bit,' she said brightly, thinking of all those men still at sea, risking their lives to keep the supply lines open.

The fear of invasion had receded since Germany had invaded Russia, and air raids over Liverpool had been few and far between since those terrible nights in May. Although in its aftermath with so many ships sunk in the river and at their berths, with the dock road blocked in places, the port's vital role as front door to the nation's larder and entry for vital equipment from across the Atlantic had seemed in danger of grinding to a halt. It had been Ronnie who had told her how hundreds of men had worked feverishly to clear debris and wrecks to enable the ships to dock and be unloaded.

She considered how glad she was of her brother's presence in the house. Only when Ronnie and the new lodger were there did she and Matt share any semblance of normal life. They both seemed different beings to the ones who had fallen in love in what appeared another world now. At least Ronnie did not seem to suspect there was anything wrong between them. Fortunately Lily had always been first up and last to bed so it was not out of the ordinary for her brother to find her downstairs in the early morning. An ache made itself felt in her gut and she realised how she missed the comfort and delight of sex with Matt. Hurriedly she thrust the visions the thought aroused aside and made herself a cup of tea, deciding that thinking such things would not make matters easier for her. But for the first time she wondered why she had not set a time limit on his sentence.

She switched off the tap on the urn and eased her back, gazing across the cleared bomb site where grass and weeds were already finding a tentative hold. Suddenly her name was called and a voluptuous figure, dark against the sun, came running towards her.

'Wotcha, Lil!' said May, her eyes abrim with merriment. 'How's the good works going?'

'What are you doing here?' Her mood lightened as she gazed at her sister's bright young face.

'Aunt Dora gave me her clothing coupons and with what I've got I might just about have enough to buy a new winter frock – so I thought I'd have a look round town. Not that everywhere isn't a mess these days.' She glanced towards where the men were working and one of the young lads wolf-whistled. She tossed her head but there was a smile on her lips as she met Lily's gaze.

'You'd better watch yourself, my girl,' said Lily, amused.

May winked. 'That's what Aunt Dora says, but I'm not stupid, Lil.'

'What set Aunt Dora off?'

'We had men-type visitors.'

She was instantly alert. 'Who? Tell me more.'

'You'll say I'm far too young to be thinking about men and I'd say I can't stop thinking about them.' Her eyes twinkled. 'It was the two Aussies. One asked after you, wanted to know if you were all right. I told him you'd lost the baby.'

The muscles of Lily's face froze. 'Which Aussie?'

'The Rob Aussie. He kissed me on the cheek and told me I was fair dinkum.'

Lily was more than annoyed. 'Bloody cheek!'

May moved her tongue inside her mouth. 'I told him he was too old for me and he said I'd get older but he'd still be young. Anyway he only kissed me because I helped him.'

'How did you help him?'

May frowned. 'I don't know. It could be because I gave him and his mate a drink of elderberry wine and a slice of cake but somehow I don't think it was that.' She shrugged. 'I'd better get along. I've left Vera with the kids in TJs. We'll probably drop in later and see you at the dairy so make sure you're home.' She rushed away.

Lily stared after her, feeling like a hedgehog who'd had its spines pushed the wrong way. What the hell was Rob playing at, kissing her sister? She would get Vera's opinion on what had gone on when she saw her.

Lily thought she had problems until she saw Vera. The younger woman looked strained but that was not surprising with Ben in North Africa and letters being infrequent. Every two weeks, with the help of Lily and Dora, Vera got together a parcel to send to him. Aunt Dora generally made him some kind of cake. This week Mrs Draper had offered hand-knitted socks and several hankerchiefs made from part of an old sheet. Lily had rummaged for and found a couple of Jules Verne on the second-hand bookstall, and there were sweets and chocolate, fortunately not rationed yet.

'He'll enjoy these,' said Vera, placing the books in a bag. The twins were outside being initiated into the basic rules of hopscotch, drawn on the pavement with a chunk of plaster and using a piece of slate for a counter from a cleared bombed site. May had gone to visit her old friend Jean McGuire who was now working for the British American Tobacco Company in Kirkdale, where according to her, they were rearing pigs on the site of the bombed fitting shop, fed on leftovers from the canteen.

Lily decided to get straight to the point, but before she could speak Vera said tentatively, fiddling with the scone on her plate so that it crumbled, 'Andy the Aussie called, saying he wanted to speak to Matt on a spiritual matter. Matt being an Aussie, he said he'd understand his needs better than a Pom.'

'You didn't tell him where we lived?' responded Lily swiftly.

'I didn't know what to do,' said Vera, her brows knitting. 'So I told him the name of Matt's church. Did I do right?'

Lily shrugged. 'Right enough if he was being truthful and it's not some trick of Rob's.'

Vera looked at her curiously. 'I wish . . .' she began.

'Don't ask me to explain any more than that we met in Australia and Matt was away so he asked me out,' said Lily drily.

There was silence.

Vera said slowly, 'Andy asked me out.'

Lily stared at her and knew exactly how she was feeling. 'You were tempted.'

'How did you know?'

'Rob – Australia.'

'I didn't say yes!'

'You wouldn't be telling me if you had.' Lily kissed her impulsively. 'I know it's not easy . . .'

'Nowt's easy at the moment,' said Vera, flushing. 'But you've all been good to me and the twins and I'd feel like I'd be betraying the whole family if I said yes. Besides it must be worse for Ben. As long as he comes home it'll be worth the wait.' Lily agreed but pitied her and damned the war, while wondering what might be the outcome of Andy's knowing the name of Matt's church.


A couple of weeks later Lily and Ronnie were doing the second milking when they heard the sound of some lads the other side of the wall in the entry. One of the cows bellowed and pulled its head back. There were several giggles. Lily put a finger to her lips and reached for the cane in the corner by the door. Then she crept up the yard, through the house and up the entry. She was behind the boys before they realised.

'Gotcha!' she said, whacking the nearest one across the seat of his pants, causing him to splutter as the peashooter dropped from his lips. The two others fled.

'I wasn't doin' any harm, missus,' cried the lad, hopping from one foot to the other in an attempt to dodge the cane.

'Weren't you?' said Lily grimly, catching him a stinging blow on his leg. 'Cows have feelings. How would you like bits of grain up your nose and in your ears, Jimmy Jones? Besides, don't you know there's food shortages? I'll tell your mother.'

'Mam's at work in the munition factory. Don't tell her! Ouch! I won't do it again.'

'You better hadn't or I'll have your guts for garters. Now scram!'

The lad legged it and Lily turned to go in the back gate but a figure in air force blue was leaning against it and although with part of her mind she had half expected something like this one day, the sight of him startled her. She remembered just in time Ronnie was the other side of the wall and walked swiftly past Rob and round the corner.

He followed her, just as large and handsome as ever. 'May told me you'd lost the baby. It must have been meant, Lil, so you've got nothing to tie you to Matt.'

Pain mingled with sudden fury. Bringing the cane down, she slashed him across the back of the hand.

'Hell, Lil, what are you playing at?' he cried, nursing his hand. 'You don't still believe he's innocent, do you?'

'He doesn't remember. He was knocked unconscious. Besides, that's got nothing to do with it,' she hissed. 'The baby was mine as well. You have no idea how much it hurts to lose a child.'

'I'm sorry. I didn't think.'

'That doesn't surprise me. Did you really think before you came here?'

'Only of you.' He seized her hand.

'Don't give me that soft soap!' She struggled to free her fingers, worried in case Ronnie should come out. 'If you were thinking of me you wouldn't be here.'

'I'm not noble, Lil. I want you, and as I've said before I'll do anything to get you. Pity Matt survived the blitz.' His eyes gleamed as they gazed into hers.

She remembered Matt's worried, weary face and also that it was Rob's words that had caused her to fly in a fury to confront Matt that day she had begun to lose the baby. 'It is my husband you're talking about! He might have his faults but so have you,' she muttered.

'But mine are faults you can accept, his aren't. Come on, Lily, you can't believe that cock and bull story he's told you? Come out with me and I'll tell you again how it really happened.'

'No thanks,' she said stiffly.

He shook his head and said softly, 'You'll regret it.'

Lily smiled tight-lipped. 'I don't think so.' She walked away, half expecting him to follow, but he did not and she determined to put him out of her mind for ever.

'Lily, I want to talk to you,' said Matt.

She looked up at him and immediately was on her guard. They were alone for once. Ronnie had gone to the pictures with the new lodger, a middle-aged but spry Irishman who worked as a horse delivery man at Scott's bakery and helped look after the horses. He had lost his sister and home in the blitz while at the stables freeing his team during the raid. He had told her and

Matt how the horses always found their way back afterwards. Lily put aside the cardigan she was knitting Josie for Christmas and turned off the wireless. The Japanese had bombed American ships at Pearl Harbor and it appeared the Yanks would enter the war. 'What is it?'

'An Australian airman called at the vicarage today.' Matt's expression was inscrutable.

Lily stilled and her nerves jumped. She was unsure how to respond. 'Who was it?' she said at last.

'It was Rob Fraser but I wasn't there unfortunately.' He tapped an envelope against the palm of his hand and his expression hardened. 'I'd have liked to have him tell me to my face what he told you about Abby all those months ago.'

She was immediately very unsure of herself. Matt sounded so honest, as if he didn't have anything to hide from Rob. 'He came here,' she said hesitantly. 'I told him I'd rather he didn't. I don't want to be reminded of the past and his part in it. Maybe it's time we put everything behind us, Matt.'

He did not respond immediately as she hoped. 'What did he say?' His expression was probing and she felt herself flushing as if she had something to hide.

A sharp laugh escaped her. 'The same old thing!'

'If he comes again, delay him. I want to talk to him.'

Suddenly she was apprehensive. 'What's the point? He's talked of knocking your block off.'

Matt's eyes glinted. 'Should that change my mind? Do you think I'm frightened of him?'

'I didn't say that.' She frowned. 'But he's a big man. It's pointless the two of you meeting, only to fight.'

'You're forgetting my calling.' He sounded slightly amused. 'We won't fight. I just want to ask him a few questions. You will tell him?'

'He won't be back!' She was impatient at his insistence.

'But you will if he does?' He dropped the envelope he had been toying with and leaned towards her, taking one of her hands and lifting it to his lips. It was the first show of affection between them in months and she felt a lessening of the unhappiness inside her.

'I hope he doesn't come,' she muttered, letting her fingers curl about his. 'But yes, I'll do as you ask.'

'Good girl.' His smile still possessed that charm which in the past always had the power to melt her heart.

It made her realise just how long it was since Matt had smiled in her company. 'I'm not good, Matt,' she said slowly. 'We all make mistakes and perhaps with time we'll get through this after all.'

'I hope so, Lily.' He touched her hair and traced the curve of her cheek with a finger. Then his hand dropped and he picked up the envelope from the table. 'I've got good news. This is from Aunt Jane! I wanted to tell you about it yesterday but I wasn't sure if you'd be interested.'

'Not interested in a letter from your aunt when we thought she was dead? You must be joking!' The pleasure the news gave her was there in her voice but she was hurt he had kept it from her until now. 'What does she have to say? Where is she?'

'Ormskirk. Do you know it?' He handed the letter to
Lily. 'She would have got in touch sooner, only Amelia
took bad and got worse and worse and apparently she's
just died. The interesting thing is that she knows we're
all right because she bumped into Nora in some market
they hold there. Because they both had Liverpudlian
accents they got talking about their old homes and the
bombing, although apparently the bombers gave Ormskirk
a slight scare last spring too.'

Lily perused the letter eagerly. 'I see she's living on
the money you gave her.'

'She had to because Amelia needed her full-time care.'

'We should go and see her,' said Lily, then almost
hesitantly she smiled at him. 'If you think that's a good
idea and you can spare the time?'

His set expression stilled. He smoothed back the tuft
of tawny hair sticking up from his crown and nodded.
'I'm due a day off. We'll ask William if we can borrow
the car.'

They did so and a few days later headed for Lancashire.
They conversed little but Lily did not mind. She was not
quite ready for a heart to heart but found it immensely
comforting being in his company and away from the city.
They travelled through lanes hemmed in by hedges and
trees stripped of their leaves, leading between fields which
stretched for miles towards the coast. The road rose before
dropping steeply into Ormskirk and it was not long before
they were making their way through narrow streets.

Lily glanced about her curiously. In her letter Jane had
mentioned the town beginning its existence as a coaching

stage on the road north to Lancaster. It had developed as
a market town only after the surrounding area had been
drained by the Scarisbrick family a couple of hundred
years ago and now the land was heavily farmed. Lily
enjoyed finding out these things. It gave her a sense of
Britain and what fighting the war was all about.

They soon ran into trouble in the crowded streets
because it was a Thursday and market day. Matt parked
the car by a convenient pavement and suggested they
walked round the stalls. The slower Lancashire dialect
mingled with a surprisingly high number of nasal Scouse
accents. It appeared that Nora and Jane were not the only
Liverpudlians to take refuge there.

Their own conversation was desultory and concerned
mainly with whether to buy some ginger parkin for Jane
and home-made pink and white coconut ice for the twins.
Lily bought both and Matt, who had wandered off, came
back with two bunches of Michaelmas daises, one of
which he handed to Lily without a word. She was touched
by the gesture and although the shadow of depression was
still there at the back of her mind somewhere she felt
it lift.

They found Jane brushing up leaves with a besom in
the front garden of the small terraced cottage she rented.
As soon as she saw them, the broom slipped from her
hands and she flew to the gate to open it. She hugged them
both. Her hair was greyer and she had cut it short, but it
seemed to Lily she had not changed in any other way.

'It's the gear to see you!' she cried, ushering them into
the house, talking non-stop.

It was not until after they'd eaten a hastily prepared
meal of brawn, mashed potatoes and turnip cooked in a
frying pan over the fire that Jane shooed Matt out. 'Go and
look at the church! It has a steeple and a tower 'specially
made for some bells from Burscough Priory in the time of
Henry VIII. There's a bit of Lancashire history for you,
lad! I want to talk to Lily.' He went with good grace.

Jane waved Lily to the rocking chair in front of the
blackleaded fireplace and seated herself a couple of feet
away. She fixed her eyes on her, gimlet fashion. 'Nora
told me you lost a baby and that you and our Matt were
having trouble,' she said.

Coming so bluntly and out of the blue this caused
memories to come flooding back and for a moment Lily
was unable to speak. Then she managed to say, 'It's been
a difficult time for both of us.'

'Aye! Nora said you'd gone into yourself and Matt was
lost as to how to winkle you out.'

'I didn't think she'd noticed,' murmured Lily, slipping
off her shoes and holding her stockinged feet out to the
fire, more for something to do than because her feet were
cold.

'Well, she did! I remember myself doing the very same
thing after I lost my baby. I never had the chance of
another. Reg was killed on the Somme.' For a brief second
moisture glistened in the inner corners of Jane's eyes.
'Thousands of my generation lost our men. You've got
yours. He mightn't be perfect, Lily, because none of us
are, but don't let the time go by, only half living.' She
picked up the poker and shoved it into the fire. 'I've said

me piece. Now tell me how the rest of your family's doing and then we'll go and meet Matt at the church.'

All the way home Lily was thinking about Jane's words, nursing Matt's flowers in her arms as if they were a baby, and imagining if she was the older woman or even Vera. She was fortunate having Matt with her but that did not make it any easier to cross bridges.

Yet she had it in mind to start bridging the gap that night, but Matt was called out to a dying woman. The next day he was tired and it seemed harder than ever to attempt the seduction of a husband who was distracted by other people's woes.

Christmas came but Rob did not, much to Lily's relief. She believed violence would be the only outcome of him and Matt meeting. There was enough of that in the world, she thought, as they came out of church on Christmas morning.

'Mr O'Hara is coming with us to Aunt Dora's, isn't he, Lil?' asked Ronnie, as they walked home in bright sunlight. Matt and Mr O'Hara were bringing up the rear.

Lily glanced at her brother, considering how he had grown up in more ways than one in the last year. The tweed overcoat he wore belonged to Ben but only just fitted him. 'I've told Aunt Dora that he's clean, respectable, Protestant, and all alone in the world except for us,' she murmured, her eyes twinkling, 'and she has condescended to extend an invitation.' She had asked Jane as well, but she was spending Christmas with Nora.

Ronnie's face brightened. Lily knew her brother had taken a real shine to the old man, who possessed more knowledge where horses were concerned than William or her father. In truth he was swiftly becoming a father figure to Ronnie.

Mr O'Hara's leathery face creased into a smile when Lily told him of Dora's invitation. 'Sure, and you're a gorgeous woman, Mrs Gibson, lovely in looks and lovely in nature. Because I'm sure your aunt would not have thought of asking me if you hadn't thought of it first.'

Lily smiled. 'You're a flatterer, Mr O'Hara. I'm sure you'll say as much to my aunt, but I warn you, she's suspicious of compliments and fine words.'

He winked at her, a devilish gleam in his other eye as he placed on his head a brown Derby with a sprig of mistletoe in its curling brim. 'I've yet to meet the woman who doesn't enjoy being told she's a beauty, Mrs Gibson.'

'Yes, Lily, don't put Dermot off,' said Matt, smiling. 'I wouldn't mind borrowing that hat of his for purposes of my own.' She turned and looked at him and was suddenly breathless.

Dermot's shrewd eyes passed from wife to husband. 'Now, Matt. I'm sure you don't need a sprig of mistletoe as an excuse to kiss your lovely wife whenever you feel like it. Although maybe me and the boy cramp your style at times.' He smiled and hobbled slightly bow-legged out of the room, accompanied by Ronnie.

Lily went to follow them but Matt pulled her back and the expression in his eyes was intense. 'Is it true, Lily, that I don't need the excuse of a pagan custom to give my wife a Christmas kiss?'

She barely hesitated before pulling his arm around her waist. She was aware of a stir of excitement. How would it feel being kissed by him after all this time? His mouth came slowly down over hers. It felt good and her lips parted beneath his, prepared to extend the moment, but her brother called, 'Time we were moving, Lil. We've got the tram to catch!'

Lily and Matt drew apart but she was aware of a warmth inside her that had been missing for a long time. He pulled her hand through his arm and they went to join the others.

The old farm kitchen rang with chatter as they gathered round the oak table. Both leaves had been pulled out to accommodate them all and it was covered by Dora's best lace-trimmed linen tablecloth. In the centre was a cut glass bowl of apples and pears from the farm orchard and four precious Jaffa oranges. Firelight sparkled on crystal glasses, bought at Litherland and Co. in Bold Street in the year of the King's coronation.

'I told Dora that we have to make the most of these occasions,' said William as he waved Lily and Matt to places either side of him. 'It's been a sad year for all of us in one way or another, and last Christmas we weren't sure we'd survive it but we have.'

'Yes. Let's look on the bright side of life,' said May, sliding on to a chair next to Matt. She picked up her glass and wiggled it under William's nose. 'I hope you've got something stronger than lemonade to fill this, dear uncle?'

'Show a little decorum, May,' said her aunt severely. 'I don't know what Mr O'Hara must think of you.'

'Dermot, dear lady, and I'm thinking that the young miss is very pretty and charming.' He seated himself next to Lily and smiled across at May.

'I think you're charming too,' she said, tilting her head and grinning at him. 'I suppose you've kissed the Blarney Stone?'

'It was too far away, my dear. I'm just telling God's own truth about you.'

Dora plonked another chicken down between the two of them. Her cheeks were flushed. 'I think Matt should say grace and we get started or it'll be supper time before we have dinner.'

Matt took the hint, adding a prayer for Ben's safety and for peace in the world.

William opened one of the bottles of champagne he had bought in anticipation of Lily and Matt's baby's christening and they drank a toast to absent family and friends.

After the meal Ronnie, Matt, May and the twins took Dermot off to show him round the farm while William and Dora napped and Vera and Lily dealt with the washing up.

Lily had dried several plates before she realised Vera was dripping tears into the washing-up water. 'What is it, love? Not bad news?' she said with a mixture of anxiety and sympathy.

'No! I was just thinking that this time last year Ben was here.' Her voice had a desperate note to it as she plunged more plates into the sinkful of steaming water.

'We were so happy! But now I can't stop thinking – what if he doesn't return? How'll I bear it?'

'You'll bear it,' said Lily, putting an arm round her. 'You're strong, love.'

'I'm not!' Tears brimmed in her eyes. She made to rub them away but only succeeded in getting soap in her eye. Lily handed her a dry tea towel. 'Why don't you leave these to me?' she said quietly. 'Go and get some fresh air. It'll do you good.'

Vera nodded, and taking off her apron went outside. Hearing voices from the direction of the stables but wanting to be alone she went down the drive and through the gates. She had walked nearly the length of the lane when she saw a man coming towards her. He wore a tweed suit with a thick jumper underneath and the trilby on top of his dark head was pushed to the back. It was not until he spoke that she realised it was Rob. 'Hi there, Vera!' he called. 'Anybody at home?'

Instantly she thought, I've got to get him away. 'They've gone to Lily's,' she said swiftly. 'Aunt Dora does Christmas dinner most years but this time Lily thought she'd give her a rest.'

'Is that straight up?' He drew closer and she caught a whiff of beer fumes.

She looked at him squarely. 'Why should I say it if it isn't?'

'Why aren't you with them?'

'Someone has to stay behind and look after everything.' A smile lit her face. 'What is it you wanted?'

He swayed slightly. 'I just wondered how Lily was. I've met her husband, you know.'

'Have you?' Vera could not conceal her surprise. 'I suppose it was in Australia.'

'Sure was.' He paused and scowled. 'Would you say they're happy?'

'Why shouldn't they be?' she prevaricated. Something had been wrong in the last months between them but she had put that down to their losing the baby. Now she wondered if Rob had anything to do with it.

'Why not indeed?' he muttered. 'They're together while thousands of couples are apart.' He gazed at her from bleary eyes. 'Your husband's in the army, isn't he? So's my younger brother. Me and them are fighting for our countries while Matt gets away with it. Doesn't seem right.' He reached inside a pocket and taking out a pencil and a scrap of paper began to write.

She watched him crossly, knowing how hard Matt had worked during the blitz and since. How hard they all worked on the farm. She thought, there's more than one way to fight a war, and who does he think he is, judging Matt?

Rob folded the paper and held it out to her. 'Do me a favour, Vera. Give this note to Matt when you see him.'

His words puzzled her and she hesitated. 'Are you sure this is for Matt and not Lily?'

'Matt!' He stared at her fixedly. 'You make sure and do what I say.' He saluted before turning and marching slightly unsteadily back up the lane.

Vera watched him until he was out of sight before going back to the farm. The first person she saw was May standing behind a tree. 'What are you doing there?' she whispered.

'Playing hide and seek with the twins.' May's bright eyes looked her over. 'You look guilty. Where've you been?'

'For a walk.' She hesitated. 'Where's Matt?'

'He's playing, too. I think he's in that rhododendron over there.' May's expression was curious. 'Why d'you want him?'

Vera hesitated. 'I met Rob up the lane.'

May sighed. 'Why didn't you invite him in? He's really my kind of dreamboat.'

'I didn't think it would be wise,' said Vera slowly, her brows knitting. 'I think he and your Lil nearly had a thing in Australia.'

'What!' May's eyes widened and she let out a low whistle. 'So that's why she doesn't want him hanging round. What did he have to say?'

Vera took out the note. 'He gave me this to give to Matt. They knew each other in Australia apparently. I got the impression he didn't like Matt.'

The two girls stared at each other.

'Curiouser and curiouser as Alice said,' murmured May. 'I wonder what's in the note.'

There was an uneasy silence and Vera picked at a corner of the paper hesitantly. May groaned, snatched it from her and unfolded the note. Vera looked over her shoulder and they read: 'Matt, Ask Lily what we did in Cairns, Adelaide and on Bondi Beach. Rob Fraser.'

Their eyes met. 'What do you think they did?' whispered May.

'Nothing!' said Vera positively, wondering just how much May knew about sex and things. 'Lily wouldn't. He's just out to cause trouble between them for some reason.'

May gnawed on her lip. 'We'll have to warn our Lil – and the best way of doing that is to give her the note.' She pocketed it. 'She'll know exactly what to do with it.'

May passed the note to Lily as the family were having a light supper and she was handing round slices of Aunt Dora's fruit cake, made with the extra ration of dried fruit for Christmas, and sugar saved for the purpose. 'Look at it in private,' she whispered.

Lily gave her an amused look. 'What is it? Something out of an old cracker?'

'You'll see. Just don't let Matt see it,' she hissed.

Lily was startled. 'Why shouldn't I?'

'Shhh! He's looking. Just remember Vera and I are here if you need us.'

'Thanks,' said Lily, wondering what was up. She slipped the note up her sleeve and curiosity took her to the bathroom.

As she read the note she went rigid with shock. How had May come into possession of the note? Matt must not see it. Not now when things were starting to get better between them. The note hinted at so much. What had Rob thought Matt would do? Throw her out in his direction? She could have laughed at the thought if she had not been so worried and angry. How could he say he loved her and do this to her? It was she who would get hurt as much as Matt.

Before she could think any more Josie knocked on the door, saying she was desperate to wee. Lily ripped the note into tiny pieces and flushed it down the lavatory, washed her hands and came out smiling. 'It's all yours, sugar plum.'

'Fanks!' Josie darted inside the bathroom, not bothering in her haste to close the door behind her, and would have hit the lavatory bowl with her head as her knickers fell down her ankles if Lily had not grabbed her in time.

She sat her on the lavatory, smiling at her. Longing for the child she had lost swept over her. He was gone from her but she could have another. She walked slowly downstairs, having decided it was time for action.

# Chapter Seventeen

'I've wanted to be alone with you all day.' Lily's voice was low and seductive as she sat naked on Matt's bed, shivering slightly in the cold room.

'Are you sure about this?' The fire in his gaze sent a thrill through her. 'We can wait a bit longer if you've any doubts.' He sat beside her, still fully dressed, but she could almost feel the heat of his desire as his gaze washed slowly over her, lingering on her mouth, breasts, stomach and thighs.

'Don't be so nice to me, Matt. I don't deserve it,' she said unsteadily, adding inwardly, and don't ask me to be absolutely honest. I still have a tiny lingering doubt about you and Abby because we're all human, but I've had enough of this so close but far apart life and I don't know if Rob is telling the truth or not.

He touched her bare shoulder and his fingers were trembling. 'Are you sure?' he repeated.

'Absolutely,' she whispered, placing her arms about his neck and moving against him. 'I was hurt but now I'm healed.'

'God be praised,' he breathed, and kissed her with a passion that sent vibrations to the soles of her feet. He forced her flat on her back and took her with a swiftness that took her breath away before beginning all over, but this time he did it much more slowly and it seemed to her that all the months without had been worth it to experience the pleasure that followed.

'Again soon,' said Lily, drowsy with lovemaking. 'I can't understand myself now for cutting my nose off to spite my face.'

'I hope it proved something,' murmured Matt, raising her arm to his lips and licking along its length before biting a finger gently. 'I love you, Lily, not just your body. You do believe me when I say I couldn't have slept with that girl? It's against all I believe in.' He gazed into her eyes with an intensity that made her feel she should be utterly honest but she couldn't be because it would hurt him.

'Yes. I believe you.' She turned, snuggling into him and feeling at peace. They could never know for sure the truth about Abby but she believed he believed what he said. They were back in each other's arms and that was enough for now.

It was as if spring had entered Lily's heart. As she passed fog-shrouded bomb sites she thought, if only I could conceive again, the war end, Ben come home, and I knew for sure Rob was not going to turn up again, I could be perfectly happy. They had seen no sight of Rob and she really hoped he had gone for good. Perhaps everything was going to go her way now.

Then unexpectedly William had a heart attack which proved fatal, saddening them all. He had always been there to turn to and would leave a big gap in their lives. The farm, not quite as he promised, was left to Ben and Ronnie, with the added proviso that Dora should live there for as long as she wanted.

It brought change to all their lives. Ronnie decided to move to the farm and work there full-time. He asked Dermot if he would like to take over his carting job and work from the farm. The Irishman accepted with alacrity and Ronnie, at Lily's instigation, wrote to Ben telling him of all he had done.

There was a letter from Daisy who had moved to Yorkshire to a training college. She hoped to be drafted to Liverpool in the not too distant future. Again Lily spoke to Matt about the possibility of her living with them. 'You won't mind, will you? Things have changed between us.'

He pulled her on to his knee, wrapping his arms round her and nuzzling her throat. 'I don't mind. Although do you realise, with Dermot gone, this is the first time we've had the house to ourselves? Just over five years we've known each other, Lily, and out of that we spend nearly three of them apart. I wish things had been different. I wish I could have shown you Australia. I wish . . .'

Lily closed his mouth with hers, not wanting to be reminded of how she had spent her time in Australia. The memory of Rob was like a spectre, haunting her happiness, but Australia was very much on Matt's mind. They listened to the wireless with anxious hearts and read the newspapers. Matt wrote to friends far and wide. News came of heavy Allied naval losses in the Java Sea and the fall of Singapore sent shock waves through the whole country. Then came the bombing of Darwin on Australia's north coast. She began to sense a restlessness in Matt but did not worry overmuch. She considered it was natural he would feel some concern for the country he had grown up in. She was more worried about Ben.

In June news came of fighting in Africa and the fall of Tobruk. A white-faced Vera called at the dairy in a distraught state. 'I don't know what to do! I can't think straight. What if Ben gets killed in the fighting to come?' She wrung her hands.

Lily felt helpless. What could she say to comfort? She could only think, don't let Ben be killed, Lord!

Vera turned to Matt. 'Do you really think prayer works, Matt? What about all those who have died? Someone must have been praying for them!'

He took her hand and held it tightly. 'We're in a battle on two fronts, the physical and the spiritual. We're fighting against real evil. You can't touch that but it's there. To win often involves personal sacrifice and suffering. Giving in to despair won't solve anything. You have to carry on praying and doing what you can practically.'

Vera freed a breath and nodded. 'I won't say thanks for that, Matt, but you've made me look at things differently.' A smile trembled on her lips and leaning forward she kissed him on the cheek. 'You must be worried about your own country. I'd never thought before of Japan being a threat to Australia. Do you think Andy and Rob will be going out . . .' She stopped abruptly and glanced at Lily.

She felt she had to say something. 'They're in the RAF not the Australian Air Force. I shouldn't think they'd go to the Far East. Am I right, Matt?' She did not look at him.

'I should think they'd stay here.' He hesitated. 'I didn't realise you were on first name terms with Rob, Vera?'

'Not him so much as Andy.' She pleated a fold of her skirt. 'But you don't have to worry about me. Lil put me straight and I haven't seen him in weeks.' She stood. 'I'd best be going.' Before they could comment further she hurried out of the dairy.

There was a silence after Vera left. Her words had left a distinct impression that Andy had been on the scene not so long ago. Perhaps Rob was still around?

'How did you put Vera straight?' asked Matt, his eyes on Lily's face.

She chose her words carefully. 'Andy asked her out. She was feeling low and asked me whether I thought it would be all right if she accepted. I said I thought it would be a mistake even if she sees him just as a friend.'

'Do you really believe she sees him just as a friend?' he asked sardonically.

She flushed but was saved from answering by the jangle of the shop doorbell. She responded swiftly, knowing that a crack had appeared in the fragile structure of her newfound happiness. Something else was going to go wrong, she thought. Uncle William was dead. Ben was in danger. These things always went in threes.

Lily managed to shrug off her sense of impending gloom when May called and suggested they went to the pictures. Matt was visiting a newly bereaved family and then going on to a meeting so she knew he could be out for some time. She scribbled him a note and left it propped up against the clock on the mantelshelf.

They were out of the pictures in time for May to catch the tram back to the farm. She was turning into a proper land girl, much to Lily's amused amazement. It was hard to relate the May of today with the girl who had hated farmyard smells and getting her hands dirty.

Lily was almost home when a uniformed figure detached itself from the corner shop doorway and, seizing hold of her arm, pulled her into its darkness. With almost a sense of fatalism, she thought, how strangely right our instincts can be.

'Hello, Lil,' drawled Rob, seeming to tower over her. 'I take it Matt never got my note?'

'I tore it up,' she said, determined not to be cowered.

His mouth tightened. 'I should have known better than to have trusted a woman.'

'Shouldn't you just?' she said lightly. 'What is it you want, Rob?'

'You. I was hoping Matt might throw you out.'

Lily's laugh had an edge to it. 'Twisted thinking! You're forgetting the dairy belongs to me. Anyway, why should he throw me out? I haven't done anything wrong.'

'Then why rip up the note?'

'Because I thought it despicable! Trying to get at Matt by blackening my name.'

'I didn't say much.'

'You insinuated!' Her eyes blazed up at him. 'It was a lousy thing to do.'

'All's fair in love and war.' He grinned. 'I posted another and I saw him go in not five minutes ago. He'll have read it by now.'

Lily did not speak but pulled away from him and raced up the street.

She had just opened the door when Rob came up behind her and pushed her inside. He slammed the door and she held her breath, waiting for Matt to call out, but there was no sound. He's left me, she thought, her stomach lurching as she hurried along the darkened lobby into the kitchen. That, too, was in darkness but for the glow of the embers in the fireplace. She pressed down the switch and flooded the room with light.

'Tricked you,' said Rob, smiling as he leaned against the door jamb. 'I haven't seen sight nor sound of him but I'm aiming to. I've been waiting a long time to face him with what he did.'

'I used to like you,' said Lily breathlessly. 'But thinking about things, I've realised I only have your word for it that your sister said any of those things you've told me.'

A dull red ran along his cheekbones and he straightened and took a stride towards her. 'So you have. But she'd lie to protect him.'

Lily experienced a tremendous sense of release. 'There was no baby, was there?'

'You were ready to believe it, though!' He seized her by the shoulders and shook her. 'Why was that? Because deep down you wanted to because you love me!'

'You're deceiving yourself,' she said fiercely, struggling in his grasp. 'It was because I was feeling tired and ugly when I was having the baby and you said nice things. I was frightened! I was jealous! When I lost the baby I hurt so much I wanted to blame someone for my suffering and I blamed Matt instead of you. I hurt him a lot because when you love someone you know exactly how to hurt them.'

He looked disbelieving. 'You can't love him! He could still have slept with her. They stayed in the same hotel.'

'So did we but nothing happened.'

He stared at her. 'That doesn't matter. You can't love him, Lil. I wanted you, almost from the first moment I saw you. You have to love me. I'm more handsome, I'm richer—'

'You've got an overwhelming conceit, Rob Fraser!' She laughed scornfully. 'Go on, tell me more about your assets. You're strong. You're tough. You're God's gift to women.'

He smiled at her. 'You've got it all figured right, Lil. You mightn't love me but you still fancy me, admit it?'

She felt like hitting him and was about to tell him a few home truths when she heard a key turn in the lock. 'Let me go,' she whispered.

'You're joking!' He forced her against him as Matt entered.

'It's not what you think,' she said swiftly.

Rob said, 'It's exactly what you think.'

'Shut up, Rob,' she snapped, her eyes on her husband's face. 'He's out to cause trouble, Matt.'

'Too damn' right I am.' Rob smiled. 'Ask her about us having sex on Bondi Beach.'

'We did nothing of the sort when we were there,' she said hotly. Almost instantly she realised by Matt's change of expression that she had fallen into the trap which Rob had set.

Matt's hand tightened on his Bible. 'You were on Bondi Beach together?' His voice lacked emotion.

'Sure we were, while you were converting the natives,' drawled Rob. 'And Cairns and Adelaide! You name it, we went there.'

'I was looking for you! He followed me,' said Lily, controlling a desire to shout.

Matt's eyes met hers briefly but she could not tell if he believed her or not. His gaze moved to Rob. 'Release my wife.'

Rob smiled. 'You going to make me?'

'If I have to.'

'Surely not part of your calling, preacher?'

'There's such a thing as righteous anger,' said Matt softly, placing the Bible on the table. 'You told my wife I'm an adulterer. We have matters to discuss. I want her out of this so let her go.'

Rob released Lily and she moved swiftly to Matt's side. 'It's not true about you and Abby. He as good as told me he'd lied.'

Matt did not look at her but took off his coat and flung it on a chair. His clerical collar followed. 'Leave the room, Lily. This is between Rob and me.'

She moved, then stopped and turned. 'But it concerns me too. Why should I go?'

Suddenly Matt's eyes blazed. 'For once, Lily, do as I damn' well ask you! Sometimes I am in the right, you know!'

'Go, Lil,' said Rob, his eyes bright as he rubbed the palms of his hands down the side of his trousers. 'How can I bash his head in with you looking on? You've got too much of a soft heart.'

She stared at them both. It seemed incredible that two men, so different, should fight over her. Would the victor come to claim her for his own? Oh God! What was she thinking? This was no Hollywood swashbuckler, nor were they kids playing games. This was for real, but she could tell there was no reasoning with either of them while they were in this mood. 'I'll check the cows,' she muttered. 'let me know when it's all over.'

It seemed hours before Matt opened the door of the shippon but it was only just over an hour and instantly Lily knew that it was definitely no game to him. There was an angry red mark on a cheekbone and his eyes were as hard as pebbles. 'Out!' he ordered.

'You're hurt!' She went to touch his cheek but he flicked her hand away and pushed her out of the door.

'You don't have to pretend to care, Lily.'

'But I do care! What's he told you?'

'It's not so much what he told me as what you didn't tell me!' A slap on her back sent her flying up the yard.

'Matt, I didn't do anything wrong,' she gasped.

'I can forgive what you might have done wrong,' he said, undoing her coat and dragging it off, 'what I hate is him telling me what you should have told me! What you hid from me! Why, I ask myself, if there was nothing in it didn't you tell me? I slept apart from you for months, believing it might be possible I'd gone against all I believed in and sinned. I wanted your forgiveness and all the time you withheld it and kept silent about having been with him!' He almost choked on the words, and seizing her by the wrist flung her through the open doorway along with her coat.

Her hand banged against the easy chair as she landed on the floor. She could not believe this was happening. 'Matt, I didn't do anything wrong with Rob!' she repeated desperately. 'I'm sorry I doubted you. Sorry I didn't tell you.' She attempted to get up.

'So am I,' he said, pushing her down. 'My wife whom I kept away from for night after night, week after week, month after month, when all the time I needed her. When the bombs were falling and my life was in danger, when I was exhausted and grieving and wanted comforting, you gave me nothing!' His voice dropped to a whisper. 'Perhaps it was because you were making love to him?'

'Matt, you can't believe that!' she cried, striving to sit up. 'I didn't tell you at first because I didn't want to mention Abby and spoil things between us!'

But he didn't seem to be listening. He forced her down, straddling her and holding both her wrists with one hand. 'Perhaps the baby wasn't even mine?'

That stung and she began to feel really angry. 'What a thing to say! As if I would betray you in such a way—'

'You believed I could!' His voice shook with fury. 'You took his word over mine!'

'I was feeling neglected and then I lost our child! I wasn't thinking straight,' yelled Lily, attempting to prise his fingers from a wrist.

He shook her violently. 'You took his word over mine,' he repeated. 'Do you know how much that hurts?' He choked on the words and released her abruptly so that her head hit the floor.

She was barely aware of the pain. 'Matt, I'm sorry!'

'Sorry isn't always enough.'

'But you preach repentance and forgiveness,' she whispered, feeling sick inside.

A grim smile darkened his eyes. 'Perhaps I've been preaching the wrong thing all these years?' He hesitated. 'I need some fresh air before I do something to you I might regret.' Without another word he left the room. A couple of minutes later the outside door slammed.

Lily forced herself to her feet, thinking to follow him but her legs felt wobbly and her head ached. She sat down again. Her brain felt numb and she was cold and shivery. Her coat was on the floor where he had thrown it and she picked it up and covered herself. He'll come back, she thought.

She must have dozed. Rising fuzzy-headed she went to the bathroom, then she made tea. She wondered if Matt had returned but did not go and look for him. There was a lump on her head and her wrists hurt where he had gripped them. He called himself a man of God and yet he had flung her on to the floor and wouldn't accept her apology! She felt angry and had an overwhelming desire to burst into tears but instead she made herself a hot water bottle and crawled inside the Morrison shelter with another cup of tea.

Two weeks passed and Lily was furious with Matt, with all men in fact. He had not returned but the vicar, David, had called and she had lied to him, saying Matt's aunt was seriously ill and he had rushed off to take care of her as he was her only relative. It had been a stupid thing to say but she felt unable to speak to anyone about their quarrel.

A month went by but still no word from Matt and by then Lily was starting to suspect she might be pregnant. Her feelings were in turmoil but her overriding emotion was a strange sense of bereavement and anger. How dare he leave her without letting her know where he was going, causing her to lie to David and her family!

Why had she lied? Why couldn't she tell the truth? she thought fiercely. Suddenly she realised with an awesome sense of shock it was because, if she was honest, she was responsible for his leaving. She should never have used sex as a punishment. Never withheld that special bond of comfort from him. And he had been right in saying she should have trusted his word above Rob's and that she should have told him about Rob's part in her search for him in Australia. Dear God, she'd made a mess of things. If only they had talked more. If only he would get in touch. Her head ached and she could not keep still. She told herself she had to control her feelings or her blood pressure would rise and that wasn't good for the baby. She pressed a hand to her belly. At least she still had part of Matt with her.

The next month brought an envelope written in Matt's handwriting. Lily's stomach turned over at the sight of it and for a moment she hesitated before tearing it open. Inside was a single sheet of paper with the word 'Sorry' written on it. The envelope was postmarked Liverpool, NSW.

She was stunned, barely able to take in that single word of apology, the lack of an address or that he could be in Australia. She felt a sense of helplessness. The physical rift between them was now so wide it seemed it could never be bridged.

# Chapter Eighteen

Lily put the lid on the freshly scalded pail as the shop door bell jangled and hurried through the kitchen into the lobby. Even after that unsatisfactory letter from Matt she still hoped that one day he would come through the doorway and they could clear the air and sort things out. She stopped abruptly, shielding her eyes from the unexpectedly bright December sun, and knew a familiar disappointment.

'Hello, Lil!'

For a second she did not recognise the woman in the navy blue uniform, who smiled, clicked her black heels together and saluted, hand over her right eye. 'Leading WRN Turner at your service, ma'am, and hopefully here to stay.'

Lily's disappointment vanished and she felt a flood of what she could only describe as joy. 'Daisy!' She threw her arms around her sister. 'You never said when you were coming. Last I heard you were still at that college in Headingley.'

'Wesley College. Very holy, Lil! Used by the Methodists before the navy took it over.'

'Let me look at you.' Lily held her at arm's length.

'Let me look at you,' echoed Daisy, her eyes narrowing. 'You look better than I thought. I hope you're taking care of yourself, seeing as Matt's not around to do it? Where is he, by the way? If you think the family's swallowed all that about his going to take care of his Aunt Jane, then you're daft.'

'Shush,' murmured Lily, taking in her sister's appearance from the navy blue hat with its HMS badge in gold, the V-shaped chevrons on one sleeve and the paler blue-ringed S on the other, to the smart skirt and the black stockings. She debated whether she could tell the truth to this unexpectedly mature-looking Daisy. 'What do the fancy things on the sleeves mean?'

'The S means I'm a trained supply assistant,' said Daisy proudly. 'I've been drafted to the naval hospital at Seaforth. I'll be sleeping in so you don't have to worry about finding me a bed.'

Lily said wryly, 'I've got a couple of lodgers so it would be a problem.'

'Poor you!'

'They're out all day and most evenings, so they're not much trouble.' She linked an arm through her sister's. 'Come on in and have a cuppa. You can't imagine how lovely it is to have you here after all this time, and looking so well.'

Daisy sighed and her head dropped on Lily's shoulder. 'It hasn't been easy getting over Ted's death but there's so many others in the same boat. You just have to get on with it. And at least we all have a common aim – to blast the bloody U-boats out of the water! That's why

I'm so glad to be back here at the centre of things. The battle of the Atlantic is the big one we have to win, Lil.'

She nodded and motioned Daisy to a chair. 'I agree! The newspapers might talk about the victory of El Alamein and the tide of war having turned but, oh God, all the suffering so far. Still, at least Ben's out of it now.'

'What's happened to him?' cried Daisy, starting up.

'Calm down,' said Lily in a soothing voice. 'He's in hospital in Cambridgeshire. He's got a nasty deep gash through muscle and into the bone of his thigh and will probably be left with a limp.' She paused. 'Vera tells me too that he's hurt in another very delicate place.' They stared at each other and giggled.

'We're awful!' said Daisy. 'Poor Ben!'

'I don't know why it makes us snigger. I hope he won't be left with any permanent damage. Vera's desperate to have a baby.'

'Looking at you won't help her.'

'No,' said Lily quietly, seating herself opposite.

Daisy promptly got up and placed a low stool close to her sister's chair and lifted her feet on to it. 'You rest. I'll make the tea while you tell me where Matt is. Unless he's on a secret mission?'

'A secret mission!' A tiny laugh escaped Lily. 'Why didn't I think of telling people that? He's left me.'

The lid of the kettle fell with a dull thunk onto the rag rug. 'You're joking!'

'Oh, it's very funny.' There was a catch in her voice as she was overwhelmed by an unexpected storm of emotion. Linking her hands across her swollen stomach, she forced back tears.

'But he's—' Daisy stopped, her expression unhappy.

'Yes, I know what he is,' said Lily, gaining control of herself.

'But you loved each other so much.'

'We were in love. We didn't know what real loving meant.'

Daisy picked up the lid and did not look at her sister as she said, 'I suppose it has something to do with that Aussie, Rob?'

Lily's head shot up. 'Who wrote to you?'

'May.' Daisy perched on the edge of the stool. 'She was really worried . . . said this Rob tried to cause trouble between you and Matt last Christmas.'

'It's true.' Lily clenched her fists. 'I could hit him when I think of it now! I should have realised but I was stupid. You think if you ignore people and unpleasantness long enough they'll go away, but Rob was, is, one of those fellas who goes on pushing, pushing, determined to make things go his way even if people get hurt in the process.'

'Can you tell me about it?'

She stared at Daisy and said hesitantly, 'It won't be what you think.'

Daisy's mouth twisted. 'Tell me something that is.'

Still Lily hesitated. 'This is difficult,' she said with a slight laugh.

'Don't tell me then.' Daisy shrugged. 'Stew in your own misery.'

Lily's eyes flashed. 'Is that what May said? That I'm a misery?'

'Something like that.'

'Well, if I am it's because I've got something to be miserable about! If you knew the half of—'

'But I don't,' interrupted Daisy, leaning towards her.

'Oh, damn!' Lily eyed her sister ruefully and slowly began to tell her everything.

The instant she finished, Daisy said thoughtfully, 'It never fails to amaze me the things that go on beneath the surface in people. Matt must really love you to have reacted in such a way.'

'This time it's you who must be joking!' Lily closed her eyes and rubbed the area between her eyebrows which was aching dreadfully. 'He probably hates me. He must have to have left.'

'Hate's akin to love and we often hurt the ones we love,' murmured Daisy. 'Probably because we have this rosy picture of our true love being perfect. We never think they'll make a wrong move. Even more so if they're supposed to be one of the goodies. But when you think of it, Lil, you were always going on about wanting a man who was strong, and when Matt gets tough—'

'I didn't mean strong like that!'

'What about this Rob being overbearing? You sounded like you accepted it in him.'

Lily frowned. 'It made me mad but he was that kind of bloke.'

'And Matt isn't, of course,' she said triumphantly. 'He acted out of character – with just cause, I'd say.

'I don't know why you're taking Matt's side,' said Lily crossly, putting her feet on the floor and sitting up straight. 'You always wanted him out of my life before. But you're right in one thing – I didn't expect Matt to act in such a way. He completely ignored what I had to say. I know I was at fault too, but even so I didn't expect him not to listen to me. I'm not used to that.'

'Too right you're not,' murmured Daisy. 'You've ruled the roost in this house for years, our Lil. When you married Matt what you still expected, though perhaps didn't realise it, was a man who would do what you wanted when you wanted but not when you didn't.'

'Say that again!'

'You want to have your cake and eat it, and you can't do that. There has to be give and take.'

Lily laughed sharply. 'How is it you're suddenly an expert on marriage? You were hardly married five minutes.'

There was a silence and Lily realised what she had said and felt terrible. She put out a hand. 'Sorry, Dais. I spoke without thinking.'

Daisy shrugged. 'Don't we all? As it happens I know so much because I listen to people talking – and I've had to learn to give and take living with strangers if we're not all to scratch each other's eyes out.'

Lily squeezed her hand. 'I know you're trying to help. . . .'

'But you'd rather I mind my own business?'

She smiled. 'It's helped, talking. Neither Matt nor I come out of this looking good. If we'd trusted and been honest with each other—'

'You're forgetting Rob's fibs and Joy messing about with your letters,' interrupted Daisy. 'It wasn't all down to the pair of you. What did Matt do about her? Is she still living in his house in Sydney?'

'She decided to leave and live in naval quarters. As far as I know he's let the house to someone else, leaving deciding what to do with it until the war's over.'

Daisy said thoughtfully, 'You could write to him there. A letter might get to him.'

Lily stiffened. 'You're presuming I want to and that he'd like to hear from me?'

'He has said sorry.'

Lily scowled and folded her arms across her chest. 'I could scream when I think of that one word. He could have written more.'

'Perhaps he was too choked for words? You should forgive him anyway. You're not exactly the Angel Gabriel.'

'Don't preach,' groaned Lily, and covered her eyes with a hand. 'You're turning into a proper Miss Goody Two Shoes.'

'Don't be insulting,' said Daisy indignantly. 'You might never see him again!' She rose. 'I'll make the tea while you put your thinking cap on.'

Lily gazed into the fire, knowing the white-hot flame of fury she had directed against Matt had long cooled. There was still hurt and some anger but she could reason sensibly. 'Matt's not in Sydney,' she said as she took the cup from her sister. 'He's in Liverpool.'

'But you said—'

'Liverpool, New South Wales,' she said swiftly, her forehead creasing. 'There's something I know about the place but I can't remember what it is.'

'If it's important, it'll come back,' said Daisy. 'What is important is whether you're going to write to him or not?'

Lily smiled slightly. 'I'm not going to rush into it. I'm rather choked for words when it comes to knowing what to say.'

'You could start by telling him about the baby.'

Lily wondered if that was a good idea. After what Matt had said he might believe the baby was Rob's. The thought sent a chill through her as she recalled him saying, 'I want to tell you to believe I wouldn't do it, but if you can't then what do we do? Can you forgive me? Perhaps you'd like me to serve some kind of penance?'

Dear Lord, why had she been so determined to hurt him? Why do we hurt the people we love? Because as Daisy said we expect them to be perfect, to be all things to us, never to make a wrong move. She still didn't know if Matt and Abby had slept together. Abby who lived in Australia where Matt now was. The realisation caused her more pain. What if he turned to Abby because Lily's pride prevented her from making a reconciliatory move?

'I'll write saying I accept his apology,' she said abruptly, 'and I'll leave the next move to him.'

'It's a start, I suppose,' said Daisy. 'But with all that distance between you, I can see the baby arriving before the pair of you see each other again and that'll come as a shock to him.'

Lily was silent. Her sister's words could prove only too true. Should she tell him about the baby and risk his believing it could be Rob's? After all, the word 'Sorry' could have meant 'Sorry, it's over, and I don't want ever to see you again.' No, she thought immediately. It couldn't. She'd had a letter from Martin's bank saying money was being paid into an account for her by her husband. When she'd asked from where the manager had replied, 'Liverpool, Australia,' and smiled austerely. Would Matt do that if he had wanted to break all links between them? She had not touched the money – her pride again, the deadliest of sins. She decided to write a brief note, knowing if it reached its destination at best it could be seven or eight weeks before she received a reply. From previous experience she knew it was possible that Matt could have moved on to another state, another country, but all she could do this time was stay put and wait to hear from him.

# Chapter Nineteen

' "Over here, over here! O the Yanks are coming, the Yanks are coming!' sang May as she emptied the scraps into the pig bucket in the yard. Several hens came running but she pushed them away.

'They're already here. Haven't you seen the uniforms all over town?' said Lily, putting down the garment she was making for the baby from 'no points needed' packets of lint from the chemist. Her blue eyes rested on her younger sister's shapely figure. 'Don't you be letting the promise of a pair of nylons persuade you that anything goes during this war, my girl! You're only seventeen. Have some fun and don't get too serious.' She eased her back and put a hand to the lower part of her belly where the baby was flexing its muscles again. Months had passed and it seemed it would be as Daisy had said about the birth.

'As if I'd be so daft.' May sat on the back step and smiled up at Lily seated in a chair in the spring sunshine. 'Do you want me to help you find your feet so you can put your stockings on before we go to the farm?'

Lily's lips twitched. 'Are you suggesting I'm too big to find my boots?'

'You're enormous! Our Ben'll never recognise you. He'll say you've been eating for six. You haven't got six in there, have you?' she said, patting Lily's bump.

She thought ruefully, May really is a tonic. Just what I need. 'What time's Vera arriving with Ben?' she asked, squaring her shoulders.

'Dunno. But they should be at the farm by suppertime. Aunt Dora's making a real meal of it so you tell that baby not to choose tonight to arrive.' May reached inside the kitchen for the other bucket in which she had mashed bran with minced bread and a handful of grass pulled up when she passed the park. The hens clucked and scurried after her as she went down the yard to their trough.

'Is Daisy coming?' called Lily.

'She said she'd try and make it. If not there'll be other days.'

Lily sighed. 'It would have been good to have the whole family together.'

May glanced over her shoulder. 'You're forgetting Matt and Aunt Jane.'

'If you're fishing for information about Matt,' she said crossly, 'I haven't heard from him.'

'I wonder where he is exactly?'

Lily spent half her nights wondering. 'Don't let's talk about it,' she murmured. 'Tell me what the twins are up to instead.'

May pulled a face but proceeded to inform her that she had now succeeded in teaching them the alphabet backwards as well as forwards and they could count up to a hundred. 'Vera should be finding them a school but there isn't one close by. So I'll have a go at teaching them to read and do a few simple sums.'

'Do you enjoy teaching them?' she asked with a blend of curiosity and amusement, remembering the trouble it had been getting her sister up for school years ago.

'When they don't mess about I do.' She smiled and tossed back her long, naturally wavy, blonde hair. 'I was thinking, though, of coming back here to live now you've lost a lodger to King and country. You could do with a helping hand once the baby comes.'

Pleasure feathered Lily's skin like a warm breeze. 'I'd appreciate that, but how will they manage on the farm without you? Ben won't be able to do much physically at first with his wound refusing to heal properly, but thank God he's been invalided out of the army.'

'He'll be of more use on the farm organisation-wise because Ronnie and Aunt Dora squabble so. I'll still have to do some farm work or I'll have the government finding me other war work . . . but I can stay here nights and help with the milking.' May leaned down and kissed Lily's cheek. 'I reckon I owe you something for all those years you acted "me Mam".' Before Lily could say anything she slipped past and went inside the house.

Lily was deeply touched by the unexpected tenderness in her sister's gesture and it brought on a positive avalanche of longing to be held, to be caressed and kissed, to have Matt say he still loved and desired her. She wanted to cry and cry because despite having people round her she felt so alone without him. If only she knew what was happening to him it would help in coping with the fear surrounding the birth of the baby she desperately wanted – fear she had spoken of to no one. Again and again she had told herself it would be all right this time round. There had been no air raids to cope with and all the emotional trauma and weariness they had caused. There was no Rob to work her up into that frenzy of anger, jealousy and guilt which had led to the accident that caused the premature birth. For an instant she wondered what had happened to him and how Matt had persuaded him to leave that terrible night he had left her.

Remembering, a few tears rolled down her cheeks and she felt as if there was an enormous sob inside her struggling to be released, but fought against giving in to it. What good would crying do? If things did not go well with her and the baby, then would be the time to cry. Now she had to smile because Ben was coming home and that was something to rejoice about.

'Do you think everything looks all right?' said Dora, gazing anxiously at Lily. 'Will there be enough food?'

Lily stared at the table with its array of scones, cakes, pies, cooked meats, slices of buttered home-made bread, jelly with slices of banana set in it, and shook her head in a bemused fashion. 'I know people who would believe they'd died and gone to heaven if they saw this. Where did you get the banana?'

Dora sniffed. 'I paid five pounds for it and the money's gone to the Lord Mayor's War Fund. This is a one-off, Lily. You don't have to tell me there's a war on. Now you sit and rest. They'll be here soon.'

Lily had no sooner sat down than May said, 'They're here now! The car's just driven up!' She turned from the window and hurried across the room. She seized Lily's hands and heaved her to her feet. They moved as fast as they could and arrived outside just as Ben eased himself off the running board with the aid of a stick.

Lily was aware of the heavy sweet smell of wallflowers growing beneath the window, and of being shocked. 'See the conquering hero comes,' she thought. 'Sound the trumpets, beat the drums!' She felt a sob swell inside her chest. Pain had drawn lines in her brother's face and his hair was completely white. She had been warned but now she was reminded of her father and could not think of anything to say.

Ben smiled and said, 'Good God, our Lil, you look worse than me! You're as big as a tank!'

'Ben, you shouldn't make remarks like that!' exclaimed Dora, clasping her hands to her black silk bosom. 'It's indecent.'

'No, you should have said she's in a delicate condition,' said May, her eyes dancing. 'Only she doesn't look delicate, does our Lil.'

'Shut up, you!' Lily was glad of their words. Smiling, she held out a hand to Ben. 'I'd give you a hug only I doubt you can get close enough.'

His fingers tightened about hers and she could see the query in his eyes. 'You OK?' was all he said.

She nodded, knowing there were some things neither of them would ever be able to tell the other now. They'd changed, but it was a comfort knowing he was near at hand to lean on if need be.

A pale but determinedly smiling Vera took Ben's arm. 'You must meet Dermot,' she said. 'He's been of great help to Ronnie.'

'To us all,' said Dora gruffly, falling back alongside them. 'He's getting a quick spit and polish out in the stables after mucking out with the girls and your brother.'

Ben glanced about him. 'Where are Ronnie and the twins?'

'Ron's still in the bath. He's worse than me for wallowing,' said May brightly, slipping her hand through Ben's other arm and hugging it tightly. 'The twins are in the house somewhere.'

Lily caught the sheen of tears in her sister's eyes before the curtain of her hair fell forward and hid her face. May might not have suffered much in this war but was definitely more caring now because of it. The sight of Ben had upset her but she was doing her best to appear her old cheerful self.

They all went inside to find the twins in the kitchen, kneeling on a chair, leaning over the jelly bowl.

'You dare!' shrieked Dora, and flew across the room.

The twins' heads shot round and Joe fell off the chair and dropped his spoon but Josie rammed the contents of hers in her mouth. She received a swift smack on the bottom but by then Joe was out of sight under the table. 'You come out of there,' ordered Dora. No answer. 'Joseph!'

'I'll get him.' May got down on her hands and knees, her scarlet-patterned skirts billowing about her.

'No, leave him,' said Dora, eyeing the crater-like surface of the jelly, depleted of nearly every bit of banana. 'He can stay there and do without while we eat everything else.' She took a spoon and lifted out the last of the jellied banana and proffered it to Ben, with a glass bowl beneath it to catch any bits. 'Not much for a returning hero but it's all yours and it didn't come cheap.'

'Thanks, Aunt Dora.' He grinned and took the food straight from the spoon. 'It's great to be home.'

They all laughed and Joe crawled out from under the table. At the same time Ronnie and Dermot and the four land girls walked into the kitchen. Joe's misdemeanour was forgotten as introductions were made, and the level of conversation rose as they all sat round the table. 'Ben, say grace,' commanded Dora.

In the silence that descended came the sound of footsteps along the paved passage leading to the room. The door opened and Daisy entered, accompanied by a man in sailor's uniform. A chorus of voices welcomed them and Dora said, 'Sit down quick, do. We're all starving.'

Daisy pressed her cheek against Ben's and dragged her sailor to where there was a space on a bench. 'For what we are about to receive,' said her brother.

'May the Lord make us truly thankful,' chorused everyone.

There was rattle of cutlery, a chink of plates. Dermot and Ronnie opened several bottles of peapod, parsnip and blackberry wine which had been fermenting in the cellar since the year war had been declared.

'Potent stuff,' said the sailor, draining his glass.

Daisy smiled across the table at Lily. 'You OK?'

'You'll soon know if I'm not.' She returned the smile. Now was definitely not the time for tears or speaking of her fears.


Lily's pains started the next day just as she was pouring the last of the milk into the cooler after the second milking, but she waited half an hour just to be sure before telling May.

'You get up to bed,' said her sister immediately, undoing her apron. 'Who do I get? And where do they live?'

Lily told her, adding, 'Fetch Mrs Draper first if she's in. I – I'd rather not be on my own.'

May stared. 'You're not scared?'

'Of course not,' said Lily crossly, clutching the back of a chair and breathing deeply. 'I just want company.'

Her sister hesitated. 'Perhaps I should stay and send Mrs Draper? I'd hate—'

'Don't be daft!' interrupted Lily in mid-breath. 'She's an old lady. She can't run!'

May swallowed. 'It's not going to come that fast, is it?'

'Just get the midwife,' she cried. 'I'll get Mrs Draper.'

'But can you— ? began May.

Lily lost patience and pushed her sister out of the door and followed her to fetch Mrs Draper, her apprehension firmly under control.


Lily felt as if she had done a week's work without stopping but it was all over now and had been worth it. She glanced at the screwed-up features of her son and felt the tug as his tiny mouth worked to draw nourishment from her breast. She brushed her cheek against the soft down on his head and thought, my little hero, it must have been as hard for you as me. If only your father knew about you. Hopefully he'd come running home. She was not going to dwell on the thought that Matt might not want to see his son.

An hour later May entered the sunlit room with Ronnie. She took the baby out of the old Moses basket and rocked him in her arms. 'I hope you're going to let me be godmother?'

'I haven't been to church for ages,' murmured Lily, realising she would have to make some decisions. David had called several times but she had told him she could not talk about what had happened with Matt. It was too soon and she was hurting. He had returned to Australia was all she would tell him.

'You've got to have him christened,' said her sister. 'Matt would want him done.'

'You've got no tact,' said Ronnie, sitting on the bed and placing a box of chocolates on the cover.

Lily pretended not to have heard either of them. 'You must have really done without to buy these,' she said, undoing the cellophane on the box of Black Magic.

'We all decided to do without an Easter egg and our weekly sweeties,' said May. 'But getting back to godmothers . . .'

Lily smiled. 'You like him then?'

'He's beautiful, but not when he wees over me.' She shook her arm and handed her nephew to Lily. 'Somebody should come up with something to stop them doing that.'

'Put a cork in it,' drawled Ronnie.

'Exactly,' said May, grinning.

Her brother ignored her. 'Ben said he'd visit later.'

'What about Vera?'

'Someone's got to look after the twins. Aunt Dora is going to see Clark Gable at the flicks with Dermot.'

Lily and May exchanged smiling glances but made no comment.

Later when Ben called, Lily asked him what he thought of Dermot.

'I was going to ask you that,' said Ben, fetching a chair and placing it beside the bed. He sat, his wounded leg stretched out in front of him.

'I like him.' She thought how much more relaxed her brother seemed today. Close up, his face only appeared a little older than his twenty-seven years.

He took a pipe from his pocket and fiddled with it. 'He's asked me if he may court Aunt Dora.'

Lily smiled. 'How lovely and old-fashioned. I presume it's because he sees you as the head of the house?'

'I'm the eldest male and that goes for something in his book.' He paused to take tobacco out of a pouch. 'He's considering going back to Ulster and buying a bit of land with a cottage on it . . . rear a few hens, a couple of pigs, a cow and some horses. He thinks Aunt Dora'll make the perfect companion.'

'Is he madly in love with her?'

Ben raised his eyebrows and grinned. 'At their age? He thinks she's a damn' good cook if the truth is known!'

Lily mused, 'The way to a man's heart. If it wasn't for Matt they'd never have . . .' Her voice trailed off. There was a long silence before she continued, 'Do you think she'll go?'

He shrugged. 'She's definitely got a soft spot for him and she told me she misses Uncle William dreadfully. Someone of her own age, you see.'

'I miss Uncle William.'

'It seems strange without him – but I've seen too many die young to grieve overmuch for a man who had a fairly good life and lived to see sixty.' He rammed tobacco into the bowl of the pipe, lit it and got it going before continuing. 'Besides, that's how life is, a generation moves on and the next moves up.' He stood and limped round the bed to where the baby slept. He gazed down at him for what felt a long time.

Lily waited for him to say something and when he did it was only partly what she expected. 'What are you going to do about Matt? Daisy told me he was in the Aussie Liverpool.'

She nodded, a flush on her cheeks, wondering what else Daisy had said.

Ben drew on his pipe before saying, 'Do you remember me reading that bit out of the *Echo* to you about that Aussie Liverpool? It was just before the Coronation when the papers were full of fascinating snippets about people from here, there and everywhere.'

She sat up straighter, her interest roused. 'I remember, but I've forgotten what it said.'

'It was about a bishop who'd popped off. He was ordained here on Merseyside but had also been a chaplain at an army base in Aussie Liverpool.'

Lily's pulses quickened. 'Are you saying you think Matt's joined the Australian Army as a chaplain?'

Ben lowered himself on to the bed. 'It's a thought.'

She swallowed. 'He got restless when there was news about Aussies involved in the war.' Her voice was barely audible. 'When Singapore fell, and when Darwin was bombed.' Her eyes met Ben's. 'Chaplains don't go into battle, though.'

'They don't fight but they should be up there some-where with the men, giving them moral support.'

She tried to think about that, calmly, logically. He prob-ably wasn't in danger. 'We can find out for sure, can't we?'

'I should think so. Write a letter to him c/o the Commanding Officer. That should get to him if he's been there.'

'He mightn't have told them he has a wife!' A nervous laugh escaped her. 'And he mightn't believe the baby's his when he does get to know.'

Ben's expression changed and he looked irritated. 'You two haven't half made a muck-up of things! I know events and the war have messed your life up a bit but it's done that for thousands of couples. You and Matt should at least believe that God can do something about straightening the kinks out in your marriage. In the meantime give Him a helping hand! Write to Matt telling him the truth about you loving him and having had his baby and about what exactly happened between you and Rob Fraser. Tell him of your fears and hopes where he is concerned. I know it's a tall order but he's only heard Rob's version in depth. It could make the difference between life and death to Matt, and I'm not joking, Lil. A man needs to know there's something worth returning to when he's in a war. Because of his faith, Matt'll have tortured himself more than some of us would, thinking of things he shouldn't have said or done and vice versa. As for his telling the army about you – he will have done because he's honest and got some sense. You're his next of kin. If he gets killed they need to know you exist.'

She felt she'd been steamrollered. 'OK! OK! But do you have to be so brutal about his being killed?'

His eyes softened. 'But that's what should be at the top line. Think how you'd feel if he was killed, and don't leave things too late.'

He stood, leaning on his stick, looking down at the baby once more. There was something in his face that made Lily forget her problems and wonder about his. 'Will you be one of his godfathers?' she said quietly.

He nodded and she knew he was pleased despite his walking out without saying another word.

Lily wrote the letter, being as honest as she could, put it in an envelope with her name and address on the back. Then she wrote a note to David asking if he could please call She needed to be churched before her son's baptism and that had to be arranged. Naturally having a good reason to see David would make it easier to talk about Matt to him.

She handed both letters to May, praying this time Matt's would not go unanswered.

# Chapter Twenty

Lily turned the sheet of paper over between her hands and did not know whether to laugh or cry. For security reasons her letter had been opened and some cheeky Aussie sergeant was sending his congratulations on the birth of Paul Matthew Gibson and informing her that her husband was no longer at the base but her letter would be sent on. He was just letting her know because there'd probably be a bit of a delay before she'd hear anything. He couldn't tell her any more for security reasons. 'Damn security,' she muttered.

May stopped bouncing the baby on her knee and looked up at her. 'What's up?'

'The security blinkin' read my letter to Matt! I could screw myself into a ball and go and hide in a corner.' She sighed heavily and allowed the letter to fall from her fingers into the fire where it quickly caught light and disintegrated.

'Do they tell you where Matt is?'

'No.' Lily sank on to a chair and fought back that sob inside her.

'At least you know he's been there and they're sending your letter on to him.' said May.

'Thanks for the words of comfort!' She rested her head against the back of the chair and closed her eyes. 'But I get so tired of wondering and worrying about him.'

'You're tired altogether. What you need is a break.'

'Chance would be a fine thing.'

'Sometimes you have to make your chances,' said May sagely. 'When's our Daisy coming again?'

'When she arrives.'

'Let's hope she makes it soon.'

A few days later Lily was serving Frank his daily pinta when Daisy entered the shop. 'You're early,' said Lily, immediately feeling heaps better for seeing her. She had suffered nightmares since the letter had come about Matt, imagining all sorts of things happening to him wherever the Australian forces were involved in fighting the Japanese.

'It's not that early. It's almost dinner time!' Daisy flashed Frank a teasing glance. 'Hello, you! Still keeping the street in order?'

His face, which was much thinner than before the war, turned brick red but he bounced back with, 'Someone has to do it. You haven't lived here for a good while now, Dais. Half the kids not evacuated are running wild because it's the school hols and mams are working in factories and dads are away in the forces. Some of the lads have been up by the railway line where the ammunition train exploded, collecting shrapnel. A couple came home with live ammo. They could have blown themselves up if I hadn't copped them and given them a warning and a good clip round the ear.'

She looked at him approvingly. 'You have come out of your shell. Does this new masterful you extend to your mother?'

'Keep Mam out of this,' he said shortly. 'She's been going funny lately – had to have the doctor to her.' He picked up his milk, raised his hat and walked out.

'He's gone better-looking,' mused Daisy, following Lily into the back premises. 'But what does he mean about his mam going funny?'

'She's been going out into the street in the early hours with nothing on.' Lily's voice quivered slightly. Daisy stopped and stared at her. 'I know it isn't funny, but she always has her handbag with her and slippers on.'

Daisy's lips twitched. 'It's the war.'

'She's probably worrying about her business, poor thing. No oranges or bananas. People growing their own stuff as much as they can. Shortages of this, that and the other . . . queues. Now they're bombing Italy.'

'What's Italy got to do with it?'

'Can't help feeling sorry for the Eyeties,' said Lily shortly, putting on the kettle. 'I've never been able to feel the same way over them as I feel over the Nazis.'

'What's the other option? It'll make it easier for the Allied soldiers who'll be doing the ground fighting if there's less resistance. We've got to isolate Germany and throw the lot at them when we do.'

Lily said quietly, 'You've gone hard.'

Daisy's face set. 'The Jerries killed my husband, and thousands of other sailors have gone to the bottom of the sea!' She paused, sighed. 'Anyway, I thought you'd be more concerned about Matt than the enemy. Think how you'd feel if it was him or my nephew here who'd been killed in the air raids.' She smiled down at Paul who was lifting the blanket in the air with his feet. Tickling him under the chin she said, 'Where's our May, by the way? She sent me a note.'

'Did she?' Lily stared in surprise. 'Why on earth would she do that?'

'She thinks you need taking out of yourself, and to all appearances she's probably right.' Her eyes passed over Lily and she shook her head. 'You're looking drab. When did you last go anywhere? And I don't mean queuing up at the fish shop or taking the baby to the park.'

Lily shrugged. 'Don't talk to me about the park! You can't walk a hundred yards without falling over a Yank from Burtonwood snogging in the grass with some girl. Anyway, I don't want to go out. I'm quite happy as I am.'

Daisy looked disbelieving. 'We all need a change some time or other. Anyway, you're going out whether you like it or not. There's a tea dance at Reece's this afternoon. You're coming with me.'

Lily shook her head. 'I don't dance.'

'You can just drink tea and eat a cake then, but you'll be out, doing something different.' Daisy smiled and shooed her in the direction of the lobby.

'But—' began Lily.

'Don't argue with me. Go and have a good soak, shampoo your hair, find a pretty dress.'

'I've got no shampoo. There's a war on, you know,' she said impatiently.

'I thought you'd make excuses.' Daisy opened her capacious shoulder bag and handed a brown paper parcel to her.

'What is it?'

Daisy raised her pencilled eyebrows and fluttered her Cherry-Blossom-boot-polish-in-place-of-mascara eyelashes. 'Go and find out!' She pushed her again. 'I'll mind the baby and the shop.'

Lily gave in and ran upstairs, clutching the parcel to her breast. She put it on her bed, tore a hole in it and brought out a block of Lux toilet soap. She could not believe it. Her sister certainly hadn't pinched this from supplies. She cradled it in her hand almost reverently and sniffed its delicate perfume, remembering how the adverts said Jessie Matthews used Lux toilet soap. She rummaged some more in the parcel to find Amani shampoo, bath salts, a face flannel and a pair of sheer nylons, not black so not naval issue. Her fingers stilled. Her sister must have got the stockings from a Yank. Should she use them? She glanced down at the white ankle socks lack of coupons and shortage of stockings had driven her to wearing when she didn't use leg tan, and made her decision. It had been kind of Daisy to give her all these goodies.

Lily opened the wardrobe and riffled through the garments hanging there. Most of her coupons went on buying wool or baby clothes because she enjoyed Paul looking and smelling nice and fresh, and besides he was growing so quickly. She found the crêpe-de-chîne dresses which had been part of her trousseau. An enormous sob swelled inside, her body began to shake and she burst into tears.

How long she lay on the bed crying she had no idea, but by the time the emotional storm had passed, her face was blotchy but she was feeling a lot better. She ran a bath and enjoyed pampering herself. She even pushed back her cuticles and filed her nails before smoothing Pond's vanishing cream on her hands, not wanting to ladder the stockings first time on. She dressed in one of the floral dresses, pleased that it still fitted, and felt a sense of shock on gazing at her reflection. She looked much younger than yesterday and for the first time in a long while she did not feel her thirty-one years.

After the barest of hesitations, from a drawer she took a small photograph album and opened it. Slowly she turned the pages showing pictures of her and Matt on their wedding day. She had not possessed the courage to do this for a long time but today she felt strong enough to cope with the sight of their happy faces. Please God, bring him home, she prayed before closing the book.

Matt's image was clear in Lily's mind as she went downstairs. Daisy wolf-whistled as she entered the kitchen. 'If Matt could see you now his tongue would be hanging out.'

'Let's hope it will when he comes home,' she said cheerfully.

'That's the spirit, Lil.' Daisy smiled as she placed a copy of *Woman* on the table. 'What are we going to do with the baby? I thought our May would be here by now.'

Lily glanced at the clock. 'Not for another couple of hours, but Mrs Draper will probably have him till she arrives.'

'Let's drop him off then and be on our way.'

Lily glanced about the huge ballroom with its long beautifully draped windows overlooking Clayton Square where the flower girls still managed to sell their wares. The room was three storeys up. On the floor below was Reece's restaurant and below that the shop that sold meat, fruit, bread, cakes, all sorts of food. Next door was Owen Owens where she had bought her wedding dress. Her eyes took in the white linen-covered tables with all sorts of fancy cakes and then the band playing at the other side of the room. Her toes tapped out a tune despite her having second thoughts about being there. She had never seen so many men in uniform except in a Pathé newsreel and wondered what Matt would think if he knew she was here. There were some civilians whom she knew had paid half a crown to come in. Service personnel got in cheaper.

'May I have this dance?' The naval rating appeared in front of her as if by magic. He was neither tall, dark or handsome nor very young but his expression was hopeful.

'I don't dance very—' she began.

Daisy trod on her foot and smiled at the seaman. 'She's been ill, so you'll have to go easy with her, sailor.' She forced her sister off her chair and on to her feet.

Lily had no option but to go with him as he pulled her into his arms to join the dancing throng circling the floor to a Glenn Miller number. She sought for something to say but the next moment she had forgotten her partner because, as she glanced over his shoulder in Daisy's direction, she saw a man in RAF uniform stopping in front of her sister. There was something about his stance that made her wonder. But it couldn't be, she told herself. What were the odds of Rob's being here on the very day she was here for the first time? Besides this kind of thing surely wasn't his cup of tea? She tried to catch a glimpse of the man's face as her sister stood up but as her partner swirled her around, she lost sight of them.

For the rest of the dance Lily's mind was only half on what her partner was saying as she tried to catch sight of Daisy. The music came to an end. Her partner inclined his head but did not ask for another dance or offer to escort her back to her place. And who could blame him? she thought as she made her way to her table.

Daisy was not there and it suddenly struck Lily that if she stayed at the table, and the man was Rob, he would recognise her and might be tempted to interfere in her life again. Before she had a chance to worry overmuch, a Canadian airman asked her for the next waltz. She accepted with alacrity and was soon part of the swirling scene again. This time she tried to concentrate on what her partner was saying. He told her he came from Ottawa and talked of his family back home. He seemed quite happy for her just to listen and her mind drifted as her eyes scanned passing couples. When the music stopped, he asked her to dance again and she accepted.

Two dances later and Lily had heard enough about Canada and its beautiful scenery and made the excuse she had to powder her nose. It was on the way back from the

Ladies that she bumped into her sister. She seemed to be in another world. Her eyes were sparkly and she was humming a tune to herself.

'Who was that you were with?' said Lily, steadying her.

'Which who?' said Daisy.

'The first RAF officer who?'

'The Aussie? He didn't give his name. They don't always. They're just whiling away the hours at this kind of dance. He was a bit of a dead loss actually. He trod on my foot and kept looking over my shoulder and didn't listen to a word . . .' She stopped abruptly. 'Why d'you ask? It wasn't . . .?'

'Of course not!' She knew immediately she had spoken too quickly and added in a lilting voice, 'I'm just neurotic about Aussies in blue uniforms. Tell me instead who's made your eyes sparkle and put a song in your heart?'

'Another airman who suggested the most outrageous things in a deadpan way. He's asked me out this evening but I said I couldn't go because I'm with my sister. He said he had a mate. I said you were married. He said so was his mate. So I said—'

Lily interrupted her. 'You go without me.'

Differing emotions warred with each other on Daisy's expressive face. 'Are you sure, Lil? I did plan on us making an evening of it.'

'I'm sure.' She smiled. 'I feel heaps better and I appreciate the thought behind all this.' Her waving hand encompassed the dancing couples, the noisy chat and the swinging musicians. 'But I think I'll go home now.'

Daisy could not conceal her relief. 'Our May'll be wanting to hear all about it anyway. It was partly her idea.'

'I'll tell her all about it. You go back to your man.' She squeezed her sister's arm and left.

Lily did not immediately go home. She walked up past the site on the corner of Clayton Square and Church Street where she and May had come not long after Paul's birth to see a Halifax bomber assembled during 'Wings for Victory' week. There had been crowds in Liverpool that week. The streets were still crowded. Some came from Wales and other places like sightseers to look at the devastation Hitler had caused to the main shopping area. It made Lily sad, so she caught a tram which stopped at the Victoria monument. She remembered how she and Matt had changed trams there when searching for his aunt. By some miracle the monument had survived unscathed, a landmark for all to see amidst the expanse of ruin. Rule Britannia! she thought wryly. Yet somehow it was symbolic that the bronze Victoria was still there. Her spirits lifted. T. J. Hughes and other shops and stores which had suffered bomb or fire damage were still operating, and even Lewis's was back in business. Hitler had failed.

She felt more her old optimistic self as she stood watching a ferry boat carrying goods from a cargo ship across the choppy water, and would have enjoyed a walk along the Prince's landing stage to have a closer look at the ships but most of it was fenced off and barred to all except those with legitimate business.

She walked past the Riverside station and noticed what looked like aeroplane parts being loaded on to lorries

further along the dock road. They were probably for the
aircraft factory at Speke. She took several lungfuls of salty
air, crossed the road, passing under the overhead railway,
and had a look at the ruined sailors' church. The diocese
had suffered the loss of several churches, as well as Church
House with its records and thousands of valuable books.
She thought of Matt and how he had thrown himself into
his work in Liverpool, and wondered if he did return,
whether he would stay. It was a question she had no
answer to.

Once more she gazed in the direction of the river and
breathed deeply of the sea air before looking up at the
Liver birds.

'It's all right, girl! They're still there,' said a gruff
voice.

She looked round at an elderly, grey-haired gentleman
leaning on a stick. A flush darkened her cheeks but she
smiled. 'How did you know I was checking?'

'Because us Liverpudlians think the same. While they
fly high, there'll always be life in the city.'

She nodded. 'I think you're right. It would have been
a morale crusher if Hitler had knocked them off their
perch.'

The old man chuckled deep in his throat. 'But we saw
those black eagles of his off. They won't return now.'

Lily murmured that she was sure he was right and said
tarrah before catching the tram home.

She had barely got through the kitchen door when May
started up, a book slipping from her knee, and said in a
voice that quivered, 'You've had a visitor.'

Lily stilled as their gazes caught. 'Was it Rob?'

May's expression was stormy and she did not ask how Lily knew. 'I wouldn't let him in the house! I told him he was a slimy toad trying to ruin your and Matt's marriage!'

'I bet he didn't like that.'

Her sister's eyes glinted. 'You can say that again.' She got to her feet, folding her arms across her chest. 'Then he had the cheek to say he was surprised to hear me speak like that! That he'd always thought I liked him. I told him we all make mistakes and to get lost.' Her eyes gazed unfocused across the room.

'Did you tell him that Matt wasn't here and about the baby?' Lily had to ask the question three times before May's gaze switched to her face.

'What?'

Lily repeated the question.

'I told him Matt had probably joined the Australian Army as a chaplain but we didn't know where he was because it was all hush-hush. I doubt we'll see Rob here again.'

Lily was not so sure but she kept her thoughts to herself and asked if Paul had been any trouble. May shook her head and asked whether she'd had a good time. Lily sat opposite her and began to tell her all about her outing.

'It's done you good,' said May warmly. 'I'm glad I thought of getting in touch with our Dais. But fancy you thinking Rob was there. He's not exactly a tea dance man, would you say?'

'Men can be full of surprises,' said Lily drily, getting to her feet as she suddenly heard the lowing of a cow. 'Did you do the second milking, by the way?'

May put a hand to her mouth, seized an apron and fled down the yard. Lily checked Paul was all right, rid herself of her fine feathers, and followed her sister.

Several weeks later Lily received a flimsy blue envelope. She squinted at the postmark but could not make it out. Her hands shook as she carefully opened it, not wanting to accidentally rip the paper. Relief flooded her as she caught sight of the words 'God bless you, Matt'. Then her heart sank as she took in the lack of that word 'love'. She flattened the single page out on the table, looked for a date but there was none – was that for security reasons also? She began to read.

Dear Lily,

I don't know what to say. Your letter was so brief. I suppose I shouldn't complain but I feel like a man starved. I couldn't think what to write that first time beyond that single word SORRY. My feelings were all mixed up and I didn't know what to say. I still had a lot of anger in me during the weeks after I left you. I kept wishing I'd strangled Rob Fraser instead of throwing him out of the house. So much for turning the other cheek and forgiving your brother seventy times seven. Primitive man still lives!

As you can guess I have had time to think out here. Where's here? If I told you the censors would cut it out, so suffice to say I've been here before and you worried in case I was gobbled up. My being here makes me believe that maybe those years we spent

apart were for a purpose after all. I love you. Never
forget that.

God bless you,
Matt

She reread the words greedily, realising he must have only
received her first letter because there was no mention of
Paul. The words of love reassured her. There was the
chance of a fresh start, of their being happy again if he
returned safe from the war. If, if! Where was Matt's war
being fought? Her eyes scanned the words: 'I've been
here before and you worried in case I was gobbled up.'

'New Guinea!' she said aloud, and that gut-gripping
fear which she had experienced during the blitz seized
hold of her and she could not think straight for a moment.
Then from the recesses of her mind she recalled reading
in the newspaper of American bombers destroying over a
hundred Japanese planes on airfields on the island. At
least the Aussies were not alone and Matt knew the terrain.

She felt more hopeful. The tide of war was turning.
Italy had surrendered and had declared war on Germany.
Daisy's airman boyfriend, who had been drafted south,
had flown bombing ops over Berlin, and Daisy was
convinced the Battle of the Atlantic was being won. Due,
she said proudly, to the work of Western Approaches
Command in Liverpool and Captain Johnny Walker who
operated out of Gladstone Dock, Bootle, with his flotilla
of 'chicks', as he called the sloops, named after birds,
under his command. He was relentless in his search for

U-boats, said Daisy. There was also talk of an army gathering for the invasion of Western Europe but most believed that would not happen until spring. The beginning of the end was in sight.

Lily read Matt's letter once more and was reminded of Rob's visit. Why had he come? Couldn't he let things go? Knowing him as she did, she guessed he would have hated Matt getting the upper hand. Hopefully, though, he would take May's words to heart and stay out of their lives. Casting him out of her mind, she went in search of pen, ink and paper to write to Matt.

# Chapter Twenty-One

'Lil, are you coming?' Daisy's impatient tones echoed upstairs. 'This son of yours is getting out of hand.'

'Coming!' she called, taking some money out of the cocoa tin under the bed, some of which she had taken out of Martin's bank. She thought of Matt now and sent up a prayer, trying not to worry. The Allies might be making big advances out East and in Europe, but she had no idea where Matt was since the declaration that victory was certain in New Guinea. Men could be blown apart or knived up to the last minute in a war or die of tropical diseases far from medical help. She would not be able to relax completely until he came home, but in the meantime she wanted to carry on with her life as peacefully as possible. Daisy had a day off and May had arranged some free time so they could go into town together. The singer Vera Lynn, whose grandmother came from Bootle, was said to be visiting the VI exhibition at T. J. Hughes and they were hoping to catch sight of the 'Forces' Sweetheart'.

She heard the kitchen door open and May speaking, then the sound of Daisy's sharp tones. She hoped the next few hours were not going to be difficult with the pair of them bickering. Daisy had been moody since her hero Captain Johnny Walker had died in the naval hospital last year from overwork, but she had been far worse since her RAF boyfriend had been shot down over Germany a month ago. For weeks her face had worn a blank expression as if she could not believe what had happened, but that had passed and anger with anything and everybody had followed.

Lily hurried downstairs to find Paul, who would be two in a month or so, paddling with his hands in the coal dust at the bottom of the scuttle while her sisters sat staring sullenly at each other. She leaned over and grabbed him by the wrists, holding him at a distance. 'What are the pair of you thinking of, letting him do this? We'll never get to see Vera Lynn the way things are going!'

'It's not my fault you weren't ready.' Daisy shrugged and fiddled with the strap of her shoulder bag. 'Anyway, who cares about seeing her?' She swung her leg back and forth. 'Her with her songs about love ever after and stupid bluebirds! You don't get bluebirds over cliffs, only seagulls screeching.'

'Never mind the bluebirds,' snapped May. 'Tell our Lily what you've just screeched at me!'

Crimson flooded Daisy's face. 'I shouldn't have told you! But you made me lose my temper going on about Aunt Dora and Dermot living in Ireland like two elderly lovebirds. There's no happy ever after in this world!'

'What is all this?' demanded Lily, wondering if it was going to be one of those days. She manoeuvred her son over to the sink, trying to keep his hands from touching her clothes. She stared at Daisy waiting for her to say something, saw her swallow as if it was a struggle to get the words out.

The shop door bell jangled. 'Go and see who that is, May,' said Lily, running water into a bowl and hoisting Paul up to the sink by his hands.

Daisy said, 'I'll go. You tell her, May.' With a mixture of relief and apprehension on her face, she shot out of the kitchen.

May closed the door after her and leaned against it. 'She's having a baby.' She barely paused before adding, 'Doesn't it seem utterly unfair? There's Vera desperate to have one and our Daisy frantic because she is.'

'Oh, my God!' Lily nearly dropped Paul, who was balancing on her raised knee at the sink. 'What are we going to do? We'll have to help her!'

'You mean help her get rid of it?' said May, her forehead creased in thought as she reached for a towel and came over to the sink. 'Jean McGuire once said you could do something with a knitting needle up—'

'No! I didn't mean that!' Lily shuddered at the thought. 'Besides, she mightn't want to get rid of it if she loved the bloke. It's all she's got to remember him by.'

'She said she didn't love him – said nobody could replace her Ted.'

Lily sighed. 'Isn't it strange the way people fall in love? Anyway, it's going to be her decision.'

May nodded. 'I told her you'd be OK about it but she was worried sick about telling you.'

'She was? Am I such an ogre?' Lily screwed up her face in disbelief, then remembered how apprehensive she had been about telling Matt about Rob.

At that moment the door opened but it was not Daisy who entered. The sisters stared at the man standing there.

'Hello, Lil,' said Rob. He gave May a brief nod. She flushed.

As for Lily, she just managed to bite back a 'What the hell are you doing here?' because she realised in time just how wretched he looked. 'What's happened?'

'One of my brothers has been killed,' he said forlornly.

She forced Daisy's problem to the back of her mind and without thinking switched into role of carer. 'Oh, I am sorry, Rob. Sit down. I presume it was your youngest brother? The one in the army.'

He shook his head as he lowered himself into a chair. 'It was Doug that told me about it. I could understand if it had been him, but it was my eldest brother.'

'What happened?' said May, moving closer to him.

Rob blew out a long breath and clasped his hands between his knees. 'There was a riot in a prisoner-of-war camp outside Cowra in New South Wales. The Japs attacked the guards. Most were killed or captured in the compound but some managed to escape.' He sighed again. 'They were eventually hunted down but not before one slit Gordon's throat.'

'How terrible,' whispered Lily, feeling a catch at her heart. 'Your poor mother!'

Rob nodded. 'It happened last August but it was played down for fear of reprisals from the Japs on our men in their camps. The family kept it from me and Doug, reckoning we had enough to cope with, but Doug was invalided home after being wounded in the Philippines and thought I should know.'

'I really am sorry.' Lily's eyes were sympathetic. 'I can guess how you feel. Matt and I saw enough of it here on the home front during the blitz. It seemed terribly wrong. Somehow much worse than if it had been on what we think of as a real battlefield.'

He nodded and cleared his throat. 'May told me he joined up.'

'Yes. Last heard of in New Guinea,' she said brightly.

'That's rough, but at least he'll know his way about some.' Rob smiled feebly. 'I'd have been here straight away if I'd known. Although he warned me away, no messing!'

'He meant it,' she said quietly. 'In one of his letters he spoke of strangling you. Why have you come back, Rob? Surely it wasn't just to tell us about your brother?'

His sombre eyes met hers. 'I could say it was because Matt packs quite a punch and I'd like to get my own back, but it wouldn't be true. I've changed. And besides, there's this bloke here.' Rob nodded in Paul's direction. The child was staring at him from wide, heavily fringed blue eyes as he perched on Lily's knee. 'I guess it was because I was homesick and your family is the closest to one I've got here, despite everything that went wrong between us. Anyway, I needed a bit of feminine company – I don't mean I wanted a woman,' he added hastily. 'I mean . . .'

'You wanted a listening ear or a shoulder to cry on?' She smiled, not quite believing him.

'Men don't cry,' drawled May, her hand on the back of Rob's chair. 'He wants a hug.'

He glanced over his shoulder at her, his eyes narrowing. 'I take it you're not offering after what you said to me last time?'

'You said I was just a kid and didn't understand.'

'My mistake.'

Lily stared at them and decided to change the subject. 'What are you doing now, Rob? I thought you must have moved on with not seeing you.'

'I've got a weekend off but I'm with Coastal Command. Our job's drawing to an end.' His eyes were still on May. 'The war should be over soon.'

Lily stood up, deciding it was time to get going. 'I hope so. We were going into town. Perhaps you'd like to come with us?' she said politely.

He rose to his feet and gave a ghost of a smile. 'You're hoping I'll say no.'

Lily thought, he still possesses a dangerous charm. 'You always did think you could read my mind,' she said lightly.

He pulled on his cap. 'I'll walk with you both to the tram stop.'

'OK.' She handed Paul over to May and remembered Daisy. 'I wonder what's happened to Daisy?'

'You mean the woman who came out of here earlier?' said Rob. They nodded. 'She went out.'

Figures, thought Lily, groaning inwardly. Would she be back soon or what? She'd give her five minutes to return and if she didn't she'd leave without her. 'You go ahead,' she said to May and Rob. 'I'll catch you up.'

They left and Lily stood a moment, her hand on the shop door, trying not to think about what Rob had said about the Japs, and worrying about Daisy. She waited ten minutes but there was no sign of her sister so she followed the other two.

Lily never did get to see Vera Lynn. Rob pressurised them into having lunch with him at a Kardomah and after saying goodbye to him, they had to rush round the shops to be back in time for milking. May said that she would be going out that evening and did Lily mind? She wondered why she asked but did not think about it overmuch, instead pondering on how far gone Daisy was in her pregnancy and what her plans were. She had an idea what to do with the baby herself but so much depended on the rest of the family.

Over the next few days Lily stayed close to the dairy, wishing Daisy would call, but there was no sign of her sister so she hoped to see her at the farm, as Vera had asked them all to Sunday lunch.

'I think I'll give the family a miss,' said May on the Sunday morning as she smoothed glycerine over her hands. 'I see them every day and I get tired of that journey. I'll feed the lodger and take it easy.'

'OK,' said Lily, her mind on Daisy's problem.

When she arrived at the farm there was no sign of her sister.

'Perhaps duty called at the last moment?' said Ben, smiling as he balanced himself before hoisting a chuckling Paul up on to his shoulders.

Lily shook her head. 'I don't think it's that. May said she's scared to face me, the stupid ninny!'

'Why?' asked Ben as they went inside the house.

'Because she's having a baby and left our May to tell me!'

He let out a low whistle. 'That flying bloke, was it?'

'It seems like it.' She frowned. 'I'm just praying she hasn't done anything stupid. I've heard some of these backstreet women are sheer murder! I had thought that maybe if she agrees and you—' She hesitated and glanced at Ben. It was not so easy speaking her thoughts when it actually came down to it.

'You thought what?'

She plunged straight in. 'That she could have the baby and you and Vera could adopt it. You want children and—'

He shook his head at her, his eyes smiling. 'Vera's having a baby. It's just been confirmed.'

'But I thought . . .' Lily put a hand to her mouth and groaned.

He laughed. 'I can guess what you thought but it was just a matter of time and things getting working again. Sorry, Lil, you'll have to let Daisy do her own sorting out. I know it's difficult for you to get out of the habit of looking after us but we're all grown up now. She'll come up with something.'

She nodded and reaching up, kissed him. 'Congratulations. Let's hope more things will go our way now.'

He agreed and no more was said about Daisy.

Lily arrived home to discover May was out again. After putting Paul to bed she felt lonely despite the presence of the lodger. She longed for Matt. He was the someone she wanted to talk to most about Daisy and May and life's problems. He would listen and understand. From his letters he accepted her the way she was, loved her the way she was. You're a carer, Lily, he had said, and you didn't stop caring because circumstances changed. She had been jealous of that caring aspect of his nature in the past and of his commitment to God and others, but she accepted it now. It was what made him the man she had fallen in love with. It did not matter that he was not six feet tall, handsome as a Greek god, or physically fit as Tarzan. He was her man. All she needed was for the war to end and for him to come home.

But the war lingered on, although the news was full of the German retreat across the Rhine and of more American successes against the Japanese.

The danger from air raids was past and fire watching was abolished in Britain when at last Daisy came to call.

'Where have you been?' demanded Lily, pouncing on her sister as she came through the shop door. 'How are you? I've been so worried.'

'I'm fed up!' Her face was all dragged down as she dropped against the counter. 'I've had hot baths, drank a couple of bottles of gin, taken so-called magical potions from a chemist – but it's still there! I don't know what to do next.'

Lily was not going to mention backstreet abortion if her sister wasn't. 'It looks like it wants to live,' she murmured.

Daisy gazed at Paul, sitting on the floor playing with a couple of old Dinky cars which had belonged to Ronnie.

'Paul's got Matt's lovely eyes.' She sighed. 'It's not that I hate the idea of having a baby, but what'll I do for money, Lil?'

'We'll help out. I've still got Paul's baby clothes. Although it might be a girl. And you can come and live with us,' she said firmly.

Daisy pulled a face. 'It's all right for you to say that but what about Matt when he comes home? He might cast me out.'

'He won't!' She was warmed by that 'when' not 'if'.

'You don't know,' said Daisy soberly, toying with the milk ladle. 'He'll probably want you all to himself.'

'You're forgetting the lodger and May.'

'I'm not.' She hesitated. 'But have you given thought to your having to leave the dairy? What if Matt wants to live in Australia? And what if he doesn't, but decides to stay over here? He'll want his own parish eventually, won't he? You'll have to go where he goes.'

Lily had thought of these things but only in passing because stupidly, superstitiously, she had not wanted to consider the future too much in case the one she envisaged did not come to pass. 'There's no reason why you can't stay here once the navy give you the boot.' She smiled. 'Things are changing with the Milk Marketing Board. You and our May can get rid of the cows and just buy in milk to sell.'

'Me and our May do that?' Daisy laughed. 'You must be joking! Anyway I wouldn't be surprised if wedding bells rang for our May. I saw her in town the other night with a fella.'

Lily stilled. 'What was he like?'

'I didn't get a proper look but he was in uniform.' Her mouth set. 'Another RAF bloke. But I can't see our May giving in like I did. I should have stuck with the Senior Service, Lil.'

'No guarantee of abstinence there, I would have thought,' said Lily lightly, hoping she was wrong in her guess about the RAF bloke. 'Anyway, come in and have a cuppa.' She scooped Paul up off the floor. He let out a wail as he dropped a car. Daisy picked it up and they went inside.

Lily had no sooner put the kettle on and was spreading jam on bread when the doorbell jangled.

'I'll go,' said her sister.

Daisy was away some time but when she came back, her mouth had lost its dissatisfied droop.

'It was Frank!' she said, standing in front of Lily, her hands clasped in front of her. 'His mother's died in Rainhill Asylum and it's knocked him sideways! I told him it was a blessing and he agrees, but you know what he said that really touched my heart, Lil?' She paused for effect. '"I'm really alone now, Daisy. I've got no one." I told him I knew just how he felt and I've offered to keep him company while he makes all the arrangements. I think he still loves me because he jumped at the offer. You don't mind, do you, Lil?'

'Be gentle with him,' said Lily, trying to keep the tremor out of her voice. 'And don't be too cheerful. We mightn't have loved his mother, poor soul, but he did!'

'Yes, Lil.' A smile lit Daisy's eyes. 'I've been longing to see what lies beyond the shop and in that flat upstairs

for years.' She swung her bag over her shoulder, put her
hat on at a jaunty angle and departed.

Daisy married Frank in a quiet ceremony a few days after
President Roosevelt died. It seemed so sad to Lily that
the president had not lived to see the end of the war
because he had been a good friend to Britain. Daisy had
a wedding cake made richer from dried fruit donated from
her local NAAFI and sewed together a goodly number of
opened-up naval uniform scarves to make herself a
nightdress.

Aunt Dora and Dermot came over from Ireland. The
family had considered it only right that their oldest living
member should be at the wedding.

'A much more sensible match this time,' said Dora,
the feather in her crimson hat nodding in the breeze as
they stood outside church. 'Although if I'm not mistaken
Daisy's put on weight.'

'You're getting more tactful in your old age,' said Lily,
smiling. 'And, yes, she will be leaving the Wrens on
medical grounds.'

'I take it that it's not his?' Dora placed a hand through
her arm.

Lily's eyes widened. 'Why should you think that?'

'Because he hasn't got it in him, girl! But he'll make
a good husband and father. Can't see him straying like
that other one would have . . . although I shouldn't speak
ill of the dead. He died like many another before his time,
poor boy.' Without drawing breath she added, 'Any news
of Matt?'

Lily shook her head. 'I just live in hope and tell myself no news is good news, not that it really helps – but I try not to let my imagination run away with me.'

'His son's growing into a fine lad,' said Dora, looking towards where Josie and Joe were swinging Paul by the arms out of the way of the photographer. 'And that reminds me.' She fumbled in her black handbag and pulled out an envelope and handed it to Lily. 'If you can find anything worth having in the shops, get him something for the birthday I missed.'

'Thanks. It's kind of you.' Lily kissed her aunt's cheek.

'Don't have to make a fuss,' said Dora gruffly, patting her arm. 'Tell me, what's May up to now? I wrote and asked would she like to come and stay with us in Ireland for a holiday, but she said she didn't want to be out of Liverpool at the moment. She hasn't got a young man on the scene, has she?'

'I don't know about young,' murmured Lily, her eyes resting on May who was wearing a three-year-old blue organdie dress trimmed with a bandage frill to lengthen it. She was talking in a desultory fashion to Ronnie as they waited for the bride and groom to make a move. They were honeymooning in Blackpool and would be leaving straight after the wedding breadkfast which Ben had paid for. 'If he's who I think he is,' said Lily, 'then he's just past thirty.'

Dora glanced round. 'He's not here, though?'

'She's keeping him quiet. There's a couple more years before she's twenty-one and perhaps she thinks I won't approve.'

'Some girls are better with an older man. Surely you wouldn't prevent her from marrying him on the grounds of age? Thirty's not that old!'

'I'm not sure what I'd do,' said Lily, wondering what Matt would make of it all. 'Anyway it hasn't come up so let's not worry about it.' She smiled and changed the subject.

Life resumed a quieter pattern after the wedding, although Lily was conscious of an awkwardness growing between her and May which she found herself unable to do anything about. She had started to look forward, and with her own words ringing in her ears, asked Ben to take her cows back to the farm and requested that Ronnie deliver milk in churns to the dairy. Her brothers agreed with her foresight and bought her a bottling machine but she and May had to put all the cardboard tops on by hand. Then her sister declared there was no longer any need for her to be at the dairy and began to stay nights at the farm. Lily missed her and wished she could be open but felt unable herself to bring Rob's name up in conversation. After all, she was only going on a hunch and could be mistaken.

As each week passed an almost tangible feeling of expectancy grew in the air as news of the Allied advances across Germany was broadcast on wireless, in the Pathé news and on front pages. At the beginning of May came the news that Hitler had committed suicide and within days Germany had unconditionally surrendered.

Ronnie and May came rushing into the dairy the day peace was declared in Europe and suddenly May was her old self.

'Let's all go into town. I want to be with people!' She turned shining eyes on Lily. 'Paul has to go, Lil. This is a day he should remember all his life. We can take turns carrying him when his little legs can't keep up.'

When they reached Lime Street there were masses of people gathered there. The weather was damp and drizzly and Lily felt there were plenty like herself pleased that some of the fighting was over, but complete peace had not come yet and they wouldn't be happy until it happened in the Far East. Even so it was good to be with the crowd. Ronnie hoisted Paul on to his shoulders and somehow they managed to make their way on to St George's Plateau within touching distance of the cenotaph erected after the Great War. There were tears in Lily's eyes as she glanced at it. She could not help thinking about her father and all those men killed in both wars . . . and could not get Matt out of her mind as people cheered, sang and waved Union Jacks.

'Remember,' said May, gripping Lily's hand, 'us coming here to see the King and Queen before the war? We went shopping and you bought me shoes for your wedding.'

'Of course I remember,' said Lily, the tears rolling down her cheeks.

May squeezed her hand tightly and said no more. Lily was relieved because she felt if her sister had carried on in that vein she would have broken her heart crying.

They all went back to the farm together and Ben brought out one of the bottles of champagne which he said had been hidden away in Uncle William's cellar with a label on it saying, 'Not to be opened until the end of the war'. 'Probably been there since the beginning of it,' he added, squinting at the label. He filled the glasses bought during the year of the King's Coronation and lifted his. 'To all who have suffered and fought for the victory in Europe – and to Matt's return when we'll crack open the other bottle.' They all looked at Lily and she could see their thoughts. She smiled, drained her glass of its sparkling wine, and then with Paul's hand in hers went out into the garden.

She released her son when they got to the orchard and he immediately started jumping to try and reach the lower branch of a tree. The blossom was just opening and suddenly she felt in her blood that tingling which spring had always brought in the past. Her body yearned for Matt so strongly it was a physical pain. She dropped on to the ground and lay on her stomach. 'How much longer, God?' she whispered. 'Please make the Japanese surrender and bring him home soon.'

# Chapter Twenty-Two

In June the Japanese announced the formation of a People's Volunteer Corps, including every able-bodied man, woman and child, to resist invasion. Lily found herself remembering after Dunkirk, Ronnie repeating Churchill's speech about fighting on the streets, and felt for the ordinary people of Japan, especially the women.

In July she read of Australians with bayonets and flame-throwers capturing important ridges in New Guinea, and prayed this was the end of the war there. The Philippines were liberated and the Japanese mainland bombarded by Allied warships. Italy declared war on Japan.

A pale-faced May arrived on a visit and Lily asked if she was sickening for something. 'Someone told me some of our airmen might have to go out East. Do you think they really need them, Lil?'

Guessing the cause of her worry, Lily said, 'I wouldn't have thought so with the Yanks out there.'

May nodded and seemed comforted by what she said, asking if there was any news from Matt. Lily shook her head. 'But my money's still being paid so I'm sure he must be alive.' May hugged her and left.

There was an election and Labour won a landslide victory. Mrs Draper said she hoped this was the beginning of a new age for the working classes, but it all seemed unreal to Lily. All her thoughts were concentrated on the other side of the world.

On 6 August the first atom bomb was dropped on Hiroshima and thousands of people were killed. She remembered the blitz and Matt with a child in his arms. She wept, thinking this had to be the end of the war and soon he would be home. But another bomb was dropped before, on 14 August, the Japanese signed an unconditional surrender.

Liverpool went even wilder on VJ-Day as ships' hooters blew and bells rang. A two-day holiday was declared, flags and bunting decorated the streets and music was relayed from the floodlit Town Hall and St George's Hall. People got up for impromptu dances and Irish jigs. If the war had done anything it had partially destroyed bad housing and there was a bit of a better blend of Irish Catholic and English Protestants. The Chinese district nearer the docks had received a battering too and had needed to move up nearer the Anglican cathedral. There were bonfires, and fireworks over the Mersey. There were prayers of thanks-giving and bands played in the park all day.

Soon afterwards Lily received a letter postmarked Liverpool, NSW, dated the beginning of July. She thought ruefully of all the letters she had sent and here she was getting just one. She opened it eagerly. It was brief. Matt had been suffering from some kind of jungle fever and was in hospital. As soon as he could he would be heading home.

'Your daddy's all right!' she cried, swinging Paul up into her arms. 'He's coming home!'

'Daddy! Daddy!' He bounced in her arms.

'Poor love,' said Lily, hugging him. 'You've no idea really what a daddy is.' She took out the photograph album and showed him, not for the first time, the pictures.

He pressed a stubby finger against Matt's face. 'Daddy!'

'Yes, Daddy,' she said more soberly. Neither of them would be looking so young and radiant as the photograph when they met. Still she could not be downcast and had to tell someone the news.

She met Mrs Draper in the street and told her. 'Wonderful, my dear.' She smiled happily. 'I'm so pleased for you.'

Lily hugged her and went to tell Daisy but could not get an answer. She went to tell David. He was delighted and they thanked God together. Then she and Paul called at the greengrocer's on the corner again and this time found her sister leaning on the wooden-holed containers holding potatoes. 'Daisy, he's alive and coming home!' she cried.

'Great,' groaned Daisy, with a hand to her belly. 'I think my pains have started. I'd best tell Frank. Could you fetch the midwife?'

It seemed incredible to Lily that it should happen at such a moment but she did as asked with a smile on her face.

Her sister gave birth to a girl in the early hours of the next morning. Frank seemed pleased and for the first time Lily realised her sister had trusted him with the truth. 'I don't know how I'd have coped with a boy, Lil,' he said.

'I'd have always been thinking of the father, but this way I can just think of her as Daisy's daughter and I can love them both and maybe have a lad as well.'

'I always knew you were the right man for her,' said Lily, and kissed him affectionately.

When Ronnie came with the milk she told him both pieces of news. 'That's great, Lil! I'll tell the family. You know who'll be next?'

'Vera! I hope all goes well for her, too.'

As Lily served customers and did her housework she could not help thinking that perhaps she and Matt could have another child. She was thirty-three but that wasn't too old. As for Matt he'd be . . . She counted on her fingers. Around forty. The prime of life for some men. All she had to do was wait.

Vera's child was a boy and she and Ben were besotted with him.

'All these people having babies,' May said moodily. 'It makes me sick.'

Lily kept silent although she longed to ask May about her love life. Her sister left without saying much else beyond asking when she thought Matt would be home. 'Any time,' Lily answered.

Now she knew Matt was coming home the waiting seemed more arduous somehow. Maybe it was because every day she was expecting his arrival. The first shipload of prisoners released from the Japanese prisoner-of-war camps arrived and David told her something of their condition. Lily was horrified. He tried to reassure her quickly. 'Matt hasn't been a prisoner.'

'He's been ill, though, with some kind of tropical fever. Getting bitten by horrible insects and swallowing goodness knows what kind of food.' She prepared herself for a Matt she might not recognise, a man who was a shadow of himself.

It was David again who told her when the hospital ship Matt was on was due to dock in Liverpool. 'How do you get to know before other people?' she asked, smiling at him.

He returned her smile. 'We're expected to pass on unpleasant news and prepare people for shocks but that's not so in this case. It was I who enquired about Matt.'

'He is all right, isn't he?' Her face was suddenly drawn with anxiety. 'You're not just pretending?'

'He's fine compared to some of them.' He patted her shoulder. 'I've received permission for you to go aboard and see him for a few minutes before all the men are taken off to various hospitals.'

She thanked him and after he had gone went upstairs to pick out a dress that had lasted the war better than some. She chose one of the faithful flowery crêpe-de-chînes and made her way to the docks where the white ship was berthed. The wind was sharp and heavy with the tang of the sea and it tossed her dark curls into confusion, just as it had that very first day she had set eyes on Matt.

Somehow Lily had expected Matt to be in bed but he was sitting in a chair at a desk in the tiny cabin which the able-bodied seaman showed her to. She paused in the doorway as he looked up. He smiled and she wanted to cry but smiled instead and went into his arms. She buried her face against his scrawny neck, all the better to conceal the shock she felt. He was nowhere near skeletal but he had lost weight, his skin was more yellow than brown, even the whites of his eyes were yellow. It seemed a long time since they had been young and full of life. How did they pick all that up again? She with her idiotic thoughts of them conceiving a baby as soon as he was home. He didn't look like he could. And yet the arms holding her had a strength that belied his appearance. Still he would need building up, rest and nothing to trouble him. She would keep quiet about her suspicions about May and Rob.

'Are you all right?' she said in a muffled voice.

'I'm fine. You feel thinner, though.'

She laughed, close to tears. 'Look who's talking, skinny melink!'

'What's a melink?' There was a smile in his voice.

'*I* don't know. It's just something we say in Liverpool. Are they going to take you away for long to this hospital, and how far is it?'

'They're not taking me away at all. I'm going to a hospital in Liverpool just for tests. I've been informed the port has the best facilities for tropical diseases in the country. I should be home in a few days and then we can have a proper talk.'

'Good.' She rubbed her cheek against his. All the questions could wait until he got home.

May called that evening and Lily told her about seeing Matt.

'So he's arrived.' May ran a finger round the brim of her teacup. 'Do you think he'll be staying in Liverpool or will he go back to Australia?'

'I told you we haven't discussed anything! At the moment I don't want Matt upset,' she said in a pleading voice. 'I thought you'd be pleased he was home. You used to like him in the old days.'

'I do like him and I am glad he's safe!' said May indignantly. 'It's just that—'

'What?' Lily flashed her a challenging look. 'Rob, is it?'

May stared at her. 'How did you know?'

'So I'm right.' Her smile was taut. 'It was the way you looked at each other and the way you spoke that day he came – and you've been so secretive about this fella you've been going out with – and Daisy saw you with a chap in a blue RAF uniform.'

May's mouth drooped. 'Matt's not going to like it, is he?'

'I don't like it! Rob's a good few years older than you and he's devious.'

'I love him and he loves me!'

'Has he said so?' She was remembering Rob saying he loved her and wondered whether he could be trusted to cherish her beloved sister.

'Of course! He'll be going back to Australia soon.' She put down her cup. 'He wants me to marry him. I told him I need your permission.'

'So you do,' said Lily lightly. There was a silence while she digested this. 'How that must rankle with Rob,' she murmured.

'I said I'd probably be able to persuade you but he thought you'd say no because of Matt,' said May, playing with her fingers and not looking at Lily. 'He thinks Matt will put a spoke in our wheel.'

'Does he now?' Lily grinned, thinking of the pain Rob had caused. 'Well, he'll have to wait and see, won't he? Because I'm not going to bother Matt about it right now.'

May looked dismayed and started up from her chair. 'Damn it, Lil, you couldn't be so mean! I told you, Rob's going back soon and I want to go with him as his wife.'

'I've said my piece,' said Lily. 'You'll have to wait.' And she swept out of the kitchen.

Lily took Paul with her to fetch Matt home. Her heart was beating heavily as she gazed out of the tram window at the rows of drab houses and shops with gaps in them like missing teeth. The long weary years of war showed on some faces but others looked cheerful. She smiled herself, anticipating the moment when her son and husband would confront each other for the first time. Did Matt believe Paul was his son? He had never mentioned not doing so in his letters, just relief that they were both well. She supposed it was possible not to allow oneself to feel real emotion about someone just from a photograph. The test would be when they saw each other face to face.

'You've got your grandfather's chin, Paul,' stated Matt as he knelt on one knee in the entrance of the hospital, holding his son at arm's length.

Lily smiled with relief. 'He's got your eyes and your hair.'

'What he needs is Brylcreem.' Matt made an attempt to flatten the tuft of hair that stuck up. 'Remember, Lil, how when we talked about us being married and your travelling around Australia with me, we never took into consideration what would happen if we had a child.'

'I never thought about it at the time,' she murmured. 'It wouldn't have been much of a life dragging a baby from pillar to post in the heat or the storms, would it?'

'Not a baby,' said Matt seriously. 'It wasn't so bad for me with Dad for part of the year when I was older, but not as a way of life for a family.'

Paul, who had been silently staring at his father with his chin stuck out pugnaciously while he still stroked his hair, wriggled beneath his hand. 'It won't stay down, Daddy. Mammy says it's a waste of time trying.'

Matt stared at him, then grinned. 'Daddy! I think I've made a breakthrough, Lil.' He caught Paul up in his arms and lifted him on to his shoulders before walking out of the hospital.

Lily hurried after him. 'Do you think you should be carrying him? Let's find a taxi. You haven't been well. You might . . .'

Matt gazed down at her and his eyes were a clear serene grey. 'Don't fuss, Lil. I'm a grown man. This is my son and I want to carry him home. If he starts feeling too heavy, I'll put him down and we'll catch a tram.'

She fell into step beside him. 'Did you ever really doubt he was your son?' Her voice was low. 'After what you said that last evening . . .'

'I doubted it as much as you believed I could have fathered Abby's child.'

Ouch! she thought. 'I don't think I ever really believed it deep down,' she murmured. 'I was just hurting so much I wanted you to hurt equally as badly. Really Christian, wasn't I?'

'I haven't always turned the other cheek or found it easy to forgive – Rob, for example.'

Oh dear! thought Lily, but remained silent about May and her plans, though she told him about Rob's visit. Matt was quiet and she wondered if she should have kept her mouth shut but it would have had to come out one way or another. But his mention of forgiveness where Rob was concerned did not bode well for a quick marriage for her sister. She did not see how she could grant something that Matt would be against and which she herself was not sure about. It was a problem they could do without while they learnt to feel comfortable with each other again and made decisions about where they were going to live now that the war was over.

They reached Brunswick Road with its mixture of shops and its workplace for the blind. The road had a bit of an incline to say the least. Lily glanced at Matt and saw there was sweat on his brow. He grimaced and lifted Paul down, who immediately wanted to be lifted up again. 'No, Paul. Daddy's tired,' said Lily, taking his hand while Matt took the other. Fortuitously there was the rattling of an approaching tram.

As soon as they stepped inside the dairy, Matt said, 'There's something different in here.'

'The churn's gone. I forgot to tell you I got rid of the cows,' she said hurriedly, putting Paul down. 'It was something that I'd have had to do sooner or later with the way things are going in dairying. And besides—' She suddenly noticed that there was an envelope sticking to her shoe and bent to pick it up.

'You thought we wouldn't be staying here?' stated Matt, his eyes on her face.

'You talked of wanting your own parish. I presumed we'd be going elsewhere.'

'Australia?'

There was something in his voice and she guessed what he was thinking but knew him well enough to come up with the answer he would want. Her gaze met his squarely. 'If that's where God wants us. Where we live isn't important. It's us starting over again together.'

Relief flooded his face. 'You're coming up with the right answers. There's hope for us yet.'

'Have you doubted it?'

'Sometimes.' He leaned against the counter in the wintery sunshine. 'You start questioning and doubting when you have too much time to think.'

'I know!' she said in a heartfelt voice, remembering wondering if his 'sorry' had meant it was all over between them. She glanced down at the envelope and recognised May's writing. She opened it quickly and stiffened as her gaze alighted on two words, still listening to Matt as she read.

'It's possible when two people parted the way we did and have spent so much time away from each other, to say the right things in letters but not mean them,' said Matt. 'Who's that from?'

Lily glanced up at him.

'What's so enthralling about it?' His voice was unemotional but she knew he was hurt by her allowing herself to be distracted from what he was saying. It was an immensely important time for the two of them, trying to put their lives together. Oh, why had May's letter had to come now? He cleared his throat. 'Having your full attention would be more flattering to me than having you read that note.'

'Sorry, love.' She pinned a smile on her face and made to slip the note in her pocket. 'It's nothing for you to worry about.'

Matt stretched out a hand. 'I know you better than that. Let's have no secrets between us at a time like this.' He glanced down at the note as she gave it to him and read aloud:

Dear Lil,

By the time you read this Rob and I will be on our way to Gretna Green. I know my marrying him is not what you want so I thought it best to take the decision out of your hands. This way you won't have to worry about what Matt has to say, and there's no need for either of them to see each other again if it causes trouble. I'm going to miss you but . . .'

Matt glanced up and their eyes caught.

'We'll have to go after them,' said Lily hurriedly.

'Why don't you want them to marry?'

The question surprised her. 'Because it's Rob, of course! You said you couldn't forgive him and—'

'I said I didn't find it easy,' he said emphatically, 'but that's because my feelings were all tangled up with his saying he loved you and you'd fallen in love with him.'

'You know that's not true. Didn't I write to you that it wasn't?'

Matt folded the letter carefully. 'As I said before, it's easy to say things in letters, especially when you believe you might never see that person alive again.'

She was angry. 'I didn't lie, Matt! I was as honest with you as I hope you've been with me. I never loved him. I found him attractive at a time when I felt lonely because you'd gone off seeking solitude when you should have been with me.'

He looked relieved. 'I've said I'm sorry about that – how it took me a bit of time to realise having a wife meant considering your needs as well as my own. But why didn't you tell me about May and Rob when we were talking about him earlier?'

'Because you'd been ill. I've been used to making decisions for other people for a long time. I didn't want it disturbing you and coming between us.'

A laugh escaped him. 'I'm not a child, Lil. I can cope with this.' He tapped the letter against his palm. 'All I need to know is that your reason for wanting them not to marry isn't because you can't bear May getting him instead of you because of your being married to me for better, for worse.'

'I can bear it.' Her eyes were bright as she drew close to him. 'May always said Rob was her kind of hero but he's not the man I want to spend my life with.'

'No?' said Matt, smiling. 'Then you don't want me to chase after them like some Victorian irate father or brother? There'd be some poetic justice in that, don't you think? Although it should be up to Ben and Ronnie to do the chasing.'

'No. I never want you to leave me again,' she whispered. 'I love you. You, Matt! We've both made mistakes and will probably go on making them, but you're the man I want to make some of those dreams of the future come true with.'

The letter slipped from his fingers and his arms went round her. She gave a deep sigh and pressed against him. This was the moment she had been waiting for. Never had she been able to luxuriate in Rob's kisses like she could Matt's.

Her fingers laced behind his neck as his head came down. That kiss told her everything about their future together and was well worth waiting for, but it didn't last long enough. Their son forced his way between their legs and eventually they had to draw apart to pay him attention.

Smiling at each other, they each took one of his hands and went through into the kitchen together.